ACCLAIM FOR ADRIAN MCKINTY'S EXHILARATING THRILLER

HIDDEN RIVER

"An outstanding and complex crime novel that should appeal to fans of hard-boiled Celtic scribes such as Ken Bruen and Ian Rankin. . . . This is not only an expertly crafted suspense novel but also a revealing study of addiction."

—*Publishers Weekly*

"I really enjoyed the previous novel's combination of toughness and a striking literary style. Both those things are evident in *Hidden River* and the plot also has a great twist at the end. McKinty is going places."

—*The Observer* (London)

"McKinty's first thriller, *Dead I Well May Be*, was a wild, riveting roller-coaster of a read. This more measured and disciplined adventure is equally exciting and engaging thanks to tight plotting and vivid characterization."

—*Irish Independent*

"Brisk and energetic. . . . Reminiscent of Dennis Lehane."

—Publishers Weekly

"A startling, dark poem of a thriller that takes you to the heart of New York City's most bloody era. . . . McKinty is the real deal."

—Thomas Kelly, author of *The Rackets*

"McKinty has a keen ear for dialogue and a talent for fast-paced plotting. . . . By turns funny and tragic and always enthralling. The world he portrays is vividly rendered and not easily forgotten."

—Denver Rocky Mountain News

"A profoundly satisfying book from a major new talent."

—Booklist

More Praise for HIDDEN RIVER

"The prose is so crisp [it] reads as if it were the author's tenth book, not merely his second."

—Chicago Sun-Times

"A breakout second novel . . . a storyteller with the kind of style and panache that blur the line between genre and mainstream. Top-drawer."

—Kirkus Reviews (starred review)

"A protagonist and narrator who forces us to like him."

—*San Francisco Chronicle*

"McKinty writes with élan, and his dialogue is as hard and true as the streets. His hero's quest for vengeance and redemption kept me reading into the loneliest hours of the night."

—Thomas Kelly, author of *The Rackets* and *Payback*

ALSO BY ADRIAN McKINTY

The Dead Yard

Dead I Well May Be

Orange Rhymes with Everything

HIDDEN RIVER

A Novel

ADRIAN McKINTY

POCKET BOOKS

NEW YORK   LONDON   TORONTO   SYDNEY

This book is a work of fiction. Names, characters, places and
incidents are products of the author's imagination or are used
fictitiously. Any resemblance to actual events or locales or
persons, living or dead, is entirely coincidental.

 POCKET BOOKS, a division of Simon & Schuster, Inc.
1230 Avenue of the Americas, New York, NY 10020

Copyright © 2005 by Adrian McKinty

Originally published in hardcover in 2005 by Scribner

All rights reserved, including the right to reproduce
this book or portions thereof in any form whatsoever.
For information address Scribner, 1230 Avenue of the
Americas, New York, NY 10020

ISBN-13: 978-0-7434-7057-5
ISBN-10:   0-7434-7057-5

First Pocket Books printing January 2006

10 9 8 7 6 5 4 3 2 1

POCKET and colophon are registered trademarks of Simon &
Schuster, Inc.

Cover design by Jae Song; cover photo by Don Kim

Manufactured in the United States of America

For information regarding special discounts for bulk purchases,
please contact Simon & Schuster Special Sales at 1-800-456-6798
or business@simonandschuster.com

HIDDEN RIVER

O Arjuna. Why give in to this shameful weakness?
You who would be the terror of thine enemies.

—*Bhagavad Gita 2:3*

HIDDEN RIVER

1: CREATOR, SUSTAINER, DESTROYER

Seven time zones west of Belfast the murdered girl was alive yet and well. She was confident, popular, young and clever—this last virtue was going to be the death of her.

That and a slug from a .22.

She lay snug in the groove of the futon mattress. Over her: a cotton sheet and a fleece blanket. The fan on for noise. The humidifier for moisture. The heat in the middle of the thermostat. She was comfortable, as comfortable as one could be in this bed, in this room, in this building, in this town.

I know all this because I read the police report.

Perhaps the humidifier cast off a little light that illuminated her face. An interesting face. Imperious, marked, beautiful. Of good background, of good stock. Actually—and although she said it was unimportant—of good caste. She had dark eyes and dark hair. An aristocrat, you might have said, or someone who could play the archetypal rich girl who disdains and then ultimately falls for the poor but handsome boy in the silliest of Hindi films.

Victoria Patawasti was clever but even the cleverest can't be experts at all things. The encryption software for her computer diary had said that the FBI's Cray supercomputers would take years of processing time to break her password; all that she wrote would be safe, certainly from office gossips or other ne'er-do-wells. Of course, the encryption software meant nothing if the password wasn't secure. But who would ever think of a long word like *Carrickfergus*—the small town where she'd grown up, in Ireland.

She had confided everything to her computer diary: her thoughts, her ideas, her suspicions. Suspicions. What a big word. Probably nothing she should worry about. Klimmer had been right. Not the sort of thing that should keep her up at night.

Not the sort of thing that would get her killed.

She lived in Denver, where the mountains met the plains in the middle of the continent and where seemingly all climatic conditions were possible within one twenty-four-hour period. She hailed from a place where the moderating currents of the Gulf Stream turned every day into a hazy rain, warm and temperate, even in winter. A place of fog and sea spray and men with flat caps; cows, sheep, stone walls, muck, slurry, more rain. The weather as predictable as bad news.

Even where her grandparents lived, in Allahabad, India, on the rolling brown plain along the Ganges, it wasn't hard to guess what the day would be like. Hot and dry nine months a year, hot and wet three. No mystery. Here, though, things were different. The mountains brought down snow and the deserts kicked up sand and the wide expanse of prairie could conjure up just about anything. They'd had drought for years, drought punctuated by big storms. Drive a few hours east and apparently a tornado could transport you to the wonderful land of Oz. Yes, here weather was weather, and thunderstorms and ball lightning and rains of frogs all seemed as likely to occur as anything else.

Perhaps she woke for a time. She told her mother she woke five or six times a night, having never really adapted to the wooden futon bed or the altitude or the aridity. Tonight it would actually be good that she was awake, she had only had about thirty minutes of consciousness left. Better to make the most of it.

She could have read the book next to her bed. Kerouac. Or she could have pulled on the toggle on the furry musical sheep that Hans Klimmer had given her. It played "Beautiful Dreamer" over and over and as it slowed and stopped perhaps she yawned and threw it on the floor.

Or maybe she looked out the window. She'd be surprised. A blizzard. She couldn't have been expecting that in June.

Monday, June 5, 1995, two-thirty Mountain Time . . .

At precisely the same moment, it was raining in Belfast, and the man who would eventually find Victoria's killer was not yet up.

Me.

I was half awake in a boat I'd broken into at Carrick-fergus Marina, a girl with me whom I'd met in Dolan's the night before.

I was twenty-four, underweight, bearded, pale and sickly, with black curly hair that badly needed a cut. The girl: pretty, redheaded, skinny, and (unknown to me) only seventeen, at Carrickfergus Grammar School, a prefect, a member of the choir and scripture union but rebelling and well on her way to dropping out, failing her A levels, moving to Dublin and becoming a singer/model/prostitute/junkie. Breaking and entering and plying her with stolen gin would do nothing to alter the course of this trajectory.

And yet it was not such an illogical leap that, two weeks later, I'd be on my way west to the United States to investigate a murder that confused the local police. No, it wasn't so strange because in fact I'd been a detective for the Royal Ulster Constabulary—Northern Ireland's police force. A copper for six years, a detective for three of those and a DC/DS for my last six months on the force. Those last six months the key to my current geographical, moral, physical, and spiritual condition.

Detective Constable/Drug Squad.

The girl rolled over sleepily in the bunk, went back to sleep. I stroked my beard and lit the remains of her joint. I never smoked pot, never, it made you stupid. My drug of choice . . .

But that's another story. Well, part of this one, but we'll get to that.

Still raining. Cold. Pissing down.

The boat stank. Why a boat? I couldn't go home—my father, retired from teaching math, always bloody there. And her house was out of the question. The marina had an emergency turnstile locked with a Yale standard. Easy. You break in and you find a boat that looks expensive. The bunks were narrow, though, and there was no way to get warm unless you turned on the power on the dock but that would set off a light in the marina office. Suffer for your sin.

I had things to do but the rain had hypnotized me into apathy. I slid out of the bunk and went along the passage to the head. For it to work properly, you had to turn a cistern on, piss, pump it out, and turn it off again. A lot of effort. I went down there in my boxers, T-shirt, jacket. Trailing a duvet. Shivering. Smoking. A notice on the wall: "Trust in God and keep your bowels clean—Cromwell." I regarded it for some time. Was it supposed to be funny? My brain felt addled.

I looked out through the thick glass. Pissing was right. The sort of gray, heavy downpour chief constables pray for during riot season. Not that I cared about it, not anymore. Nope, all over, done with. I was no longer part of the solution but had migrated to become part of the problem. I smiled.

I tugged the blanket around me. I smoked and rested my head against the bog wall. Something troubled me still. Something I didn't want to forget. I searched my memory and then the jacket pocket, but neither place revealed its mystery.

Sleep on it, I told myself.

I got up and walked to the chart table. I found the gin bottle and a square of Cadbury's chocolate from the night before. I threw the square in my mouth. Stale. I reached down again, found some fags, and lit one. Climbed in the bunk next to the girl.

Filthy habit, smoking in bed, for God's sake. I took a few puffs, coughed for half a minute, and added the cigarette to what I hoped was an ashtray lying down there.

I pulled the covers up over my head and kicked away a hot water bottle, icy and rubbery as a dead seal pup. I folded the duvet tighter. All now quiet—only the easing rain on the window ledge and a drip, drip, drip coming from off the mainmast and down the hatch. The girl woke, whimpered. I slept. . . .

And as the sky above eastern Ulster started to clear, on another continent, in the foothills of the Rocky Mountains and a thousand miles into the Great Plains, a wide, suffocating blanket of snow had closed down the railways, the highways, and every other road to all but the hardiest of souls. Cops, night shift workers, emergency personnel, stranded drivers, or the horde of high-altitude insomniacs staring through their windows.

And, of course, Victoria Patawasti's murderer.

Few vehicles moving, fewer people around, everywhere an eerie quiet.

Denver smothered in low clouds reflecting back the street and building lights, turning them sickly orange and neon red. Snow falling slantwise and hard but then diminishing as the pressure systems rotated around themselves in enormous anticlockwise ellipses. And in those moments of relative tranquillity, from high apartment windows came the peculiar sight of the snow falling upward, bobbing on heat thermals and heading into some icy purgatory in those awful clouds.

A truly impressive storm system that stretched from Canada all the way down into the Sangre de Cristos. Great swirls of low pressure that bounced off the Rockies and sucked up moisture from as far away as Puget Sound and the Gulf of California. The overnight man on the Weather Channel was dizzy with excitement. After a winter of drought, this was the biggest snowfall of the year. In fact, this was the biggest June storm since 1924, snow in six states, sixteen inches in Aspen, power outages in Utah, fourteen airports closed, all the east-west highways, America effectively cut in two, families trapped in cars, trucks overturned, El Niño, La Niña, Global Warming, Instability, the End Times, the Second Coming. . . .

Not that it bothered Victoria's killer.

No, you didn't care, did you?

You had already murdered Alan Houghton up on Lookout Mountain.

And now it was three in the morning. Perfect. They say that that's when the body is at its weakest. The storm had come out of the blue. But it wouldn't matter. It would erase your footprints like a shaken Etch-A-Sketch. You probably liked the darkness, the low clouds, the fresh snow. The deciduous trees like scarecrows, the pine and spruce drenched in white. Trails on the path from people walking their dogs. Here and there a glimpse of the mountains. How long did you stand outside Victoria's apartment building?

You must have come in by the fire exit next to the garage. The only entrance that did not have a security camera. What would you have done if some old lady had spotted you down there?

You're going in late? Don't I know you? You're the—

You wouldn't hesitate. Jump down, rush her, kick the dog, take out the knife, slit her throat, knee drop on the dog, break its neck. That's the sort of thing you didn't want. Messy. Ugly. A whole night's adventures and you wouldn't even be in the building yet. And besides, you'd had quite the night already.

Absolutely no turning back now. Alan Houghton already dead. His body probably dumped in a quarry or under the extension of Interstate 70. What an effort that must have been for you, lifting his dead weight into the plastic sheeting in the trunk, driving through the snow, finding the trench you'd picked out yesterday. Necessary.

As was this.

Houghton had no proof of Charles's involvement in the murder but once the smear got out there it wouldn't go away. The bleeding had to stop. It had literally been millions of dollars over decades. If Charles was going to go anywhere, Houghton had to be silenced. And now with the first step taken, the job had to be finished. Oh, the surprise on his face. I'm sure he'd been expecting an envelope stuffed with benjamins. . . .

The fire exit. You took out a magnet and greased it over the pass sensor. The light went green, the lock clicked. Easy as pie.

The door. A blast of heat. You rode the lift to the thirteenth floor.

Unlucky for some.

The apartment. You produced the copy of Victoria's key that you'd had ample time to make. You turned the lock. You applied the bolt cutters of the Leatherman multitool to the security chain. The chain snapped. You listened for a sound. Nothing. You opened the door.

You went into the apartment.

It wasn't your first time here.

It would be your last.

You closed the door behind you.

Smooth. Very smooth. You took out the revolver— hopefully that wouldn't be necessary. You'd shot Alan far from anyone on Lookout Mountain. You'd probably met him there once before so that he wouldn't be suspicious. But even a .22 would make noise. Still, if you had to use it again you would. A superb gun. Handmade by Beretta in Italy, "from CM to AM with love" engraved in gold on the butt. Incriminating, to say the least. They'd never find Houghton, but even if you didn't have to use it on Victoria it would be safer to get rid of it.

You reached in your pocket and found Hector Martinez's driver's license. You dropped it near the door.

You took out the knife. Adjusted to the darkness.

The lights were off, but through the living room window you could see the storm had started up again. You walked across the living room. Opened the bedroom door. The humidifier glowed in the corner. The fan whirred. Victoria slept. So beautiful. Peaceful.

The knife glinted.

Victoria.

Breathing.

Closer.

Closer.

Her golden neck exposed to the ambient light. Victoria's carotid artery pulsing slightly. You gripped the knife tighter. A slash rather than a stab.

Closer. But something happened. A loud noise. Maybe you stood on something, a stuffed animal that moaned and played a bar of "Beautiful Dreamer."

Victoria sat up, opened her mouth to scream. But didn't scream. Instead maybe she smiled and said in a half question:

"Amber?"

The .22 flashed. A single bullet wiped out that pretty face forever.

o o o

I shivered. Suddenly woke. Looked around. The last of the rain drizzling down the portholes, weaving patterns and rivulets. The boat moving up and down against the dock. The halyards gently clanking against the metal mast.

"I'm going to be late for school," the girl said.

"School or college?" I said.

"School."

"Oh, God."

"I told ya last night," she said.

"How old are you?" I asked.

"Seventeen."

"I could go to prison," I groaned.

"Also for possession of cannabis resin, peddling controlled substances to a minor, criminal trespass, breaking and entering, theft, and a couple of other things," the girl said, getting up and lowering herself onto the floor.

She had red hair, curly, long, pale skin with freckles, and she looked a lot younger in the cold light, et cetera.

"How old are *you*?" she asked.

"Twenty-four, almost twenty-five."

"You look older."

"Thanks. So do you."

"Yeah, but you *really* look older."

"Aye, well, I'm a bad lad, hard living," I said, and fumbled for the smokes.

"Yeah right," she said, putting on her blouse. "Here, you want some coffee?"

"Sure. What time is it?"

"Just after ten. I've study until eleven, so no one will miss me," she said.

"Your parents?"

"Said I was staying at Jane's before I left."

"So you went out looking for trouble?"

She didn't reply. She went to the range and hit the gas. Struck a match on a ring, found some distilled water, put it in a pot. I got up on my elbow, swung my legs out.

"How do you know all the law stuff?" I asked.

"Read a book, *Introduction to English Law.* I was thinking of doing law at uni, either that or journalism."

"Was thinking?"

"Bored with A levels, school, load of rubbish, going to become a singer," she said, finding a biscuit tin and opening it.

"I went to Queens," I said. "And coincidentally I was a law student. Best time of my life, seriously, you should suck it up, do your A levels, get to college. It's fun, you can party, good advice."

The water boiled and she added some coffee to a cup. She brought me the coffee and a couple of digestive biscuits.

"Thanks," I said. I took a sip and a tiny bite of biscuit.

She sat on the chart table, brushing her hair, looking at me.

"So your advice is don't do drugs and stay in school," she said with mild irony.

"Uh, yeah," I said.

"And through this I, too, can reach the high plateau of your success as a man who breaks into other people's boats?"

I took the joint out of her hand and stubbed it out.

"Too young for that," I said.

"Ok, dad," she said laughing.

"Seriously, not good for you," I said.

"Your friend John gave it to me," she said.

"Yeah, well, he's not very responsible."

"He said he was a policeman."

"Exactly."

"He said I should go with him. He said you were a bit of a druggie," she said quietly.

I did not reply. The girl looked at me. Her young face twisted by concern.

"John said you used to be a cop too. What happened to ya? The police lay off the old men first. Were you fired? Did you get shot?"

"I resigned," I said, and offered nothing more. I was infected with caution, even this early.

"You resigned? Why?"

"You answer one question, million others behind it," I said with mock exhaustion.

"Are you saying I talk a wee bit too much?" she asked.

"No. But I am saying go to uni. Seriously, don't bugger up your life. Do yourself a favor, finish school."

"What did you get in the A levels?" she asked.

"Four As."

"Four As, shit, are you a genius or something?"

"Or something," I said, shivered again.

"You look way older with that beard. It doesn't suit you at all, you grew it because you got too thin and you think the beard hides it but it doesn't. You can tell that you were handsome, you know, the green eyes, the dark eyebrows, the cute nose, but you seem ill, to tell you the truth. All tall and stooped over. You should look after yourself better."

"Jesus. If I look so rough, how on earth did I manage to persuade such a doyenne of fashion to—"

"Slumming it," she said, interrupting me. "Besides, your friend John insisted on telling me in excruciating detail how he was going to fix his motorcycle."

"Not a very exciting topic," I agreed, and sighed. And she was right. This silly seventeen-year-old was right about everything. Ridiculous. My skin was starting to crawl. Nearly time, but this wasn't the place and not with a child around.

"We should hit the road," she said, anticipating my thoughts. "But I'm going to shower first."

"Are you sure there's a shower?"

"Checked already, there is," she explained, and made her way to the back of the boat.

I leaned back in the bunk. Smart girl. Screwing up her life, none of my business. Her stuff on the chart table, hair clip, brush, purse. I opened her purse, stole a ten-pound note, put it in my pocket, changed my mind, put it back in the purse, changed my mind again, put it back in my pocket.

I heard the shower come on. Eventually the girl appeared in a towel.

"Good shower," she said.

"You're tougher than me," I said.

"How so?"

"I can't handle a cold shower, I like my creature comforts."

"It wasn't cold."

"What do you mean?" I asked.

"I put the water heater on," she said, matter-of-factly.

"But the boat's not plugged in," I said, a tear of panic starting to go through me.

"I plugged it in, out there, on the dock, I've been on a boat before, my uncle F—"

"Jesus. A light goes on in the marina office to let them know what boats are powered up," I said, and ran to the back of the cockpit. I looked up and across the three rows of boats to the office. Sure enough, the security guard was coming over to check why no one had signed in for the boat but its power was on.

"Jesus Christ, get your shit together, bloody hell."

I grabbed her by the arm as she desperately tried to get her trousers and T-shirt on at the same time. I fumbled into my jacket, scrambled on deck. The guard probably thought it was routine. Just starting down the ramp, not exactly racing, eating crisps, but regardless we were screwed because there was only one way in and out of the marina—past him. We would have to hide in another boat, or swim to the jetty wall, or walk by him and brazen it out.

"Look respectable," I said, helping her on with her sweater.

"Ha, coming from you—"

"Shut it, he hasn't seen us, come on."

We climbed over the safety rail and stepped onto the wooden dock. The guard two aisles over, munching his crisps, lost in thought. We began walking casually.

"Talk to me," I said.

"So Mother and I decided to go to the same psychiatrist but he said—"

"Talk sensible," I interrupted.

"In English I have to write an essay on a personal hell. We're reading *No Exit*, the Sartre play. You know—hell is other people," she said.

"Other French people, certainly," I said.

"Well, yes, so, what's your personal hell?" she asked.

"I don't know. Um, being trapped in a lift with Robin Williams?"

We turned the curve on the dock, past the guard. He gave us a look, but one of relative unconcern. We hastened our pace and walked fast to the exit. We were nearly at the turnstile when the guard yelled at us to stop. Or at least our translation of a strangled "Hey, youse, get back harble garble, trabba dap."

We ducked through the turnstile.

"This is where we split," I said.

"Sex, drugs, a brush with the law—you certainly know how to show a girl a good time. How can I get in contact with—"

"You don't until you turn eighteen," I said.

"What's your name at least?" she began to say but I was already jogging across the park.

"Wanker," she called after me.

I didn't reply.

I realized what I'd forgotten. I reached into the inside pocket of my jacket. I had left one of my baggies of ketch on the boat. It had gotten wet in last night's downpour and I'd left it somewhere on that bloody chart table to dry. Now I had only one small bag left. Damn it. And I had been trying to avoid Spider. Just enough now for a couple of days: I'd have to go crawling to him. Have to get some money somehow. Have to show up at that pub quiz and of course Spider would be there too.

Bugger. I cursed myself for five minutes. Finally calmed down.

Take care of the day at hand, Alex, I told myself. First things first. I had to get my free supply of needles, using John's dad's diabetic prescription. A different drugstore every week just to erase suspicion.

Today: Smith's Chemist. Ok, do that. I went in with my prescription, browsed the newspapers while they took their sweet time filling it.

"Hello, Alex, how's your dad?" a voice behind me said. Mr. Patawasti.

"Oh, he's fine, how are you?"

"I'm fine, the knees, you know, but still have to get out. I'm just getting the papers, *The Times* for me, *Guardian* for the wife. Poison and antidote, I like to call them. Though I never let on which is which," Mr. Patawasti said in that upper-class Indian accent of his.

I laughed but before I could reply the clerk said that my prescription was ready.

"See you another time, Mr. P.," I said.

"Another time, Alex," Mr. Patawasti said.

I walked out of the drugstore, satisfied that at least I had needles for another week. I suppose I should have asked Mr. Patawasti about Victoria. The last I'd heard, she had some new job in America. Still, it would keep. I'd see him around.

I walked home. I had things to do. Plans for the coming day or days. But no further than that. I couldn't live further than that. A sensible policy, for I didn't know that it was done now. Done. Events set in motion that would carry me away from this depressing little scene, to Belfast Airport, Heathrow Airport, the brand-new Denver International Airport, to Boulder, to Denver, to a gun battle in Fort Morgan, to a bloody mess in a ballroom, another flight, the Old Continent, the Hidden River. . . .

Aye, it was done.

The .22 was being walked to the frothing waters of Cherry Creek, where it would be cast in and would remain for years before being nudged along to the South Platte River. From there it would make its sliding way to the Platte, from the Platte to the Missouri to the Mississippi and finally the Gulf of Mexico. From there to some deep trench in the Atlantic. The seawater would break down the steel into its component molecules, the molecules would break down into their component atoms, the sun would expand, the oceans would boil off, the Earth would fry, all the stars would go out, the last remnants of intelligence in the universe would cobble together light from somewhere, but the second law of thermodynamics always wins and eventually blackness would reign in perpetuity, all remaining atomic nuclei disintegrating, electrons losing their spin and dissolving and the whole of creation a void of nothingness, a few faceless neutrinos separated by oceans of night.

Perhaps.

2: THE FIRST INCARNATION OF VISHNU

I was being tailed. He'd been on me since I'd left the house. I'd tried to give him the slip by going out the side door of the Joymount Arms but he was wise to that. Bastard. Maybe Internal Affairs from the peelers following me to see if he could get me on anything—but I'd made a deal with the cops, so that seemed unlikely. Maybe one of Spider's goons after his dough. Maybe that seventeen-year-old from yesterday had told her father or brother or uncle and he'd come to knock me into next week. Maybe a lot of things.

He was good, so I decided to ignore him. My maneuvers had already made me late.

I hurried up, arrived at Dolan's breathless.

Dolan's, our local pub, a coaching inn back in the sixteenth century. Low ceilings, timber frame, whitewashed walls, nautical theme in the public bar, and the highlight of the pub—the large open-plan front room containing a huge fireplace, originally used for roasting spits. The fire always lit except in the very warmest days of summer, which tonight wasn't.

I walked in. It was nine o'clock. The quiz had already started. Facey fumed at me for being late. John smiled and patted me on the back.

"How do, mate?" John said.

"Not bad," I said.

"It's Facey's shout," John said. But Facey was too pissed off to buy me a drink at the moment. Facey was a reasonably good-natured guy who played prop forward—the enforcer—in rugby, so obviously the good nature only went so far. Facey was the only one of the three of us that had a real job, though. He was in the full-time Reserve of the Royal Ulster Constabulary, which meant he worked about twelve days a month. John was also a peeler, but he was in the part-time Reserve, working only two or three days a month. John worked so little they allowed him to claim unemployment benefit.

I'd been the real supercop of the bunch. A high flyer in the RUC. A detective. John didn't care about rank but Facey, desperate to get out of the Reserve and into the real cops, had always been envious of me. For the last six months, since my resignation, the positions were, if not reversed, at least more complicated.

If you think of me as Lenin in the coma, Facey is Stalin seizing the leadership of our little group, which only really meant he held the pencil at the pub quiz and you could hit him up for dough. He had tried unsuccessfully to change our team name from the Pigs to the Peelers, which he thought more dignified.

"Alex, are you having a Guinness?" John asked, a broad hint in Facey's direction.

"Aye," I said, taking off my sweater.

Facey, seething, had to bloody say something:

"Because of your lateness we could have dropped a point," he growled, his eyes narrowing, a thing to behold, for Facey was heavy, pale, squat, with squashed features. Tight eyes on that face made him look like a constipated sumo wrestler.

"You look like a constipated sumo wrestler," I said.

"You look like someone who nearly cost us a hundred and twenty quid. Nearly dropped a point or a couple even," he said.

"And did you drop a point? Did you get any questions wrong?" I asked him.

"No, we didn't but we could have."

"But you didn't."

"But we could have."

"But you didn't."

John interposed to stop this regression continuing to infinity and asked if things had gone ok with the girl we had met on Sunday night.

"Actually, John, things did not go well, she was underage," I said.

"Really? Heard they try to castrate statutory rapists in prison," John said, grinning.

"Thank you, John, reassuring as always."

"I thought I had a chance with her, she was very interested in hearing about how I was repairing the Triumph. I told her my You-Must-Become-the-Motorcycle theory," John said.

"She mentioned that. Seventeen-year-olds are very

impressed by Plato, Zen, and greasy mechanics. You gave her pot as well, didn't you?"

"I suppose you told her your interesting theory about Batman villains and American presidents," John mocked.

"It is a legitimate theory," I said, but before I could elaborate Facey finally took the hint that we were ignoring him and figured out that he should be getting us some drinks.

"Two Guinnesses," John said.

Facey went off and came back with three pints of Guinness before the next round started. The Pigs had only one serious opponent, the Army Brats. We were coppers or ex-coppers and they were part-time soldiers, so we all had a lot of time on our hands to bone up on trivia. The pub quiz had six rounds of team questions and then a rapid-fire round of five minutes dictated by a buzzer. Tonight's jackpot would be fifty pounds but with the rollover from last week it would be a hundred and twenty, which was forty quid each.

"Round Two," Marty, the wiry quizmaster, said over his microphone.

"How much do the Brats have?" I asked Facey.

"Sshhhh," he said, getting his pencil ready.

"'Tainted Love' was a hit for what band?"

"Soft C—" I began.

"Already have it," Facey whispered.

"Which country has more coastline, Japan or the Soviet Union?" Marty asked.

"Russia," John, Facey, and I whispered together.

And on the questions went. We finished the round, Facey handed up our answers. They were marked. We got ten out of ten. The Brats got ten out of ten. Everyone else now hopelessly out of contention. At the end of six rounds we had fifty-eight points, the Brats fifty-nine, the next team thirty-five.

John and I went for a piss. I always went with John in case there were cute girls on the way to the bathroom. John, you could be seen with. Facey, too squat and violent. John had the hengie thing going. Vain, longish blond hair, earring, pretty good-looking chap, frilly shirt. Big shoulders—he looked like Fabio's younger, tackier, even stupider brother. But still it attracted a better class of impressionable seventeen-year-old skank. And no one looked less like a cop than John, good for getting girls, but probably why the police seldom gave him work.

We scoped the bar and the back bar but there was no one around. We went in the bathroom for a pee.

"So tell me, how are you feeling, Alex?" John asked me from a little farther down the trough.

"Ok."

"No, but really, how's life treating you?"

"John, I don't want to be rude but in general one does not speak at the urinal trough," I said.

"Is that right?" John said diffidently.

"It's these little taboos that keep society together. We are trying to build a civilization here and you speaking at the urinal trough does not help matters."

"Bombs are going off in Belfast every day. People

are being shot. Heroin is flooding the country. Riots in Derry, but me asking about your health and well-being is somehow contributing to the collapse of Western civilization? An interesting thesis, Alexander Lawson, and yet it reeks of utter shite."

"You break this social norm here, that rule of etiquette there and next thing you know you're kneecapping your neighbor and throwing Molotovs at the peelers," I said.

"And you think both of us are susceptible to this?"

"Chaos theory, John. Butterfly . . . tornado; urinal . . . the Dark Ages," I said.

"And yet if I had kept my mouth shut we would have just pissed and left and yet here we are debating philosophies," John replied.

He had me there, the bastard, but I wasn't going to admit it. I'd finished. I grunted, washed my hands, left. A mistake, for right there was my dealer: Spider McKeenan. Even his ma admitted that Spider was a nasty piece of work. Rangy, powerful arms, orange hair, from a distance a bit like a clothed orangutan. A good way of getting a kicking was to mention this to him.

"You owe me—" Spider began.

I stopped him with a hand.

"Spider, my simian pal, let's go outside."

"It's raining," Spider said.

"Takes you back, does it, the tropical rain forests of Sumatra?"

"What are you talking about?" Spider asked.

"Spider, seriously, let's leave the pub," I said. "John Campbell is about to come out of the bog, and you know he's in the peelers."

I had to go outside with Spider. I had to buy ketch and keep those track marks fresh. Being a user kept the police off my back, but getting caught buying drugs could get me arrested by the cops. Delicate balance, Catch-22, call it what you like, bloody tight spot was what it was. I followed Spider out of the pub and under the overhang.

"Alex, before you speak just shut the fuck up and listen to me, you owe me fifty quid and my patience is at an end."

"Pub quiz tonight," I said. "Forty quid each."

"I am none the wiser, Alex," Spider said.

"No, not wiser, but better informed," I said.

Spider smiled and nodded. He seemed a little drunk, clumsy, I could have dodged him but what was the point? I'd have to get this sooner or later.

"You know, Alex, don't think because you were a peeler and your mates are peelers that you'll be treated any differently, because you won't," he said, and punched me in the stomach. Then he hit me with a combination, left jab to the rib cage, right jab to the gut, hard left to the kidneys, hard right to the gut. If it had been on someone else I'm sure I would have been very impressed at his speed, range, and location but instead I fell to the pavement, gasped, heaved up half a pint of beer, choked, and spat.

"You bastard, I said I'd get it," I managed.

"How?"

"In the pub quiz, you son of a bitch."

"You better. Forty quid before you leave the bar. You know yourself, Alex, I'm the only supplier in town. Piss me off and I'll cut you off. Where will you be then? Eh? You'd rather have me use you as a punching bag. Wouldn't ya? Course I'd do that too."

He went back inside. I lay there. He'd been bloody right. It ate up all my dole money and I had the indignity of scrounging off my broke da. And again I thought back to that night in my apartment half a year ago. The right decision? Not brave. But at least I was alive. At least Da was alive. And ketch itself. Not the bogeyman of the government ads. Life. I could thank it for that. I dusted myself off, went back inside. John gave me a look. Facey was raging at me as usual.

"The rapid fire is just about to start, Alexander," he complained.

"Keep your hair on, Facey, just getting a breath of air, so much bloody smoke in here, hard to breathe," I said.

Marty started the rapid fire. I was anxious now, normally I didn't give a damn about the pub quiz but we had to win tonight. I had to get Spider that fifty quid. I really couldn't afford to piss Spider off. Where would I score ketch without him? You either dealt with the paramilitaries or didn't deal. Spider was the local UDA rep. You didn't need years of policing experience to know that Northern Ireland was divided into Catholic paramilitary (IRA) and Protestant paramilitary (UDA) districts. Try to be an independent pusher and you would end up naked in a bog with a hole in your head.

"History: In what country is Waterloo—"

Facey and I pressed the buzzer and said simultaneously: "Belgium."

"Van Morrison was formerly part of which band?"

"Them," Facey said.

"The High Kings of Ireland were crowned where?"

"Tara," one of the Brats said, getting in before me.

"Science: Boyle's law . . ."

The questions went on and at the end we were tied. Marty needed time to prepare a tiebreaker. I went to the loo again. Just as I had relaxed my bladder in came Mr. McCarthy, one of Da's friends from the old cricket club. Dolan's was that kind of bar. People from the cricket club, aldermen, drug dealers. Carrickfergus had many bars, some paramilitary hangouts, some for locals only, but Dolan's was for everyone.

"Sandy," he said.

"Mr. McCarthy," I said.

"Sandy, I respect your dad very much but he can't win the election, you know."

I nearly gave Mr. McCarthy my spiel about how the decline of the west begins at the urinal, but he was a friend of my father's, so I had to humor him.

"I know, Mr. McCarthy, he lost his deposit last time and in a ward of a thousand people, which means that fewer than fifty voted for him. Told him not to run. But he says it's the principle of the thing."

"He's a good man, your dad, a good man. If he was

in my ward I'd vote for him. Well, anyway . . . Oh, terrible about Victoria Patawasti, wasn't it?" Mr. Mc-Carthy said.

"What?"

"It was terrible about Victoria Patawasti," he said again.

"What was?"

"Didn't you hear?"

"No."

"Maybe I'm mistaken, but I heard this morning that she'd been in an awful accident or something in America."

"I don't think so," I said, "I saw her dad just yesterday."

"Oh well, maybe I'm wrong," he said.

I went back to the quiz, unsettled. Victoria Patawasti? What was he talking about? He must be mistaken.

"Jesus Christ," Facey said, "we're about to have the tiebreaker."

I sat down.

"Who was the Roman Emperor who conquered Britain?" Marty asked.

I buzzed. I hadn't even heard the question. I was thinking about Victoria.

"Julius Caesar, no, Claudius," I said.

Facey groaned.

"I must accept your first answer," Marty said.

"It must be bloody Claudius then," one of the Brats said.

Facey didn't even speak. I felt sick. I went outside. I waited for John. What an idiot. How would I pay Spider now? A minute passed.

There was some kind of commotion.

I looked in through the windows. A depressingly familiar scene. John and Facey right in the thick of an argument, yelling at Davy Bannion—the Brats' captain, a tough-bastard sergeant in the military police. Shite, I supposed I had to go help. I went back inside. I caught John's eye and shook my head ironically at him, trying to convey the impression that this sorry state of affairs had begun with his speech in the toilet. But before John could respond, Davy swung a punch. It hammered John backward into the picture over the fireplace.

"Oh, shit," I moaned.

Facey immediately piled into a skinny corporal called Blaine and I jumped the third member of the Brats, a stuck-up officer called McGuigan, from behind. I enjoyed smacking him a good right hook on the side of the head. A fight between cops and the army, so you knew no one in the bar was going to break it up.

McGuigan turned around and tried to head-butt me, but I used his forward momentum to grab him by the hair and hurl him into one of the ceiling-support columns. He crunched into it with a sickening crash. Blood squirted everywhere and he fell dazed onto the big wooden tables.

"I think I broke his nose," I said to a disgusted female noncombatant who'd come out for a quiet drink, not a John Ford movie.

"What's happening?" I shouted across to John.

"Marty doesn't want to give them the rollover money from last week's quiz, because technically it was a tie," John somehow managed to explain.

Facey and Blaine suddenly went skewing across a table, turned over three more tables, and there was chaos now, people screaming, yelling, trying to save their pints; in the melee, somehow two other quite separate fights had broken out. Violence always bubbling beneath the surface here in the north Belfast suburbs.

I turned to my left. John and Bannion were wrestling on the floor. I was going to go and kick Bannion but I happened to notice Spider sprawled in a mess on the ground. His back was to me, so I went and gave him five or six good kicks in the ribs. He was already half concussed from whatever had justly befallen him. I took a moment and rifled his pockets. No dough, but a nice little tinfoil turd of ketch that would last the likes of me a week or more. Make up for the one I left in the boat. Just hope he didn't guess who took it. I kicked him once more for luck.

Now John had pulled himself up, and that eejit Bannion was fighting with someone else completely. John and I rescued Facey and ran out of there before the Carrick peelers showed up and had the embarrassing task of arresting the lot of us.

o o o

Belfast Lough to our right, the town to our left, Carrickfergus Castle behind us, the stunted palm trees

surviving in the Gulf Stream breeze. I knew it wasn't
the fight. John was quiet for some other reason. A
deeper reason. He gave me a long look. He wanted to
say something. It had been building all evening. It had
been building for weeks. I knew what it was. He
wanted to give me a lecture.

The peelers had hired John because they thought he
could be a big bruiser but in fact he was a lazy, pot-
smoking, terrible cop. But he knew it had been my vo-
cation. He was three years older than me, we'd grown
up almost next door to each other and in lieu of a de
jure older brother who lived in England, John considered himself the de facto one. Sometimes he felt he
should tell me off. I looked at him. Quiet, reflective.
He really was going to say it, he'd prepared a spiel. He
took a breath. I had to stop him.

"John, look, before you start. I don't want to hear
that shit you read in some pamphlet. About three hundred people die a year of straight ketch overdoses.
More people die in lightning strikes. Tobacco kills ten
thousand times as many. No bloody lectures."

He smiled and choked on his cig.

"Alex, two things. First, I'm very impressed with
your psychic abilities and second, who do you think
you're bloody kidding, you know it's killing you."

"No, it's not. I don't want to hear it. You don't understand. I'm not you. I am the driver, it's the driven. I'm
in control. You should understand that. I'm not even
an addict."

"Do you not see? You're the worst kind of addict,

that thinks he's not even an addict," John said with a sad smile on his big face.

"Bullshit, John, total bullshit," I said with more than a little anger.

"It's not. And you have to deal with that scumbag Spider. Come on, Alex, you were a bloody *detective*, what's happened to you? Look at you now, it's humiliating."

"You know the rules, John, we don't talk about this."

John stared at me and shook his head. But I'd taken the wind out of his sails and he didn't want to go on.

"Ah fuck it," he said, angry at himself for blowing his chance. I was pissed off at him for trying to get heavy with me. We walked in silence past the Royal Oak.

"Some peeler you are," I said after a while.

"Why?"

"Bloke back there following us."

"One of the soldiers?"

"No. Picked him up outside Dolan's, in the phone box. Stupid place to hide—phone doesn't work. Waited till we went by, looked back, there he was. We crossed the Marine Highway, he crossed with us and back again."

"Shit, he's after me. I, I owe a guy some money . . ." John began and trailed off, embarrassed.

"I owe a guy some money too," I said.

John looked me in the eye and for some reason we both started laughing.

"You know, we're both a couple of fuckups," John said.

"We'll lose him by cutting over the railway lines. Course, if chain-smoking has killed your lung capacity . . ." I said.

John grunted. We ambled back behind the Royal Oak pub and pretended to take a piss against the wall. As soon as we were out of sight, we legged it into the shadows, climbed over the car park wall, scrambled over the wire fence that led up the railway embankment, cut over the railway lines and up the other side. We threw ourselves into the field and hit the road running.

We looked back but the tail had to be still looking for us in the shadows of the Oak's car park. Laughing, breathless, we parted ways.

"Last we'll see of that bastard," John yelled, waving at me as I walked up the road.

"Aye," I yelled back happily.

I laughed. John laughed. And if only we'd bloody known. The man, of course, was none of the things I'd suspected he was. No. Someone quite different. For two lines of force were converging that night. Two pieces of information. Two motivators. From the man following me. And from what Dad was about to tell me when I got home. . . .

The house. A bungalow on a side street near the supermarket. Overgrown garden, peeling paint, Greenpeace posters, a peaty smell from the blackened chimney, boxes of recyclables in the yard. "A disgrace to the street," some of the neighbors called it.

Da stood in the kitchen checking his flyers for the millionth time. The place a mess of papers, even more of a mess than usual. Da was running for the local council as a Green Party candidate. He was up against the popular deputy mayor. Poor Da, on a hiding to nothing. One could only hope that it would be such an easy campaign for the deputy mayor that he wouldn't smear Da with his son's mysterious resignation from the police.

"Dad, what are you doing up, it's almost one o'clock?" I asked.

"Working," he said.

"Dad, please, I hate to be a broken record, but everyone agrees you won't win."

"I know I won't win. Not this time, maybe not next time but soon. Momentum is growing. Speaking down at the Castle Green for an hour this morning."

"Dad, can you lend me some money?"

"You know I can't."

"I don't mean a lot, I mean, like twenty quid."

"Alex, I'm trying to run a campaign, I'm totally strapped," he said, his melancholy blue eyes blinking slowly. He yawned and ran a bony hand through his short gray hair.

"Listen, if I get more than five percent of the vote in the election, I get my thousand-pound deposit back and I'll give you money for anything you want."

"Yeah, white Christmas in Algeria, pigs flying, and so on."

"Why Algeria?"

"Why not? There's the Sahara."

"Well, because there's also the Atlas Mountains in

Algeria, where it might actually snow, so your little analogy—"

"Dad, are you going to lend me any money or not?" I interrupted.

"Alex, I don't have it," he said sadly and shook his head.

"Ok, forget it," I said.

I opened the cupboard and tried to find a clean mug to get a drink of water. The kitchen was as messy as the rest of the house. Old wooden cupboards, filthy with dust and stains. Fungi in Tupperware, weird grains in bags, chai teas, bits of food that had long since become living entities. It was as if he'd cleaned nothing since Ma died six years ago. I'd only been back living here for the last two months, ever since they foreclosed my mortgage, but it was so disgusting I was thinking of moving in with John.

"Don't forget the dry cleaning stub, you're to pick up our suits tomorrow while I'm in Belfast," Dad said.

"Suits. . . . What are you talking about, did somebody die?"

"Didn't I tell you already, don't you know?"

"Victoria Patawasti," I said, aghast.

"Aye. America, it was a mugging that went wrong, a Mexican man or something, I heard."

"Oh my God, she was murdered? I went out with her, you know."

"I know."

"For, for two months. She, she, uh, she was my first real girlfriend."

"I know. Son, I'm sorry. Are you ok?"

I wasn't ok. Victoria had been more than my first girlfriend. She'd been my first real anything. A year older than me, a year more experienced. At the time I thought that I was in love with her.

"Jesus Christ, Victoria Patawasti," I said.

"I know," Dad said glumly. Scholarly, bespectacled, he looked a little like Samuel Beckett on a bad day.

"I saw Vicky's dad just yesterday," I said.

"Well, someone said that they thought the funeral would be at the weekend and I figured we should get our suits cleaned just in case," Dad said.

"She was mugged in America? Was she on holiday? No, she was working there, wasn't she?"

"I don't know," Dad said, shaking his head. "They told me in the newsagent's. I don't know any more. Alex, I'm really sorry, I thought I told you."

He got up, patted me on the shoulder, sat down, waited for a decent amount of time, stared at his flyers again.

"Alex, I don't have my slippers on, will you lock the garage?" he asked after a while.

I said nothing, took the key, and went outside.

The stars. The cold air. Victoria Patawasti. Bloody hell. I wanted to walk down to the water, to my place. I had my ketch now. But that would be the thing a junkie would do. I was in control.

I'd known Victoria since I'd gone to the grammar school. Our sixth form was so small: thirty boys, thirty girls, you couldn't help but know everyone. Victoria

Patawasti. Jesus. She was head girl, of course, captain of the field hockey team, beautiful. We'd gone out for a couple of months. We had gone on maybe seven or eight actual dates. To the leisure center cafeteria, to the cinema in Belfast a few times, and sailing in Belfast Lough. She'd taken me out in her dad's thirty-two-foot cruiser. She knew what she was doing but I'd never sailed before. God. I remembered it all. I knew why we were really going out there.

I'd been nervous. Small talk. I asked her about Hindu mythology and on the lee rail in the middle of Belfast Lough she'd told me a story. It was about the first incarnation of Lord Vishnu. In the Hindu pantheon Brahma was the Creator, Vishnu was the Sustainer, and Shiva the Destroyer. Vishnu repeatedly comes to Earth to help mankind, the first time as a fish to tell some guy there's going to be a big flood and he has to get all the animals and people into a boat. I told Victoria that a fish would be the last person to be concerned about too much water, but she said that the guy bought the yarn and thus saved mankind. I bought it too. There's a similar story in the Torah.

And then. Then she took me down below. And we took off her clothes. Not the first time for her, but the first for me.

Victoria.

I went back inside the house. Dad still there. I didn't want to think about her but I wanted to talk. Clear my mind. Anything would do.

"Dad, what's the deal with Noah and the flood?" I asked him.

Dad, of course, had studied it in Hebrew but he and Mum were old hippies and had kept my brother, my sister, and myself from such superstition. Mum and Dad were both from Belfast's tiny Jewish community, but we'd been raised with no organized religion. They'd felt, with abundant evidence, that religion was the cause of most of the problems in Ireland, Western Europe, Earth. So we were taught Darwin and Copernicus from an early age. No bris, no bar mitzvah, no Shabbat, Passover, or Chanukah. Nothing. We got presents at the winter solstice, not Christmas. Crappy presents, too.

"What do you know about Noah?" Dad asked, his eyes narrowing with skepticism.

"Well, uh, he got all the animals, right, in twos and put them in an ark, they ended up in Turkey," I said.

"That's about it, rain for forty days, forty nights, the floods covered the highest mountains, a dove brought back an olive branch showing when the rains had subsided. They all lived happily ever after."

"How did the olive tree survive under all the pressure of water?"

"What do you mean?"

"Covers highest mountain, Everest. That's almost thirty thousand feet of water pressure, that's going to crush an olive tree to bits."

"Yes, I see," Dad said.

"All the forests would be wiped out. Osmosis would kill the sea creatures. Also, too many animals to fit."

"Alex, I get your point," Dad said wearily.

"It's unlikely is what I'm saying."

"But I agree," Dad said, concern in that wrinkled brow and those eyes like dried-up wells.

"Look, Alex, what's the matter? Are you depressed? Not upset about the police still?"

I was suddenly pissed off.

"Dad, I'll tell you what is depressing. It's depressing hearing the same questions day in and day out. I mean, do you want me to move out? I'm going to have to. If you keep this up it's going to drive me mental. I mean, how about a moratorium on the words 'police force,' or 'are you ok,' or 'maybe you should go back to university,' you know, one week without any nagging, how does that bloody sound?"

"Sorry, Alex, I'm tired. . . . Look, do you want some tea?"

"No. Oh, wait, I'd love some."

He boiled the kettle and made the tea and gave me a mug. He took off his glasses, smiled.

"One time Noah got so drunk, he was rolling about naked in his tent and one of his kids came in, saw him naked, and got really upset. The Book of Genesis. There's a whole racial dimension too, ugly stuff," he said.

"Sounds like an interesting book. Probably I'll read the Bible, rebel against your atheistic ways and become a rabbi or a minister or something, it's always the case," I said.

"I'd probably deserve it," he said with a little laugh.

I was feeling conciliatory and guilty. Da looked old and tired.

"Sorry for yelling, it's just, well, it's just my life's very complicated at the moment."

"Your life's complicated? You're unemployed, you've nothing to do all day."

We sat in silence. America. Of course you'd die of a mugging in America. You grow up in Northern Ireland, schools and trains being bombed. You go to America and you get mugged, killed. I watched the moon through the window. A trapdoor of green light in the cold, unfathomable night. Clouds came and obscured the sky. I shivered, stood.

"I'm going for a walk," I said. I could wait no more.

o o o

There is a place, a quiet place where the drunks go, or the boys out sniffing glue, or girls with their boys, or people with kids or dogs. Or people alone. In the dark, behind the railway lines, at Downshire Halt where the tracks have come, ten miles out of Belfast, to be near their reflection in the water. Night is the time. When the trains have stopped. And it's quiet and you're in the place, on the compacted sand and grass, and before you is the still lough and everywhere is lights.

Behind you, Carrickfergus. And in front. Left to right. Bangor, Cultra, Belfast in a curve of silence and color giving up their presence to the brooding of the black clouds and the yawning sky and the stars.

And you sit there in the cold and you boil the heroin and take a nip. And it's moving. The whole of the Earth. Everything rotating about that one spot. The city. The houses. The ambulances and cars. The water itself. And no one knows.

But you.

The cold of the ground working its way through your jeans and your boxers and the sandy grass under your fingertips. Birds down in the pale of the moonlight and the planes coming from Scotland, a light and then another, and a faint sound of closeness and then gone over to the ocean and the other countries.

Ketch dissolving into the water. You add a piece of cotton and it puffs up, you draw the heroin through the cotton and into the needle and then tighten the pajama cord on your arm. You find a vein. You need illumination for this. You go lengthwise on the vein. You draw back the needle so that you can tell if there's blood in there. It is a vein. You inject yourself.

Clouds. A breeze. And the world moves about you. Bairns and old men and dogs and cats. Slumbering. The city on the mudflats struggling like a man in quicksand to keep itself from oozing under. Its beacons. Its cranes. Its waves of radio that speak unto itself and that bounce off granite and anvil stone and slip into the heavens and across the plain of night. The souls asleep. All of them, save you.

Here, water and birds and the phosphorescence of the lights. Beautiful. The shape in the darkness is the quiet of a tanker heading for the working power plant and with it a dark familiar, a pilot boat nudging the waves and gently put-putting out of the muted harbor mouth.

It's unfashionable, heroin.

It broke here only two years ago, but already it's going out of style. The scene from Manchester is drifting over. We're always about five years behind England—acid house and dance music dictate that uppers are what's in now. Cocaine, crack cocaine, methamphetamine, and the hep and current recreational drug of today—ecstasy.

Heroin peaked in 1971. Who does heroin now but losers? Sad sacks. Kids on a path toward self-mutilation and suicide.

Ecstasy is fun, it's a trip. Heroin, the posters say, kills. But better than that, it fucks with your skin and your hair and makes it so you can't dance. Heroin is so over.

It's a drug without trendiness or cool.

For them. For the common herd. But you know its secret. You've mastered it. You are the king. One long hit a day to even you out, to take you to the place. Who ever heard of a junkie who only needed a hit a day? Junkies are slaves to ketch. Not you. And every day you inject or buy it saves your life. Yes. Makes you not care that you're an ex-cop. An ex-detective and that your love affair with truth is long since done.

You sit there and smile. The waves, the water, the moonlight on the vapor trails. Time elapses. You rub at the numbness on your thigh. You fidget. You look around and about you. There is a still torpor over everything. The nighttime dormancy. It adds to the depth of your emptiness.

You cough.

The wind picks up a little. The water breathes. A gull. An oystercatcher. A ripple of noise on the sewage outfall. The sound of steam escaping from a cooling tower.

The moon tugs you. The lost sun. The mountains. But it's so cold.

And finally you stand and shake the stiffness from yourself and you're about to walk back up the rocks away from the harmonic of wave and sand over the lines to the platform on the other side, but you don't.

Something stops you.

The second part of the high. A wave. A big one. Spider's been holding out on me. This is grade-one shit.

Jesus.

It smothers me. Makes me sit. Lie down.

Makes me remember . . .

Autumn fog drifted in from the water. The clock tower in the Marine Garden pointed at three different times. Leaves clogged the gutters of the drains. The swings in the swing park damp, sad. The castle shrouded in mist so you could see only the gate tower and the portcullis. The rain, a drizzle—soft, temperate. Full dark now. My watch said seven o'clock. I'd been here since six-thirty. Time ebbed slowly. Puddles formed. There was no one around. That kind of night. I let the hood fall on my duffle coat. Victoria wasn't coming. I drank the rainwater. Watched the fog drape itself over the highway. At seven-thirty a car pulled in. Lights on, radio playing. She exited. She was still wearing her school uniform. Raincoat, umbrella. She came over. The car waited.

I stepped out from under the overhang.

"I'm so sorry I'm late but I was at a debate," she said in that elocution voice.

"It's ok. Is that your dad?"

She waved the car away angrily. Mr. Patawasti got out of the car, waved back.

"Hello, Alex," he shouted.

"Hello, Mr. Patawasti," I said. He stood there looking at us, grinning.

"Dad," Victoria said desperately.

He got back in the car and reversed into the mist.

"Well," she said, taking out a lipstick and applying it.

"Well," I said.

"Sort of awkward, isn't it?" she said, touching up the lipstick with her long fingers.

"Yes. Who won the debate?"

"We did. It was about the European Union. It was a Catholic school on the Falls Road and there we were in our red-white-and-blue uniforms."

"Tough crowd."

She nodded. I looked at her, her hair was wet. She was tired.

"What do you want to do?" I asked.

"I don't know," she said, wiping rainwater from her dark green eyes.

"Do you want to just go for a walk, maybe talk a little?"

"I'd really like that," she said, her face lighting up.

I wanted to ask what she'd done with Peter on their dates, but it wouldn't be smart to bring him up. She'd gone out with Peter for a year and he'd dumped her for a girl in the fifth form. John had said that this was the moment to swoop in and ask her out. "Ok, she's older, sophisticated, but now she's vulnerable, she wants to show the world she's ok. She'll go out with you."

And sure enough, a little late, but here she was.

"But, Alex, remember she's on the rebound, she might just want someone to tide her through, till she gets her bearings," John had also cautioned. Bastard had been right about that one, too. Peter owned a car, so they'd probably gone places—Belfast, the Antrim coast. They'd probably gone to pubs. I wasn't old enough to get into pubs. I was only sixteen. What must this feel like for her? Walking around with some lanky wanker in Carrickfergus in the rain. A step down, tedious, a real sham—

"What are you thinking about?" she asked.

"Uh, poetry."

"Poetry?"

"Yes."

"You don't seem the type."

"What is the type?"

"I don't know, but you don't seem it."

She was right, too. I didn't fit into any of the cliques. I

didn't play rugby, so I didn't fit in with the jocks. I wasn't into Dungeons and Dragons, so I didn't fit in with the nerds. I wasn't sniffing glue, so I wasn't in with the bad kids. Not tight with the creative types who worked on the school magazine. I didn't quite fit in anywhere.

"Yeats, I like Yeats," I said.

"You don't find the fairy stuff wears a bit thin?" she asked.

"Uh, no."

Silence again. And yes, there's her back then and there's me back then. Me, fifteen pounds heavier, no beard, tidy hair, clean and sober. She, Indian, beautiful, exotic. Me, of the hippie parents, the wunderkind with the discipline problem. She, the head girl. Both of us, though, outsiders. Aye. We were made for each other.

"It's all Celtic mythology," I said.

"It is?"

"It is. For instance, you know why Celtic crosses have a circle on them?"

"No."

"That's the symbol of Lugh, the sun god. That's also why the Romans made the Sabbath a Sunday."

"You know about that stuff?"

"Not really," I admitted, and caught her tiny smile.

"I know a lot of Indian mythology," she said.

"Tell me some," I said, breaking into a grin.

"It's pretty wacky. I'll save it for next time," she said coyly.

"Will there be a next time?" I asked.

"Maybe."

We walked to the cafeteria at the swimming pool, watched the swimmers go back and forth in lanes. We talked about school and books. Still raining. I saw her home. She was soaked. We stood outside her gate. Her father's big house. A thirties folly in white stucco with Romanesque windows, gargoyles, three floors, and a little Gothic tower on the roof. I'd heard about this place, but I hadn't been here before.

The house had a name, the "Tiny Taj."

"The Tiny Taj?" I said, trying not to grin.

She groaned.

"It's been called that since the 1930s when it was built by a retired member of the Indian Civil Service. Of course Dad couldn't resist when he saw that. It's totally embarrassing. Living in a house with a name is bad enough, but the Tiny Taj?"

She laughed. Her face shone under the porch light.

"You'll see me again?" I asked.

"I will."

"We'll talk in school?"

"Yes. We'll go out next week. Give you a chance to actually read a Yeats poem."

"It will that."

"Ok. Night."

"Night."

She looked at me. Her eyes, dark, heavy, beautiful. Her lips full, red.

"Well," she said, "are you going to kiss me?"

I didn't say anything. I leaned forward and with great care, as if she were some delicate rose, I put my hand on her wet cheek and kissed her lips. She tasted of peaches. We stood there kissing in the rain and caught our breaths and she went up that big path to her house. And I walked home thinking, I don't believe I'll ever be this happy again.

I was right.

3: THE BURNING GHAT

We hadn't brought umbrellas. The day had started sunny. But it's a funeral in eastern Ulster and who ever heard of sun for such an affair? Now from Donegal to the Mournes a smear of black cloud and thrashing rain. Raining so hard it makes divots in the clay.

St. Nicholas's Parish Church, Carrickfergus, June 12, 1995.

Cold, hard to see what's happening at the front. Impossible to hear. The funeral mass is in the style of the Church of Ireland. The simple pine coffin beside the font. Hymns. A memorial read by her older brother, Colin. The church dating back to the twelfth century. William Congreve and Jonathan Swift worshiped here. I stand there reluctantly. I didn't want to come. The last funeral I was at . . . Ma. And where *do* you bury a Jewish atheist-humanist in Belfast? Not the synagogue. A rented hall. And who conducts the service? A man Dad met. An actor with a booming voice. Talking about Mum, whom he didn't really know. He goes on forever until it becomes a farce. It is the opposite of catharsis—whatever that is.

"Shit."

"Ssshhh," John says.

The service, handshakes. Tears. John, Facey, myself squeezed soaked into Facey's Ford Fiesta.

Rain guttering down Facey's broken window wiper. The funeral procession. Facey dipping the clutch, stalling the car. Out along the sea front. White water on the lough. Black clouds. The turn up Downshire Road. The graveyard. Exiting. Hats on, umbrellas up and sucked outward by the wind. Cars parked. Only the men walking to the graveside. The women, as is traditional in Protestant Ulster, outside the cemetery gates or at home preparing the wake.

The graves. Markings. Pictures on some. Wet flowers on others. Pitiful messages over children. And that one grave. The saddest here. Don't even look down that row. Don't even look. Visited it three times in six years. Pain. Numbing. Panic rising in my throat. A flash to that bed in the hospital, Mum on full meds, the pain racking her body, just me and her. Oh, God. John and Facey still beside me. I lean on John for a moment to steady myself.

Mr. Patawasti, Colin and Stephen Patawasti and an uncle I don't know carrying the coffin. Slipping in the mud with that deadweight inside the box. The story's out now. Victoria murdered by a Mexican burglar at her apartment in Denver. So pointless. Such a waste.

Mist on the hills. The Knockagh from the side in pale loops of gray and green. A smell. Damp earth. Around the graveyard the dungy aroma of a churned field. The service. The priest's white cassock sodden and blowing around his face. Sixty men soaked in their dark suits. No one can hear what the priest says.

It belatedly dawns on me. This is a Christian burial. She was a Christian. All that Hindu mythology had been what? A pose? An embrace of the exotic in dyadic, sectarian Ulster.

Oh, Victoria. We are so similar. Can you not see, you there, the rain hammering off your coffin top, your brothers stumbling on the earth. We are so alike. You, the third child, the last born, the youngest. You and I, both of ancient peoples, alien here in this atavistic god-intoxicated land. You and I, the punch line of a joke. We both have failed. You are dead and I am a specter of a man. I look away. Down from the Knockagh, the forest and the beginnings of the town.

Stand still and gaze anywhere but the fourth row.

The cemetery is pitched on the high ground above the main body of Carrickfergus. Winds coming down from the Antrim Plateau and up from the lough. John complains about the rain and he and Facey move discreetly toward the lone tree.

"We commend to Almighty God our daughter," the priest must be saying. "Ashes to ashes." And they try to lower the coffin but the rainwater has caved in earth on either side of the grave, and it won't go down. Mr. Patawasti asks them to try again. They attempt it three more times but she will not go.

I remember that. Stubborn, proud, the only dark-skinned girl in a school of six hundred. Captain of the debate and field hockey teams.

Everyone is getting soaked. Mr. Patawasti says that that's enough. He walks off with his two sons and the uncle and my da and other members of the disbanded cricket club. Great solace you will be, Da. Don't think I didn't see you sneak on your yarmulke. Hypocrite. Did you say Kaddish that previous burial? Did you convince us that she would live again, somehow? Did you offer us one ounce of comfort? "Your mother's gone for good, but her memory lives inside of us." I needed more than that, you bastard. They walk right past me. And oh God, Mr. Patawasti is coming right over with Da. I back up against a gravestone. I want to run. He opens his mouth to say something but he doesn't. His face is torn apart, his eyes vacant. The skull showing beneath the skin. He looks like the subject of the funeral, not one of the mourners. It's horrific. He stares at me for a second and then the party moves on. Dad looks at me and nods.

They make their way back to the cars. I stand in the shelter of the tree, shaking, waiting for the weather to break. The gravediggers leave, the cemetery keeper leaves. The coffin sits there by the grave, rain pattering on the name plaque and the memories. I walk over. The wreaths, a dozen or more. The biggest one from America: "From all at CAW, fond memories of a wonderful person—Charles, Amber, and Robert Mulholland."

I look down the pale lough. I can imagine the Viking boats, like this coffin, shaped from pine or spruce. A boat carved from pine dissolving into the bog of the next world.

"Come on," John says, "we might as well make a dash for the car, this is going to be on all day."

"What is?"

"The rain."

"We'll go to the pub," Facey says.

Go to the car, like a sleepwalker. Get in, drive to Carrick. John talking to Facey in the front. Someone has bought the Triumph brand name, will be making them, again. Motorcycles. Nonsense. John, Facey, why can't you see the ocean of pain around you? Tribulation falling from the skies. Did you ever read the Venerable Bede? Of course not. Life is like a bird at night, flying into a great hall full of feasting, behind is darkness, ahead is darkness, the journey through the wonder, brief, bewildering, awful, done.

"We're here," Facey says, takes the keys from the ignition, turns around, grins, "we're here." Aye . . .

The fire in Dolan's was lit and I stood there drying out my wet funeral-and-interview suit. A cold, nasty day but the fire helped a lot. I dried off and got some crisps from the bar. John supplied the information about the Christian burial. The Patawastis had been high-caste Hindus from Allahabad, India. But Mr. Patawasti and his brother had both been sent to public school in London at an early age and both had gradually fallen under the somnambulant spell of the Church of England.

After school Mr. Patawasti had gone to Oxford, mar-

ried an English girl, had two sons, got offered a lec-
tureship in physics and applied maths at the University
of Ulster, and had moved to Northern Ireland, just in
time for the start of the Troubles in 1967.

"Maths, eh?" I said to John. Typical. Another thing
apart from cricket and vegetarianism he had in common with my da. Cricket, vegetarianism, and maths,
surely the three most boring things in the world.

We talked about Victoria but the boys knew I'd gone
out with her and were restrained. I got up to go, Facey
offered me a lift. But I was having none of it.

Soaked to the skin, I arrived at the back door of our
house. Dad in the kitchen, nervous, upset. He had
changed out of his drenched suit into sweatshirt and
jeans. The sweatshirt said "Save the Rainforest" on it
and had a picture of a leaping whale. You wouldn't
have thought the rain forest supported many whales
but maybe that was why it needed saving.

"What is it?" I asked him.

"There's a man waiting for you in the living room.
An Englishman. Are you in some kind of trouble?"

"Not that I know of," I said.

I pulled down the ladder and went up to my bedroom in the attic. Hundreds of my old books. Teenage
manifestations. *The Catcher in the Rye, L'Etranger,
The Outsiders.* Records, train sets. I grabbed a dressing gown and sweatpants, sat there, amid the dust. I
was glad now I'd come home. I'd had a flat at the marina. I'd done it in pastels, big black stereo, a couple of
chairs, minimalism. Not many books. A few choice

records and CDs. A guitar. I wanted to impress girls with the Zen-like tranquillity of pure being. No clutter. A lie, of course. Here, despite the filth, I was more at ease. I could pull up the ladder and climb under the duvet and no one would ever get me. I could stay here, and the autumn would come and then the winter. Snow would pile up on the window ledge. I'd stay here, safe and warm until Mum yelled at me and got the hook and pulled down the ladder and brought up hot chocolate and digestive biscuits. Yes.

I shook my head, rejected the mawkishness, climbed down the ladder, walked across the hall and into the living room.

A very tall man, six six, two hundred and forty pounds, clothed in a baggy, expensive blue suit with narrow lapels. His face showed worry lines and had a gray, bitter edge to it. He had an oft-broken nose and salt-and-pepper hair. He was sipping tea and looking at the jazz records, the piles of old newspapers and the other shit. Fit and tough, and I would have pegged him for a bouncer or a debt collector if it weren't for the big mustache, which told me he was a peeler. So— an English cop. A cop from Scotland Yard. He came from the Samson Inquiry. I knew immediately why he was here and why he'd followed me. I knew immediately I was fucked.

I stuck out my hand. He shook it. Scars over his knuckles. His hand was rough. Christ, this was definitely no desk jockey, or at least he hadn't always been one.

I sat down. He opened a briefcase and removed a clipboard.

"I'm Commander Douglas," he said with an unpleasant grin.

"What's a commander?" I asked him. He looked at me, didn't know if I was taking the piss or not.

"In the Met, the Metropolitan Police, it's the rank above chief superintendent."

"Fancy that. If I was still a peeler I'd salute ya," I said.

"Well," he said, baffled, irritated.

"And you know who I am," I said.

"Yes. I'd like to ask you a few questions, Mr. Lawson." He said it so quietly I could barely hear him.

"What about?"

"Well, I want to be very informal, Mr. Lawson. If I'd wanted to, I would have had you arrested, we could have talked in Belfast or in London, tape recorders, lawyers, all that," he said with a grim little smile.

If he had meant to put the fear of fucking Jehovah in me, he had. I hid my panic in my beard, stuck my hands in the dressing gown pockets.

"Fire away, Commander. I'm ready."

"You don't, Mr. Lawson, seem surprised to see me," he said.

"Well. Your Keystone-Kop-following-me routine for the last couple of days gave the game away, didn't it?"

"Yes, well, I like to keep an eye on a suspect for a few days before I go charging in. You can only get so much from the files."

"What do you mean by the word *suspect*?" I said.

His smiled widened. Ugly, like a crack in a granite craphouse.

"What I mean, Mr. Lawson, is that you don't seem surprised to be being interviewed by a detective from Scotland Yard."

"I assume you're from the Samson Inquiry," I said.

He nodded.

In 1994, after years of pressure from the Irish lobby in America, the British government in London had launched an inquiry into the Royal Ulster Constabulary of Northern Ireland to find out three main things: Was the police force biased against Catholics, was there a shoot-to-kill policy when dealing with IRA men, and finally, was there widespread corruption? They'd put John Samson, an assistant chief constable from the Metropolitan Police—an outsider—in charge and given him free rein to investigate all aspects of the RUC's operations. Samson had seconded about twenty officers to help him, most also from the Met. Many, many people in the RUC were worried about the inquiry. I'd never shot anyone and I wasn't in charge of recruitment, so Douglas had to be part of the corruption team. I'd heard that in the last few weeks Samson's investigation was reaching a climax and he was soon to show his preliminary report to the prime minister. It made me very nervous. I sat on my hands.

Douglas took a sip of the tea and put down the jazz record. *Kind of Blue* by Miles Davis. Obviously not a connoisseur, just grabbed the one disc he'd heard of.

He had a wedding ring, married, about fifty-five. The right age to be a chief super, so no high flyer he, just a plodding efficient copper, the dangerous type. He had a gun, too. They'd issued it to him. You could see it protruding through his jacket lapel. He gave me a contented look. It scared me.

"Why did you resign from the Royal Ulster Constabulary?" he asked, lighting himself a cigarette and putting the ash into one of Mum's long-dead-plant pots.

"What?"

"Six good years as a policeman and suddenly you pack it in. Why did you resign from the RUC, Mr. Lawson?"

"Well, Commander, I'd had enough of the police, it wasn't the place for me. I didn't want anymore to be part of a predominantly Protestant force, largely seen by Catholics as a repressive instrument. My father, as you probably noticed, is a progressive; me, too. I realized I was in the wrong line of work, I resigned."

"I have your dossier. Joined at eighteen, made detective after three years. You know who makes detective after three years? At the age of twenty-fucking-one?

"No, but you're going to tell me," I said, attempting insouciance.

"No one makes detective at that age. No one. Practically unheard of."

"Yeah, they hated the way I saluted them. They wanted me in plainclothes. Honestly, that was the reason. Buck McConnell told me that."

"You were quite brilliant, Mr. Lawson. In Belfast it's an accelerated learning curve, but even so, a detective at twenty-one? After three years? You were destined for great things. You obviously had mentors. Inspector John McGuinness, Chief Inspector Michael McClare, Superintendent William McConnell. I've read all their comments about you."

"What's your point?"

"My point, Mr. Lawson, is that you were an outstanding police officer. I pulled your police boards. You finished top of your class. And your IQ test. The top third of the ninety-ninth percentile."

"No serious person believes IQ tests anymore. And the ninety-ninth percentile, five billion people on Earth, at least fifty million people with that score. No shakes there, mate," I said.

"And your A-level results?" Douglas said with a smile.

"What about my university results? That throws a spanner in the works, doesn't it," I said. "I was a total failure at university. I flunked out in my second year."

"Your mother was dying throughout your second year at university. I would say you were distracted."

"Well, ok, so I'm the original Jesus Christ, what exactly—"

"You worked on fourteen cases in your first two years as a detective and all fourteen were broken. That represents a fifty percent higher success rate than the RUC's norm. You solved two closed-book homicide cases."

"Yeah. You know, I'm not being modest here but you're from England and you probably think the quality of peelers over here is equivalent to what it is over there, but it's not, mate. Most of the coppers I worked with were hoodlums, drunks, thickos, the other day I was in a bloody bar fight with two of them, it really—"

"What I'm suggesting, Mr. Lawson, is that you were destined to rise very high in the RUC and yet for some reason, out of the blue, you resigned. I checked, you'd just passed the sergeant's exam. Hell, you could have been a detective inspector by thirty. It makes no sense. There was no reason given in the report. But I want to know. Why did you resign, Mr. Lawson?"

"Look. I'd had enough, I had two really ugly domestic violence cases. Murders. I had one where a child was killed. That doesn't take much solving, but it takes some time to get it out of your head. I had just had enough."

"Lies," he said, stubbing the cigarette violently into Mum's pot.

"What?"

"I am not a very patient man, Mr. Lawson," Douglas said, angrily.

"Look it up, that's in your files. That was my case, Donovan McGleish, had him arrested. Life imprisonment they gave him. In the Kesh. Don't call me a liar."

"You're too young to be a burnout. That's not why you resigned," he said, stroking the mustache. He picked up his clipboard and read something. His cuff went up on his shirt. There was a tattoo on his wrist. A pair of wings. An ex-paratrooper. A hard case. Just great.

"After two and a half years as a detective constable, you were assigned to the drugs squad," he said, matter-of-factly.

"Correct."

"Did you ask to be transferred?"

"I did, I told you I'd had enough of homicide."

"You solved not one case in the drugs squad, and then mysteriously you resigned."

"Not mysteriously, nothing mysterious about it, I had had enough. Many peelers quit after their very first year or blow their brains out. Look up the suicide rate for RUC men, I think you'll find that it is—"

"Mr. Lawson, your behavior is just not fucking cricket. But you are going to cooperate with me and I will explain why. As part of the Samson Inquiry, I have extremely wide-ranging powers. Arrest. Summoning before a magistrate, prosecution of uncooperative material witnesses. Contempt of court. You name it. I will have you arrested, I will throw you in jail."

Now I was starting to sweat. Not an empty threat. He didn't make empty threats. I could see it in his eyes. Cold, indifferent. All business. He lit himself another cigarette.

"There's an old Belfast rule for when you're being questioned by the police—whatever you say, say nothing," I announced, attempting levity. He wasn't impressed.

"I'm not sure yet what happened with you, Mr. Lawson, or what you found out in the drug squad, but I do know that a meteoric detective does not suddenly resign for no reason. I will get to the bottom of this and I will make you talk. I want the names and I'm going to get the names. If you were intimidated, we can give you protection."

"Protection. Ha. Not as smart as you look. What do you think? I'd uncovered a big bloody plot to flood Ulster with drugs? Some enormous protection racket? You're way off base, mate. You think they would have forced me to resign and that would have been it? They would have fucking killed me already. There's no plot, no racket, I don't know anything. I resigned because I was sick of it."

"Who is they?"

"What?"

"You said 'they.' Who is 'they,' who would have killed you?"

"There's no 'they,' there's no mystery. You don't get it, mate, I resigned because I'd had enough policing for a lifetime. Fed up. Forget your plots, forget your conspiracies. They don't exist. People like you and Samson believe in the conspiracy theory of history, well I believe in the fuck-up theory of history. Stupid things happen for no reason."

Douglas sat for a moment, listened to the sound of the rain on the rooftop. He looked at me and a wave of disgust seemed to go through him. His face contorted with rage. What was he doing here? I knew what he was thinking. These fucking Micks. Even the so-called smart ones, bog stupid. Eight hundred years England had been entangled with this awful place. Eight hundred bloody years. And he was a paratrooper, he'd probably been over here in the army and taken all kinds of shit. This time he stamped his cigarette out on the carpet.

He seemed to make a decision, got up, came over, grabbed me by the lapels of my dressing gown and pulled them so tight that he was effectively choking me.

"Now you will listen to me, you Paddy fuck," Douglas said, leaning in close. His breath stank, he was grinning. I gasped for air.

"You'll listen to me, Micky boy. I will fucking break you. I will have you, you Paddy piece of shit. I want the names. I am not someone to be fucked with," he said.

"I can't breathe—"

Douglas tightened his choke hold, I really couldn't breathe, seeing stars, blacking out, I grabbed at his big wrists, tried to push them off, but it was no good.

"Listen to me, bastard, fucking potato head. We will arrest you. We will force you to testify. I personally will make sure you do hard time for whatever it is you're hiding."

Suffocating. Choking.

"Stop it, I'll tell you," I managed to get out.

He eased up on the stranglehold, let me fall back to my chair.

"Speak," he said.

I took a couple of big breaths.

All policemen in Northern Ireland go on a survival course, and one aspect is how to respond if you're kidnapped by the IRA, tortured, questioned. At the first stage of the interrogation you say nothing, then you let them break you to the second stage, where you give them a lie and then, if the torture continues, you let them break you to the third stage, where you give them a story that is nearly the truth but not quite but close enough, so they'll think that that's finally it and they'll buy it. I had already told two stories about my resignation, so unfortunately I was at the third stage quicker than I would have liked. Nearly the truth.

"Ok, look, Douglas, here it is. It's the oldest bloody story in the book. I was an undercover cop. I had to pretend to be a junkie. I started taking heroin. It got ahold of me, took over, I really was a junkie, I was taking heroin from the police evidence room to support my habit. One time they caught me. The RUC found out and they made me resign. They were nice to me, they didn't prosecute me for theft, they just made me resign. No conspiracy, no corruption. I just fucked up. I know it's the bloody cliché of the narcs squad. But it's true."

He stared at me for a moment. He wasn't sure. He sat back down in the chair and lit another fag. He smoked nearly the whole thing. Thinking. I tried not to show that my fingers were crossed. He coughed, weighed his words.

"Mr. Lawson, I'm disappointed in you, I'd guessed that that was the story you would tell me, but I thought you'd be more creative."

"But it's fucking true."

"Part of it may be true, Mr. Lawson. Pathetic, I'm sure. But I don't want part of the truth, I want all of it."

He sighed melodramatically, got up again, walked over, suddenly grabbed both my wrists with one hand, and then pinned my arms with his knee and body weight. He smiled at me and brought the hand holding the cigarette up to my face. I started to yell but he shoved his free hand over my mouth. His knee and entire body forcing me into the chair. I struggled. He brought the cigarette to my eyebrow and let the ash singe it. I tried to wriggle away from him, but he was too strong. Strong and obviously a real psycho. He let the cigarette burn me for five agonizing seconds, then he let me go.

I gasped for air.

He stood. He picked up his briefcase, his clipboard.

"I'm flying back to London tonight. It's not just fucks like you we have to deal with. Other cases, too. That's why I have no time for your shit. But I'll be back two weeks from today. Yours is the most interesting. Monday the twenty-second. Keep your appointment book free. It's a good thing. Give you time to think. You will cooperate or I will shit upon you from a great height. I will destroy your fucking life. I will see you do ten years in Wormwood fucking Scrubs. And they will know that you were a copper. Oh yeah. I will see you fucking broke, you pathetic little shit. I'll see myself out."

He walked across the living room, turned, grinned at me, spat, and left.

I leaned back in the chair, got my breath back, tried not to puke. I heard the front door bang. Dad came in.

"What was that all about? Did he touch you? Are you ok?"

"Dad, how much money do you have?" I gasped.

"Nothing. I told you. I used it all for my deposit in the election but I do get it back if I win. Are you ok? What happened?"

"So, in other words, you've nothing."

"Are you in trouble?"

"No, but I might have to go somewhere for a while till the heat cools down."

"Who was that man, what did he want?"

"A policeman. He wants me to rat on my brother officers."

"Is he part of that Samson thing? But you've done nothing wrong," Dad said.

"I know, but he's going to persecute me, I've got to go somewhere."

"Your brother would put you up in London."

"England's no good. Besides, he wouldn't put me up anyway."

"He would, Alexander. Look, what's going on?"

I got up and went into the hall. I climbed up into the attic, I felt I was nearly going to cry. I was pathetic. Douglas was right. I stopped myself, found my coat, came back down the ladder.

"Where are you going?" Dad asked.

"Out."

I knew what I had to do, I had to get to the water. I had to get to my place. Raining again. But I had to get down there. That's where everything would become clear.

"Where are you going?" Dad insisted.

"Nowhere."

"Do you want some tea? You have to eat, Alex, you never eat," Dad said, shaking his head, worried.

"I'll get something."

I put on my coat and hat and ran out the door.

Pissing down. Hard. Bouncing off the stones and making lakes on the tar macadam. My wool hat was drenched in a minute. My place. Not going to panic. My place. Close, soon. Yes. Think. Think, man. Maybe John could lend me some money. Maybe Dad would come through. In any case, I had to lie low. Where? My brother and sister, in England. Hardly talked to them since the funeral. We weren't that close and Mum had been the glue holding the family together. And wasn't I right? They'd find me.

I shook my head. No. No money for a bus ticket to the airport, never mind an airfare. My left eyebrow hurt, everything hurt. What to do? Keep out of the shit. I could lie low. I had enough ketch for a couple of weeks. I could avoid Spider until then. Yeah, everything be fine. Yeah, all work out somehow. Douglas, looking at my personal file. Bastard. What does he know? Used me. Buck McConnell used me. Transferred me to narcotics because they knew I'd been arrogant. Curious. Knew I'd pursue the leads wherever they went. So stupid. Messed up. They were smarter than me. Thank God for ketch, ketch saved my life. . . .

The railway lines. The beach. The heroin. Thank God.

Everything in my coat pocket. Lunch box. Dry. I find my spot under the tiny cliff. Out of the wind, out of the rain. Open the lunch box. Ketch in a cellophane bag. Needles and syringe. New needles as important as supply. Can't share needle, ever. AIDS, hepatitis B and C. Death. Distilled water. Cotton balls. Some people use citric acid to make it dissolve better. Basic safety. New needle, alcohol swab, cotton filter. Spoon. Heroin so pure now some smoke it. Smoke it off aluminum foil. Eejits. Get brain damage, lung cancer. Injection safe. Safe as houses. Spoon, water, heroin, lighter under spoon. It boils. Ketch, beautiful. Check it's a vein. Draw it in. Draw it in. . . .

The beach.

The beach is not a beach. The sea is not a sea. The clouds are not clouds.

The beach is a slick of seaweed, jetsam, garbage, and shopping carts embedded in the sand like abstract sculpture. The sea, a tongue of lough. The clouds, oil burn-off from the smokestacks at the power station, two chimneys that fuck any residual hope of loveliness in the Irish landscape.

Belfast just across the water, its yellow cranes, its ferry terminus, its back-to-backs, its poison of estates. Everything dissolves. The rain stops. The sky clears. The world ceases to spin. Time slows. The power station vanishes into the sludge of history. The sky quiet. Birds. Gray seals. Sun. It's Ireland before people came. Before that Viking bark, that pine coffin of this morning, before the coracle. An Eden. A meditation of hill and forest. I stand there—an anachronism. A dead girl walks past me, in bare feet along the golden shore.

"Hey, you're a Christian really. What was all that Hindu stuff you were always going on about?"

"My heritage."

"You're really beautiful."

"Death doth improve my face."

"No, it never needed improving. But it is true, you are dead."

"I am and you're what, now, a junkie?"

"Why does no one understand? I'm not a junkie, you have to really try to become a junkie. I'm not a functioning heroin addict, because I'm not an addict."

"Sounds like you have that all rehearsed."

"Did you come here to give me a hard time?"

"I didn't come here at all."

"Oh yeah."

"It's just you and me on the boat."

"I remember."

"I know."

Your lips, your hair, oh, Victoria. I was terrified. My first time ever. Your breasts and those dark eyes. Jesus. And it was something you wanted too. You pushed away the silk spinnaker sail and made room. You kissed me and the saliva caught the light as you sat up and climbed on top of me. And you said, "This is position twenty-one from the Kama Sutra" in an Indian princess accent. A joke against yourself, the exotic Oriental. And I thought it was the funniest thing ever and laughed and relaxed and we screwed for an hour and a half. I remember. Truth, is that what heroin brings?

"No," she says.

But that was truth. Her words fade. Gone into the smoke in the air above the river. And in every gasp I can't help but breathe in ash, little particles of sandalwood and cherrywood and her. The wind changes its direction and the rain comes down and I open my mouth and it's cold, like the coldness in my heart.

°   °   °

Things happen to fuck you up. Little things. You get chased from a boat and you accidentally forget your heroin. It forces you to go to the pub quiz but you get the crucial question wrong and have to steal more heroin from your dealer—Spider. Spider realizes it could only be you that stole from him and wants to get you. And how to get me? Tell the peelers that an English copper has been seen going into my house. That's all it would take. Everyone would know what that meant.

And they got me. A week after Victoria Patawasti's funeral. Walking along the sea front. They were so smooth that I didn't even notice the Land Rover pull in beside me.

"Lawson," a voice said.

I turned, saw the open door at the back of the Land Rover, legged it, got about twenty feet. A burly man tap-tackling me to the ground. I didn't recognize him. In his forties, alcoholic face. Leather jacket. Old stager. Reliable. He had two fingers missing from his left hand. Bombing, shooting, accident?

"You're under arrest, Lawson," he said.

"What for?"

"Shut the fuck up."

The man slapped cuffs on me, hauled me up, dragged me to the Land Rover. Three more men inside. One was Facey, looking guilty. The second, a copper in a flat cap, green sweater, tanned face, and finally a bald man with glasses and a raincoat, trying to cover a police uniform. High one, too, chief super or above. The Land Rover drove off. It came back—that familiar stench of diesel and lead paint and ammunition. Same claustrophobia.

"Alex, I'm sorry, they needed someone to ID you," Facey said.

Flat Cap turned to Facey: "You shut up and don't speak again," he said.

The bald man nodded at the big guy, he held my

arms, Baldy leaned over and punched me in the stomach. I retched. I looked at Facey but he was looking away. Flat Cap grabbed me by the hair. Shook me. Shit, they weren't going to kill me, were they?

"What do you want?" I managed.

"We heard you were talking to the Old Bill, the Metropolitan fucking Police," the bald man screamed in my face.

"Think we don't know about everything that happens in this town, in this country? Your mate Spider told us. Wipe your fucking arse and we know," Flat Cap continued.

"You know what we'll fucking do to you. You'll go down. You'll go down, Lawson. I don't care what they promise you," Baldy said.

"Aye, whatever they threaten you with, Lawson, it'll be a thousand times worse if you ever fuck us over. Remember that. You'd be dead if you weren't such a fuckup. You owe us. You owe us. We've been lenient. We could kill you now. We could do anything we like, Lawson. Do you understand? Do you understand?" Flat Cap said.

"I understand," I gasped, shaking.

"Says on your file you're Jewish, not even Protestant at all. Is your loyalty a question we should be worrying about?" Baldy said.

"No," I spat, somehow managing to answer this humiliating question.

"Hope fucking not. You're a fucking sorry excuse for a human being," Baldy said.

"Aye, he is, but he gets it. Good. Stop the vehicle," Flat Cap commanded.

"Stop the vehicle," the big guy yelled to the driver.

The Land Rover stopped. Through the armored windows I could see that we were in the middle of nowhere. They uncuffed me, pushed me out the back of the vehicle. I stumbled and fell.

"Think about it. We know where you live, we know everything you do, we know everyone you fucking see," Baldy said, closing the door.

The Land Rover drove off in a slew of mud. I got up and brushed myself down. Smiled. The icing on the cake. If I didn't cooperate with Douglas, he'd have me arrested. If I did cooperate, the RUC would at the very least release my confession. Worse. Get me, get Da. Or that age-old drama. A car, a gun, a struggle, a field far from anywhere, a bullet in the neck . . .

I got my bearings. They had dumped me way up Empire Lane. I calmed myself. Walked down the hill. My wrists hurt. I went past the big, asymmetrical Patawasti house. Farther down. The rich neighborhood giving way to the poor. Council houses, bungalows. A bonfire being built for the twelfth of July holiday.

My house. Kitchen. Da gone campaigning. I tried to find something to drink but there was nothing. What to do? Escape? Go to Douglas? Borrow some dough? I racked my brain but couldn't come up with anything.

I picked the bills from off the hall floor. Final demands on electricity, oil heat, ground rent. Place was a mess. Ma would have cleaned it. Made Da clean it when she was sick. Ma. Jesus . . . What the hell was I going to do? I needed to think but I couldn't do ketch again today. Twice in one day. Never. Back to the kitchen, opened the fridge.

The phone rang. I picked it up. It was Mrs. Patawasti. She asked if I had been up Empire Lane this morning near their house. I said I had. She said that Mr. Patawasti had come out after me, but his knees were bad, couldn't keep up. She said that they would very much like to see me. Would this afternoon be convenient? I said it would.

I hung up the receiver. It didn't take a genius to see what they wanted. All the pieces were there now. I would never have gone to America. I knew Victoria and I loved her and I was sorry that she was dead, but I had given up police work forever. I had failed in that aspect of my life and it was only heroin that kept me together at all. I had not, like so many RUC officers, put a bullet in my own brain. Detective work had destroyed me. Why had I resigned from the police? Because I had unearthed the case, because I had broken the case. The truth had imprisoned me, not set me free.

But everything had come together, leaving me one way out. The British cops were down on my neck, the Irish cops were on my head. I had to run. But it was all of it. The boat. The drugs. The quiz. Spider. And now the murder case. That English peeler was just the stoker, the driver of this great derailing train. And within a week we were in America.

Aye, within a week we were in America, we had killed a man, fucked up the case, and were on the run there, too.

4: THE FLOWER OF JOY

Two days after her murder, Victoria's brother Colin had flown to Denver to pick up her effects. The murderer was already caught. The case was open and shut. Nearly half of all murders that are solved are done so within the first twenty-four hours. The Denver police had a known criminal in custody. His Mexican driver's license had been found in Victoria's room. In the U.S. he had previous convictions for theft and burglary. He wasn't particularly bright—he had been arrested by the police at his brother's house. The police had assured Colin that they had their man, that prosecution would be easy, that he could go home with at least the thought that Victoria's killer would be brought to book. And that since the murder was committed during the commission of another crime, he might even get the death penalty.

The Denver police had an air of competence that impressed Colin and he was convinced. In violation of the rules, the cops took him to the jail to see the man who had killed his little sister. After that, Colin drove the forty-five minutes to Victoria's office in Boulder, Colorado. He got a great deal of sympathy. She had been well liked. She worked for a nonprofit called the

Campaign for the American Wilderness. A charitable organization that explored new ways of looking at environmental policy. A very successful group, so successful, in fact, that they were moving out of their Boulder headquarters to a shiny new office in downtown Denver. Victoria had been in charge of many aspects of the Denver move and it was difficult without her. Everyone had been sweet and kind, especially the copresidents of CAW, Charles and Robert Mulholland. Charles and his wife, Amber, took Colin to the Brown Palace Hotel and bought him lunch.

Colin gathered Victoria's effects and gave them to a thrift shop. No will had been found, but, of course, Victoria had only been twenty-six. The cops released the body. Colin met with an undertaker and they flew her home.

Four days after Victoria Patawasti's funeral, on June 16, Mr. Patawasti received a letter with a Boulder postmark. It was slightly faded, computer printed (rather than typed), and said simply:

```
Don't let him get away with you'r
        daughter's murder.
```

A lead. Revealing something about the sender, but the family didn't know that and the local peelers hadn't seen it either.

The family called Carrickfergus RUC. A Constable Pollock came to see them. He checked for prints, found nothing, held the note up to the light, found nothing, and on that basis somehow decided it was probably the work of a crank. After all, didn't the Americans already have the murderer in custody? America was full of cranks. They should throw the letter out, burn it.

Mr. Patawasti was an Oxford graduate, a professor; Constable Pollock's analysis did not satisfy him.

He called up the Denver police and after a great deal of trouble got through to the investigating officer. Detective Anthony Miller. Detective Miller assured Mr. Patawasti that they had their man and that everything was under control. Of course, he could send the letter to them and they would add it to the investigation, but really the Northern Irish police were probably correct, it sounded like a crank.

Mr. Patawasti had seen me at the funeral, talked to Dad, had a think. . . .

A phone call. A change of clothes. Shirt, tie, jeans, Doc Martens. Mr. Patawasti's house on Empire Lane. That big house from the 1930s. The two wings. The Gothic tower. The servants' steps. The massive front garden with a lawn and roses. A view down to Belfast Lough. On a clear day you could probably see parts of Scotland.

Doorbell, living room: Mrs. Patawasti, Colin, Stephen, Mr. Patawasti.

Stephen, six years older than me; Colin, four. I knew them both vaguely from school. Stephen had been captain of the rugby team. Colin had been head boy and a prefect who had given me lines and detention at least a dozen times. Even now he intimidated me.

The living room. Pictures of her: playing hockey for Carrickfergus Grammar School, matriculating at Oxford, with the family in front of the Red Fort in Delhi, dressed in a sari and stepping out of an Indian river. The rest of the room was academic, tidy, scrubbed. A bookcase, framed cricket posters, shining surfaces.

I stared at everyone while we sat. Mr. Patawasti looking a hundred years old. Colin: angry, impatient. Stephen: aloof, sad. Mrs. Patawasti: utterly destroyed.

"Would you like some tea, Alexander?" Mrs. Patawasti asked, her face deathly pale, her hair gray.

I shook my head. I was supposed to take charge here, ask the questions, but I wasn't sure of the protocol, I hesitated, stumbled over words.

"Um, well, uh . . ."

Colin glared at me. His lips white with mounting fury.

"Look at him. Just look at the state of him. Can we end this farce now, please?" Colin said to his father.

Clearly, Colin remembered me as the screwed-up wiseass from school. And here I was confirming it all, looking like a wreck. Hadn't I quit the police under mysterious circumstances? Didn't I have money troubles, too? Now come like a vulture to exploit his parents' grief.

"Colin, please," Mrs. Patawasti said.

"Look at him, what can he do that the Denver police can't?" Colin insisted.

"Um, Mr. Patawasti, you said in your phone call that

there was an anonymous note. Maybe I could take a wee look at it, if you don't mind," I finally managed.

"Oh, yes, of course," Mr. Patawasti said, standing, going upstairs. After he left, silence descended.

A clock ticking. The gables rattling. Victoria staring at me from the photograph. The unspoken person in the room so badly needed now, so adept at defusing a situation such as this.

"Sure you wouldn't like some tea, Alex?" Mrs. Patawasti asked.

"I wouldn't mind some tea now, please," I said to give her something to do. She went to the kitchen.

Another long pause. Colin, Stephen, and I stared at the floor. Mr. Patawasti came back down. I took the note gratefully and examined it.

"Hmmm, very interesting," I said. I knew I would have to bullshit them a bit to get the case. Not exactly ethical. But this was life and death.

"Why? How so? Constable Pollock said it was a crank," Colin said.

I began slowly: "It says a lot. Obviously a great deal of thought went into this."

"What are you talking about?" Colin interrupted. "Everyone agrees it's a nutter."

"No, I don't think so. It's a very deliberate piece of work. Taking the trouble to avoid fingerprints. And look at the mistake, 'you'r' instead of 'your.'"

"Constable Pollock tells us it was an uneducated person," Mrs. Patawasti said, coming back in with no tea.

"Aye, could be, but I don't think so. I think that's what he wants you to think. He wants you to think he's stupid. He's disguising himself by making a mistake, but would he (I say 'he' but of course it could be 'she') really make the mistake 'you'r' on a word-processed document? Most word processors have a spell check that would have caught that. The more common mistake is to mix up 'your' and 'you're,' which a word processor won't catch. Also, he doesn't misuse the apostrophe after 'daughter.' I'd say that if he were an ignoramus, he would have blundered over the apostrophe first. You could say he was in a hurry, he didn't have time to do a spell check. But it only takes a second and in any case this note was written with a great deal of consideration. An anonymous note about a murder. It's not the sort of thing you dash off."

"Ok, where does this get us then, Alex?" Colin asked a little less aggressively.

"Well, we want to know who wrote it. Someone that knew Victoria personally, someone who knows or suspects he knows who the killer is, someone who doesn't believe the police have arrested the right man, someone educated enough to be worried about appearing too educated, so he makes a deliberate mistake in the anonymous note. I'd say someone who worked with Victoria or was a neighbor or close friend. He wants us to take an interest in this case and expose whoever did this crime but he's not sure he wants to be involved. Do you still have the envelope it came in?"

"I think I threw it out," Mrs. Patawasti said. "The RUC didn't want to see it."

However, she went into the back room and appeared with it a few minutes later. The envelope was more revealing than the note. A lot of times that's the case. It was postmarked June 12 in Boulder, also slightly faded, and said:

```
             Mr. Patawasti
              The Tiny Taj
             78 Empire Lane
      Carrickfergus, Co. Antrim,
          N. Ireland BT38 7JG
             United Kingdom
```

"Any help, Alexander?" Mrs. Patawasti asked.

"Yes. Postmarked June the twelfth in Boulder. Your daughter was killed on June the fifth. The Denver police arrested their suspect two days after that. He thought about this for five days. He was frightened to reveal what he knew. He didn't want to go to the police, but he wanted you to do something. To stir the pot, to lead the police in the right direction. He couldn't do it—he'd be implicated because he's already very close. Like I say, friend, neighbor, coworker. It's interesting that Victoria lived in Denver, but commuted to her office in Boulder. Possibly a coworker," I said.

"He could have just driven there, and posted it there," Colin said sharply.

"Yes," I agreed.

"Victoria had an address book," Mrs. Patawasti said.

"I'd like to see it," I said.

"She didn't know that many people, she didn't have time to socialize much outside of work," Colin said defensively.

"Well, I think we can eliminate some of the names. We know the writer owns or has fairly exclusive access to a computer. This isn't the sort of thing you print out at the local library. I don't want to leap to conclusions, but did you notice the way the note and the address were slightly faded?"

"I did," Mr. Patawasti said.

"The cartridge was running out. Could it be that he didn't know how to change the cartridge, that that was his secretary's job?"

"You can't know that," Colin said.

"No," I agreed. "Anyway, now I'd like to see her passport and her letters, the things that were in her apartment with her home address on them."

With a heavy sadness, Mrs. Patawasti brought the meager box of things I wanted. I skimmed through them, saw what I needed. I knew I was on to something. Something significant.

"And do you still have an unlisted phone number?" I asked, remembering the frantic time eight years ago when I had temporarily lost her number.

"It's not listed, so what?" Colin said.

"Well, it's the name of the house. Victoria would never have told anyone that this house was called the

'Tiny Taj.' It embarrassed her. It's not on any of her letters or her passport, or other personal items. The post office doesn't give out addresses. So how could anyone know? It's not here on any of her documents. When you wrote to her, did you put the name of the house on the sender's address?" I asked.

Everyone turned to Mrs. Patawasti.

"No, I never write Tiny Taj, or mention it," she said, "it *is* embarrassing."

"So how could anyone know that this house is called the Tiny Taj? Victoria would never have told anyone. I'll bet the only way someone could know was if he had access to her personnel file at work and saw it written there as her full postal address. She would never have spoken about it, but she might have written her full home address on her personnel file. It would fit. And who could know that but someone who worked with her in Boulder and had access to her file? It's just a guess, but I'd say if you were to go to her office and ask around, you might be close to finding who wrote the note."

I put the note and envelope and the effects down on the coffee table. A little silence. Some of it had been flimflam, but some of it real enough. Colin unfolded his arms. Mr. Patawasti's face broke into a little half smile. I'd impressed them. Like I'd been trying to do.

"Alexander, do you think you can find the man who killed my daughter?"

I looked at him, nodded.

"Find him, find who did it, Alex," Colin said, his voice breaking.

"It might well be the man they have in custody," I said.

"Find out the truth," Mr. Patawasti said.

"I will," I said.

Mrs. Patawasti and the boys left so Mr. Patawasti and I could agree on terms. He'd pay me three hundred quid a week plus my airfare and any other expenses I'd need. I tried not to see it as a way out of my difficulties. A case. I was working for a family friend. I was doing them a favor using the skills I'd learned in the peelers. Everything I'd promised myself never to do again. But it wasn't me. It was altruism. Victoria. The fact that it would be the perfect excuse for getting out of Ireland, getting money, away from Douglas, away from the RUC, was beside the point.

I went home and read all the documents. Mr. Patawasti had given me Victoria's personal effects, employment documents, apartment receipts, company personnel profile, a copy of the Denver County Police report. Victoria had been shot during a struggle in her apartment. According to her cleaning lady, a number of things were missing. The police theory was that the assailant, Hector Martinez, had botched the robbery, killed Victoria. During the struggle his Mexican driver's license had fallen out of his jacket or trouser pocket. It was too soon for forensic evidence, but the circumstantial evidence was pretty good. He had two previous convictions for theft and had fled the jurisdiction once on a grand theft auto rap. He'd been living with his brother and they'd picked him up easily. Martinez's lawyer, Enrique Monroe, had been denied bail for his client. Martinez was considered a flight risk. Pretty damning, but clearly the note writer believed they had the wrong man. Either that or he wanted to muddy the waters to get Mr. Martinez off or implicate someone else. Worth checking out. I called John and asked him to do some snooping for me, using the police computers.

John met me in Dolan's that night. He was happy. I'd given him a lot to do.

"Ok, Alex. Envelope and letter normal office stuff. No help there. But the font is New Courier 2. An updated version of Courier that is only available on the latest packages of WordPerfect. It's been out about three months and is only in office suite packages. No, don't ask, I already checked. Victoria's employers, the Campaign for the American Wilderness, do indeed run WordPerfect rather than Word. And yes, they have the latest release. However, so do tens of thousands of other businesses. Hundreds in Colorado. Tough getting through to CAW, spoke to a college student, they're moving the whole office from Boulder to Denver, Denver's not set up yet and they only have a skeleton staff. But anyway, yeah, it's not impossible the note writer could be someone who worked with her in Boulder and printed it out there."

I grinned at him. He'd done well. Everything I'd

asked. If you kept John on message, he could be pretty efficient.

"Aye, well, that's plenty, that's more than enough, it's up to me now," I said.

"Listen, you've got to admit that I've been a help," John began.

"Yeah," I said suspiciously.

"Well, I've always wanted to go to America and the peelers owe me months of leave, and I work at the station only a day or two per month, for whatever reason," John said.

"Maybe because of your stupid haircut, it looks like you should be on the cover of romance novels, not writing traffic tickets or—" I began but John cut me off.

"Let me finish, Alexander. My point is, I've been a big help to you, British Airways are doing two-for-one flights, you need me. I want to come with you," John blurted out.

I looked at him. That big goofy face. Grinning. I didn't see why not. He just might be able to help with the legwork. Watson to my Holmes. He was a peeler, after all, my best friend, and I didn't want to go alone.

o o o

Blue meets blue at the curve of the Atlantic Ocean and the sky. America looming. An hour away. But I'm not here, I'm somewhere on the other side of the world.

The peaks, high valleys of the western Himalaya.

The highest mountains on Earth. Formed fifty million years ago when India crashed into the continent of Asia and pushed them up.

I close my eyes and I can see them. Glaciers in Kashmir. Tarn lakes in Ladakh. Snow over the opium fields of the Hindu Kush.

I am crawling in my airplane seat. My body is craving heroin.

A village. Cooking fires. A weather-beaten old man down among his crop. He lovingly removes his penknife and scores the bud of the opium plant. The flower's botanical name is *Papaver somniferum*. The Sumerians and ancient peoples of the Indus valley called it Hul Gil, the "flower of joy." When the Aryans came to India, they discovered that the flower allowed you to see Brahma, the creator of the Universe.

Only a few weeks ago, red and yellow petals bloomed at the tips of tubular green stems. The old man is content. The petals have fallen away, but the plants have survived the snow. The egg-shaped seed pod is unharmed. Under the penknife an opaque, milky sap oozes out. This is the opium in its crudest form.

He calls his sons. The sap is extracted by slitting the pods vertically. On exposure to the high mountain air the sap turns darker and thicker, becoming a brownish-black gum. The family collects the gum, laughing, making a real harvest of it, the older boys molding it into bricks or cakes and wrapping them in plastic bags.

The big money isn't in opium, but even so, the villagers are content to sell their crop to experts who will know what to do next. On a bright January day, a mule train shows up and takes the village supply of opium over the Afghan border and into Pakistan. The opium refinery is a rickety factory in a residential neighborhood of Lahore. The opium is mixed with lime in boiling water. The morphine is skimmed off the top, reheated with ammonia, boiled and filtered again. The brown morphine paste is heated with acetic anhydride for six or seven hours at 85 degrees centigrade. Water and chloroform are added to precipitate impurities. The solution is drained and sodium carbonate added to solidify the heroin. The heroin is filtered through charcoal and alcohol. Purification in the fourth stage, involving ether and hydrochloric acid, is notoriously risky and can blow up the lab. But assuming everyone survives, it is filtered again and stamped ready for shipping. The final fluffy white powder is known to everyone as number four. It has taken ten kilos of opium to make one kilo of heroin, but it's worth it. One kilo of number four costs about a hundred thousand dollars.

The first person to process heroin was C. R. Wright, an English researcher who synthesized it in 1874 at St. Mary's Hospital in London. He thought it was too dangerous to use. In 1897 Heinrich Dreser of the Bayer Pharmaceutical Company was presented with two new drugs, acetylsalicylic acid and diacetyl morphine: the first became known as aspirin, the second, heroin. Dreser tested both, deciding there was no future for the former, but the latter he called heroin, for it would be the "heroic" cure-all drug of the twentieth century.

From that heroin-refining factory in Lahore to a cargo flight carrying expensive cashmere shirts from Karachi to Newark Airport in the United States. It comes in under the noses of customs inspectors (who are too swamped to inspect every shipment of textiles from Pakistan to the United States) and makes its way to a warehouse in Union City, New Jersey. From Union City to a van traveling west.

The imaginary journey of my ketch. Aye, something like that or more likely a ship rather than a plane. But how to get it? I'm not fool enough to smuggle what's left of my own supply with me. I have to get it in Denver. As soon as I get in. Fast. Now.

I mean, I know there is a case to be solved. A lot of questions. Who killed Victoria Patawasti? Who sent the anonymous note? How long can I stay in America before the English peelers or Irish peelers track me down? But the most important of all—how in the name of God am I going to score heroin within a few hours of touching down in Denver?

Thirty thousand feet. Greenland. John watching the movie, hardly able to contain his excitement. Back to my book. I'm reading a dual-language Bhagavad Gita. I suppose it's because of Victoria. Lame, I know.

The coast. Islands. Lakes. Brown fields, irrigated to form huge circles. Rivers. Plains. We both stare as we cross the Mississippi. More fields, the odd sprawling settlement. A highway. The colors faded—like giants' clothes washed and patched too many times.

Mountains like the barrier at the world's edge. How did the settlers get through those? Why didn't everyone just stop here? A squeal of wheels, a bounce. The plane touches down at the brand-new Denver International Airport. White tepees over the big terminal. Immigration. My skin is starting to burn. My hands are shaking. Shit, here goes. There are five desks. The man at one desk is called O'Reilly. He'll do, in case I mess up somehow.

"What's the purpose of your visit to the United States?"

"Tourism."

"Been here before?"

"Yes, I was here when I was a student; I came for a few months and traveled around on Amtrak. Just the East Coast," I say, shivering.

"Are you cold?" the man asks.

"I don't like air-conditioning, it's always too cold," I say, keeping the panic out of my voice. I get momentarily worried, but the man's not interested now that he sees I'm Irish.

"Ireland. Love to go there. Wonderful golf courses, I'll bet," he says.

"Oh yeah, great courses, Royal Portrush, great views of Scotland," I say.

"How long do you intend to stay in the United States?"

"We're here for a few months."

He stamps the passport, smiles. I smile back. Walk off.

The luggage rack. The automatic sorting machine in the airport has misplaced about a third of our flight's luggage. "Teething troubles," a harried airport official says, trying hard to placate the potential lynch mob. But we get our rucksacks with no problems.

The customs desk. A blue form. We have nothing to declare, although I do have a lunch box filled with needles that I've marked "Diabetic Syringes." I'd been concerned that this was far too obvious and customs was going to confiscate it and figure out I was a user or something; but we walk through the channel and no one says a thing. I could have brought the bloody heroin. Typical.

Outside. Christ, it's hot. A cloudless sky. Three in the afternoon. One hundred degrees, says the temperature gauge above an ad for a bank. So many commercials. Even on the taxi. We get in the cab.

"We need a hotel, not too expensive," I say before John can speak.

"It needs to be downtown, but not the Brown Palace, or the Adam's Mark, cheaper than that," John says, reading from *Lonely Planet USA*.

The taxi driver turns around. He's an older black man with a gravelly voice. "I know the very place, boys," he says, driving off.

"How come it's so hot, didn't it snow just a couple of weeks ago?" John asks incredulously.

"That's Denver," the driver says, laughing. "We get over three hundred days of sunshine a year. More than Arizona. Sometimes it snows at night and by lunchtime it's gone. The traces of that big snowstorm we had a couple of weeks back, gone in two days. Year's been real bad for weather. Need rain, we're in the middle of a big drought."

He's not kidding. I look out the window. Yellow and brown fields, an unforgiving sky. No animals. In fact, from the highway it looks like it's semidesert. The city, a line of big buildings and then the mountains. A punchy, aggressive sun.

Most people don't know Denver. Maybe they came skiing here once, or went to a conference. Drove in from the airport, stayed downtown, went to the mountains. Maybe they live here in the white 'burbs. But even they don't know it. They don't know the Denver of Kerouac and Cassidy, of the hobos getting off the freight trains at the biggest intersection in the West. They don't know because the bums have been pushed off the streets, the downtown has been regenerated, lofts, wine bars, trendy eateries and coffeehouses instead of dive bars and diners. John Elway's toothy grin on the posters for his auto dealerships. But the old Denver still exists out on Colfax Avenue where they never go. Or on Federal or in the black section north of the city center.

Colfax for us. Desperate-looking motels, armored liquor stores, Spanish restaurants and bodegas. Prostitutes, pushers, hangers-on at the corners. What are they selling? Is everyone still on crack in this country, or is heroin coming back?

We turn on Broadway past two of the ugliest buildings I've ever seen. One is a tall windowless slab the color of baby puke, the other a demented Lego assemblage of blocks and pyramids.

"Art museum and library," the cabbie explains and then stops at a place called the Western Palace Hotel 1922—pink and flat with a swimming pool. It looks slightly rundown and cheap. It'll do. The Denver city center is about half a mile down the baking white strip of Broadway.

We pay the driver and remember to tip him 15 percent. Get our bags. Walk to the front desk.

"This is so cool," John says.

I look at him. I'm sweating, jumpy, in no mood to talk. I'd woken early, gone to the beach. Injected myself. Gone home, spent two hours packing and hiding my drug paraphernalia. It took an hour to pick up John and get to the airport, Facey driving slowly and carefully in his Ford Fiesta. Facey still too embarrassed to talk to me following the Land Rover incident even though I'd forgiven him, for if not him, who? They would have found me. Anyway, that long airport drive. Then a two-hour wait to go through security, then an hour-long flight from Belfast to London, then a five-hour wait at Heathrow to board our flight. A ten-hour flight from London to Denver. Three hours getting our bags and going through customs and the ride here. It's been twenty-four hours since I had a fix.

The hotel lobby exudes desperation and a hint of better days. The harsh setting sun streaming in through venetian blinds and illuminating an enormous cracked mirror above a chipped art deco check-in desk. A man at the desk reading a comic. An image of ourselves on a black-and-white security camera monitor. A dead or hibernating cactus plant. Dust vortices in the strobed sunlight. Tiles missing from a checkerboard floor and, on an orange sofa, a hatchet-faced old man with a portable oxygen tank. He and the desk clerk both smoking.

"Careful you don't blow yourself up, old timer," John says cheerfully to the old man.

"What's it to you, shithead?" the man replies, incredibly slowly.

We go to the desk and the clerk gives us a room. We pay up front for a week. He doesn't ask to see our passports or tell us the hotel rules or anything. He gives us keys and motions us upstairs. He's reading *Justice League of America*.

The stairs, a long line of identical rooms. The key.

The door. In. Broadway out the windows. Hot, clogged with traffic.

"Shit, there's an air conditioner," John says enthusiastically.

He drops his stuff, runs to the AC, turns it on. By the time we've done a very quick unpack, the room is twenty-five degrees cooler.

John cannot contain his excitement.

"America, bloody America," he says.

"Yes."

"I mean, Jesus Christ, it's *America* we're talking about here."

"I know."

"You've been, but I haven't. I always wanted to come. Did you see the bikes? On the ride in I saw two Harleys and an Indian. An Indian, can you believe it? And the cars, the cars are bloody huge. It's just like *Starsky and Hutch* or—"

"John, listen, I need to score some ketch."

John shakes his head.

"No. No, no, no. Come on, Alexander, couldn't you use this as an opportunity to go cold turkey?" John asks. An excellent question.

I stare at him.

"No," I say.

"Alex, if you—" but then he stops and sees the state I'm in. Shaking, pale, trying to keep down my meager stomach contents.

"Alex, ok, look. I can't convince you?" he says.

"No."

"Ok, if you really insist on going, go. Look, and score me some pot as well, ok?"

"Maybe. John, you're what they call an enabler."

"Sure. Just don't get arrested."

"If I do, I'll tell them you put me up to it."

◦   ◦   ◦

Heat. Sun. I walked down Broadway. Wide streets, flat pavements, ramps on the sidewalk. I found Colfax again. A lot of pedestrian traffic. Roasting, too, my beard itched. The Capitol Building. A statue of a Civil War soldier. The Ten Commandments.

Homeless people, desperate people, alcoholics on the sidewalk.

Ah, a scumball bar.

The bar, dark, smoky. Sun like laser light through cracks in the paint of the blacked-out windows. Very American. Budweiser signs, Coors signs, a pool table, strange things on tap. People on their own staring at shot glasses, hugging their beer. No women. Is this the right place?

Barkeep. Black guy, forty-five, bald, big strong hands that looked like they could wring your neck.

"A beer please," I said.

"You got ID?"

"What?"

"ID."

"What for?"

"Are you from out of town?"

"Yes."

"You have to be twenty-one to drink here."

"I'm twenty-four. Most people think I look older," I said.

"I don't give a shit, you got ID?"

"Uh, wait, yeah, I got my passport."

"That'll do, let me see it."

I showed him my passport, he looked it over, I don't how he read it, so dark in there.

"You from England?"

"Yeah."

"Tourist?"

"Yeah."

"Been to Denver before?"

"No."

"You're too late to ski," he said, his face contorting into a disconcerting chuckle.

"I don't ski."

"What type of beer you want?"

"I don't care."

"Coors ok?"

"Yeah."

The barman pulled me a Coors and set it down.

"Three dollars," he said.

I gave him a five and as I'd seen in the movie, I left a dollar of the change back on the bar.

"Tourist, huh. I was born here. Native, very rare. You know what the first permanent building in Denver was?"

"No."

"A bar," he said with satisfaction.

"Really?"

"Yup, you know what the second was?"

"No."

"A brothel."

"Fascinating."

"You know that TV show *Dynasty*?"

"Yeah."

"That's Denver."

"Really?"

"Uh-huh."

I finished the beer and bought another. I was getting increasingly anxious. It's not that I needed a hit, I told myself. I just wanted one. The bar began to fill. A few more desperate types but also a party of college students. Four guys, two girls. Maybe they would know. The guys all had buzz cuts and were well muscled, they actually all looked like undercover cops, so maybe it wouldn't be too clever asking them. It would have to be the barman. I cleared my throat.

"So," I said, "I hear there's a big drug problem around here."

"You heard that?" His face frozen, revealing nothing.

"Yeah."

"Huh."

"You know, pot, smack, that sort of thing."

"Is that a fact?" he said, giving me a quizzical look.

"It's what I heard."

He wiped the bar and served a customer at the far end. Obviously thinking something over. Clearly, I was from out of town, he had seen my passport, for Christ's sake. It wasn't a sting operation. Suspicious, but not a sting.

"Bar tab's twenty bucks," he said, coming back to me.

I owed him nothing, I had paid and tipped for each drink. I took a twenty from my wallet and put it on the bar. He lifted it and put it in his pocket.

"I heard," he began slowly, "I heard that the biggest problem with product was behind the Salvation Army shelter on Colfax and Grant. That's what I heard. I heard, you should say Hacky sent you."

"Hacky sent me?"

"Hacky."

I left the beer, grabbed my baseball hat, practically ran out into the dusk. I went east. Night was falling fast and there were many more prostitutes out on Colfax, skinny black and Latino girls who looked as if they were about fifteen. Most of them on something. Crack, presumably. They were wired, nervous, looked for vehicle trade. Pimps on the corner, big guys, little guys, enforcers, all of them obvious, unconcerned about peelers or being seen. I found the Salvation Army hostel and walked around the back. Garbage, a small fire. A dozen men drinking from brown paper bags. Older guys, mostly white.

First character I saw, old for his years, pale, thin, drinking vodka. Rotted gums and teeth, horrible smell.

"Listen, I need to score, Hacky sent me," I said.

The man looked at me.

"You want the kid. Are you a cop?" he asked.

"No."

"Better not be a cop."

I shook my head, what would he do about it anyway? Breathe on me?

"Hey, kid," he yelled, "guy wants to book you."

The kid came from out of the shadows. He really was a child. Maybe sixteen years old. Spanish, obviously, well dressed in jeans and a black cowboy shirt. Walking slow, smoking a cigarette. Was he the dealer?

If so, why was he hanging out with a bunch of indigent white guys three times his age?

He came over.

"You're no cop. I know all the cops."

"I know. Hacky sent me."

"Hacky sent you?"

"Yeah."

"What you want?" he asked, suspicion flitting around his eyes.

"Ketch, I mean, horse, smack, heroin."

"How much?"

"I don't know, a few grams, seven good hits."

"What you talking about? Where you from?"

"Ireland."

"Where's that at?"

"England."

"See your money," he said, the light gleaming on his smooth baby-face cheeks.

I opened up my wallet, he looked at me. His face had a scar under the chin. I stroked my beard nervously. He took out five twenty-dollar bills, put them in his pocket, said nothing, walked off to a door, went inside. I waited for about ten minutes. Had they stroked me? Was I ripped off? It would be the easiest scam in the world. Who would I complain to? I didn't care about the money. I wanted the goddamn heroin. Let them rip me off, just give me the bloody ketch.

The sun disappeared behind the mountains and I stood there watching the oblique light illuminate the vapor trails of airplanes flying west.

Venus came out. The sky turned a deep blue.

From the Colfax side of the alley a homeless man shambled over to me with a brown paper bag.

"This is for you," he said.

I opened the bag, inside was a plastic bag containing a white powder. Easy to get bait and switch in a situation like this, so I opened the bag, tasted the heroin. Milky, acidic, the real McCoy.

"Where's this from?" I asked the homeless man.

"I don't know," he answered. I wanted to know where the heroin had originated—Burma, Afghanistan, South America. I wanted to know its purity, but the man was drunk, he knew nothing, just the fall guy on the outside chance that I was a peeler. I put it in my pocket and jogged back to the hotel. Night. Almost no pedestrians. I took a shortcut through the grounds of the state capitol, no one paying me any mind at all.

When I slid back into the motel room, John was asleep and the place stank of shampoo and hair conditioner. John washed that long mane of his twice a day.

"Who the hell is that?" he muttered from the bed.

"Me."

"Did you get your ketch?" John asked from under the covers.

"I did. No pot, though."

"Shit, ok. Was the guy trustworthy? I mean, you're going to shoot that stuff into your veins. Did he look trustworthy?"

"He looked fine."

"Ok, then it's your life."

"It is."

I took out my syringes. I went into the bathroom and brought out my spoon and the distilled water. I took the heroin out of the plastic bag. I sieved it through my fingers. I boiled it in the spoon. Injected, drew it in, saw there was blood, I always find a vein first time, always. I injected myself.

A weird hit. A deep high.

I lay down on the bathroom floor. Goddamn, this stuff was purer than the gear that made it to Ireland. Wow. Everything that was hurt in my body disappeared. My thoughts became clear. The shower curtain, the tiles on the bathroom floor, the cream-colored ceiling. The traffic on Broadway. The fan from the AC in the bedroom, the bathroom pipes. One irritation. Helicopter, probably from the TV news. In Belfast there are no civilian choppers, all belong to the British Army. A copter is an ominous sound meaning trouble. I had to get rid of it. Blend it into the cars, pipes, air conditioner. Going, going, gone.

Noises, absence of pain.

Until you take heroin you don't know how much pain there is in your body. Most humans just get used to it. With heroin every little ache disappears. Every ache of body and spirit. The wound of memory, the fear. That nagging fear that never quite goes away. For how can you live happily on Earth, knowing that your consciousness will be annihilated along with everything else you cherish? All the matter in the universe will someday decay into random photons and neutrinos. Diamonds are not forever. Nothing is forever. All the works of man will be lost in the Heat Death of the universe. Doesn't that make everything pointless?

The girl is dead? We are all dead.

Heroin relieves you of these thoughts. And it was heroin, after all, that had saved my life. But for heroin I would be dead in a ditch somewhere in Ulster. Rain on my beaten body.

But I was smarter than them. Maybe not smart. But smarter than them.

The cars. The fading light. The airplanes. Men yelling. A fat June night. An urban symphony. A heavy overcoat of emptiness. I drift on an air bed over the ocean of eternity. On the infinite nothingness of a black sky.

The list of a diesel engine. The air horn of a freight train. Vehicles. Voices. A TV in another room. A breathing city. We are clawed by the past. I have read up on the history of this town. I think of the Spanish, the gold rush, of hard-faced Denver men throwing the bodies of the Indian women and children into Sand Creek. I think of Oscar Wilde at Denver's Union Station. The golden spike. Walt Whitman's beard. A father's tears.

A beautiful girl in an orange sari, beaming from a photograph.

Everything eased. . . .

Later.

Denver ketch.

The purest heroin I've ever had. Enough to make you become an addict. Lying there. Floating. Remembering the poet Novalis. "Inward goes the way full of mystery." I don't even have to take heroin now. Now I'm out of Ireland. I don't even have to take it. I could be free of it. It has served its purpose. It's been my shield. Like the beard, like the skinny stoop and the broken voice.

No reason now. Yeah, I'll stop, quit. Solve the murder. Save myself. Yes. Thoughts. Coming down from a deep high. Heroin doesn't end like anesthesia. The world slides you out.

Not today, though.

John shook me.

"Up, you bastard."

"What time is it, you dick?"

"Ten o'clock," he explained.

"In the morning?"

"Night."

"Jesus Christ, what did I tell you about jet lag?"

"I'm hungry, I wanted to see if you wanted to go out and get something to eat. Besides, it's America, we want to get out there, see stuff, do things, you know."

"Yeah, but John, you're supposed to sleep through the night, adapt to a new time zone."

"Were you going to sleep on the bathroom floor in your underpants all night?"

"No."

"Come on, then. I'm going to get something to eat. Are you coming or not?"

We dressed and went downstairs. The man behind the desk was watching baseball on a portable TV.

"Is there somewhere we could get something to eat around here?" John asked.

"White Spot Diner, three blocks south," the man said, not looking up.

The diner. A waitress, ashen skin, dyed blond hair, a smoker, forties, exhausted, beaten down by the day and life. We looked at the menu. There were at least a dozen things we had never heard of: sloppy joes, meat loaf, submarine sandwiches, huevos rancheros; so we plumped for cheeseburgers and french fries, which was pretty bloody American in any case. When my burger came, I'd lost my appetite but John ate his and half of mine and I had a few fries. We drank Coke and John smoked and left. A nice night. I was feeling better now.

We walked down Broadway. The city of Denver ahead of us. The sky filled with stars and airplanes crossing the vast continent from coast to coast. Amazing to be here. Very different from living on an island as small as Ireland. You could get in your car in Ireland and the farthest you could drive from home was two hundred miles. Here, you could get in your car and drive to the top of Alaska or to the jungles of El Salvador.

Neon lights. The warm night. Police cruisers. Sirens. Big American cars. A club letting in a line of kids. John turned to look at me.

"No way, no way," I said. "I'm going home and I'm going to get a good night's sleep. No way, mate. No way."

The nightclub . . .

Girls at the upstairs bar. A redhead in the PhD astronomy program at the University of Colorado. Brown eyes, feline, intelligent. John with an Asian girl in Daisy Dukes and sandals, John explaining that in *The Wild One*, Brando rode a Triumph, not a Harley. The girl feigning interest wonderfully.

John got us a round and his big smile infected all of us. He took the brunette to the dance floor and I talked to the redhead about astronomy. I told her my dad was a maths teacher and she said that astronomy was about 80 percent maths.

For possibly the only time in history our talk of mathematics proved mutually seductive and I found myself biting her pink, moist lower lip. She kissed me and moved from her stool to my seat so that the breasts under the R.E.M. T-shirt were touching my chest. We kissed and she tasted of beer and honey.

She stopped to get a breath.

"Hey, you know what day it is today?" the girl asked.

"Apart from my lucky day, no."

"Ain't lucky yet, mister."

"Ok, what day is it?"

"It's the start of the solstice. Began at sundown. You know what the solstice is?"

"Longest day of the year."

"That's right," she said, surprised. "We're going to a

rave on the Flat Irons behind Boulder. Have you been to Boulder yet?"

"We only got in today," I said.

"Denver sucks, man. Boulder's where it's at. Have you been to a rave before? You'll need a sleeping bag. I can rustle one up. Do you take e? We're going to dance all night until the sun comes up."

"Why?"

"Haven't you been listening? It's the shortest night of the year. Midsummer night. Wait, I've got a flyer."

She rummaged in her tight jeans back pocket. Raves were impromptu illegal affairs on public land. They were organized in secret and news of them spread through word of mouth. The ecstasy/rave scene was new to America. Rave culture here was in its infancy. Still enthusiastic, unironic. You could tell. The flyer had a big lowercase e and underneath it the words "Midsummer Madness Rave. Acid House. Party Till the Sun Comes Up."

"Sounds like a lot of activity," I said with a slight air of skepticism.

"Forget it then," she said.

I stared at her. She was pretty and I liked her. I wanted to placate her. Words from Heine, my favorite writer about the poppy.

"What did you say?" she asked, unable to understand me.

"*Du bist wie eine Blume,* you are like a flower," I said.

Her face reddened. She breathed in. Amazingly, it

was a line unknown to her, maybe it was the German, although no one's ever said it's the most romantic of tongues.

She leaned forward and we kissed again until John came back up from the dance floor with his girl.

"You look serious, you weren't talking about why beards are coming back, are you?" he asked me with a wink.

"No, were you talking about the Platonic embodiment of your Triumph Bonneville?"

"No, and by the way, that was far too long a sentence to work as sarcasm. Anyway, did you hear about the rave, are you in, man?" John asked, with a big, hopeful grin.

"I don't know where you get the energy from, but I think I want to go home," I said.

"No, no, no, the rave is in Boulder, we have to go to Boulder tomorrow, right? To go to Victoria's office?" John said.

"So?"

"So it'll save us the trip," John said.

I had no resistance and the girl was cute.

"Ok," I said. . . .

A small thing but, who knows, with a good night's sleep what happened the next day might not have happened.

An hour later. The highway to Boulder. The drive to the university. Drunk kids saying "Ssshhh," very loud. Jeeps and SUVs up into the mountains. A long walk through a forest to the top. A clearing. The city of Boulder a few thousand feet below.

Tents. Speakers. A DJ. About three hundred kids. Ecstasy being passed around in solemn little tablets. The DJ faking a British accent. A smiley-face poster. All of it Manchester, 1989. The generator started up. The spotlights came on. The speakers kicked in. Dutch trance music. The mountains. The city. Everybody yelled and started dancing. She passed me an ecstasy tab. But I might be unemployed, I might be a druggie, I might be in the throes of existential crisis, but I wasn't stupid. A few hundred people die of heroin overdoses every year. There are about four thousand heroin cocktail deaths. Heroin and coke, heroin and speed, heroin and e. You don't mess with that shit.

I palmed the pill, fake-swallowed, kissed the girl. We danced. They played acid house and Euro dance and trip-hop and for variety the Soup Dragons and the Stone Roses and Radiohead. At two we drifted away.

We laid out sleeping bags and we took off our T-shirts and our jeans and I stole beside her and kissed her breasts and her long legs.

We had sex and I still didn't know her name and in the dark she could have been anyone. And our moves were theater and our words rituals. You are beautiful. You are my little flower. You are the negation of the enemy. But a substitute. Oh yes, my dear, a substitute.

And I ground my hips and my heart pumped and from nowhere some last residue of that wonderfully refined opium plant changed the chemistry of my brain. I smiled and the world's pain eased. We got to our feet and we walked naked to the tent and the stars lit our way and our feet trod lightly on these subtle and unforgiving grasses of the New World.

5: THE LONGEST DAY OF THE YEAR

The blue flame of the paraffin lamp was almost cobalt in the darkness of the tent. It burned clear with only a fragile light that dripped color and a little heat, taking the dark, molding it into tiny shapes and forms that were weird and spectral under the aged canvas of khaki and muck black and burnt sienna.

The tube around the wick was hot and the green metal of the vessel buckled slightly as the heat rose. I adjusted the intake valve to make it consume more oxygen. The smell of the oil was strong and rich, like some exotic opiate or sleep inducer, and I drank it in and kneeled there for a while like a devotee before his idol.

I sighed, and leaned back, and sat, still in the moment, holding my breath and then slowly letting it out again into the cool night air.

The heroin easing out of my body now.

I shook myself. The lamp burned on, seeping a brittle indigo onto the cheek of the sleeping girl. I hadn't slept at all. I climbed out of the tent. There were a few people awake waiting for the dawn. John, one of them, smoking by a fire.

"How do, mate?" John asked, grinning at me.

"Not bad," I said.

"You look terrible. You shot up again, didn't you?"

"I did."

"What about your 'Only an addict would shoot up twice in twenty-four hours' spiel?"

"Jet lag. Doesn't count," I said.

"Why even bring your gear with you to the bar? Do you carry it everywhere now?"

"John, I was up all night and I couldn't sleep, so I thought I would take a hit. I am exhausted beyond belief. We should have just gone back to the hotel."

"Yeah, blame me," John said, his face showing a little irritation.

"I'm not going to get into this with you again. I'm really not."

"Ok."

And what was I going to say? John, the heroin in America is not to be believed? John, I'm having serious misgivings about trying to be a cop again? But the bastard was right. I didn't have to do heroin now. It wasn't necessary. The fact that I had shot up this morning meant something huge.

"Hey, at least did it go ok with the girl?" John asked.

I didn't answer. I was thinking now about the day ahead. We had much to do. Victoria Patawasti's neighbors had to be interviewed, her work colleagues, the police, the supposed murderer and his attorney, and if possible the murder scene had to be examined, her movements explored, a thorough, slow, precise investigation. Haste is the enemy of the investigator. Haste makes you jump to conclusions, miss things. The ally of lies is speed. I'd solved about two dozen cases in the RUC as detective and ordinary cop. All of them broken by solid police work, a slow growth of fact and evidence until the picture had formed itself. In my experience no one cracked under questioning, no one confessed, there were no sudden lightning flashes of insight. An assembling of a jigsaw full of detail. Detail upon detail until its weight breaks through the lies and ambiguity, and truth rings out.

That was the way to solve this case, too.

But it wasn't to be that way. I mean, did I want to fail? Did I want to escape from the awful injunction over me? Did I want to sabotage myself? Maybe the peeler wants to be nabbed himself, trapped, found out. Maybe he has had enough of truth.

"You don't buy into this summer solstice shit?" John asked, taking off his Belfast Blues Festival baseball hat, wiping his forehead, and shaking his long hair in a way he knew really annoyed me. I was determined not to let him piss me off.

"Well, John, they say it's the holiest day of the year. In Hinduism and Buddhism it was a propitious day to reach enlightenment."

"You ever been to Newgrange in County Meath?" John asked.

"No."

"I went down there on the bike once, now it's aligned with the winter solstice, not the summer, that's more like it, that makes more sense, you're begging the sun to come back again, see. . . ."

But I wasn't listening. I was still obsessing on me and Victoria and that big word: truth—I don't buy into the existential solipsism of fucking defense lawyers: "Everything's relative, subjective." I'm old school. Aristotle, who says there are five ways of finding things out: *techne*, which is practical technique; *episteme*, or scientific method; *phronesis*, which is sagacity; *sophia*, which is wisdom; and, finally, intelligence or *nous*. Techne is the most important for a policeman. The most important for me. And before heroin, my technique was killer: patient, focused, incremental, deep.

Aristotle was wrong about nearly everything. Galileo disproved his physics, Darwin his biology, his pupil Alexander his politics, but he was right about technique. More important than being smart is being meticulous. We had a lot to do today and it was the longest day of the year and we could have done it if we'd been patient. But instead of techne—fuckups; instead of breaking the case—disaster.

In fourteen hours the sun had finally gone down on this long midsummer day and we were on the run from the Denver police, the state police, and any other law enforcement agency you care to mention.

John patted me on the shoulder and we turned from the sunrise, walked back to the tents.

∘ ∘ ∘

We decided on a division of the labor. I'd do Victoria's old office in Boulder to see if the anonymous note writer was still around. I'd let John interview Victoria's neighbors at her building in Denver. I'd have to do it again myself but it would give him something to do and there might be inconsistencies in their stories. John was a peeler, but I told him again how to interview someone. You don't offer information and you take all they say with equanimity. You write down everything and if they're going too fast you ask them to slow down.

Also at some point, I'd call the lawyer representing Hector Martinez—the supposed killer. Then I'd call up the police and book a talk with the lead detective.

The girls drove us to Boulder and we had eggs for breakfast. The girls had things to do, so we split and John caught the bus back to Denver. I was wearing a shirt and jeans, but I bought a tie to look more respectable.

Boulder had an interesting vibe, it was what happened when Grateful Dead fans became rich, yuppie, and comfortable. Every third store sold crystals and Tibetan prayer flags. The parking lot outside the yoga center was stuffed with brand-new Volvos and Range Rovers. The L.L.Bean-clad citizens were white, thin, smelling of soy and vitamins—the sort of smug baby-boom wankers so caught up in their path toward self-actualization that they really didn't see the scores of homeless people begging on the pedestrian mall.

I found a phone booth that contained a potpourri

basket to mitigate the stench of urine. I dialed my first number. Before I got through, I hung up. I had to rethink my story. I wanted to be very low-key at first. I know as a cop I hated private detectives with a passion. So instead, I decided I'd be a newspaperman.

I dialed the Denver police department.

"Detective Miller, please, my name is Jones, I work for the *Irish Times,* I'm looking into the Victoria Pat—"

"Detective Miller is out of town for a few days," a woman said.

"Oh. Uh, well, can I speak to any other detectives on the Victoria Patawasti case?"

"Detective Hopkins is on leave."

"Ok, is there a supervisor?"

"Detective Redhorse hasn't come in yet."

Dead air on the line.

"Ok, I'll call back," I said and hung up.

Damn. Better luck with the next call. The phone book was still attached to the booth. I looked it up and found Enrique Monroe, public defender, attorney-at-law, who was representing the accused. I dialed his number. Got a secretary, told her I was a reporter from Ireland looking into the Victoria Patawasti murder.

"Hello," the lawyer said in a friendly manner.

"Hello, Mr. Monroe, my name is, uh, Simon Jones, I'm a reporter from Ireland. I'm investigating the Victoria Patawasti case and I'd very much like to speak to you."

"I'll give you all the help I can. I would be delighted to talk to you. Are you in town soon?"

"Yes, I'll be in Denver very soon, I—"

"Well, let me tell you something, the police have got the wrong man, Mr. Jones. You can tell your readers that my client has an alibi for the night of the murder, if only I can persuade his friends to speak up for him."

"What's the problem?" I asked.

"Well, to be frank, they're all illegal immigrants and they're worried about their status. I think, though, that I'll be able to turn them around, the police have no physical evidence at all. Nothing, this is an outrageous case. What newspaper did you say you worked for?"

"Uh, the *Irish Times*."

"Listen, I know the people of Ireland want justice, I want justice, but my client is innocent. I've checked his alibi, it's watertight. I'm working on his friends. Working on them. And with an alibi the DA will have to drop the charges."

"That sounds interesting. Mr. Monroe, could we talk later in the week?"

"Impossible. I always want to talk to gentlemen of the press, but this week is impossible. I have to go to Pueblo then juve court. Look, how about Monday, next Monday? Nine o'clock."

"What's your address?"

"Evans and Downing. The Calendar Building, Suite Eleven, Denver, easy to find, I promise you. Well, look, I have to fly—"

"Let me ask you something. What did your client do for a living?" I asked.

"Hector's a mover. He works for Grant Moving."

"Where does he work?"

"Oh, he works all over the city, the whole metro area."

"Boulder?"

"I believe so."

"Let me guess, he'd done some moving work at the CAW headquarters in Boulder, right? They were moving from Boulder to Denver, isn't that right?" I said.

"I don't know," Monroe said, sounding a little embarrassed.

"Don't you think that's where he could have dropped his driver's license?" I suggested.

"I don't know. I haven't really looked at that in much detail. I've been trying so hard to get the alibi witnesses on board, I haven't been working on anything else. I had just thought that the victim somehow found Hector's license, put it in her purse, and was going to turn it in to the police. But yes, that's possible. That license is the only piece of physical evidence linking my client to the murder. If I can dismiss that or if I can get the alibi to work I honestly think we're home free."

"No fingerprints, no hand prints or powder residue on your client?"

"Well, this isn't the sort of thing I would want to discuss over the phone, but what I'm hearing from the DA is that their whole case is based on that license. Pretty thin stuff. They say he picked the lock but there were no scratches on the outside. They say he shot her because he panicked. But Hector's a big guy, he could have just knocked her out. It's weak, very weak."

"I'll bet you money that Hector's firm did the moving in the CAW building. That's why Victoria had his license. She found it there. Or even better, someone else picked it up, used it to frame Hector."

There was a long pause on the line.

"Now that you mention it, it's so plausible," he said finally.

"Well, look, can you find out for me by Monday?" I asked.

"Of course, I'll ask him. This could be very helpful."

"Mr. Monroe, *you've* been very helpful. I'll look forward to meeting you."

"Thank you, I'll see you then."

I hung up. Typical overworked immigration lawyer, and I'd learned from bitter experience that you only believed half of what a defense attorney said. But even so. Maybe the murderer had found this poor guy's Mexican driving license, knew he was almost certainly an illegal immigrant with no credibility, maybe even chatted to him, found out that he had a criminal record, decided to set him up. It would be very interesting to talk to Hector Martinez, could be he'd met the murderer or at least come into close physical contact with him. And it pointed again to that Boulder office.

It was noon. I was so tired. The temperature hovered around ninety degrees. Being five thousand feet up didn't seem to help cool things down. I decided to skip lunch and walk over to the CAW building, which was just off the main pedestrian mall.

The narrow building sat on an empty lot with construction all around it. Four floors, built in the fifties, air conditioners jury-rigged in most of the offices. Maybe this was one reason CAW was moving out. Now that Boulder had become rich this was prime real estate, whoever bought the building would probably demolish it and build a new, much taller, more modern office block.

I put my tie back on and went through the swing doors.

An empty reception desk on the first floor. A large sign that said

```
CAW call Denver 303 782 9555.
```

Not an expert on fonts, but that looked like New Courier to me. I stood in the lobby for a minute or two.

"Hello?" I said.

No answer.

I walked to the elevator and pushed the button for the second floor. When the elevator doors opened on two the lights were off, the floor empty, no one around. I got back on and tried three and finally four. Here the lights were on and I could hear the sound of a photocopy machine. The whole floor had been stripped down to a stained white carpet, deserted except for one corner where a man was working at a computer. He was surrounded by boxes, a photocopier, a few black filing cabinets, a chrome filing cabinet, a minifridge, a shredding machine, and black plastic bags. He didn't see me walk up to him.

"Hello," I said.

He stood. Six five. Pale, thin, tall, balding, saturnine, around forty-five years old. The sort of lived-in face that hinted at experience, though once he spoke you saw that it wasn't experience, just years of rage, you could take your pick why: thwarted ambition, unhappy marriage, poor health. His nose had a network of dying capillaries. A bit of a drinker, too.

"You shouldn't be in here," he said sharply, advancing toward me like a huge praying mantis.

"My name is, uh, Jones," I said, still for some reason reluctant to give my real identity.

"We're closed, we're done here. The whole organization has moved to Denver, there's just me and Margaret and a couple of students and they left this morning and I'm supposed to be gone too. You have to take up your business with the Denver office, it's already opened. How did you get in here, anyway?"

"I just walked in."

"Well, walk out."

"Listen, uh, Mister . . ."

"Name's Klimmer, vice president in charge of operations. How did you get past Margaret?" he said accusingly.

"I didn't see anyone," I said.

"Hold on," he said, and picked up a phone. He dialed a number. No one picked up.

"She must be getting me lunch, ok, well, what do you want? If it's about leasing the floor space you can forget it, this building's coming down," he said.

"I wanted to speak to someone about Victoria Patawasti," I said.

"What?" he said, visibly shaken. He backed away from me and sat down.

"It's about her murder. I'm a private investigator, sent by her family."

"Uh, oh, ok. Um, yes, of course. Ok, you better sit, look, there's a chair over there, you can move that box. What did you say your name was?"

"Jones."

"Jones, and her family sent you, from Ireland?"

"Yes."

"Well, well, well," he said with a half smile.

"Did you know her?"

"You want a Coke? I have a cooler full of Coke," he said, crossing his long legs.

"No. Thank you."

"You're very lucky to catch anyone here. I'm finishing up, today, at the latest tomorrow. We're closing the office here completely, moving everything to Denver."

"Did you know Victoria?" I asked.

"Did I know her? I knew her very well. Very well indeed."

"Did you work with her?"

"Yes. She was a bit of a floater between departments. She worked for me and the brothers. Supposed to be getting her own secretary when we moved. Much bigger building, accommodate more staff."

I looked at him for a moment. He had said all this very quickly. Cheerfully. It was a little suspicious.

"How many people worked here?" I asked.

"At CAW we had about twenty-five employees. A dozen full-time staff, a dozen campaigners. Something like that. We're a very small organization. Before the move we let most of the campaigners go. CU students. Of course, some of them will come to the Denver office. It's only a forty-five-minute commute, if you avoid the rush hour. I do it every day. Bus, easy."

"So you don't live in Boulder?"

"No, almost none of us did. That's why the move is good. I live in Denver, Victoria lived in Denver, the Mulhollands. Boulder is a very expensive town."

"What does CAW stand for again?" I asked, although I knew the answer.

"The Campaign for the American Wilderness."

"What does that mean?" I asked.

"We're a nonprofit organization, we lobby government to get changes in environmental policy, we have a membership, a growing membership, we're a very young organization, one of the youngest, in fact. Charles and Robert founded it just three years ago."

"Charles and Robert?"

"Mulholland. Ryan Mulholland's boys," he said significantly.

I gave him a blank expression.

"You've heard of Ryan Mulholland?" he said.

"No."

"No. No, why would you? You're from Ireland. Yes? Well, Charles and Robert are the boys from his second marriage."

"Well, who is he?"

"He's a banker, a financier. He runs the Mulholland Trust. Rich guy. One of those. You know the type. Fortune 500."

"His second marriage?"

"Yeah, one girl from the first marriage, Arlene, the two boys from the second. He just got married for the third time. Wife's expecting, the boys are pissed, I could tell."

"How old are the boys?"

"I suppose they're not really boys. Robert's thirty-two or thirty-three. Charles is about thirty-eight or thirty-nine, something like that."

"Why are you moving to Denver?"

"More space, higher profile, closer to the networks. We're growing very fast, we need a bigger building. Boulder City Council wouldn't let us expand. You don't have to be a genius to see that that would be a clash of temperaments. They call it the People's Republic of Boulder up here. We're a right-of-center organization. Boulder is slightly to the left of Che Guevera. Also, in terms of media coverage Boulder might as well be on the moon. Denver's a better fit. It's the state capital, HQ of all the media outlets, new airport, new library, fastest-growing city in the West next to Vegas and LA."

"And what do *you* do here?" I asked.

"I'm in charge of mass mailings and, for my sins, this big move we're doing," Klimmer said with a trace of annoyance. I inched my chair a little closer to him.

"How long did you know Victoria?"

"Nearly a year," he said hesitantly.

"And you said she worked for you?"

"She worked for me and she worked for Charles and Robert, she had virtually no administrative experience at all. Actually, she'd been working for one of Ryan Mulholland's companies in England. They head-hunted her. She was very intelligent, very gifted."

"What did she do for you?"

"Oh, well, everything's been upside down for the last couple of months, she's been helping me coordinate the move. It's very complex, you know. The two cities are only a few miles apart, but, my God, you wouldn't believe the crap we have had to deal with."

"What sort of crap?"

"Well, the new building, the lease, putting in the phones, that kind of thing. Also the company that owned this building, Hughes Developments, owned several apartments in Denver that CAW leased. Giving up the lease on this building meant giving up the Denver apartments, too. Mine, for one. So several of us have had to look for new apartments in the middle of all this. You wouldn't believe the hassle."

"Was Victoria one of the people who had to look for a new apartment?"

"Yes, as a matter of fact, I think she was," he said, his

eyes narrowing with the recollection. He dabbed at a bead of sweat on his forehead. He got up and grabbed a Coke to conceal how tense he was. I was glad when he sat that big skinny frame down again. He opened the can and drank little sips.

"When did the rest of the organization leave for Denver?" I asked.

"More or less everyone was gone by the tenth. I know that because it was Robert's birthday and they had the party at the new building in Denver. So neither Peg or I were there, although you would have thought it was bad taste having a party in light of what happened," he said a little angrily.

"Victoria's murder," I said.

"Yes."

"So everyone was gone by the tenth?"

"Pretty much."

"And it's just been you here since then?"

"No, myself, Margaret, two of the CU students, Julie and Anne. But I was put in charge of winding things up. We needed a senior person for that."

"What's the command structure? Where are you in the hierarchy?"

"Why do you need to know that?" he asked.

"I'm just curious."

"Oh, ok, well, Charles and Robert at the top, joint presidents, and then myself, Steve West, Abe Childan are vice presidents. I know what you're thinking— three vice presidents for a permanent staff of twelve, but we plan to grow and—"

"Did Margaret, Julie, or Anne know Victoria?"

"Well, it's a small organization, everyone knew everyone."

"Let me put it another way. Did they know her well, were they confidantes?"

"Uh, I really don't know."

"So, Mr. Klimmer, for the last ten days you've been more or less running the show since the move to Denver?"

"At this end, yes."

"And Victoria was killed right before the move?"

"That's right. A very difficult time."

"On June fifth. Just days before the move," I said flatly.

"Yes."

"That's interesting, isn't it?" I said.

"What is?"

"That she was killed just before she got a new apartment in Denver, a whole new set of circumstances. If someone was going to murder her at her old apartment they were running out of time. They had to strike soon."

"I suppose," he said, again taking tense sips from his soda.

"What was the name of the moving company that you used to relocate from Boulder to Denver?"

"I can't quite remember, it was a Spanish name, I could find out pretty easily. I can ask Charles when I talk to him."

"Yeah, I'd like to know. Tell me, Mr. Klimmer, where did you go to college?"

"Cornell University."

"Good school. Charles and Robert?"

"They went to Harvard. Why do you want to know that?"

"If you'll bear with me."

"Fine," he said submissively.

"Did you have access to Victoria's personnel file?"

"What are you saying?" he asked, again a trace of irritation in his upper lip.

"Did you have access to her personnel file?"

"Yes, but what's that got to do with anything?"

"What about Margaret and the students, would they have had access to it?"

"Of course not. It's confidential."

"Ok. Let me ask you something else. I see you don't have a printer here. If you wanted to print out a document, where would you print it out?"

"What?"

"If you could answer the question, please," I said.

"All the printers have been moved to Denver. Margaret has one at her desk, I believe. What exactly is the relevance of that question?"

"Could I see Victoria's personnel file?"

"Again, most of the personnel files have been sent on to Denver," he said, but from his tone I knew that Victoria's had not.

"But not hers, because she's not personnel anymore," I said.

He nodded and put down his soda. For some reason he had kept the file. And of course he knew exactly where it was. He stood, unlocked the big chrome filing cabinet, reached inside, and handed it over without another mutter about it being confidential or none of my business. He smiled weakly, sadly. Victoria had clearly meant a lot to him.

"Did you know her back in Ireland?" he asked. The question threw me a little.

"No, I didn't," I managed.

"Oh, she was really a wonderful person. Not just beautiful, clever, too," he said absently, putting the filing cabinet key back in his pocket.

The cream folder contained six sheets of paper. I scanned them, checked that she had written "Tiny Taj" as part of her home address. Of course she had. I gave the folder back. He put it carefully back in the file cabinet. I looked at him for a moment. He and three other people could have sent the anonymous note. It was postmarked June 12 and by then everyone else had left for the Denver office. He worked closely with Victoria. I would have to check out Margaret, Julie, and Anne but my gut told me it was him. He was educated, at a very good university, pretending in the note not to be. A secretary might not have thought to do that. But a secretary would have had time to reprint a letter if she was interrupted. A boss using the printer, say while the secretaries went for lunch, would be in a rush, possibly making do with a faded copy. Most telling of all, only he of the four people here could have found out Victoria's home address in the personnel file. Probably he sent the note. It all fit. Why? Why did he do it? Because he liked Victoria? Why not go to the cops? Was he afraid of something? Someone? Frightened for his own life? If Hector Martinez had dropped his driver's license here at CAW, the murderer had picked it up to frame him. Someone here. Someone in CAW. Perhaps Klimmer was the murderer himself and this was his oblique confession.

"What's the difference between CAW and Greenpeace or Friends of the Earth or the Sierra Club or whatever?" I asked.

"Oh, we're quite different," he said.

"How so?"

"Well, we're in favor of a policy called Wise Use."

"What's that?"

"It's a more balanced approach to the environment. We've become very successful at counteracting some of the more biased approaches to environmental policy foisted on us by the media."

"Who do you think killed Victoria?"

Klimmer blanched for a second. It was standard cop procedure to throw a lot of secondary questions and then hit the person with the big question. Standard procedure, but it often worked.

"I—I don't know," he stammered, telling me, incredibly, that he did know. Or at the very least he didn't buy the story about the burglar. Hector Martinez killed Victoria Patawasti. The police had him in custody. It was an open-and-shut case. Or so it appeared to be. Unless you had a different piece of evidence. Unless you thought you knew who really did it. The phone rang.

Klimmer picked it up.

"Yes . . . oh, yes . . . uh-huh, it's been very busy."

He put his hand over the receiver.

"Mr. Jones, I am extremely busy, perhaps we can meet here again in a few days or maybe early next week."

"You said you would be gone by the weekend."

"Oh, oh yes, sorry, yes, well . . . here, take a card, and give me a call and we can talk, this isn't a good time."

I shook my head. I didn't want to go, I felt I was right on the verge of a breakthrough. I remained in my seat.

"I have a few more questions," I said.

Klimmer suddenly stood, towering above me, his face paler.

"I said this isn't a good time, give me a call and we can talk," he said more forcefully, almost angrily.

"It will just take a minute," I said, wanting to push him a little.

"No, I'm on the phone, I'm busy, it will have to be another time," he said, his voice rising half an octave, becoming more aggressive.

I didn't want to upset him that much. He was important to the case. I nodded, took his card, walked back to the elevator, left the office. When I got outside I dialed the number on the card. The operator informed me that this number had been disconnected.

It didn't matter. If he didn't send the note, then at the very least he knew something that he was having a hard time trying to hide. I would have to see him again.

I sat for a minute in the pedestrian mall. A busker came up to me and began singing Phish songs. I got the bus back to Denver, returned to the motel. John appeared, haggard, out of sorts. He hadn't been able to get into Victoria's building to interview the neighbors. Because of the murder, they had beefed up security, you needed the code to enter.

"John, you just press all the buttons and someone will buzz you in," I said, exhausted now.

John was chagrined, but excited by my news. His voice poured in my ear and I listened to him.

"Alex, we should press our advantage, we should see him tonight, as soon as possible, crack him, you've rumbled him, see? You did it, mate. We'll go over there together, sort it out, make him come with us to the peelers, free an innocent man, get the investigation on the right track. Crack the case, get a big bonus from Mr. Patawasti."

John spoke and I stared, tired, through the windows. The sun in the sky, heavy, loitering. Planes. Helicopters.

Oh, take from me this day. Unmake it. Please. All it needs is for me to say, no, John, tomorrow will do. All it takes is for me to say no. In Irish there is no word for "no." Maybe that's the trouble. All I have to do is refuse and none of the bad stuff goes down.

But I didn't say no. I was knackered from the rave and the sleepless night. I was weak.

I said nothing.

I took the easy way.

"Come on," John said and helped me to my feet.

Another of those wee things that fuck you up. Little things with big consequences. Paul of Tarsus has a fit and Christianity is born. Franz Ferdinand's chauffeur turns left instead of right and a hundred million Europeans die.

Poor John. I will not be there at your tide burial. Tractors and the cries of seagulls will wing you to your resting place. Seagulls a thousand miles from the ocean, in the landfill on the road to Kansas, your body rotting there under earth and garbage piles.

Lead on chaos, pandemonium, death. And weary, I muttered:

"Ok, eejit. Let's go."

o o o

We went to the bus station at three o'clock and took turns staking it out. I read the newspapers on John's watch. Very different from the UK. In America, the main story wasn't the Oklahoma bombing, which had taken place just two months ago and killed 168 people. No, it was all about a former American football player I had never heard of, O. J. Simpson, who apparently had murdered his wife and was now on trial in California.

In Colorado the big story was the continuing

drought, the bankruptcy of several ski resorts, and the dreary prospects for a long, hot summer.

Klimmer showed up at the Denver bus station just after four-thirty. He was carrying a briefcase and didn't look nervous in the least. John and I followed him. We were both wearing baseball caps and sunglasses. We didn't stand out.

He walked to the Sixteenth Street pedestrian mall and cut up through the park next to the hideous central library.

It was our first chance to really see Denver in the daylight. It looked ok. Dead grass in the parks, granite government buildings, a world trade center, office towers, a university building, several imposing masonic lodges within a block of the state capitol, which must have given conspiracy theorists food for thought.

Klimmer resided in a large apartment building overlooking Cheesman Park in the Capitol Hill section of Denver. John pointed out that he lived only a couple of hundred yards from Victoria Patawasti's building, though whether this meant something or not, I didn't know.

We waited outside his building for about fifteen minutes until he was settled, then we buzzed his apartment.

"Mr. Klimmer?"

"Yes?" he said through the intercom.

"Mr. Klimmer, it's Peter Jones from this morning, I wonder if you wouldn't mind answering a few more questions."

There was a long pause on the intercom but finally he said:

"Come on up. It's apartment 714."

He buzzed us in, we took the elevator.

"Remember, my name's Jones," I told John.

"Why did you tell him that?"

"I don't know."

"Well, my name's going to be John Smith then," John said.

"You can't have Smith and Jones, for God's sake," I muttered.

"Well, what then, we're nearly there," John said in a panic.

"You're Wilson, now you just shut up and leave the talking to me, ok?"

We got off the lift and walked to 714. Klimmer answered, wearing flip-flops, sweatpants, and a thin cotton T-shirt. He was drinking from a large brandy glass. It wasn't his first one, either. His breath stank of booze, and he'd been home only fifteen minutes. I'd forgotten how tall he was too, taller than even John, and that was something I didn't see much.

"Mr. Klimmer, allow me to present my partner, John Wilson," I said.

Klimmer nodded, looked John up and down thoughtfully.

"Delighted to meet you. Why don't you all come in," Klimmer said demurely.

We stepped inside. The apartment was bare, save for a sofa and a few lounge chairs. It was a big space with a balcony that looked west toward the mountains. Doors to bedrooms. Boxes with shipping labels on them.

"Spartan, I'm afraid, everything else in transit, I'm moving just across the park. Bigger, of course, but I'll lose the sunset," Klimmer said.

"You'll get the dawn," I said.

"The dawn's nothing. Can I get you fellows anything to drink?" Klimmer asked.

"Whatever you're having."

Klimmer went to the kitchen unit, came back with two more large brandies.

"This is the good stuff," he said, giving John a wink.

"Oh aye?" John said. Klimmer grinned and patted John cheerfully on the back.

"Let's sit on the balcony," Klimmer said. "When the sun sets behind the front range, it's really quite spectacular, the light's diffused because it's so dry, so much dust in the air, ash, too, from wild fires, quite lovely, you'll see what I'm talking about."

We moved to the balcony. It was narrow, with barely room for the three wicker chairs. I put my hand on the safety rail, which was only as high as my waist, and it came back covered in a thick layer of dust or possibly ash. Everything was coated in this thin red film, the chairs included.

"Very dry summer," Klimmer said apologetically, attempting to wipe my chair before I sat on it.

He seemed relaxed, not at all surprised to see us, not irritated by our visit. Unusual behavior, I would have said, in a busy man organizing his firm's move from one city to another while he himself is getting a new apartment.

He sat there and waited for me to begin. They always did that. It was as if the last half year had never happened. I was back in the old routine. They wait for you to start. On television or in books, people are always doing something interesting while they're being questioned, but in real life, they sit there, patient, ready, marshaling their thoughts. How to begin? How to approach the conversation? Start off with chitchat, build up slowly like this morning, or hit him with what I knew and get him to deny it?

"Mr. Klimmer," I asked, "why did you write Victoria Patawasti's father an anonymous letter stating that the police had arrested the wrong man in connection with her murder?"

Klimmer's smile evaporated. His face had become instantly gray, nervous, he was no poker player, that's for sure.

"I don't know what you're talking about," he said calmly and finished his brandy.

"I'll lay it out for you in easy steps. The letter was postmarked from Boulder on the twelfth of June. By someone who knew Victoria's home address. None of her neighbors knew her home address, so it had to be someone at work. Crucially, only someone with access to her personnel file could know that her house was called the Tiny Taj. Victoria never told anyone that. You and three others were the only ones left at CAW.

You were the only one with access to her personnel file. There was a partial print on the inside of the envelope itself, and I'll bet if I took it to the police they'd find it matched your fingerprints."

"That's impossible," Klimmer said angrily.

"It's impossible that there was a print on the envelope? Impossible because you used gloves? Is that right, Mr. Klimmer? Perhaps we'll let the police decide that."

Klimmer groaned. The bluff had worked. He wasn't used to this sort of thing. He was no informer, or blackmailer. He really thought that he had screwed up somehow and left a print. He frowned in disbelief.

"Shit. Shit, shit, shit. I should never have sent that letter, I should never have got involved," he said, putting his head in his hands.

John opened his mouth to speak, but I shook my head at him. We had to go very carefully now.

"Mr. Klimmer, I feel you wanted me to find you. You wanted this. The mere fact that you postmarked this in Boulder. That you sent it at all. You wanted someone to come looking for you, to investigate. Please, Mr. Klimmer, tell me what you know," I said.

"Oh, God, I don't know anything, not really, not anything," he said.

"Mr. Klimmer, you liked Victoria and you seem to know that the man the police are holding didn't kill her. You think you know who did kill her, so tell me. You sent the note because you didn't want him to get away with it. Tell me who did it, tell me what you know. I'll take care of everything, you won't have to be involved."

Klimmer looked at me and then at John, went to the kitchen, took a drink, and came back with another full glass of brandy. His eyes suddenly bleary, red, tired.

"What if I ask you to leave right now?" he said.

"We'll go straight to the police," I said.

"Damn it," Klimmer said, taking a gulp from his glass. "I am so stupid, I'll be next. He's killed two people. I'll be next. What was I thinking? I should have stayed out of it. I should have stayed on for a couple of months and then resigned. It would have been ok. Work till Christmas, say I don't like the new atmosphere, quit. I had to stick my stupid nose in."

"Who has killed two people?" I asked.

"Are you taping this?" he said suddenly, his eyes wild. He stood up awkwardly. He came over to John and patted him down, then he lurched to the other side of the balcony, did the same to me.

"No wire, your word against mine," he said with triumph, his tall frame blotting out the sun.

"Mr. Klimmer, take a seat, we're not taping you, we want to help. Now tell me who has killed two people?" I said very softly.

"One of them. One of them," Klimmer muttered, sitting, wiping his mouth.

"Who are you talking about?"

"One of them, one of the brothers," he said with irritation, his knuckles white around his brandy glass.

"The Mulhollands?"

"Yes, the Mulhollands, of course the Mulhollands, who else? Either Charles or Robert, I don't know which one, but it is one of them, that's the only possibility."

I sipped my brandy and remained silent. I had to go easy, tease out the information, slowly, deliberately.

"Mr. Klimmer, why don't you start at the beginning? Tell us everything."

"The beginning. Ha. You don't know," he said, smiling sadly.

"Tell me about Victoria," I said.

"Victoria, oh, God . . . She was charming. We got on wonderfully. She couldn't sleep. Woke up a lot at night. I bought her a Go-to-Sleep Sheep. It played 'Beautiful Dreamer.'"

"Ok, go on, please."

"I suppose I was almost jealous when the brothers wanted her to work for them, too, coordinating the move, before that, you see, she worked for me. She was sweet. Charles and Robert probably just wanted her around. She didn't have the experience to do all that stuff with the move. She did mass mailings for me."

"She was killed because one of them was in love with her?" I asked.

"No, why don't you listen? Robert wasn't interested and Charles's wife is Amber Mulholland. Have you seen her yet? *Amber Mulholland.* Believe me, he wasn't going anywhere. Very beautiful. Drop-dead gorgeous. Even put Victoria in the shade."

"So what if she's beautiful?" John said. "That never bloody stopped anyone before. People cheated on Marilyn Monroe."

"No one cheats on Amber Mulholland, but anyway, this is way off the point. We're not talking about an affair. No one had a goddamn affair with Victoria," Klimmer said testily.

"How can you be so sure?" John said, and I glared at him.

"No, no, no, if you would just listen. It was the stupid move to Denver. Victoria would never have seen the accounts. She'd be alive today," Klimmer said with marked irritation. He was a little spiky now, jumping out of his skin. Pale, sweating.

"Mr. Klimmer, take it easy, you're going to tell me everything very slowly," I said.

"I need a drink," Klimmer said, draining his glass.

"John, get the man another brandy," I said, giving him Klimmer's glass. "Just a small one, John."

John went, made a large one, brought it back. Klimmer took it greedily.

"There we go, the sun's setting, now we'll see some stuff," Klimmer said.

"Just start at the beginning," I said again softly.

"The beginning again. Ok. Victoria kept a computer diary. The only people who had access to her office were Charles, Robert, and myself. I didn't kill her, so it had to be one of them. You see?"

"Or both of them," John said, looking at me. I shook

my head at him again. I didn't need him bloody interrupting.

"Tell me more," I said.

"Victoria was helping me coordinate the move. She had a lot of new responsibilities. One of them was to close down our bank accounts in Boulder and open new ones in Denver. We were with the Bank of Boulder, it was too small, anyway. We should have done that years ago."

"Mr. Klimmer, back to Victoria," I said.

"She noticed some sort of discrepancy, a payment problem. Victoria was discreet. It had come from an account owned by CAW but only accessible to Charles and Robert. They're not as rich as you would think, did you know that? Obviously millionaires and their father is a billionaire, but their trust income is tiny. CAW pays them a good salary and Charles is a partner in his firm, but clearly it wasn't enough to pay Houghton. You see?"

"I don't see, who is Houghton?"

"He probably thought they had more money than they really had. Everyone does. It's part of their image. Look at Charles. He's a successful lawyer, but that doesn't put him in Bill Gates territory. Right? You understand now? Not if he's being asked to pay millions."

"Who's paying millions?" I asked, desperate for Klimmer to slow down a bit.

"One of the brothers. Maybe both, I don't know. The point is, they're wealthy, but not wealthy enough. But that's fine, you see, because obviously they began tapping the CAW accounts, get it? You see what I am saying?"

"I'm sorry, Mr. Klimmer, but I don't see. Who's Houghton? What are you talking about?" I asked.

"You should pay attention then. It's ok for Charles or Robert to take money from the CAW account for purposes related to the organization, but those sums have to be itemized, accounted for. CAW is a charity, not a slush fund. The thing is, these payments didn't show up in the accounts. Money had been withdrawn and not entered as expenditure and, worse, it had been paid not to an institution but to an individual named Houghton. Victoria tracked the payments over two years. It was more than a million dollars. It worried her. She came to me, I was her boss."

"What did you do?"

"I told her to forget it. I told her it was none of her business. I told her it was none of our business. That CAW was Charles and Robert Mulholland's baby and if they wanted to pay their contractor or their fucking driver or gay lover or whatever out of CAW money, it didn't matter. I said that she was very young, and she had a lot to learn and she should concentrate on her job and forget she ever saw those payments. I meant it too, I was only looking out for her."

"What did she do then?"

"She took my advice. She took no further action, but Victoria was a smart girl and she wanted to protect herself."

"How?"

"She said she was going to keep a journal so that if we ever got audited or investigated she'd be in the clear."

"What did you say to that?"

"I hit the ceiling. I told her that she couldn't leave a paper trail, that that was how they fucking got Nixon."

"And what did she say?" I asked.

"She told me it was the only way she could stay at CAW," Klimmer said sorrowfully.

"And you wanted her to stay, you liked her, you liked her very much."

"I wanted her to stay. I said fine, keep your journal, but not on paper, encrypt it on your computer and leave me out of it and never mention it to me or anyone else again."

"And what then?"

"She was murdered," Klimmer said, fear creeping into his voice and eyes.

"That doesn't prove Charles or Robert did it," I said.

"Don't you listen? Only Charles, Robert, and myself had access to her office."

"The cleaning lady? The secretaries. The sandwich delivery boy. I'm sure there were more people in her office than that."

"Yeah, sure, the sandwich boy did it, Mrs. Mulholland did it when she was playing secret Santa. The electrician fixing the lights decided to risk his job, break into a stranger's computer, read Victoria's journal, brutally kill her, and frame a Mexican for it. Listen to me, you idiot. Only Charles and Robert had access to the private bank account records. Only Charles and Robert could have accessed her computer journal. Don't you see?"

"Frankly, I don't," I said.

Klimmer pursed his lips, bit his tongue, stood, sat down again. He was exasperated. Angry.

"Why can't you understand this? Whatever brother was making the payments must have noticed that someone had been looking into the private bank account. I don't know, an access log, a trace back. In any case, it could only have been Victoria. He must have found that she'd been looking at the account, checked her computer, and then discovered her journal. Killed her. Fraud on this level would mean jail time, public disgrace."

"I don't know, it's not enough to kill someone," I said.

"Yeah, well, I thought so too for a while. For a couple of days, I almost believed that cock-and-bull story about the break-in at Victoria's place. That is, until Alan Houghton disappeared. And Alan Houghton, my dear Mr. Jones, was the man who was receiving the payments, the one getting the money from the secret account. The police found his car abandoned near Lookout Mountain. It was on the local news. I remembered the name. He's vanished off the face of the Earth. Call the cops if you don't believe me. Missing persons. Never find him, know why? Because he's dead. Do you see now, the man who killed Victoria killed him, too. Don't you see that that's why Victoria had to die? Because Alan Houghton's murder had already been planned. He disappeared the same night Victoria was killed."

"It's possible," I said, and nodded. Klimmer had been clever. Maybe he was right. This Houghton person was getting payments from one or perhaps both of the brothers. Blackmailing them? A million dollars. That's not nothing. Maybe the demands were going up. The murderer had had enough. He had been getting ready to kill him. He had already planned out Houghton's whole death. But then Victoria had been put in charge of closing the bank accounts. She had found out about the illegal payments. The killer discovered that someone had seen the secret accounts, reckoned it was Victoria, checked her computer. Made a decision.

I would have to check out who Alan Houghton was and whether he had really disappeared. If there actually was a missing persons report. If so, things might be fitting nicely into place. Perhaps whichever brother did it had left some physical evidence at the murder scene, or perhaps at Alan Houghton's house. The police could find out. Undoubtedly, the killer would have swept his trail, destroyed Victoria's computer, wiped the accounts evidence, scoured Houghton's apartment, but there might be something left. The police would need some convincing that they had arrested the wrong man, that the real killer was a respected and influential member of the community, but Klimmer was a convincing person. He had convinced me.

"What happened to Victoria's computer?"

"Oh, it disappeared, believe me, I looked, I was told it had probably been sent back for repairs. Likely story."

"But you said Victoria's computer journal was encrypted, how could they have broken the encryption?"

"I don't know, both brothers went to Harvard, they're sharp, I really don't know. Victoria told me she had encrypted the files herself, maybe she did it wrong."

"Maybe she did it right, the brothers never found out about her, and she was killed for some other reason," John said.

"Maybe a million things, I'm telling you what I know, someone killed her and I think I know who," Klimmer said angrily. A tic in his left eye now. He fought it down.

I needed him to be a lot calmer. I needed him to come with me to the police station. We had to get him there while he was in a cooperative mood. Tonight, tomorrow, soon. Perhaps we could have this wrapped up quicker than any of us hoped.

The killer had undoubtedly been clever but had already made one dreadful mistake. He had completely discounted the possibility that Victoria had told someone of her suspicions, assuming she had not. But how could he have been so sure of her? He must have known her intimately. Maybe, despite what Klimmer said, he'd even been having an affair with her. So why not try and buy her off? Why resort to murder? No, he'd known Victoria was not the type. And he was putting a stop to the rot, ending the blackmail. He couldn't afford to have around someone else who knew—someone who could start the blackmail again. And he couldn't set her up as a fall guy, he didn't want her speaking, telling her side. She had to be got rid of. Doubling her salary and posting her to South America wouldn't work. He knew Victoria and he knew if ever she was asked, she would tell the truth. That was my girl, honest, smart, beautiful. He had seen all that and had chosen to end her life.

"Tell me about Charles and Robert Mulholland," I said.

"They both have doctorates in some pointless social science thing, Charles has a law degree. Grew up rich in Boulder. Robert never had a proper job. Never worked a day in his life. Charles became an attorney with Cutter and May. A firm here. He worked in environmental law. They both wrote for those magazines, you know, *Commentary, The National Review,* that kind of paper. One of them had a brainchild to found an environmental group, get start-up dough from Daddy, I told you this before—"

"Tell me again, please."

"Ok, so they set up CAW. Charles got made partner at Cutter and May and when CAW really started to take off, everyone benefited. I believe they have political ambitions. That's why we're moving the office to

Denver, plus Daddy has remarried, so who knows, maybe they're worried about the will," Klimmer said with a leer, wiping brandy off his thin lips with a big clumsy paw.

"How long have you worked for them?" I asked.

Klimmer drank some more of his brandy, went to the kitchen, crashed something down on a tabletop, groaned, came back with the bottle.

"You know what I think?" he said.

"What?"

"I think I'm done with these fucking stupid questions, that's what I think," he said bellicosely.

"Well, Mr. Klimmer, don't get—"

"I think I've told you more than enough, in fact, I've told you far too much," he said loudly.

I nodded.

"Mr. Klimmer, you have been very cooperative and I'm very grateful. I, I suspect we'll just have to do this one more time."

"No more times," Klimmer said, laughing, slurring his words. He sat down heavily, dropped the bottle, brandy spilling everywhere.

"Mr. Klimmer, you know we're going to have to go to the police with this information," I said.

"Go, I don't care, I'll deny everything. I'll deny I ever saw you. Margaret was on lunch, she can't back up your story, you were never at CAW today. You never came here. Don't you see, if he can kill Victoria and Houghton he can kill me."

"No, the police will protect you."

"The police. The police can't do anything. I don't know what I was thinking. I never told you anything. I never saw you. I never fucking saw you," he said, raising his voice and gripping the sides of his chair. He pointed his finger at me and shook his head.

"Ok, Mr. Klimmer, well, look, I think we'll go, we'll discuss this tomorrow," I began.

"We're discussing nothing tomorrow, I make a huge mistake, I don't know what I was thinking. I thought I wanted someone to come looking for me, but I was wrong. Goddamnit, you tricked me, you tricked me. I don't know what you're talking about. I invented the whole thing. No, I never saw you."

"Mr. Klimmer—"

"You weren't here, you made it all up," Klimmer said, angrily, on the verge of hysteria. It was time to leave, we had to let him calm down. I gave John the nod.

John tried to get up.

"Where are you going?" Klimmer said, furiously, "what are you doing? I'm not going with you. Sit down, sit down, I tell you."

Klimmer was right on the edge. We had pushed it too far. Shouldn't have come here again today. This was a catch to be taken easy, on a light line, not brutally hauled in. Tomorrow morning, the three of us walking to the police station together. Bad call hounding him again today.

Klimmer got up and backed away from us. He was furious. He looked unhinged. More than just the drink. He slapped himself on the face. Made a fist. John was standing right next to him on the balcony. Three chairs, me and two big guys, we could barely fit at the best of times. Now, with all of us standing, it was crowded, horribly tense.

"Back off," he shouted at John. "I'm not going with you."

"Calm down, mate, we're leaving you alone, we're not touching you," John said.

"I don't know who you are, leave me alone," Klimmer said, his body shaking with fury. Was he drunk? Was he having a breakdown? All those pent-up weeks, knowing what he knew, and now it was released. Now it was all coming out, his anger, his fear, his love for the dead girl. His fury at the spoiled rich kid who had killed her. And it was John and me who had stirred these emotions in him. Somehow we were the enemy.

The veins throbbed in his head, his pale skin had turned red.

"Leave me alone," he yelled at John, standing a few inches from him, his face almost up against John's.

"Steady on, mate," John said.

"Everything's fine," I assured him.

But his eyes were wild. His cheeks crimson, then white, then ashen. He bit his lip. He bit it until it bled.

"Get out, get out, both of you, I don't know anything."

"We're leaving," I said, and started backing away, except there was nowhere to back to.

"I'm not going anywhere," Klimmer said.

"It's ok, everything's fine," I said. "Come on, John, we're leaving."

"Go, leave, now," Klimmer said.

John turned his back and began squeezing past the chair, trying to go back into the living room. Klimmer shoved him. John grabbed Klimmer's hand. Klimmer shoved him again.

It all happened in slow motion now. Time paused on its journey to eternity. I don't know what John was doing. Steadying himself? Shoving Klimmer back? What did Klimmer think? That John was trying to grab him, trying to wrestle him to the ground as a precursor to frog-marching him to the police station? He punched John, hit him in the throat, started shoving him back into the seat, John reacted violently, pushed Klimmer away from him. Klimmer snarled, went for John again, grabbed at his collar, John pushed Klimmer off him. Harder this time. Cop fashion. Aggressive. John had big shoulders. Klimmer was all height, but John had bulk, too. The balcony was very narrow. Too crowded. Klimmer six-five, six-six, with that high center of gravity. The rail came up only to the top of his hips. I could see it before it happened. I reached out my hand.

Klimmer stumbled. The momentum carried him into and onto the balcony rail. He toppled backward, lay horizontal on the rail for a fraction of a second.

"John," I said in a frozen whisper.

Klimmer clawed the air. John made a grab for him but Klimmer had lost his balance, the momentum carrying him tumbling over the balcony. He fell at a rate of thirty-two feet per second per second, his eyes stunned, his mouth open, his voice gone. He had, perhaps, a second to prepare himself. He landed on his feet but his femurs burst out through his knees. His internal organs smashed into one another. Parts of his brain liquefied inside his skull. The body snapped and crumpled sickeningly on the concrete path. He died instantly without uttering a sound.

6: THE DWARF

West across the park and the city—five layers of mountains and the setting sun. A halo over the foothills like an enormous chrysalis. A trap enclosing us in this town, in this state. Forever. We stood on the balcony for an amazed moment—caught in our own theologies of panic, fear, retribution. It was the longest day of the year and it wasn't to be over for a long time yet. A dozen witnesses in the park. At least two or three had seen the whole thing.

We moved back from the edge of the balcony.

John was stunned, his eyes wide, his face white.

"W-what now?" he asked. "The police?"

"We make a run for it," I said.

"What?"

"We'll get twenty years for this," I said.

"It was an accident."

"It was goddamn manslaughter, twenty years," I insisted.

"We won't get out," John said.

"We'll try."

I grabbed his arm and backed him off the balcony and into the apartment. I found the brandy glasses we'd drunk from, wiped them with a piece of paper towel. Tried to think of any other surfaces I'd touched, wiped them, too.

Police sirens now. John sat down on the chair, dazed.

"Oh, Jesus," he was saying over and over.

"Get up," I yelled at him.

He sat there, incredulous. Stunned into catalepsia. And to think I was the heroin user. I grabbed him, pulled him to the door. Wiped the handle, went out, left the apartment, closed the door behind us. Marched him to the fire escape.

"We'll just walk out," I said.

He nodded, I don't think he knew what was going on. John was a peeler and back in Ireland he owned a gun but he'd never bargained on killing anyone. Out of his depth here, this whole scene wasn't his, this whole story had turned into a bad dream. John had hitched his star to mine in the hope of getting somewhere better. Getting out of rain-swept, war-torn, depressing Ulster for America. And I should have resisted. John, the anchor dragging us down. Going to drown us both.

"Where's your hat?" I asked.

"My what?"

"Your fucking baseball hat," I said.

I sprinted back to the apartment.

"Where are you going?" he wailed.

"John, you better snap out of it, we're in the shit, I'm going back to get your hat."

"We got to get out of here," he said, his voice quavering.

"John, shut the fuck up, stay here, I'll be back."

I went to the door. Pulled the sleeve of my shirt down, turned the handle, it wouldn't open. Thoughts raced through my head. The apartment door naturally had a self-locking mechanism. I wouldn't be able to get in. The cops would find John's print-encrusted hat that said on it: Belfast Blues Festival. Maybe, if they were really smart, they'd cross-check the recent arrivals at DIA, to see if any had come from Belfast. Well, that would be that. Best-case scenario, we do get away from this building, out of Denver, back to the UK. They'd find our names, put two and two together. Extradite us, try us.

Had to get back into that apartment, get that goddamn hat. I looked down the corridor. Mercifully, no one had come out to see what all the bloody commotion was. A fancy building—most people on this floor probably had fancy jobs that kept them out during the day.

Arms on my back, pulling me.

I turned.

John, wild, gesticulating. Losing it.

"Alex, forget the fucking hat, we have to go."

"John, if we don't get the hat, we're fucked, your prints are on it, so are mine, and since we're peelers we're on Interpol's computer. We have to get back into the apartment to get it. Trust me. We gotta break the door down."

"Can you take prints off cloth?"

"Aye and take them off the bloody peak," I said.

"Leave it, we have to get out of here," he said.

I grabbed his face and made him look at me. His whole body was shaking. He was drenched with sweat. This close to a nervous collapse, I could tell. No point trying to convince him, I grabbed him by the collar, dragged him over to the door.

Again I could hear sirens.

"We gotta go, Alex, they are going to nail us," John pleaded.

"We're going to charge the door, shoulder it, break it down," I said.

The corridor was wide, it would give us a bit of a run at least.

"Alex, we don't have the time," John said.

"Now listen, you wanker, if we don't get that hat, we are fucking going to prison, do you understand?" I said as calm as I could.

"Alex, we have to—" John began, but his voice trailed off, his eyes closed, he didn't know what he was doing. His body slumped and I could see he was giving over his will to mine, it was the path of least resistance.

We backed up from the door, maybe a good ten paces. I'd never broken a door down before. I had no idea how difficult it would be. Nice strong building, too, the door probably wouldn't give like they did in cop shows and the movies. We'd try for it, anyway.

"Now," I said.

We ran at the door and jumped into it with our shoulders. A huge crash. We bounced off, fell, without noticeable effect on the door. Shoulders killing us.

The sirens were louder now too. At least a couple of different vehicles. John looked at me. Desperate.

"We go again," I said.

We backed up, ran at the door, shouldered it, again bounced off without any noticeable change.

"And again," I said.

We backed up and this time as we did so, a man came out of his apartment. A very old man, in checked trousers, white shirt, slippers.

"What's all this noise?" he said.

"We have to take him out," John said under his breath.

"We're police, sir," I said in what I hoped was an American accent, "someone jumped from their balcony, suicide, we think. I'd like you to return to you apartment, we're going to be questioning everyone."

"A suicide, where?" the old man asked.

"In the park, the body's right out there," I said.

"I gotta see this," the old geezer said and went back inside.

"Now we have to go," John said.

"One more try," I said.

We backed up, charged the door, bounced off.

"One more," I said, "I felt something give."

"You said that was the last," John said.

"One more," I insisted.

We rammed the door and this time the metal screws holding the lock into the wood popped out and the door gave a little. If I could smash it with something, it would go. I looked down the hall.

"The fire extinguisher," I said.

I grabbed the fire extinguisher out of the glass case. Thumped it into the door. The lock gave. I shoved the door open.

"John, wipe my prints off the extinguisher and the handle and the case the extinguisher was in, ok?"

He looked blank. I slapped him upside the head.

"Ok?"

He nodded. I ran into the apartment, searched for the hat, saw it on the coffee table, grabbed it, ran out.

"It's clean," John said. I nodded. John and I bolted for the fire escape.

"Get that cap down again, real low," I said.

He pulled down the baseball cap as low as it would go, I pulled mine down too. Not much of an aid in concealing our identities, but it would have to serve.

"When we get out of the building, we walk away calmly, and then when we're clear, we run, ok?" I said.

"What?"

"John, you eejit, get with the fucking program, just do everything I tell you, ok?"

"Ok," he said sullenly.

We ran down the concrete corridor of the fire escape. Came out in a side lobby. A few potted plants, green-painted concrete walls, a mirror, a notice about trash, but otherwise empty. We sprinted through a door and outside into the sunlight.

A black guy stood there blocking our way. Tall guy,

shorts, sneakers, sweat-stained gray T-shirt with the words "United States Army" printed on the front. He'd been jogging, seen the whole thing, come around to the front of the building to stop the murderers or anyone else getting out.

"Por favor, señor, muy urgente, es tarde," I explained, and went to go past him.

"No one's leaving this building till the cops show up," he said.

John tried to shove past him, but with a big hand the soldier pushed him to the ground. A clear violation of Posse Comitatus, but this wasn't the time to mention that. John spun on the ground, knocking the legs from under the soldier. He went down like a ton of bricks and I kicked him in the head, knocking him out, nearly breaking his neck.

Interfering bastard. I pulled John up. We didn't know which way to go. East into the streets, west into the park. A cop car appeared ten blocks east, heading for the building. It made up our minds. We went across the park. A crowd of about twenty people around the body.

We walked as calmly as we could muster. Got about fifty feet.

"What about those two?" someone called out.

John started to run. I ran after him.

Six years as a copper in the Royal Ulster Constabulary (which has one of the highest death rates in the Western world) and I never once fired a gun in anger and never once had a gun fired at me. My greatest danger there was from my own side, five pay grades above me. No guns. Nothing so blunt. But now . . .

We were halfway across the park when we heard the peelers shouting:

"Stop. Police. Stop or we'll shoot."

The sky swimming-pool blue. The grass a dirty copper color. The temperature 92. My lungs aching. My eyes filled with streaks of white light. The front range all across the horizon to the west. Green foothills, blue mountains behind, and then more behind that. A big one in the middle with a horn peak and a bowl of curved magenta. Beautiful. One even had a trace of snow on it from Victoria Patawasti's storm.

We cut another fifty yards through pine trees and some kind of open-air theater. It was late afternoon and hot. Few people. A man was jogging in front of us but he had his earphones on, didn't hear the peelers yelling.

We made it to the edge of the park.

I looked back.

Three coppers in tan uniforms. Guns out. Two fat guys and an older skinny bastard another seventy yards back but bearing down like a greyhound.

John ran up the grass slope out of the park and onto Sixth Street and I ran after him. Sirens everywhere. It registered in a second that they were all coming for us. I slipped in a pool of water from a broken sprinkler and skidded in front of a building and John, turning to see what was happening, ran into an old man with a beard who was carrying a Scottie dog. All three went sprawling. I pulled John up. The dog was biting him.

"Christ," John screamed, and tried to shake the dog off.

The old man started yelling in Russian.

I grabbed the dog by its hind legs and threw it twenty feet away. The old man ran after it, swearing.

"Come on," I said to John.

We darted out into the street between massive condominium buildings and a few large private houses with high, ivy-clad walls and iron railings. No way over them.

"Hey, you," someone shouted behind us.

John turned.

"Run, you bastard," I said. We sprinted along the sidewalk. A doorman in front of a luxury condominium complex put his arm out, whether to stop us or hail a cab or see if it was bloody raining, I don't know.

I shouldered him and he went down.

"Fucksake, Alex, never get away from the peelers," John said.

"Run, you eejit, and save your fucking breath."

There were more sirens and I knew the cops running across the park would be radioing our position so they'd block our road ahead.

They knew the town, we didn't. They were acclimatized to altitude, we weren't. They were on local time, we were jet-lagged. They were in shape, we were a couple of druggies.

Things didn't look good.

"Down here," John said, and we turned at an alley.

No people. High walls between condominium complexes. Trash bins. Baking asphalt. Harsh transition from sunlight to shadow.

Cops still on our trail.

"Here," I said. Another alley, smaller. Heading west again, view of the mountains. Lungs exploding, heart so loud in my ears I couldn't hear anything else.

A side street: no pedestrians, concrete walls, town houses.

"I hear a helicopter," John said.

I didn't look up.

A big alley. North this time. Kids playing catch with huge baseball mitts. A white kid, a black kid, a Spanish kid, all in bright T-shirts, like a scene from bloody *Sesame Street*. We weaved through them and a few seconds later the cops came busting through as well.

Another turn. The alley ahead wide and clear. Houses and garages backing onto smooth tar macadam.

John a good ten feet ahead now. A main road seven or eight blocks ahead that looked like Colfax Avenue. Getting darker, too, and if we could just get to Colfax, where traffic was heavy and there were many people, we might just make it.

Perhaps the peelers felt the same, for at that moment they decided to shoot. They didn't bother with a warning. Just a loud crack and then four more cracks. Bullets smattered into a trash compactor. The police are allowed to fire their weapons only if the suspect is a potential danger to the public or a potential danger to the arresting officer. I think it was reasonably clear that we were in neither category. These guys just wanted to fucking shoot us. A bullet screamed off the concrete in front of me. The cops firing wildly and the bullets skidding by. Close, though. And they weren't shooting on the run. They were stopping to shoot, which lengthened the distance between us. I took a look back. They were about two tennis courts behind us. Strangely, not the cops from the park. Two chunky guys in blue-and-green uniforms. Hard to tell with all the sunlight glaring off the concrete walls, but they looked like older men. Maybe out of shape, but they should have known better.

And they were shooting to kill. Only on TV do coppers aim at legs or arms, real cops aim at the torso. I ran on. More bullets.

"Zigzag," I yelled to John.

"What?"

"Zig, zag," I said, and started running zigs. If you're firing at a moving target with a nine-millimeter semi-automatic, you'll miss if that target changes direction fast and unpredictably.

The peelers unloaded nearly a clip each at us. The bullets kicking up fragments of tar and concrete. Echoing horribly off the walls and the condo complexes.

They were yelling at us now, too, but you couldn't make it out. They started up again. Bloody pigs. The same peelers whose stellar work would be highlighted in the JonBenet Ramsey murder case and the Columbine massacre. They burned off the rest of their clips, bullets tearing down the alley and carrying on for a thousand yards. Then they must have been reloading, since the shooting stopped.

"I'm surrendering," John said.

"They'll give you the fucking chair, you asshole."

"They're going to kill us."

"Run, you big shite, they're reloading, we'll make it," I said.

John started running. And the heroin hurt and helped. Crippled my running but eased my mind. Stringing out the ketch from this morning so that I saw myself from way above. Me: calm, in slow motion, fleeing from peeler Pete through wide alleys, in the golden hour, with the sun behind the mountains and the sky crimson and the brilliant white cirrus clouds in lines between the buildings. Almost a moment of transcendence. The two of us running between piles of tires and wooden pallets, cardboard boxes, bins, machinery, car parts, garbage. And shadows across the alley and our reflections back at us off black-glass apartment windows.

"Nearly there," I said.

One of the cops fired twice more. Bullets flying past us, hitting nothing. Well, hitting many things, but not us. How were they going to explain this in their log? Probably say we were carrying sawed-off shotguns or Armalites or something.

Colfax closer and closer.

And the ketch lets you exist outside of time, outside of place, as if you are a being seeing yourself from above. Can't get caught up in that. Disembodied. Running.

Hubris, saying they were hitting nothing.

A bullet nicked a soda can, then clattered sideways in front of me, I fell, spun, smashed my shoulder into the ground.

"I'm hit," I said to John in a panic.

This time it was John who had his shit together. He pulled me up with one arm.

"You're not hit, you're ok," he said.

Quick look at my shoulder. A slice through the sweat-drenched jacket and T-shirt and a nasty cut on my shoulder. But I was ok. I had been lucky. He looked at me for another quarter of a second and then we both gazed back. Only one cop, staring at us, frustrated. We were too near Colfax, he couldn't risk a shot now. He had that much sense, at least.

"Let's go," John said.

We cut down the first alley on our left and dodged back up, running north to Colfax Avenue.

Seven at night. The main strip of Denver, busy, packed. This part of Colfax was like all those main streets in Westerns: wide avenues, big storefronts, low-rise buildings. But past its peak, run-down, decaying, dirty. Prostitutes everywhere. Scores of them. Same as yesterday. Black and Latina girls in short skirts and tank tops, pimps, men cruising the drag, checking out the talent, looking for regulars. Pushers, users, hangers-on. No cops.

"You ok?" John asked.

I looked at my shoulder, it was bleeding, but not deep.

"I'm ok," I said.

We caught our breaths. The sidewalks were thronged and it was easy for us to blend into the masses of people.

"Just walk, don't run, don't run, I think we're safe," I gasped.

My shoulder was stiffening up but already the bleeding was less. No one was looking at us. No one paid us any attention at all.

After about five blocks we juked behind a car and took a check back. Peeler Pete scoping for us, inventive—standing on top of a parked car, looking everywhere, speaking into a radio. We were lost in the sidewalk crowd and backlit against the sunset.

"No chance, peeler," John said with satisfaction.

"Yeah."

"What now?" John asked.

"Hotel, get our stuff, leave town," I said.

"Forget Victoria?"

I looked at him to see if he was fucking insane.

"Of course, forget Victoria," I barked.

We walked all the way to the state capitol and downtown. We got back to our hotel. Desk clerk watching a game show. Ignoring us.

We entered the room. It hadn't been cleaned. Our stuff was all still there. The beds hadn't been slept in. We packed quickly, saying nothing. At one point John went to the bathroom and threw up.

"Ok, now, John, listen to me and listen good, you're going to cut your hair short, just do the best you can, and I'm going to shave my beard off, ok?" I said gently.

He nodded.

I got my razor and clippers and trimmed the beard and then shaved the bastard. I had a quick shower and looked for something to use as a bandage on my shoulder. There wasn't anything, so instead I stuck on four or five Band-Aids. When I came out, John had done a reasonable job on his hair. It didn't look crazy, at least.

"John, you got any aspirin or anything?"

"No. How's your shoulder?"

"Ok."

"You took a spill."

"I know."

"I killed a man, Jesus Christ, Alex, I fucking killed somebody. Oh my God, oh my God, I can't believe it."

John put his head in his hands. He sat on the edge of the bed and started to cry. I let him get on with it for a minute or two. Good thing. Let him cry it out.

"Listen, John, he went for you, it was an accident. It was like a car accident. It wasn't anybody's fault. He wasn't Mother Teresa, either. Remember, he was a bad man, he was an accessory after the fact to a murder, withholding evidence," I said softly.

It wasn't true, Klimmer was just scared and we really might have talked him into going to the peelers. John had fucked up big time.

"Yeah, I suppose," John said.

"Ok, we have to get out of town."

"How?"

"Greyhound bus, anywhere, now."

We went downstairs and left the desk clerk our keys.

"Checking out?" he asked.

"Aye."

"Ok."

He didn't seem a bit interested, so I didn't spin him any kind of story. We walked out onto Broadway. Dark now. We asked the way to the bus station and someone told us it was downtown, but there was a free shuttle bus that took you there.

The outdoor Sixteenth Street Mall was stuffed with people. The Colorado Rockies were playing a baseball game. People kept bumping into our luggage on the free mall bus, giving us dirty looks. Final stop. Two coppers standing outside the bus station. Could have been there because of the baseball game, they could have always been stationed there. But we couldn't take the chance that they had our descriptions. It had been well over an hour since Klimmer's fall, plenty of time to get the word out.

"Fuck," John muttered. "What now?"

We were concealed by the crowds going to the game but we couldn't wait out here forever.

"Walk with the crowd," I said, "follow them away from the cops."

A lucky break. We walked nearly all the way to Coors Field and when we were close we saw a train waiting in Union Station.

"The train, John, we'll get the train," I said.

"Aye."

We tried to cross the street with our backpacks, but traffic was again heavy because of the baseball game.

A loud air horn, a pause, and the massive train began to move.

"Holy shit, it's leaving," I said. When I'd come to America before, I'd traveled on Amtrak. I knew that the east-west trains were very infrequent. This might be the only train leaving Denver's Union Station that day.

"John, we gotta get this train," I said.

John nodded.

We ran across the street, dodging the traffic. Brakes squealing, people honking, swearing. We sprinted up the wheelchair ramp and onto the platform. The train was moving very slowly, but it's hard to get onto any kind of moving thing with a backpack on your back and your shoulder hurting and exhaustion and jet lag eating at your coordination.

A really little guy in front of us hopped on one carriage down. John found an open door and jumped in. He put out his hand and pulled me on too.

○ ○ ○

Darkness. The train shunting out of Denver in big curves. It took me a while to realize we were heading west. I went to the bathroom and looked at my shoulder. There was a nasty scrape where the bone met the skin, the whole area an ugly scab of blood. The Band-Aids had fallen off. It didn't hurt much, but there was always the possibility of infection. I stripped, scooped water from the sink, and bathed it. I cleaned the wound with soap and water and bandaged it with paper towels. Changed my T-shirt, put my jacket back on. We found a couple of seats in the bar car and ordered beers and a sandwich. We asked the barman what train it was and he was used to dealing with stupid questions and said it was the California Zephyr going to San Francisco—which suited us just fine. California was ok. We could fly from San Francisco to London or Frankfurt or anywhere, really, just as long as it was bloody miles from here.

The train climbed up into the mountains and the track went through tunnels and curved back on itself. On those big bends you could see the whole of Denver in lights all the way up to Boulder and down to Castle Rock. We had just finished our beer when the ticket lady came up to us. An Afro stood eight inches from her short frame and thick neck. Long lacquered nails—painted with the stars and stripes—were pointing at us.

"Where you sitting?" she asked.

"Here," John said, not trying to be funny.

She took it the wrong way.

"Where are you sitting on the train?" she asked a little more sharply.

"We just got on, we're not sitting anywhere."

"Let me see your tickets," she said, glaring at John.

"We don't have any tickets," John said.

"The train was just pulling out and they told us we could buy tickets on board, we're tourists," I said quickly and gave her a big smile.

"Who told you that?" she asked me.

"Uh, the man at the station," I said.

"What man?"

"I don't know, just the man, he was in a uniform, I don't know," I said placatingly.

"Well, I don't know why he told you that because no one is allowed on the train without a ticket, this isn't a commuter train, this is a transcontinental Amtrak, you're going to have to get off at the next stop and buy a ticket at the station and then get back on again."

"Ok," I said.

"Ok," John said.

"The next stop is Fraser, Colorado, get off there and buy your ticket," the woman said curtly.

"Ok," we both said again, smiling.

She wandered off down the car.

"Fucking bitch," John muttered. "Bet she could have sold us a ticket if she'd wanted."

"Aye, but it won't make any difference," I said. "We'll just get it at the station."

"Yes," John agreed.

"No difference," I said again, and we drank our beers in agreement. Two people who couldn't have been more wrong, since getting off the train at Fraser, Colorado, was to make all the difference in the world. Our fates weren't taking us to California, to the Golden Gate Park, to Chinatown, to the airport and a ten-hour flight to Europe. No, the center of gravity in our story, the one dragging us like a black hole, was the one who had cast the first stone, the one who had killed Victoria Patawasti. We were going back to Denver, but we didn't know it yet.

° ° °

When Vishnu came to the Earth as a midget, he called himself Vamana. He stopped the demon Bali from destroying the planet. He tricked Bali with his diminutive size and sent him to the Underworld, telling him that appearances can be deceiving and that you should always watch out for the little guy.

I thought of this as John and I stared angrily at the midget. We weren't upset at him. It wasn't his fault that the ticket office had been closed, that a sign said "Buy rail tickets at the Continental Divide Saloon," that the saloon was a quarter of a mile into the town of Fraser, that the Amtrak train was late leaving Denver and had to make up time by departing Fraser earlier than planned, that we had heard the air horn too late, and that the train had left without us.

The next westbound train was coming this time tomorrow but there was a train going to Chicago in half an hour, the man selling the tickets had explained. John and I had decided Chicago would do just fine without, of course, considering that the Chicago train would have to go back through Denver.

The midget had gotten off the train at Fraser too, but he hadn't gone to the ticket office. Instead, he'd gone to a bar for a while and now he was standing a little down the platform from us. It made me a bit nervous.

Especially since the Chicago train was late.

It hadn't come in half an hour. It hadn't come in an hour.

It hadn't come by midnight.

When you called up Amtrak's toll-free number, an undead voice told you that the train was just arriving in Fraser. The voice had been claiming this for several hours. . . .

Birds. The air. The moon so bright you could see vapor trails. The cold. Snow on the mountains circling the little half-assed ski town. The steel train tracks going nineteenth-century straight into the mountain.

John waxing philosophical:

"Waiting's good for you. You notice things. You slow time down into its components. Too often we put our consciousness on cruise control. You autopilot your way through the day, the week, your existence in this world. . . ."

Pop psychology from that motorcycle book, I imagined, but I wasn't going to rise to the bait. It was very cold. You wouldn't have thought it was the summer. Much chillier than those mountains behind Boulder.

I looked up the long platform. The midget was smoking. We had no smokes, I considered going up and asking him for one to keep out the cold.

"Look at all those stars," John said.

He was annoying me and I purposely did not look up.

"I should have done astronomy. I should have gone to Oxford or Cambridge. I didn't have the A levels.

You had, Alex, you should have gone. But I suppose you needed to be near your ma."

I gave him a look that he didn't see.

"Terrible business, your ma. I was very close to her too, you know. You know, I agreed with their decision. Your da and ma," John said.

Never a good time for this topic and especially not when John had bloody killed someone and I'd been shot at and the cops were after us and I hadn't had a hit of heroin after a long, stressful day that still was not coming to a fucking end.

"What decision was that?" I said coldly.

"You know, not to do the chemotherapy," John said almost breezily. I could have punched the bastard.

"You supported their embrace of death," I said incredulously.

"Now, Alex, that's not fair. Homeopathy could have worked, those alternative treatments are not nonsense, there's more things in heaven and earth than are dreamt of in your philosophy and all that. You're awful hard on your dad, Alex. It was your ma's decision too."

John had no idea how close he was to having the shit beaten out of him. I was seething. This, he well knew, was a subject we did not ever talk about. This and my resignation from the cops, but more so this. Was he trying to provoke me into a fight to forget what had happened? Or was he just being stupid? My blood was boiling, and after all, this was all his fault. I bit my tongue and walked over to the midget.

Maybe, technically, he wasn't a midget. If he'd been a

woman, you would have said she was petite. He stood about five feet tall, with a beard, leather jacket, jeans, Denver Nuggets cap. Forties, I would have guessed.

"Couldn't bum a smoke, could I?" I said.

"Certainly," he said and handed over a pack of Marlboro Lights. I took one and lit mine from his.

"I don't normally smoke, but it's freezing," I explained.

"Yeah, we're nine thousand feet up, it makes a difference," he said.

"Train's late," I said, drawing in the tobacco gratefully.

"Yeah, the California Zephyr's late. The California Zephyr's always late. It goes at forty miles an hour and stops anytime the engineer wants to let people off."

"Really?"

"Uh-huh. Did you know that in Greek zephyr means 'fast wind'? Amtrak employs a satirist to name its trains."

I grinned.

"You're pretty funny," I said.

"David Redhorse," he said, and offered me his hand.

I shook it. The name sounded odd and familiar. Though probably Redhorse out here was like Lawson back home. Millions of the buggers.

"Alex, uh, Wilson, Alexander Wilson," I said. "Did you get stuck too? I noticed you getting on at Denver and then getting off the train a little behind us at Fraser."

"No, no, I have relatives up here, I was just visiting

them. I get to ride the train free," he said. "What were you doing in Fraser?"

"Uh, nothing, just traveling, we're tourists."

"I thought I detected an accent. Australian?" he asked.

"Yeah, yeah, we're Australian," I said, and then, realizing that John might blow the gaff and make the man suspicious, called him over.

"John, come over, David here was asking where we were from and I was saying we're just a couple of bums from Australia, traveling around the world."

"Yeah, we're from Sydney, Sydney, Australia, going to Chicago now," John said, giving me a look. The North Belfast accent was so unlike the well-known accent from the south of Ireland that you *could* conceivably confuse it with Australian.

"Chicago, how come you came out here?" Redhorse asked.

I looked at him. There was something about him. Something not quite right. Where had I heard that name before?

"We got on the wrong train at Denver," I said, "we were heading to Chicago but we got on the wrong train. West instead of east. Going to Chicago, then New York and then Europe."

"Wrong train, huh? Not surprised, they don't tell you anything at Denver. Lucky you noticed you were going west. The life, though. I'd love to travel the world, but I'm afraid to fly, always have been, you'll never get me on a plane," Redhorse said.

"Statistically, it's the safest way to travel, safer than the train, much safer than a car," John said.

"Well, that's not the way I see it. If you have a car crash or a train crash it's not necessarily fatal, but in almost every plane crash everybody dies," Redhorse said.

John said something back, but I was having trouble concentrating. The ketch wanted to find a home. Redhorse was making me nervous. He said something to John. They both looked at me.

"Alex, David was asking what sports we play in Australia," John said, giving me a nudge.

"Oh, lots of sports, Australian Rules football, cricket, rugby, that sort of thing, you don't play them in America," I said.

"You'll never guess what my favorite sport is," Redhorse said with a big grin.

John shrugged.

"Go on, guess," Redhorse said, nodding.

"I don't know, baseball?" I suggested.

"No. Think about it, what would be the most unlikely sport I could play?" he said, barely able to contain a chuckle.

"I really don't know, football, I mean, soccer," I said.

"No, basketball," he said impatiently, and then cracked up laughing.

Neither John nor I got the joke.

"Don't you see?" he said, choking with giggles.

"Not really," John said.

"You have to be six foot plus. Seven foot plus. Jeez. I thought basketball was big in Australia, that's what I heard, I heard it was getting big over there," Redhorse said.

"Oh, oh, yeah, it is, sure we watch it, don't we, Alex?" John said.

"Yeah, yeah," I said, regretting this whole Australian thing now.

"What's your favorite NBA team?" Redhorse asked without suspicion.

"Um, favorite team, well, um, oh yeah, I like the, uh, Harlem Globetrotters, they're pretty good, they always seem to win," John said, and I nodded in agreement.

Redhorse looked at us strangely for a second and decided to change the subject.

"So are you boys students?"

"Yes, we're on our gap year, we're traveling the world before going back to university," I said.

"Yeah, like I say, love to do that, but you can't go by boat, it's too expensive. Besides, I don't like to be away from the reservation for too long, my family lives there, I am the only one that lives in Denver."

"You're an Indian?" John asked.

"Yes."

"Cool," John said.

"From what I read, the Native Americans around Denver got treated pretty rough," I said.

"I suppose you read about the Sand Creek Massacre," Redhorse muttered, and threw away his cigarette, immediately lighting another.

"Yeah."

"Well, it's good that people know that history, but it's

the wrong focus, there were many little massacres and killings that never got recorded, they stole all this land from us, Denver is stolen land, these mountains are stolen land, not that we claimed to own them, we were the guardians of it, the white man claims to own it," Redhorse explained quickly and deliberately like he'd said this all before many times.

"Is that what you do for a living, then? You're a lawyer, an advocacy person?" I asked him.

"No, no, I'm a cop," Redhorse said with a little grin.

John looked at me, froze. I shook my head slightly. We weren't going to react, we weren't going to run for it, we weren't going to do anything stupid at all.

"You're a policeman?" John asked hesitantly.

"Yes."

"What type, like traffic or drugs or—"

"I'm a homicide detective," he said flatly.

"You're a homicide detective?" I found myself asking.

"Yes, I know what you're thinking, I'm too short to impress people, I can't intimidate witnesses, that sort of thing?" Redhorse said, again, like he'd done this speech many times before too.

"No, I wasn't thinking that."

"No? Well, a lot of people do think that, they think I'm too short and they think because I'm an Indian and my parents live on a reservation that I get drunk all the time. Well, they don't and I don't and I've got one of the highest clearance rates in the department."

"I'm sure you have, I wasn't thinking any of those

things, I'm sure you're a great detective," I said.

"I am," he agreed.

"W-what are you working on at the moment?" I asked.

John had turned white, lapsed into silence; he was sucking desperately on his cigarette and generally drawing attention to himself.

"Where's that train?" he was mumbling quietly.

"Oh, well, I'm running the RH department. Not leading any particular case," he said.

"Ok," I said. "What's RH?"

"Robbery Homicide," he said flatly.

"No interesting cases you can talk about?"

"Well, my big headache is a felonious assault that's become a murder now the victim's died. The lawyers are saying that the suspect didn't have his Miranda rights read to him in Chinese within twenty-four hours of his arrest. Both victim and suspect were Chinese. A lot of eyewitnesses, but we might have to let him go. That sort of thing is out of our hands, though. DA's problem, not ours. Still, if he gets off, it's in our files. It makes me crazy."

He shook his head, clenched his fists, obviously upsetting him a bit to think about this, to think about guilty men getting away with a terrible crime. I smiled nervously.

"Where is that bloody train?" John said again.

I smoked and told myself to relax. The cop seemed ok. Like most cops, he'd want to complain about his work. The best thing to do was ease him by keeping him talking until the train came. Still, my mind wasn't thinking as clearly as it could and we had obviously fucked up somehow by mentioning the Harlem Globetrotters. Any question would do.

"So this Miranda, whatever happened to him? You always hear about the Miranda rights on TV. *NYPD Blue, Law and Order,* all that, but you never hear about Miranda. He must have got off because they didn't read him his rights? Is that right?" I said.

"Yeah, it is, Ernesto Miranda got away with kidnap, torture, and rape on a retarded girl. Shit, man. But the story has a happy ending," Redhorse said with grim satisfaction, his eyes lighting up, so that even in the moonlight I could tell they were a deep brown.

"Oh, yeah?"

"Yeah, a few years later he got stabbed to death in a bar. Nice play, I'd do the same if it was my kid, wait a few years, kill the bastard."

"Yeah," I said.

And it was only then I remembered my phone call to the police department. That was only this morning? Detective Redhorse. Jesus. And he was a good 'un. I could see he was a digger. He was one of those who would keep after you. And was he here just by chance? No. Bad cops believe in coincidence. At Denver he got on the train with us. He got off with us at Fraser and was now going back to Denver with us. I looked at him. Not coincidence. This was the type who played a hunch. Hear about two guys running from a murder scene. Go to the train station, follow a couple of guys, see what happens.

"What happened to your shoulder?" he asked sharply.

"What?"

"You're bleeding."

I looked at my shoulder and, sure enough, blood was soaking through the paper towels and onto my jacket. Just a spatter or two. I decided to play it casual.

"You know anything about first aid?" I asked.

"A little."

"Yeah, we were climbing up some rocks in Boulder yesterday," I began, but Redhorse interrupted.

"You don't need to finish, you didn't have the proper equipment, you fell, am I right?" Redhorse asked, shaking his head.

"Uh, yeah," I said, trying to sound embarrassed.

"It's always the same, you don't know how many kids get injured every year. Some die, you know. You kids, you just can't go off into the mountains unprepared. Wow, it's always the same. So dry around here too, because of the drought, tree limb, root can just snap on you. Better let me take a look at it," Redhorse said with a sigh.

It would be suspicious to refuse, so I rolled down my T-shirt and bent down so he could take a look. John staring at me aghast. I shot him a glance to bloody play it cool.

"Ok, ok, let me see. Yeah, it's just a scrape. Keep it clean, get a big Band-Aid on it, don't pick it when it scabs over. And don't go climbing without proper safety gear," Redhorse said.

"The train," John yelled, "it's the train."

I looked down the line.

A tiny light in the distance. John frantic:

"Look, what's that light? Do you see that light? That's not a truck. I tell you, it's the train, it has to be, it's the train, believe me. Alex, have you got our tickets? Look, it's getting bigger. It's the bloody train. It's coming. Maybe it's a house light. No, it's it."

The sound of an air horn, the massive engine, the bell on the crossing. It pulled in aggressively, slowed and stopped. We piled into the carriage, bumping people with our luggage and belongings, looking for seats, but it was slim pickings. The dirty train sweating with exhausted people who had just come through the desert and over the Rockies in thirty hours of Amtrak's version of hell. Eventually, the steward found three seats together in the nonsmoking section.

Redhorse sat next to a hairy man who asked him if Jesus was his personal savior. He didn't reply, lit himself a cigarette, took out *The Grapes of Wrath,* and began reading furiously.

"Have you accepted Jesus into your life?" the man asked me.

"I have," I said solemnly, the only sensible answer on these occasions.

"That's great, and what about you?" the man asked John.

"Well, no, not really," John said.

I groaned.

"If you don't mind, I'd like to tell you a little bit about our Lord Jesus Christ," the man said.

"I don't mind at all," John said.

Having killed someone a few hours earlier, John was obviously vulnerable at this point. I stood up and found my soap bag.

"John, I'm away to the bathroom, ok?" I said, and closed my lips very tight, which I hoped communicated my desire that he should keep his bloody mouth shut, even if the Messiah himself showed up and asked him to confess. A peeler on one side, a bloody missionary on the other. Fantastic. I was sure at the next stop a man with a lie detector would get on.

The bathroom was remarkably clean, considering the length of the journey and the busyness of the train. I found my heroin, boiled it, got a clean needle, exposed a vein, tied it off, and sank away from all this madness. The rattling train, the long tracks, the mountain air. I nodded off, slept a little, woke up as the train went over a set of points.

Back to my seat. Redhorse had gone.

"Where's the cop?" I asked John.

"They moved him to the smoking section," John said.

"And Jesus said unto the nonbelievers, ye must be born again, it's not enough to just keep the commandments," the missionary said.

I sat down. The ketch had calmed me. Didn't matter now, let them convert John, arrest me, didn't bloody matter.

Three in the morning when we got into Denver. David Redhorse came back and wished us a pleasant trip. I said good luck in catching killers. Without further ado, he said goodbye. So his appearance here had been coincidence after all. He hadn't been watching the train for a couple of runaways or, if he had, he figured we didn't seem the murdering type. And for a peeler he wasn't a bad sort. I just hoped he wouldn't put two and two together. Most cops can be pretty stupid, but Redhorse clearly wasn't. I was relieved to see him go and bloody shocked when he got back on twenty minutes later.

Oh, shit, he has put it together, he's come to arrest us, I thought, and grabbed John's shoulder and tried to pull him up. We could run down the train, exit the next car, get back out into Denver. Probably Redhorse wouldn't have had time to seal off the station.

"John, we have to get up," I said.

I pulled him to his feet, but it was too late. David Redhorse walked over to us.

I took a deep breath and got ready for fight or flight. Take this wee shite easy.

"Guys, I just thought I'd come back and tell you, because I know you don't have a sleeper, the train is going to be stuck here all night, there's a big derailment up ahead on the line. Track's blocked. Nobody hurt, but if I know Amtrak, no one's going to tell you anything about it until the morning and the train isn't going to get going till tomorrow afternoon, if then."

"Shit," I said.

"You boys need the name of a hotel?" Redhorse asked.

"Sure," I said.

"The Holburn on Sherman, always got rooms, even this time of night," he said.

"Thanks, we'll check it out," I said.

"Ok, well, nice meeting you," he said.

I shook his hand and he headed off back down the track. Now I really believed that he had decided we were harmless.

"What are we going to do, Alex?" John asked.

"We're getting off this train, that's for damn sure," I whispered.

Later . . .

It's four a.m.

A dead time in a dead town. The prostitutes are gone from Colfax Avenue, the patrons home from the LoDo bars. Magpies, crows debate the labyrinth of alleys and deserted cul-de-sacs. The lights are on at Coors Field, but the game is long since done.

Fuck the Holburn. No way am I going there. So instead we go back to our old place, but the bastard there wants us to pay for another week, cash in advance, which is suspicious and makes me think that he thinks we're in some kind of trouble. I don't like it, and breezily refuse.

I explain it to John, and reading *Lonely Planet* he suggests the youth hostel on Seventeenth Street. On the way there, they're delivering *The Denver Post*. I pay a quarter, find the story on page three.

A man fell to his death from the fourth floor of the Mountain View apartment complex on Cheesman Park today. Eyewitnesses spoke of a struggle with an assailant. "The building has been burglarized twice in the last month," said Jean Simmons, a neighbor. Police are looking for two men said to be light-skinned Hispanic males in their twenties or early thirties. A DPD officer is believed to have shot and seriously wounded one of the assailants.

I stop reading, put the paper down. The first thing I have to do is reassure John:

"John, you can relax, a dozen eyewitnesses, three of them cops, and they have us pegged as wetbacks. Jesus Christ. That little crack in Spanish to the dude in the army T-shirt worked."

He grins at me. "Aye. Typical. You see what you want to see. Bloody racists. Xenophobes. All burglars are fucking Latinos," he says.

I nod. It doesn't let us off the hook, but it helps. Maybe that was why Redhorse had changed his mind about us. Of course, I don't tell John that sometimes the cops are tricky about what information they release. In any case, he looks visibly relieved.

An exhausting walk. The youth hostel. Overhead fans. Insomniac Swedish boys flirting with German girls. Clean, nice, inviting. John collapses into a chair, I go to the desk.

The receptionist, bald guy, sweating in a white wife-beater shirt and thinking he's part of the Christmas story: "There's no room at the inn, we're full."

"Look, we're desperate," I say.

"Plenty of motels out on Colfax near the airport," he suggests.

"How far?"

"Three, four miles, I don't know," he says.

"Isn't there anywhere closer?" I plead.

The man looks at me for a minute.

"Where you from? What's that accent?" he says a little unexpectedly.

"We're from Ireland," I say, too exhausted to lie anymore.

"I thought so," he says, "I thought so. Sean Dillon, ex–Denver Fire Department," he says, sticking out his hand.

I shake it wearily.

"Alex Flaherty," I say.

"I golfed the ring of Kerry once," Sean says.

"Is that so?"

"Rained every day. Miserable. Yeah, look, about the room. How picky are you?"

"We want anywhere, we're desperate."

"It doesn't necessarily have to be a hotel, right? Just a room, right?"

"Yeah."

"Let me see your passports."

We take out our passports, show the man, they're British passports but they're registered and stamped in Belfast. He doesn't notice I gave him a fake name, seems satisfied.

"Yeah, look. If Pat lets you, there's a building, a few

blocks east on Colfax. Noisy out there, but Pat'll let you stay for, I don't know, ten bucks a night."

"That's fine, anything," I say.

"Finder's fee, give me twenty bucks, see what I can do," Sean says.

I give him twenty bucks.

"Ok, it's late. I'll call Patrick and see if it's ok," he says, picks up the phone, dials a number.

"Sorry, Pat, I knew you'd be up. Yeah, I know, me too, but at least I'm paid for it. Couple of possibles for you. I told them you'd charge ten bucks for that room. Irish kids. . . . No, from Ireland, for real. . . . They seem ok, one looks like Big Foot on a bad hair day, the other, I don't know, Val Kilmer's skinny brother."

He puts down the phone.

"Pat says you can come over. You're very lucky, you can have one of the furnished rooms for a while. It's on the fifth floor. He'll meet you in the lobby."

We walk all the way from the youth hostel to the building. Not just a few blocks. Twenty bloody blocks. The front door is open. We go in. No sign of Pat. The elevator is busted, too, so we hike up to the fifth floor. On one apartment there's a note and a key taped to the door. It says, "For the two Irish boys, I'll see you tomorrow."

A studio apartment. Foldout bed. Tiny bedroom–box room off to one side, kitchenette. Damp on the walls, crumbling ceiling, plastic–fake wood tiles on all the floors. Small bathroom, a great view over Colfax and the mountains to the west.

"It'll do," John says.

"I want the bed in the wee room," I tell him.

John is too exhausted to argue. I slouch into the little room and close the door, John bursts into tears and weeps for I don't know how long, since within ten minutes I'm out for the bloody count.

7: STORM BRINGER

John woke first. He'd had trouble resting on the pull-out bed. There were no sheets and it was far too hot to kip in his sleeping bag. I'd had a good night since I'd brought a sheet bag and a sleeping bag to America. We checked out the apartment, small but surprisingly tidy. We learned later that Pat cleaned it when he was healthy. We climbed out onto the fire escape to examine the view. We were only about a mile east of our hotel on Broadway, but Colfax Avenue was a different animal. This was the original way into the city for travelers heading west and you could still see the traces of the old frontier town under the facades. No tall buildings, and if you evacuated the cars, the concrete road, the fast-food restaurants and tattoo parlors, it could have stood in for Hadleyville in *High Noon*. And it seemed hotter here, a seething heat that mingled with the vehicular pollution.

It also appeared to be one of Denver's few black neighborhoods, or if not black, certainly poorer. East Colfax was the opposite of everything that Boulder stood for. Down at heel, black, grungy, dirty, honest, and a little bit scary. I liked it.

John, however, was horrified. Where I saw character

in the odd derelict building or empty lot, he saw Berlin, June 1945, or—

"Bloody West Belfast on a bad day," he said. "Not the way I imagined America at all."

Before I could reply, a knock at the door. We climbed in off the fire escape, opened the door.

Patrick. Six feet tall, a hundred pounds, pale as a banshee, red eyes, cold sores, coughing, in fact, full-blown AIDS. Patrick O'Leary was thirty-three, about a year ago he'd been a two-hundred-pound, ripped, good-looking firefighter. Clearly going down fast. He introduced himself, claimed we were in the second-nicest apartment in the building, showed us how the appliances worked, made us coffee, told us his whole story. When we heard about the AIDS, neither John nor I drank the coffee. He was from Fort Morgan, Colorado, and had been a nine-year veteran paramedic with the Denver Fire Department; unfortunately the DFD had fired him as soon as they had found out that he was HIV positive. The union could see the fire department's point of view, claiming he put at risk not only patients but also his fellow coworkers. He had lied about his condition too, so the union denied him benefits. He was in the middle of a lawsuit with the union and the fire department, but that, he admitted, would be settled long after he was dead.

Pat, though, had a friend in the DFD who owned a few buildings in Denver and who had let him stay rent-free in this place. All Pat had to do was keep the building as full as possible of tenants but it was harder than it looked, only four apartments were properly furnished, it had erratic plumbing, worse heating, it occupied a dangerous part of town, it had no super and no one to do maintenance. Also Denver was undergoing a building boom, they had closed the old air force base at Lowry Campus and thousands of much nicer lots were becoming available. The suburbs were opening up to the east around Aurora, to the west at Lakewood, and in the south around Littleton. Rich people heading out where they thought it would be safer for their kids. And in 1995 Denver the last place anyone wanted to live was the seedy strip around Colfax Avenue, liquor stores, porn stores, prostitutes, and junkies and everything grown worse since it had become a feeder road for the new airport.

Pat told us that in the other furnished apartments were a retired schoolteacher in his seventies, a nurse in her fifties, and an Ethiopian family of six on the first floor.

Pat was the de facto landlord, took a minimal rent, listened to no complaints, carried a gun. We told him that we were in Denver for only a couple of days until we could change our ticket and fly back to Ireland. He said we should stay longer, that the neighborhood wasn't as bad as it looked and they had finally dealt with the roach and rat problem with a sonic vermin device. Comforting to know, but our minds were made up.

Pat had a phone in his apartment. We could use it.

I called British Airways. To change our departure

flight would cost only a hundred dollars. I changed the tickets. I hung up. That was that. Our American adventure was done. Ending in shambles and disaster. Finito. We were all set to go and we would have gone, flying Denver to London, London to Belfast, and Victoria's murderer would never have been found and I would have been assassinated by a secret cadre inside the RUC within twenty-four hours of landing on Irish soil, had not Patrick, at that precise moment, said:

"Boys, listen, make any call you like, I get ten cents a minute to Ireland."

"Any call?" I said.

"Yeah."

"Well, I could call up my dad and let him know we're coming back," I said after a pause.

"Go ahead," Pat said.

I dialed the number for home. Dad picked up after a minute.

"Noel, is that you?" he said.

"No, Dad, it's me."

"Alex," he said, "it's good to hear from you. I thought it was Noel with the new flyers. The Green Party in Dublin gave me a hundred pounds and—"

"Dad, I'm coming home," I said, ignoring him.

"Did you find anything out?"

"Yeah, the man who sent the note is just a local nut, nothing to do with anything. But as a matter of fact, I think the police have arrested the wrong man. I'm pretty sure they'll release him soon. He's got a good lawyer and I think I've helped him a bit. They'll be opening the case again, it's the cops' job now, nothing more I can do. Coming home."

"There's nothing else you can do?" Dad asked, sounding disappointed.

"No. Will you tell Mr. Patawasti? I'll be home in a couple of days, see him myself, but I'd like you to fill him in, if you can."

"I'm very busy, but I'll make a point of going to see him. Actually, I want to talk to him, I think he might want to come on the campaign trail with me, take his mind off things," Dad said.

"Dad, for God's sake, don't ask him to campaign with you, give the man some peace, just tell him I found the guy who sent the note and it was unimportant, ok?"

"I will."

"Ok, look, this is someone else's phone, I better hang—" I began.

"Oh, Alex, wait a minute, your friend Ivan called three times yesterday, he was looking for you. I got him on the third call."

"Facey called you up?"

"Yes."

"What did he want?"

"He said that it was urgent that he speak to you. I told him you were still in America and he said that it was good that you were away. I thought that was a bit odd."

"That is odd."

"He said, wherever you are, you should call him, reverse the charges, if necessary, he said it was very, very important."

"Shit."

"I know, he didn't sound like himself at all."

"What did he sound like?"

"He sounded, I don't know, worried, frightened. You're not in any trouble, are you?"

"No. Did he leave a number?"

"He did, let me see, six-seven-oh-nine-three, got that?"

"Yeah."

"Ok, Alex."

"Ok, Dad, tell Mr. Patawasti, ok?"

"Ok."

I hung up, called Facey, he wasn't home.

Pat brought me some milk.

"Alex, do you want milk in your coffee? I take mine black, but I always forget how other people like theirs."

"No, thanks. Look, uh, can I use your phone later? I've an important call to make."

Pat looked at John and myself wistfully. He cleared his throat, wiped his skinny hand over his forehead. He had something to say:

"Of course, use the phone anytime, and listen, um, the building gets quite lonely, no one wants to visit me, they're prejudiced against coming out here, even though we're only a few blocks from East High School, which is a lovely building, uh, anyway. Look, so I was thinking, you boys can stay as long as you like. Rent-free until you get jobs. How does that sound? You don't get an offer like that every day."

"Uh, no. Thanks for the offer but, sorry, we, we have to go back home. I've already changed our flight to Sunday," I said.

Pat's face fell.

"Ok. Well, it's nice to have you even for a few days," he said cheerfully, "and if you want to reconsider, there's no bugs anymore and no rent."

I thanked him and went back to the apartment. I took a shower, and when I came out, John was dressed in shorts and a T-shirt. He was going out.

"Where the hell you think you're going?" I asked.

"I've got to get out of here, I'm going nuts, just a walk up and down the street."

"John, are you fucking out of your mind? Half the cops in Denver are looking for us, you think a haircut and a beard cut are going to fool them forever?"

"Listen, I can't be cooped up in here, it's too damn hot, I want out, I want to go to the cinema or something. I'll wear my baseball cap, change my shirt, you said yourself they're searching for Spanish guys."

I looked at John, he did seem a bit jittery, but I was insistent.

"First of all, that baseball cap goes in the garbage. Second of all, not today, not today at least, maybe tomorrow when the heat's cooled down, but for today, we are staying put, ok?"

"Ok," John said reluctantly.

About an hour later, Pat saw that we weren't leaving

and came by with martinis. For someone in the throes of a major life-threatening health crisis, after a few drinks, Pat became quite the chatterbox. When he got a wind, he became an entertaining, angry son of a bitch, and we both found ourselves liking him. He particularly had it in for Colorado's white Christian population, whom he blamed for the infamous antigay referendum that had changed the state's constitution, allowing organizations such as the Denver Fire Department to fire gay people because of their lifestyle, never mind their HIV status. Odd, though, for with Pat's red hair and ghostly complexion, he was the whitest person I'd ever seen and, technically, he was a Christian.

"Yeah, boys, they fucked the constitution. It's going to the Supreme Court next year. Hope I live to see it overturned. Wipe the smile off their fat white faces. This is the only state in the country that did that. Colorado. The hate state. White, bourgeois scum," Pat said bitterly while we sipped his martinis on the fire escape.

"And no blacks voted for it?" John asked mischievously, sucking on his olive and giving me a wink. I was glad to see that he was making himself forget about yesterday in a haze of alcohol.

"I'm sure some did, but it's the goddamn Anglos. They're all Fundamentalist Christian out here. Hate gays, hate non-Christians. They hate Catholics, Latins. Don't believe me? Drive out on Federal sometime, ask those Mexican guys how they're treated. While you're at it, look at the cars, Jesus fish all over them or, occasionally, a Jesus fish eating a fish that says 'Darwin,' I saw a bumper sticker the other day that said 'Warning. This car will become driverless in the event of the Rapture.'"

Neither John nor I got what he was talking about, so Pat explained that Fundamentalist Christians believe they will all be spirited up to heaven during the Rapture, an event that will precede the Apocalypse and the Second Coming.

Pat told us about the corruption of the Denver Fire and Police Departments, for which he blamed the white Masonic lodges. He then went off on John Elway and his series of car dealerships. He blamed the drought on the Coors people, and he even had it in for the Denver Zoo for reasons neither John nor I could fully understand. Paranoid and mad, but entertaining for a while. But we could see Pat wilt before us, he had limited energy, good enough for a few serious rants, but not a whole afternoon of it. Soon he had to lie down.

"What do you make of that Pat guy?" John asked later in the apartment.

"He's all right," I said.

"What do you think his deal is?"

"The they're-out-to-get-me thing?"

"Yeah."

"I don't know, they *are* out to get him. They bloody fired him. He feels betrayed, and I think he's gone a bit stir out here in a black neighborhood."

John nodded. The paper got delivered and the later edition of *The Denver Post* had the dismaying news that the Denver Police Department was watching bus terminals, the train station, and DIA in the hope of capturing the two assailants in yesterday's apartment murder. Jack Wegener, a congressman from Colorado's eighth congressional district, was quoted in the paper as saying that maybe now people would take seriously Pat Buchanan's idea of building an electric fence on the Mexican border.

We tried to nap for a bit, and later, when we heard Pat singing to himself, we went down the hall to pay him another visit and maybe use his phone.

Pat made us two additional martinis and told us more about his favorite subjects; he hated the suburbs, SUVs, and Starbucks coffee. He said if he ever got money, he was going to open a chain of tea shops called Queequegs.

"Pat, uh, about the phone . . ." I said.

"Oh, yes, go ahead, take it in my bedroom for privacy."

Pat's bedroom. Spartan, to say the least. A futon on the floor, one sheet, one pillow.

The sun setting behind Lookout Mountain.

The phone call that'll change everything. . . .

I dial Ireland.

"Hello?"

"Hello, Facey," I say.

"Shit, Alex, is that you?" Facey says in a whisper.

"It is."

"Alex, Jesus Christ, where are you? Still in America?"

"I'm—" I begin.

"No, don't tell me," Facey interrupts.

"Ok," I say, worried now.

"Alex, listen to me very carefully, ok? Pay attention. I've been trying to reach you. I'm only a messenger. I'm only a messenger, don't take it out on me. Ok?" he says, sounding scared.

"Ok, Facey, just tell me," I say.

"Alex, I wrote it down, let me get the piece of paper, I'm going to destroy the paper once I tell you, can you believe it?"

"Facey, just fucking tell me," I yell at him, getting impatient now.

"Alex, from channels, way above me, not me, I've been instructed to tell you, that if you come back to Northern Ireland, you will be, I don't know how to say this, Alex, I'll just say it, they say they'll see to it that you're killed. They say if you come back, they'll kill you. They'll kill you."

"Who will kill me?" I ask.

"Alex, oh God, I don't know, don't ask me anything."

"Come on, Facey, I have to know everything."

Facey, gagging, unable to get the words out. I give him a few seconds.

"Tell me, Facey," I insist.

"Oh, Jesus. I'm supposed to tell you to stay out of Northern Ireland and stay out of the UK and if they hear that you're cooperating with the Samson Inquiry in any way, you a-and your dad will be in very serious trouble."

Facey goes quiet. I can hear him breathing. Someone in the police had passed the message down to Facey. Samson must be close to uncovering some heavy shit. They didn't have to warn me. Obviously, they didn't want to kill me, but they would if I showed up in Ulster again. Things must be getting serious. If I returned to Northern Ireland as planned on Friday, by Saturday night I would be facedown in a border ditch. They'd tip off a terrorist cell and get them to kill me. Tell the Prods I was a traitor, tell the IRA I was an important cop. Wouldn't matter. Of course, it would cause a stink, but not much of one. It would be better for all concerned if I just stayed away.

"Thanks, Facey," I said.

"Are you ok, Alex?" he asked.

"I'm ok," I said.

"And you won't come back, will you?" Facey said.

"No," I said.

"Good," Facey said, relieved. He had done his bit, he had secured his career and, maybe just as important, he had stopped his good pal Alexander getting bloody topped.

. . .

In a week our money had almost gone and the novelty of living in Denver had worn off. I really didn't know what to do. I couldn't go back to Ireland, it wasn't exactly safe staying here in Denver, and attempting to travel to another city might be the most dangerous thing of all with the cops still watching the bus stations, train stations, and airport. Could always rent a car and drive somewhere. But where? And what if our descriptions had been circulated to the car rental places? Stealing a car was out of the question. Easiest way to get caught. Best thing was to do nothing. Stay put. A lot of cops are lazy and their attention wanders. In another week they'd be thinking about something besides the Klimmer case. A week after, there would be many more pressing crimes to consider and a week after that, we could leave town wearing "We are Klimmer's Murderers" T-shirts without attracting attention. Besides, we had a clean, rent-free, and safe place to stay, and scoring heroin was easily done with our dwindling bucks a mere fifteen-minute walk from the apartment.

The boy who sold the ketch behind the Salvation Army place was a Costa Rican called Manuelito, nice kid, and he liked me because heroin was a minority taste in this town that was graduating toward crack, speed, crank, and other uppers.

John could have gone home, if he'd wanted. But he chose to stay with me. Doing penance by hanging out with me in exile. I had finally told him everything. I had known John since childhood and to protect him and Dad and everyone, really, I'd kept mum about my resignation from the cops, but now he had to know. I couldn't go back to Ulster, and he said he would stay with me, at least for a while.

Pat was glad to have us, and when our dough began to run out, he told us about a man he knew who could make us a green card or a J-1 visa. We said thanks, but no, better not get caught doing anything illegal.

Pat had good days and bad days. Sometimes he had energy and would clean the apartment and talk to us, other days he would lie in bed and we would minister to him water and very weak tea. Once we saw the old man who lived on four, but we never saw the nurse. Maybe she'd left and it had slipped Pat's mind.

All the time, though, we saw the Ethiopians. There were six of them. A father, mother, grandmother, two adult boys, and an eighteen-year-old girl. Only the youngest boy, Simon, and the girl, Areea, spoke any English. Simon and Areea both worked at Denver University as janitors and both were hoping to take classes there in the next quarter. The father and mother both cleaned offices in downtown Denver and the other brother worked in a restaurant. An interesting lot and they made spectacular food and we liked hanging out with them as much as possible. Even though they paid minimal rent, dough was tight and we didn't like to inflict our presence too much. Still, the dad had character and Simon translated many stories about the corruption and general unpopularity of Haile Selassie, the crazy Jamaicans who somehow thought Selassie was the messiah, and a legend that the Ark of the Covenant was in a monastery in the Ethiopian highlands.

Simon might have had the best English but the girl,

Areea, found us the ad. Areea: slender, doe-eyed, straightened hair, tan complexion, pretty. The Ethiopians, improving their reading, took both *The Denver Post* and the *Rocky Mountain News* and when they were done Areea brought them up to us. I think she had a thing for John, which showed she was no judge of character.

The ad was in *The Denver Post*.

Red Rocks Community College seeks teaching assistants for its joint diploma in Irish and Celtic Studies. Teaching exp. a must, college teaching exp. preferred. Contact Mary Block, RRCC, 303-914-6000

Areea thought this would be perfect, considering our Irishness and everything, but neither of us had teaching experience and although short of money this seemed just about impossible. John, though, had spotted something else.

"Jesus Christ," he said, "Alex, look at this."

The ad two below Areea's.

Wanted: Young, enthusiastic activists, who care about the environment, no experience necessary, generous remuneration. Résumés to: Campaign for the American Wilderness, Suite 1306, 1 New Broadway, Denver, CO 80203.

I gave the paper back to John and shook my head. "I don't think so, Johnny boy," I said.

John took me by the arm and led me onto the balcony out of Areea's earshot.

"Alex, we just go see what it's all about, we just show up, they don't know us from Adam, they have no way of connecting us to Victoria or Klimmer. Klimmer was killed by two Hispanics, remember."

"First of all, fuck that, second of all, we don't have a work permit," I said.

"Pat's friend," John said.

"John, it's asking for trouble," I said.

"Fuck it, Alex, it's a bloody godsend, don't you see, it's why we were here, it's almost a kind of message, we're meant to work there, of all the ads Areea could have showed us, she showed us this one?"

"She showed us the one above," I said.

"Alex, come on, don't deny the significance of it."

"John, you're crazy if you think I'm walking into the lion's den, just because of some stupid ad," I insisted.

"Alex, it's a job, we have no money for food, or, I might add, ketch. No one knows that we saw Klimmer, he said so himself. We wouldn't be walking into the lion's anything. The cops are looking for Hispanic guys in his death. There is no one to connect us to that at all. And once we're back on the case, you could legitimately ask Mr. Patawasti for money again. Don't you see, this is our way out."

"Your way out of guilt," I said, and wished I hadn't.

"No, your way out of not starving and not going back to Ireland to a bullet in the brain. I'm going to see what it's all about, you can come or not, up to you. . . ."

o o o

I am seven feet away from Victoria Patawasti's murderer. Here in this room. If Klimmer was right, one of those two men a mere three weeks ago took a .22-caliber revolver and shot Victoria in the head.

Charles Mulholland, Robert Mulholland.

But also sitting at the desk in front of me, Mrs. Amber Mulholland (Charles's wife) and Steve West (vice president and personnel manager). The room: white carpet, nature scenes on the wall, a large plate-glass window that looked out on Barnes & Noble, McDonald's, and the Rocky Mountains stretching fifty miles north and south in a huge panorama that took the breath away.

And something else that took the breath away.

Klimmer had been right about Amber Mulholland. You'd have to be crazy not to want to be with her.

How could you focus on Charles or Robert, trying to figure which one was the killer, when she was there?

Amber, tall, overwhelming, a blond, more than that, an iconic blond. A strikingly beautiful American woman of the type that I didn't think they made anymore. Something old-fashioned about her. Sophisticated, clever. Hair falling in a cascade down her elegant back. A white blouse, pearl necklace, icy blue eyes, skin like porcelain, no, marble, no, vellum—soft, rich, extraordinary, in fact. Cheekbones like knife blades. Liz Taylor's eyes. Audrey Hepburn's neck. And no, again, forget comparisons. If the Führer had had his way all women would look like this. Radiant, regal, poised, strong.

She didn't look fake like Miss America. Miss America would be the girl doing Amber's nails. She was the real deal. You couldn't overwrite her. She had star quality. Grace Kelly rather than Madonna. Hitchcock rather than Chandler.

Adroit, assured, and with the sort of sneering sangfroid that made you want to give her a three-picture deal, made you want to sell your family into a silver mine to spend the night with her. And something menacing about her too. This is the sort of woman who never had to lift a heavy box in her life. This is the sort of woman who could start a war between Greeks and Trojans.

I learned later that she was about thirty years old, originally from Tennessee but, fortunately, she didn't have a Southern accent. That would have been the clincher. If she'd said "Free the South from the Yankees," you would have been out looking for guns and horses.

And as Charles is talking and I'm standing there looking at her and not looking at her, two thoughts occur to me: she's thin enough and beautiful enough to be a model or an actress or a person in her own right, not just Mrs. Amber Mulholland, and, second and more weirdly, she's the inverse of Victoria Patawasti. In mathematics it is called the reciprocal. Victoria, bronzed and brown-eyed and heavy-lidded and dark-haired and beautiful. Amber, golden-haired and azure-eyed and pale-skinned and athletic and beautiful.

And maybe there was a sexual motive, after all.

Maybe Charles was having an affair with Amber's dimensional opposite.

Maybe.

Maybe it was too much to be with her.

You can only stare so long at the sun. . . .

But anyway, the here and now.

The office, the mountains.

Charles himself. Thirty-eight, tall, clean-shaven, handsome, cool, hair in a blond wave, breaking extravagantly to the left of a large intelligent face. Gray eyes with a slightly surprised expression on pale cheeks. Linen jacket, open-necked white shirt, fluttering hands, charming, just the type who could kill someone and be blasé about it in front of the missus or the cops.

Robert Mulholland, the younger brother by five years, another blond. It's like the *Village of the* bloody *Damned* in here. The same wave breaking on a barer beach, paradoxically, although younger, he's losing his hair, but he's still lean, handsome, pale, with glasses, taller even than his brother, more of a William Hurt look about him, black T-shirt, distracted, bored. Smarter? More cold-blooded? Fingers folded in front of him on the oak desk. Steady hand on a pistol grip.

Both brothers nice, friendly, inviting. You didn't need Hannah Arendt to talk about the banality of evil, experience has taught me that either of them could be the killer.

I can't help wishing I had John around.

Is John here to support me? No, he's not. John lied. For when he'd convinced me to go to CAW and made me see the sense of it, he said that it was better I go alone, too suspicious, the pair of us, two Micks, showing up.

He was right, but even so.

I had made it through the first stage, an interview with a man called Abe, and now this was the final process.

The fourth person at the table, Steve West, a goateed, squat man, is doing most of the talking now. I don't like him, he has his hat on indoors, and people like that can't be trusted:

"Well, uh, Mr. O'Neill," he continues, looking at my J-1 visa (from Pat's mate, a proficient little forger who mostly worked with the large Mexican and Central American communities but for only another hundred dollars rustled up an Irish passport), "Abe has passed you on to us, so you must be the sort we're looking for, let me, uh, let me explain a little about the position. At this stage we're looking for another dozen campaigners, to increase name recognition and membership of CAW. It's important, especially now we've moved to Denver, that we increase membership. Membership is important for revenue and for political clout. The more members we have, the more influence we can muster and the more members we'll get."

"I see," I say. "And how many members do you have at the moment?"

"Eight thousand five hundred, or thereabouts, five thousand of whom are in Colorado. I know, it's a drop in the ocean compared to Greenpeace or the Sierra

Club or Audubon, but we're a very young organization and now we've relocated to Denver, we're hoping to grow exponentially. We do have branches in Fort Collins and Colorado Springs, but also Sante Fe, Phoenix, Salt Lake City, and Los Angeles," Steve says.

"How young an organization are you?" I ask.

"Three years old, but it's only really in the last six months that we've really begun to get things together. I've taken a leave of absence from my law firm and now that we've moved here to bigger offices, we're hoping we can really grow," Charles answers with a winning smile.

"You're from Ireland?" Mrs. Mulholland says, surprised, suddenly looking up from my entirely fictional CV. I have to not look at her to answer.

"Yes," I say.

She passes the CV to Charles.

"And you're here on a J-1 visa?" she asks.

"That's right," I say, "I'm going to be attending Red Rocks Community College for a year, doing their Celtic Studies diploma, and then I'm going back to the University of Ulster."

Charles and Mrs. Mulholland look at each other. Robert picks up the photocopy of the résumé and takes his glasses off to examine it.

"What part of Ireland are you from?" Charles asks.

"From Belfast," I say.

There is a slight pause, then Robert coughs.

"You're here studying at Red Rocks Community College?" Charles says.

"That's right."

"If you're a student you won't be able to work full-time?" Charles says.

"Well, my schedule is pretty flexible," I reassure him.

"Is this your first time in America?" Mrs. Mulholland asks.

"I came once before, traveled around a bit."

"Very different from Ireland, I would expect," Mrs. Mulholland says.

"Oh, yes, very different," I say. "It's actually warm in summer, which we don't get much."

"We went to Ireland, didn't we, Robert?" Charles says.

"Charles, we're a little pressed for time, if I could bring it back to—" Steve tries to say but is interrupted by Robert.

"Dublin," Robert says.

"Yes, only Dublin, but it was charming," Charles muses.

"It's a nice city," I agree.

"I'd like to go," Mrs. Mulholland says to Charles.

"Mr. Mulholland, please, we have a lot of people still to see," Steve says.

"Mr. O'Neill," Charles says, "look, I'll cut right to it. We've had a bit of a, well, a bit of a tragedy. We lost one of our most trusted personnel just last week, and we're actually desperately shorthanded at the moment. Not just because of the move, but because of the, er, anyway, what we're really looking for are enthusiastic, intelligent people who understand the ways in which environmental policies have been manipulated and want to see common sense prevail. You don't have to agree with us one hundred percent politically but you do have to understand where we're coming from and be willing to bring our message to the public."

He smiles at me, looks at Robert, and waits for my response. He's smooth, smug, likable.

"Well, I'll tell you the truth, Mr. Mulholland, I had never heard of your organization until very recently but I've read your brochure and your ideas seem very sensible. Although I'm not an American, I do agree that the environment shouldn't be preserved like a museum but that land and forests should be developed in manageable ways that balance the needs of nature with the needs of people," I say.

"We also need p-people who will get on with other people, it's a small environment, we need to bring everyone together as a t-team," Robert says, speaking expansively for the first time today and it's a surprise because he has a slight stutter. A stutter, though, does not mean a thing, it is no reflection of an inner life, revealing neither guilt, nor shyness, nor anything. It reveals nothing except maybe a disinclination to become a public speaker and perhaps not even that—Demosthenes and Churchill both stuttered.

"If we took you on a trial basis, could you come tonight?" Charles asks, running his long fingers through his hair.

"Yeah, but why in the evening?" I ask.

"Because that's when people will be home from work," Charles tells me.

"Perhaps Abe didn't explain, this will primarily be an evening job, will that be a problem?" Steve asks.

"Not at all," I say.

"Do you think you would fit in here?" Mrs. Mulholland asks.

"I do, it seems like an exciting opportunity to get in at the start of an organization. I like challenges and I think I would like this one."

The table looks at one another, sighs. I get the impression that I'm the first normal person they've interviewed today. Not easy finding student-age workers in July in Denver. Indeed, nothing must have been easy at the moment. They must have been swamped, really. Moving to Denver and having to deal with the deaths of two of their key employees.

"Well, maybe we'll see you tonight," Charles says.

"One or t-two more questions?" Robert asks Charles.

"We are very pressed, Robert," Charles says.

Robert bites his lip.

"Ok," he says.

"Wonderful to meet you," Mrs. Mulholland says, and everyone thanks me for my time.

Steve sees me to the door and says in a stage whisper:

"I think I can say with all honesty, Alex, that we'd like to welcome you to the family."

"Thanks," I say, and walk out into the bare reception area to wait for the formal decision.

An hour later. Charles giving me the tour of the CAW offices. Showing me everything, apologizing for the mess. CAW occupies the entire tenth and eleventh floors of the building. They have twice the space they had in Boulder and it still looks very empty. There are about a dozen employees in cubicles and several others in offices. Charles introduces me and I do my best to remember names. Charles is taller than me, he smells of a light masculine musk. I'll have to find out what it is. His accent, too, is peculiar, it's very difficult for a non-American to separate out American accents besides the obvious ones like the Deep South, or Boston or Chicago. It's slightly Anglicized, though, with a twang, did he go to England for a few years? Perhaps that's the way they teach them to speak at Harvard or prep school.

"And this is a portrait of Margaret Cheverde, our honorary president, she's the daughter of an Italian prime minister. Of course, that's pretty meaningless, in Italy they let everyone be prime minister for a week or two," Charles says, laughing at his own joke.

I laugh too. He has two nervous twitches: he keeps turning the white gold wedding ring on his finger and he keeps running his hands through his hair. I'm no Freudian, so I don't figure either means anything.

When we're done with the tour of the chaotic eleventh floor he tells me what the job will be tonight.

"Tonight, Alex, myself, Abe, and Amber will be taking a van of campaigners out to the sticks, you know, going door to door, trying to drum up members. I haven't actually done it for a while, but it'll all fall into place," Charles says, grinning.

"I'm sure it will," I agree.

"And look, I don't want you to be disturbed or anything, there's going to be a film crew following me around tonight. I know it's a dreadful bore, but it's one of those things we have to endure, you know, for publicity."

"A film crew?" I ask, surprised.

"Yes, don't worry, we'll just carry on as if nothing's happening and they'll do their job, keep out of our way, sorry it has to be on your first night, but it's just one of those things."

We talk some more about tonight, but he keeps looking at his watch. Before he goes, though, I ask him about Mrs. Mulholland, whom Klimmer didn't mention at all as a staffer. He laughs and says that Amber isn't supposed to be here at all, she's just helping out for the next couple of weeks because they're incredibly short-staffed. She's a wonder, he says, and I can't help but agree. Does she know she's married to a murderer? Or that her brother-in-law is a murderer, or maybe it's both of them. Or maybe she knows and doesn't care. Or maybe she's Lady Macbeth behind the scenes. Charles stops talking. My eyes must have glazed over for a moment.

"Everything clear?" he asks me with a look of concern.

I nod. "Everything is great," I say with enthusiasm.

"Good. I'll get you your clipboard and your fact

sheets and then Abe will get you to fill in your tax details and show you how to doorstop and how to do the rap. Tonight when you go out, probably Abe or myself will be looking after you, so you'll have a good time. Is there anything else you want to ask?"

"Uh, no, just, I don't know, about money, maybe?"

"Oh, sure, hasn't Steve told you?"

"No."

"Ok, you get a third of all the money you make over quota. Quota is eighty-five dollars. If you make under that, you get a flat rate of forty percent of what you raise. But don't worry about that. Most people make about three fifty a night, which means they get, what's a third of that?"

"One twenty."

"One hundred and twenty, that's not bad, is it?"

"Yeah," I say, and I'm doing the sums in my head. One hundred dollars is about sixty pounds, which isn't bad for a couple of hours' work. Not bad at all. Thinking about this cheers me up again. Abe comes out of the office with a clipboard and some fact sheets. He's a kid my age, fat, ginger bap, wearing a Sex Pistols T-shirt. I talked to him briefly earlier. Seemed ok.

"Ok," he says, "let's get you started."

Charles departs, casually swinging his key ring, Abe brings me into his office, sits me down.

"He told you everything?" Abe asks in a New York accent.

"Yeah, although he was a bit vague and mysterious about personnel problems. Some kind of tragedy?"

"Oh, shit. Look, Alex, Charles wants us to draw a line under it, look to the future and all that, but I should tell you that we had two terrible things happen to us in the last month."

"Oh, yeah?" I ask.

Abe tells me all about Victoria and Klimmer, explaining that they've caught one of the killers and are looking for the others. He tells me not to bring it up with anyone at CAW. He seems a bit upset, especially talking about Victoria, and I'm considering him an empathetic ally when he adds that one of the worst aspects of the whole thing is that now he can't wear his Warren Zevon "Things to Do in Denver When You're Dead" T-shirt around the office.

"Is there anything else before we get down to business?" Abe asks.

"Well, Charles said there's going to be a film crew following him tonight," I say.

"Yes, yes, there is, he tell you why?"

"No, he didn't, said it was publicity."

"Well, if he didn't tell you, I can't tell you," Abe says.

"What's the big secret?" I ask.

"We're not supposed to discuss it, in fact, I'm not even supposed to know, so if you don't mind I'd like to leave it there, ok?"

"Ok," I say, not minding because Abe looks like the sort of guy who couldn't keep a secret to save his life.

Abe pops the fridge, gives me a Coke, and explains the "rap." Tonight we're going to be asking people about the preservation of the old growth forests of

North America and if this is an important issue to them. The rap has to be memorized. He does it for me a few times and I believe I've got it:

"Hi, my name is Alexander O'Neill, I'm from the Campaign for the American Wilderness, I'm in your neighborhood tonight campaigning to preserve our ancient forests, is this an issue that concerns you at all?"

If they say no, I've learned a set of answers, if they say yes, I've learned answers. It's like a computer program.

"No, I'm too busy," Abe says.

"Well, sir, this will only take one minute of your time, one minute to preserve our nation's heritage," I say.

"Good," Abe says.

Abe role-plays me through a set of situations. A woman with a baby, a man on a phone, an angry man, etc. Always in every situation I am to be "closing the loop," bringing the conversation back to the issue of preserving the old growth forests but allowing for logging in the managed forests, highlighting the short-sightedness of the Greenpeace policy of no development, explaining that logging companies plant more trees than they cut down, further explaining that Congress is choked by environmental pressure groups and that a voice for Wise Use, commonsense use of our natural resources is sadly lacking.

All the time he's talking, I'm thinking about the Mulhollands. Charles—funny, nice, Robert cold but sympathetic, Mrs. Mulholland, Charles's wife, the beautiful mirror of Victoria. A troika of evil? Hmmm. Maybe I was way off. Way, way off.

* * *

It's six o'clock, we're on a clogged highway heading south. We're in a van. Over a dozen of us. All white, students, bubbly, irritating. No blacks, Asians, or Mexicans. Only one person I recognize from this morning's set of interviews. Both of us new hires have been introduced to all the others. The others can't be that veteran either, considering CAW only moved here a couple of weeks ago.

Charles is driving, and beside him in the front seat is Amber, twisting her hair into little ringlets, not being coy, just bored. Beside me in the back is Abe and another girl, who told me her name but I've already forgotten it. She's young and skinny and looks like a student.

I don't see the film crew and I wonder if both Charles and Abe were joking about that.

As we drive through the traffic, Abe keeps asking people to do tonight's rap. He doesn't ask me, which is good, because I'm still trying to remember it. That and all the facts and the angles. First question you're supposed to ask is whether the issue of the forests concerns them. Second question (while you pretend to fill something in your clipboard) is their political affiliation. If they're a Republican, you talk about waste, how the mining companies and timber manufacturers are going bankrupt; if they're a Democrat, you talk about deforestation and why we have to cut down the tropical rain forests, because nutty environmentalists won't let us use our own forests for managed growth. The tropical rain forests have a hoard of untapped medical potential. If a Democrat woman opens the door, you're supposed to tell her about the breast cancer drugs they found in the Amazon. If it's a man, you're to talk about prostate cancer or heart disease. Whatever's relevant to the person at the door. The most important thing of all, Charles tells us, while he's driving, is always to be closing the loop.

Charles shifts lanes expertly and looks at us in the rearview mirror.

"Ok, folks, everyone's favorite time, the getting-to-know-you questions," Charles says.

Some people groan.

"Tonight we'll do favorite superhero and why. Alex, Elena, you go first, of course, since you've just joined the family," Charles says.

"Don't make them go first, honey," Amber says. "They should go last."

"Ok, you're right. Abe, you first," Charles says.

"Uh, Spiderman," Abe says, "because he's an ordinary guy, lives in Queens, I visited his house, it's a real address in Forest Hills, 'course Peter Parker doesn't live there."

"Ok, thank you, Abe. Favorite superhero, Michael," Charles asks a tubby kid in sandals and brown T-shirt.

"Does the Bionic Man count?" Michael asks.

"Yes, of course, and why do you like him?" Charles asks.

"I don't know, because he did cool stuff," Michael says.

Charles goes around the van, getting everyone talking. By the time they get to me, the only superhero left is Batman. I give them my theory about the Batman TV show and U.S. presidents:

"The Penguin is obviously a caricature of FDR, there's the accent, the cigarette holder, et cetera. The Riddler is Richard Nixon, the energy, all humped over. The Joker is Jack Kennedy, the big grin, weird accent—"

"Who's Catwoman?" Mrs. Mulholland asks, suddenly interested.

"Jackie, sexy, dark-haired," I say.

"She wasn't sexy," one of the kids says.

"She was back then," Charles says, and gives me a grin. I can see that he's thinking we made the right decision hiring this kid.

We finish the superheroes and Charles tells us that we have to remember the rap and be always closing the loop.

He makes us chant "Always be closing the loop," and no one seems to think this is particularly embarrassing. Charles continues: "Remember, everyone, always be closing the loop, even if someone is arguing with you, always be closing the loop. Bring it back to the issue of how they can help and how they help is by joining the Campaign for the American Wilderness at fifty dollars a shot. If it's too expensive, point out that that's only a dollar a week and if they still don't budge tell them we've a special reduced membership for thirty-five dollars a person, so they could join on their own, not at the family level, and still be doing their bit. Also, if it's a flashy house, maybe a Mercedes in the drive, you can ask for a hundred-dollar membership or a life membership for five hundred dollars. You get one person to become a life member and you've made yourself a hundred and fifty dollars in one evening."

In the front, Mrs. Mulholland is reading a novel with a deerstalker on the cover, Sherlock Holmes, presumably. How can she read without getting carsick?

It would be nice if they paired me with Charles tonight, Robert tomorrow night. Get a handle on both of them. I smile and shake my head. Eejit. Here I am, still trying to solve the bloody case. After all that's happened.

"Bumps," Charles says from the front, and we go over a couple of ramps. The van jolts. At a traffic halt a man wipes the van window with a squeegee, Charles smiles, winds his window down, says thank you and gives him a dollar.

Finally, as we start to get really moving, Abe turns to us and says we're getting closer and gets us to repeat the rap. We all have a go and I manage to get through mine without too much trouble. Next, Abe gets us to pretend that we're in actual "door situations," some difficult doors, some easy. People who don't speak good English, older people. I practice my rap a couple more times and he tells Charles that we're well prepared.

Charles finally pulls the car off the expressway and we're in a small mountain town with houses instead of apartment buildings. I thought we were only doing the city and suburbs, but this is clearly no longer Denver.

Darker now and all the streetlights come on with a pale yellow color. We stop outside a police station and Charles runs in. Abe explains to me that this is because we have to let the cops know we're out collecting, in case there's any kind of trouble. We're allowed to knock on any door we want according to the law, though if we're asked to leave someone's property we have to do so.

Charles comes back to the car. It's spitting down now and rain is streaking along the windows, blurring the town and everything else. He puts the car into gear and we go off. If I had killed someone a few weeks ago, would I be able to run into a police station? Yeah, I probably would, again, it means sweet fuck all.

Charles finally stops, distributes maps, sends everyone out, tells Abe to take care of Elena, tells me to wait in the back, kisses Amber, sends her with Abe. He pulls on a tan jacket and gives me an umbrella. It's hardly raining now, and I say it's ok.

"Take it, this isn't like Ireland, it might really start pouring later, we need it, a good downpour," he says.

I take the umbrella, but the rain has already gotten under the plastic cover on my clipboard, dampening the fact sheets—nothing I can do about it. Charles grins at me and we walk over to the first house. He seems younger now. He likes doing this.

I look around. It's a fairly affluent area. New cars, and the houses have big gardens and fences. The difference from Ireland is that the houses are made of wood, not brick.

"Ok, Alexander, this is how it goes down. Each person is to get one zone to cover in an evening. Usually it's about a hundred and fifty houses. Average you can get is about seven members an evening. Seven out of a hundred and fifty, but at the others you can leave leaflets, so it's still doing a bit for the cause."

"What town is this?" I ask him as we walk toward the first big house in the street.

"It's called Colorado Springs. Nice place, the Air Force Academy's here. Good hunting ground for us. Ah, there they are."

Three men come out of a dark green Range Rover. Two are in hooded raincoats carrying a camera and a boom mike, the third is wearing a baseball cap that says Broncos on it. They are all in their thirties. Charles does not introduce me and this pisses me off a bit. He shakes the Broncos guy's hand.

"Bill, I thought you wouldn't show up because of the rain," he says.

"Typical, first rain we've had in months, but it's good for us, shows your dedication. Main problem's the light, we're losing light fast, Charles, I think we should get started."

"Ok, what do I do?" Charles asks.

"You do your normal thing, and don't worry about us," Bill says.

"Ok, come on, Alex," Charles says to me, "just ignore them if you can."

We walk up to the first house.

"Now, Alex," Charles says, "I'll do the talking and you just watch. Later I'll let you do a couple of houses on your own. But for now just let me show you how it's done. We're in a pretty affluent area as you can see. Volvos and BMWs, so I'm gonna ask for hundred-dollar memberships and, if it goes well, maybe try for a couple of life memberships. That's five hundred dollars. We'll see. Are you ready? Are you psyched?"

"Yeah," I lie.

"I said, are you ready?" he says more loudly.

"Yeah," I say with more enthusiasm.

We go through the gate and walk up the driveway, crunching our shoes in the gravel. The camera crew follows us and starts filming. Next door a dog starts barking and in the living room a TV comes on. It's cold and I suppress a shiver. Charles pushes the doorbell and pats me on the back.

"It's gonna be great," he says, grinning from ear to ear and for some reason giving me the Spock "Live long and prosper" sign from Star Trek.

"Great," I say, giving him Churchill's V for victory sign as a response. Charles beams, unaware that the V sign means something totally different back in my neck of the woods.

Man in his late thirties comes to the door. Charles gives him the rap. The man resists, looks at the camera crew, baffled, Charles keeps at him for a painful amount of time and finally the man agrees to join the CAW at the thirty-five-dollar rate.

We do two dozen more houses and Charles signs up two more people, leaves leaflets at the rest, smiling the whole time. Bill stays behind with the ones that were cooperative and gets them to sign a release form, then races to catch us up again.

"You think you can do a door on your own now, or do you want me to stand there with you?" Charles asks.

"I can do it," I tell him.

"Great. We'll try down this street, might be a little trickier. I'll do this side, you the other, meet at the end, ok?"

I nod. It's a side street, Toyotas and Hondas, rather than BMWs and Volvos, but it still looks ok. Mock Tudor houses, some with gardens, picket fences.

My first house, I ring the doorbell.

No one home, I write "N/H" on the clipboard.

I walk down the path of the second house, knock the door.

"Coming," someone says.

The door opens, and it's an elderly man in his seventies. Pale, white, wearing a dressing gown, smoking a cigarette.

"Hi, I'm from the Campaign for the American Wilderness and we're in your neighborhood tonight campaigning to save the ancient forests. . . . Er, is this an issue that concerns you at, er, all?"

"The what?" the man says.

"The CAW, we're an environmental org—"

"Nope," the man says, and closes the door in my face. I hear him muttering as he walks back down the hall.

I write a zero beside his door number.

Next house. One-floor bungalow, painted a kind of frostbite blue. Creepy-looking dolls in the window. In this house there's a screen door and a porch. I open the screen door, it shuts behind me, trapping me between the two doors in the tiny porch. It's filled with potted plants and an enamel plaque of a fat man drinking beer that says on it "Bavaria the Beautiful."

A black woman comes to the door. Early fifties.

"Hi, I'm in your neighborhood tonight campaigning to preserve the ancient forests of—"

"Wait a minute," she says, "I'll get my husband."

She goes off and calls into the back room. She returns to the front room and closes the door. Meanwhile, the kitchen door opens and a man wearing dungarees comes down the hall. There is oil all over his hands, and he's sweating. His eyes are opaque gray and dead tired.

"Whadda ya want?" he asks suspiciously.

"Hi, I'm from the, uh, Campaign for the, uh, Wilderness, we're in your neighborhood tonight campaigning to save the forests."

"Yeah?" he says, and I show him the literature on the clipboard. The pictures of the trees before and after deforestation. The quotes from logging company executives and politicians. The list of endangered species in the Amazon.

"What are you selling?" he asks gruffly.

"Nothing. I, er, I'm campaigning to save the trees, the old growth forests. There's only—"

"Do I have to pay anything?"

"No, not really. It's a—"

"Ok, where do I sign?"

I give him the clipboard and he takes a pen out of his lapel pocket and signs the sheet next to his door number. He gets oil all over the acetate cover.

"Ok?" he says.

"Yes, and if, er, you'd like to, um, make a donation?" I say to him, with a great deal of embarrassment.

"No, don't think so."

"Ok, well, thanks again."

"My pleasure, glad to help."

I turn and walk down the path. He closes the screen door behind me.

Shit, I say to myself, and mark zero on my sheet. I walk to the next house. I ring the bell and no one answers and I write down "N/H."

No answer in the next four houses and in the fifth house an Asian girl comes to the door, wearing a Girl Scout uniform.

"Are your parents in?"

"Not allowed to talk to strangers," she says bravely, and shuts the door.

I turn and walk back down the path. Smart kid, I say to myself.

Next house, no one home. Next house, no dice. Next house, old white guy in a crumpled suit, standing behind a patched screen door.

"Rain, finally, cool us down," he says.

"Yeah, listen, I'm in your neighborhood tonight campaigning to save—"

"Blue steel .44," he says. "Used to have that."

"What?"

"You know what gun I got now?"

"No."

"A Walther PPK," he says, his eyes narrowing.

"Really?" I say.

"Uh-huh. Never be too careful opening the door to strangers," he says.

I look down and I notice, sure enough, that he's holding a firearm in his left hand, bouncing it there on his hip.

"You know who has that gun?" he asks.

"Uh, no. No, I don't."

"James Bond. That's James Bond's gun," he says, and gives me an off-putting smile.

"Well, that's terrific, thank you very much, I'll have to go," I say.

"What do you want, boy?"

"I just wanted to leave you a leaflet, here you are."

"Are you Scottish?"

"Irish, Irish. Well, look, thanks very much."

"Irish, Scottish, isn't it all the same thing?" he says.

"No, no, quite different. Well, thanks anyway, have a good night," I say hastily, and back down the path.

When I meet up with Charles at the end of the street, I have signed up no one. I don't tell him about the man with the gun in case he thinks I'm hysterical. But I take twenty bucks of my own money and pretend that I got two donations of ten bucks each.

"That's pretty good, Alex, that was a more difficult street, tough test. Look, we'll do a few more houses together and meet up with the others, ok?"

"Where's the film crew?" I ask him.

"Oh, they ran out of light, but I think they got enough for tonight," Charles says.

He doesn't elaborate about who they were or what they were doing, so I let the matter drop.

Charles takes us back down to a more affluent street and I wonder if this was all a deliberate ploy to blood me on a lot of rejections to see if I got downhearted.

Sure enough, back in the richer street we get three more memberships and even a life membership.

The rain has eased and when we pick up the others, everyone is excited and happy. They've had a good night and a third of the money they raised will be going to them. We drive back to the city, everyone talking, laughing. We stop for pizza in a grungy-looking place on a slip road close to the highway.

We scrunch together several tables. The lights flicker. The pizza bakes.

Charles is in high spirits. He talks and, eventually, the attention turns to me, as the new boy.

"Alexander, what would you be doing right now in Ireland?" Charles asks.

"Well, it's five a.m. there, so I'd probably be sleeping," I say.

"No, no, no, that's not what I mean, what do you do over there, at night, for fun, are there pizza places like here?"

"Uh, not that many and they're expensive, pizza is more of a restaurant thing," I say, a bit disconcerted to be the center of attention.

"So what would you do?" Charles asks.

"Go to the pub, I suppose," I say.

"Are the pubs really full of musicians and music and stuff?" Amber asks.

"Some of them, but most aren't, they—"

"I was in this pub in Dublin and it took forever for my pint of Guinness to come, I thought they'd forgotten about me," Charles says. "They were so slow."

"It's supposed to be slow, Guinness has to be poured very slowly," I explain.

"Well, it was slow, and the smoke in those places, terrible, I felt sorry for the bar staff, really awful," Charles says.

"Don't they play that game with the sticks?" Abe asks me.

"Hurling," I say.

"Do you play it?" Abe asks.

"No."

"Charles was the lacrosse champ at Bright," Abe says. "Kind of a similar game, no?"

Amber and Charles look briefly at each other.

"What's Bright?" I ask.

"You ever read *A Separate Peace, Catcher in the Rye*, any one of those?" Abe asks.

"No."

"Well, it's a bit like their school, Colorado version, Charles and Robert both went there. Very snooty, play cricket and everything," Abe says. Clearly, he's trying to get under Charles's skin, wind him up a bit, tease him, but he's overstepped the line somehow. Amber scolds him with a look that stops him in midsentence.

"Alexander, do you have any hobbies or anything like that?" Amber asks, questioning me with those big glacial eyes.

"No, not really," I say. "I go to football matches, soccer matches, I mean, sometimes, I'm not very athletic or anything."

Mercifully, the pizza finally comes.

I don't eat any. Instead, I find myself staring at Amber Mulholland as she spills Coke on her white blouse. I hand her a napkin and she thanks me with a beautiful smile. Something about that smile, though. Beautiful like a sun-drenched cornfield above a missile silo.

How much does she know about what happened to Victoria? Would she even care if her husband or brother-in-law was a murderer? I examine her closely. Maybe I'm wrong. There's something vulnerable about her too. A touch of the Marilyn or the Lady Di.

We drive back to Denver. I'm freezing, but no one else is. I try to get warmth from a cup of coffee. Charles is talking, but I'm not listening, ticking off the seconds till I can get home. We're all exhausted. Amber, in a whisper, asks Charles how the filming went. He says it went great and gives her a kiss. The kiss makes me wince.

They drop me on Colfax Avenue.

A few hookers, a few gypsy cabs, their lemony headlights distorting in the rain.

I stand under the overhang at Kitty's East Porno store. Still a few blocks to our apartment, but I'm so tired. Junkie tired. Drizzling still. The last rain for weeks to come.

From now on a continuation of the drought. Drought until August, when freezing rain would fall in Fort Morgan. And I would beg it to come down, invoking Vishnu, Storm Bringer, Lord of Night, begging him to cover me up as I lay there in the graveyard with gunshot wounds, wondering if it was too late then, to live, to survive, to avenge yet another horrible murder in this sorry, sorry excuse for a case.

8: AIR, WATER, EARTH, FIRE

Patrick and I are both irritated. It's hot, dry, we have the fan way at the other end of the room so the cards don't get blown over and John and Areea are not taking the game seriously at all. John has his hand on her lap, Areea has her hand at the back of his shorts.

I look at Patrick and shake my head in disgust.

"The one thing, John, that I can't stand is people not taking poker seriously when there's money in the pot."

"It's only two dollars," John says, and winks at Areea.

Areea giggles for no reason at all.

"It's the principle of the thing," I say.

I can tell Patrick feels the same way. For him in particular, whose weeks remaining on planet Earth can be counted in the few dozen, minutes are precious, seconds are bloody precious.

"Are you calling or not?" I say.

"No, then," John says impatiently, throwing down his cards.

"Your hand, Patrick," I say, annoyed.

He picks up his winnings.

"I think maybe we'll take a martini break," he says.

"Good idea," I say, looking significantly at John, who has started snogging Areea on the lobe of her ear. It's been two hours since I shot up and another rule I have is that ketch and spirits don't mix, but what the hell, anything to get away from those two, who have been carrying on like this for the last few days.

I follow Patrick all the way along the corridor and into his apartment, which is minimally decorated with a few photographs of friends and a bookcase filled with art books. CD player and CDs of all descriptions but mostly classical. He puts on a piece by Stravinsky, which does nothing to soothe my mood.

It's July 10. I've been going to CAW for more than a week now, making about a hundred and fifty bucks a night, commuting downtown, buying the groceries, and also attempting to look discreetly into the Victoria Patawasti murder. John, by contrast, has been hanging out on the fire escape smoking pot, eating potato chips, drinking beer, and making out with Areea when she's off her shift. It's starting to get on my nerves.

"It's starting to get on my nerves," I tell Pat.

"Me, too. You know, I was bluffing that hand, I had nothing," Pat says.

"I know."

This is one of Pat's good days, in fact since we showed up, he says he's been doing much better. He was perishing through loneliness: the lawsuit's pissed off most of his old pals in the DFD, and his only family lives in Wyoming.

Stravinsky's violins start screeching at one another and Pat puts ice into the martini shaker. Pat makes a dry martini, a very dry martini. He informs the Bombay Sapphire gin about the existence of a substance called vermouth before he pours it in the shaker. He takes two glasses from the freezer, adds an olive to each, and asks me to do the shaking, which I do.

We retire to the fire escape.

"She's very pretty, isn't she?" Pat says.

"She is, Pat, gorgeous face, great legs, honestly, I don't know what she sees in that big ganch."

"Well, it'll all end in tears," Pat predicts, as we lean forward to watch two men attempt to beat each other senseless at a brown, grassless park on the corner.

"John and Areea?" I ask, unsure if we're still on the same subject.

"Yes," he says.

"Because of her parents?"

"She says she's eighteen, but I think she's much younger," Pat says.

"Really?"

"Yeah, really," he says.

We sip our martinis.

"What about you, is there a special someone in your life?" Pat asks, the vowel sounds making his cheeks hollow sickeningly.

"Nope. There isn't."

"Back home, I mean."

"Answer's still no. I can't seem to hold on to a steady relationship."

"You leave them or they leave you?"

"They leave me, Pat."

"You think maybe the smack doesn't help?" Pat asks.

"I'm sure it doesn't. I'm sure it does not," I say.

Pat looks at me. He's not going to lecture me or give me grief. He's just pointing out the obvious. And it's that question yet again. And the answer. I must release it from me. Let it go. I don't have to do heroin now, I don't have to. So why am I doing it?

"We all need something, Pat," I say lamely.

"Yeah, we do," Pat agrees.

"And what about you, Patrick, is there someone in your life you've been hiding away?"

"Well, actually, I was in a long-term relationship until last year. Of course, he left me when I started to get sick."

"Shit."

"Shit is right," Pat says with disgust.

The sun is making its way across Colfax and the street is yawning, waking up, putting on its usual show. Guys appearing on the street corners, women walking hand in hand with little kids, other kids playing basketball. Old men talking. Big old cars playing N.W.A. and Public Enemy, bigger, newer cars blaring Tupac and Notorious B.I.G.

And as always the professional dealers, easy and unobtrusive, and the rookie dealers looking around a million times to see how much attention they can bring to themselves.

I stretch.

"Pat, it's time I was heading," I say.

"Not yet," Pat says, and rubs his hand over his gaunt, unshaven face.

"Love to stay, Pat, but it's twelve o'clock. I'm supposed to be downtown by one."

"Don't know why you're working for those right-wing bastards. Strip-mining the national forests, polluting the skies. Drought all year, couple of snowstorms which did nothing, and they're talking about the Wise Use of water to promote business, which means less conservation. I mean, Jesus, how about telling the goddamn Coors family to give some of their surplus water to Denver."

I can't help but suppress a smile. Pat clearly cares a lot more about this than I do. I don't mind arguing for fewer environmental regulations, I'll argue any point of view if I can get some dough out of it.

"Pat, I have to go."

"Ok, mate," Pat says, which makes me grin again. Pat's taking on a bit of an Ulster accent and vernacular hanging out with us. And though we have screwed up our murder case and I am exiled from Belfast, at least it seems we are doing a bit of good for someone in this world.

◊ ◊ ◊

July in Denver. Insanely hot. One hundred and one degrees says the board outside Channel 9. Drenched with sweat, I ride the elevator up to the CAW offices. Pat says Denver is livable for a few weeks in October and a few weeks in April. Winter and summer, the rest of the time. I can well believe him. People with sense leave town at this time of year for cooler places like a blast furnace or the surface of the sun.

I walk into the office.

I'm well liked now, established.

Abe says hi, he's wearing the same Sex Pistols T-shirt he's had on for the last week. Johnny Rotten is so coated with gook he has taken on a three-dimensional quality. Still, the place is air-conditioned and the offices are losing their chaotic feel and taking on a semblance of order.

The weird thing, the really weird thing is that apart from Abe no one has mentioned either Victoria's or Klimmer's death. Charles runs a tight ship and I suppose they want things upbeat for the new staffers like me. Or maybe they're trying to be very positive in front of the camera crew, which has shown up twice more to follow Charles around.

Dozens of posters have gone up over the bare walls, nature scenes with words like "Perseverance" and "Serenity" underneath them. They've hired another couple of secretaries and the campaigners are coming together as a group. Aye, they're looking to the future, not dwelling on the unpleasantness of the past.

Every day starts the same. Abe and Steve brief us about the evening's assignment, where we're going, what the rap is for the day, what to look out for. We do rehearsals, practice raps, role-playing and if there's time left we stuff envelopes and write to our congressmen. There are about fifteen campaigners now. The organization is getting bigger.

We don't see Charles and Robert at all until around five o'clock, when the van is ready to go. Sometimes Charles drives, sometimes Robert drives, sometimes Amber comes along.

No one will admit it with Abe or Steve around, but arriving at the office at one o'clock is a waste of everyone's time. I suppose if you're dedicated to the cause it's all well and good, but I sense that most of the campaigners don't give a shit about the forests or the Wise Use policy and are only here because they hope they can make cold cash.

Yeah, it's been a week and I've been patient, laying the groundwork, being nice, friendly. I've endured Abe's theories about why the Clash, the Ramones, and the Undertones were feeble imitators of the Sex Pistols. I've listened to him talk endlessly about the New York Mets. Tedious, but necessary. I've been cultivating him. Encouraging him. None of the Mulhollands will talk, but I know Abe will.

Abe was a University of Colorado student at the Earth Sciences Institute in Boulder. He started working for CAW during his vacations and stayed on after he graduated. He's only twenty-five, but he's the fourth in command.

For the last two days we've been getting lunch at the Sixteenth Street Pub around the corner from the office. Abe's a lightweight, anyway, a 6-percent Stella Artois loosens his tongue.

We talk about the movies and when he's finished his pint and it's going to his head a wee bit I come straight out with it.

"Abe, why is there a film crew following Charles around?"

"I can't tell you because we're not supposed to talk about it. Robert would kill me. Charles would kill me."

"Abe, you know you can trust me," I say, trying to ignore Abe's choice of words.

Abe takes a bite of his burrito and looks around the bar. No one else from CAW is there. And Abe wants to tell me, he just needs that final push.

"Abe, come on, what the hell's going on? It hardly seems fair that everyone else is allowed to know and I'm not."

"Everyone else doesn't know," Abe protests.

"Come on, mate, I won't say a bloody thing, I can help better if I'm in the know."

"That's true."

"Yeah, 'course it is, come on, what's the deal with the camera crew?"

"You won't breathe a word?"

"No."

"Ok, listen, I swear to God, don't tell anyone."

"I won't, just bloody get on with it."

"Congressman Wegener will be seventy years old on August sixth," Abe says slowly and significantly.

I look at him.

"That's it?" I ask. "What the hell does that mean?"

"Everyone thinks he's going to run again next year in

1996, but he's not, he's going to announce his retirement on his birthday. He's only told the chairman of the Colorado GOP and the chairman has only told Charles."

"Who has told you? Amber, Robert—"

"Listen, Alex, you can't breathe a word of this. Once he makes his announcement, there could be a feeding frenzy. Wegener represents the Eighth Congressional District, solid Republican, a safe seat, whoever succeeds him is guaranteed a place in Congress."

"And it's going to be Charles. That's why he's taken a leave of absence from his law firm. That's why they're filming him, campaigning door to door," I say.

"The state GOP has had its eye on Charles for some time. He's thirty-eight, successful, he has a seriously photogenic wife, and he's founded an environmental organization, us, which could be the GOP's route into the environmental debate, political turf solely occupied by the Democrats. Charles will have no serious competition for the seat, he's being anointed, but it goes further than that."

"Oh yeah?"

"Maybe I shouldn't say, you know."

"Don't start that again," I tell him.

"Ok, well, but you gotta keep this quiet."

"Sure."

"Ok, look, what do you think's going to happen at the general election next year?"

"I don't know."

"Dole will lose. Dole will lose to Clinton and the

GOP will be thrown into turmoil. They're going to need to move toward the center to beat Gore in 2000. They're not going to pick someone like George W. Bush or Pat Buchanan. They're going to pick moderates, and Charles will be a young, moderate, environmentalist, outsider congressman from a Western state. Do you see?"

"See what?" I ask.

Abe's boiling with excitement. The momentum's there, he's giving me this secret, something he can't contain anymore.

"Don't you see, Alex? Charles could be an ideal vice-presidential candidate for someone like John McCain or even Colin Powell. Powell-Mulholland in 2000? This isn't penny-ante shit. This is the big enchilada."

"Jesus," I say, impressed by his seriousness about it all. But surely it's a fantasy, a long shot, more than that, a delusion. Who ever heard of a two-term congressman getting to be a vice president, no matter how good the demographics.

"Long shot," I said.

"Nah, Bill Clinton was a long shot in 1992," Abe says, and continues to explain the concept. I pretend to be entranced. Abe goes on and on in a whisper and gradually it occurs to me that whether Charles really could be vice president in 2000, or 2004, or whenever, it doesn't actually matter, for I see now why Alan Houghton had to die. It's enough that Charles has convinced himself that Congress and the vice presidency are possibilities and it gave him that final push to kill his tormentor, his shadow, his blackmailing familiar. Yes. And poor Victoria got in the way. I take a sip of beer, nod at Abe, and make a mental note that I'm going to have to find out who Alan Houghton is and what connection he has to Charles.

Abe whispering now: "Alex, listen, you didn't hear it from me, ok? And it goes for all of us. We can't rock the boat, we can't do anything official until Wegener's birthday announcement. Do you see? We all have to go hush-hush."

"I do see, and I see why they moved CAW to Denver. This is going to be a campaign HQ as well? Right?"

"Change the topic, here's Robert," Abe whispers.

Robert's in the pub looking for us. Looking for Abe. He can't find the route maps for where they're going tonight.

Abe gives me a look to say nothing, gets up, and they head out of the bar.

Later . . .

We get in a large van, almost a bus, and head south toward Littleton. Charles isn't with us again tonight and Robert's driving. Surprisingly, Amber's accompanying her brother-in-law. I've seen Amber only twice since I started here. And this is the first time I've seen her without Charles. She's dressed down in a sweatshirt and black jeans, but she still looks stunning. You'd have to be misogynistic, the president of Greenpeace, Maoist, and blind to refuse to join the CAW if she asked you.

Robert drives and talks. Robert doesn't have the charm or salesmanship of his older brother. Where Charles has us telling our favorite movies and books and gets Abe to rehearse us through doorstops and the rap (to increase group cohesion and team spirit, Charles says), Robert senses that he has to do something but is a bit of a wet blanket. He seems to have digested management guru books and gives us pep talks based largely on sports metaphors and stories about the rebirth of Chrysler.

We drive south down Broadway rather than the highway and after a time we stop in a typical leafy suburb, or what would be a leafy suburb, were not all the trees dying and the lawns turning brown.

"We're here," Robert says, and switches off the engine.

He turns around to look at us.

"You should tell them where here is," Amber whispers.

"Oh yes, Englewood. It's a borderline area, mixed incomes, so I want everyone to go in p-pairs tonight."

Everyone nods.

Amber whispers something to him.

"Oh, yes, of course, we all have to g-get pumped up, don't we?" Robert asks, almost rhetorically.

"Yes, we do," Abe says.

"Ok, then. Um, Abe, are you ready to go?" Robert asks with fake enthusiasm.

"Yes, I am," Abe says.

"I c-can't hear you," Robert says.

"Yes, I am," Abe says, louder.

"I still c-can't hear you," Robert says.

Abe yells that he's ready to go. Robert does the same routine with everyone in the van. It's cringe making. When he gets to me, he says:

"Alexander, are you r-ready to go?"

"Sir, yes, sir," I shout, USMC fashion.

And then something a little odd happens. Robert laughs. Strange noise, like a small animal drowning. Really, it wasn't that funny. In fact, it wasn't funny at all, but Robert's cracking up about something. Snot comes out of his nostrils and he takes out a tissue, wipes his eyes, blows his nose. No peeler worth his salt makes snap judgments à la Columbo, but suddenly I don't see Robert as the murdering type.

"Oh my God, that reminds me, r-really reminds me. You know, I got thrown out of the ROTC after one week? I would have made the worst s-soldier in the world," Robert says to Amber, forgetting, I think, that the rest of us are here.

"I thought they'd banned ROTC at Harvard?" Amber asks.

"At school. At B-Bright. They said the only one worse was Charles and they didn't throw him out because he was l-lacrosse captain. Oh, you should have seen me, it was—"

"Robert, the business at hand," Amber interrupts, and gives him a look that none of the rest of us can see but which freezes him.

"Oh, yes, sorry folks, f-forgot what I was doing there. Um, who's next?" Robert asks in a still-cheerful mood.

We go through the rest of the van and everyone claims that they are ready and enthused about going out tonight.

"Does everyone have their m-maps?"

We all nod and say yes.

"Does anyone not know how to read their map?" Robert asks.

One shy girl with curly brown hair puts her hand up.

"Ok, I'll go with you," Robert says.

We pile out of the van. It's another warm night. Englewood looks like everywhere we've been going. Another white 'burb. By fluke or luck or foul design, Amber and I are the only two left without a pair, but it's ok, I'm still new enough to need training by the top people.

"Looks like you're with me, marine," Amber says, twisting her hair behind her into a tight ponytail.

"Looks like," I agree, somehow managing to get the words out.

We gather our clipboards and materials and walk out into Englewood. I stare at her ass all the way to the first house and my internal monologue is: Bloody calm down, Alex, she's just a woman.

The first house we go to: a chubby lass, twenty years old, black hair, glasses, pretty, holding a wineglass. She opens the door, looks at us.

"Let me guess, you're a little bit country, he's a little bit rock and roll," she says.

I have no idea what she's talking about, and I look at Amber, baffled.

"She thinks we're Mormons," Amber says.

"What?" I say, still confused.

"We're not Mormons, uh, we're from the Campaign for—" Amber attempts.

"Let me tell you something," the girl says, taking a large sip of wine, "I do not believe that the Angel Gabriel appeared in upstate New York and said go take dozens of wives. It makes no sense. Ok? No sense."

"We're not Mormons," Amber persists.

"Damn right you're not," the girl says, "and I'm not going to be one either. And then he went to Utah? Jesus is no cowboy, I mean, come on, you people are seriously misguided."

"Does the issue of deforestation concern you at all?" I ask.

"No, but converting dead people does, that's a disgrace," she says.

She closes the screen door and then the front door, leaving us outside feeling very foolish.

"What was that all about?" I ask.

"I don't know," Amber says briskly.

"She must have been drunk," I suggest.

We turn and walk down the path.

"I just don't get the 'you're a little bit country' thing," I say.

"It's from a TV show you would never have seen, a song they used to sing, from the *Donny and Marie* show. You know, the Osmonds."

"Oh, who are Mormons, oh, I see, that was a good line, then."

"Yes," Amber says.

"Aren't their missionaries always men, though?" I ask.

"I have no idea," Amber says, a bit snootily. "I don't know anything about the Mormons."

The encounter has embarrassed her, she doesn't think it's funny at all, whereas I think it's hilarious, it'll amuse Pat and John when I tell them.

"Me neither, all I remember about the Mormon missionaries is as a kid in Belfast. Our next-door neighbor would throw a bucket of water around them because he said they were the heralds of the Antichrist or something. He probably thought that because he was so filthy and they were always so clean and neat," I say.

"That's right, you grew up in Belfast, didn't you?" she says, looking at me.

"Aye."

"That's quite near a place called Carrickfergus, isn't it?" she says.

"Yeah, I've heard of it, but I've never been there," I tell her.

My résumé is crucially different from Victoria Patawasti's in that respect. But even so, it's time to change the subject.

"Yeah, in fact, everything I know about the Mormons comes from that Sherlock Holmes story and that's hardly complimentary," I say.

"You read Sherlock Holmes?" she asks excitedly.

"Some of them."

"I love Conan Doyle, I love mysteries. Mysteries,

puzzles, figuring stuff out, I love that stuff. It's not Charles's thing," she says, her face lightening.

"Never Chuck, or Charlie, or Chaz, always Charles, eh?"

She frowns at me and I see that I've goofed up. Charles's name is not a subject for levity.

"Who's your favorite mystery writer?" I ask.

"Oh, the divine Agatha," she says, giving me a big smile.

"Are you a Poirot or a Marple?" I ask.

"Oh, a Marple, of course," she says.

I grin at her. She really is quite captivating and suddenly to think that either she is implicated in a brutal murder or closely related to the murderer seems utterly absurd. Once again I wonder if I'm completely on the wrong track about all of this. Or maybe my dick or the ketch is clouding my judgment.

In the next house an old man gives us a lecture about the low reservoirs, the yearlong drought, the importance of conservation, and refuses to take a leaflet.

In the next house no one's home. In the next house they don't want to give. Next house, fat white woman in a print dress, very heavy perfume. I give her the rap.

"You doing the whole street?" she asks.

"Yes."

"How much they give next door?"

"They weren't home."

"I'll bet they were. Mother's black, father's Japanese, Chinese, something like that."

"Really?"

"A lot of Negro families in the street now," she says.

"Is that a fact?"

"It is a fact. It is," she says conspiratorially.

"Well, that's America," I say, a little thrown by the first obvious racist I've met since coming here.

"Look at that O. J. Simpson. Would you want him next door? All on welfare. They're not really contributing anything, are they?" she says.

"Who?"

"The Negroes. Who do you think? They don't do anything. Haven't done anything."

I look at Amber for support, but she's staring at her shoes in shame and humiliation. Honey, you're going to meet a lot more people like this if you start moving in right-wing activist circles, I'm thinking. And again she looks vulnerable and slightly lost.

I smile at the woman.

"Well, they built the railroads, won the Civil War, were the workhorses of the Industrial Revolution, created an amazing literary culture, and invented four original musical forms in this century alone: jazz, blues, rock and roll, hip-hop. Boring old world without them, huh?" (I say all this with a big friendly smile. The woman looks furious.)

"What is it you want?" she asks.

"We're trying to promote Wise Use of the forests," Amber says.

"I don't think so," the woman says, and slams the screen door so hard that it rattles on its hinges. I can't help but laugh and even Amber grins.

Two more doors, we get nothing. As we head south the neighborhood is getting less affluent and the next street on our map is distinctly poorer still. The cars parked outside aren't as nice and the kids playing in the street are Mexican. I find it quite interesting the way there's almost an invisible demarcation line and I remark on this to Amber, but she doesn't reply.

Clapboard houses, most of them run-down looking. Rubbish piled up on the sidewalks in black bags. At the end of the street there's a big warehouse that looks as if it hasn't been used for about fifty years. The windows are dirty or smashed, and someone has drawn soccer goals on the walls.

It's dark now. The wind has whipped up, the sky is clouded over, and the temperature has dropped by thirty degrees. I shiver and we go down the path of the first house. A dog barking in the backyard, snarling at us through a chain-link fence. Slabbers coming out of its chops. I ring the bell and an Asian man answers. Amber does the rap, but it's impossible to hear over the dog, and anyway, he's not interested. We cross the yard to the next house and tap on the screen door.

It is answered by a huge man in a dirty white T-shirt and jeans.

"Yeah, what do you want?" he asks, like we're the millionth person to have called on him that night.

"Hi, we're from the Campaign for the American Wilderness and we're—"

"Yeah, I know," he interrupts. "I know what you are.

You guys should do your research better. You guys were around here last week for the same fucking thing."

Amber's shivering beside me, a little cold too in her thin sweatshirt.

"The old growth forests are a vital part of—"

"I know they are. Thank you," he says, and closes the door.

"It's going to be one of those nights, I can tell," I say.

She nods glumly.

"Maybe we should take a break, find a coffee shop or something," I suggest.

She shakes her head.

"No, everyone is going to do their full quota, so should we, it would upset Robert if we snuck off somewhere," she says, not very enthusiastically.

"Ok, you're the boss," I say. I didn't mind, in the last week I had had a lot of success, ok to strike out tonight, especially with such charming company around.

We cross the street to the next house. A bungalow, straggly garden, wire fence, patched screen door, scuffed paint.

Amber knocks on the screen door.

"Hold on, wait a minute, I'm getting the money," a boy says.

He opens the door. Fifteen, skinny, pale, curly hair, gormless expression.

"Dude, where's the pizza?" he asks.

"We're in your neighborhood tonight, campaigning

to promote Wise Use of . . ." Amber begins and does her whole rap uninterrupted.

The kid looks at her and shakes his head.

"Yeah, but dude, where's my pizza?" he asks.

"We're not the pizza people, we're promoting Wise Use of the forests," Amber says a little desperately and does the rap a second time. Again, I think that she seems younger than the thirty Abe says she is. Is she so naive that she doesn't see that the kid is stoned out of his fucking brains?

"What the fuck is keeping you?" another kid yells, appearing in the hall, flipping a cigarette lighter on and off.

"These guys won't give us our pizza," the first kid explains.

"Whoa, she's a babe," the second kid says.

"Come on," I say to Amber, "let's go."

She hesitates for a minute and lets me take her down the path. The power in the relationship has shifted in that moment. She, who is supposed to be training me, has cracked. She's wearing flats, is an inch or two smaller than me. But it's enough. She has to look up to ask me the question.

"What was going on there?" she asks.

"The kids were stoned," I tell her.

"At their age?" she says, sounding amazed.

"That's the age you get stoned," I say.

"Not where I come from," she says indignantly.

We get halfway down the path to the next house when the sprinkler system comes on, soaking us.

Amber is furious.

"And that's illegal too," she says. "Breaking the water rules."

When we get to the door, they're pretending not to be home and we have to brave the sprinklers down the path again. I offer her my jacket, but she says no.

No one's home in the next house, either. Her hair is damp and clinging to her face. She looks increasingly miserable, increasingly beautiful.

"So where do you come from?" I ask.

"Knoxville," she says after a pause.

"Where's that?" I ask, not entirely ignorant.

"It's in Tennessee," she says.

"Cool," I say, "it's a cool place."

"What do you, an Irishman, know about Tennessee?" she asks, finally breaking into a little smile.

"A lot," I say.

"Like?"

"Well, you've got Elvis for a start," I suggest.

"Memphis is totally the other end of the state," she says. "Although we did go on a hellishly long school trip there, if you can believe it."

"Did you go to Graceland?"

"Yeah, we did, it was so boring."

"Did you see the toilet?"

"What toilet?"

"Where Elvis died."

"Elvis died on the toilet?" she asks.

"See, now I know you're an imposter, obviously you're a Communist sleeper agent awaiting the rebirth of the Soviet Union. Every red-blooded American knows that Elvis died on the toilet," I explain.

"Well, I didn't," she says, laughing.

"You should have, your cover's blown. Every Brit knows that Evelyn Waugh and King George the Second died on the privy, we find that kind of thing funny."

"I thought you were Irish," she says.

"It's complicated. Oh, and speaking of that, another Tennessean, Andrew Jackson, President Jackson, he's big in Ireland because his parents came from, uh, Ulster."

I was going to say Carrickfergus again, but realized just in time that this word is far too likely to remind her of Victoria.

"The Hermitage is miles from Knoxville as well," she says, "and don't say Nashville, either, because that's miles away too."

"What about Dollywood?" I say.

"How do you know about Dollywood?" she laughs, amazed again.

"Are you kidding, she's huge in Ireland, country and western in general, huge, Patsy Cline is practically a saint."

"Is that so?" she says, giving me a sideways glance.

"It is."

We're at another house. I'm annoyed, we were just beginning to have a great conversation. My next line was going to be to ask why she didn't have any kind of a southern accent. We ring the bell. A black man answers the door. He's elderly and is wearing a coat as if he's on his way out.

"Yeah?" he asks.

"Hi, I'm an environmental activist in your area tonight to raise consciousness about the plight of the ancient forests."

"That a fact?"

"Yes, sir, it is. Is this an, uh, an issue that concerns you at all?"

"Trees?"

"Yes, the old growth forests, they're being cut down at a—"

"Let me tell you what concerns me. They're cutting food stamps, I can't afford to feed my kids, I hardly see my kids. Hardly ever see them. I've been unemployed for six months and there ain't no work."

He stares at me, waiting for me to reply, but I can't say anything. I look at Amber, she does her rap like a good 'un, closing back to the fifty-dollar memberships.

"I'll take a leaflet," he says politely.

I give him a couple of leaflets and say goodbye and we walk back down the path again.

"I can't believe this," Amber mutters under her breath.

Perhaps this is the first time she's ever met people immune to her charms. And we're both cold. She looks totally pissed off. Wet, lovely, and miserable, her ponytail being blown about in the wind. Her nipples erect under her sweatshirt.

"Sure you don't want to get a coffee or something?"

I ask, putting my hand on her elbow to prevent her walking. She looks at me and shakes her head.

"Charles would be upset if we stop now, a few more streets," she says quietly.

"This is getting us nowhere," I protest.

"I know," she says.

"But look down at the next street. It doesn't look at all inviting," I say.

She looks where I'm pointing. Broken windows and screen doors, refuse and bits of furniture on the sidewalk and on the barren lawns.

"Come on, Amber, we're done here, it's nine-thirty, this has been a pretty disastrous night, we'll go get something to eat and meet everyone else back at the van, hope they did better," I say.

Amber is resigned and nods. A blond hair comes loose and falls on her face, she pushes it back violently, like a drill sergeant pushing a soldier back in formation.

"They won't have done any better," she says after a minute or two.

"Why not?"

"Well, uh, do you ever go to the theater?"

"Not really."

"I love the theater, never get to go. Don't you love it?"

"I might love it, I just haven't experienced it," I say.

"Well, anyway, did you ever hear of a play called *Glengarry Glen Ross*?"

"No, never heard of it," I tell her.

"It's about these real estate men and they cold-call people, but they're all after the Glengarry leads, people who actually want to buy real estate. Well, we normally go to neighborhoods which are on the GOP list, people who have contributed to Republican causes before, like the Glengarry leads, people who are interested, so that's why we've been doing quite well, but Robert thought tonight we could just try a random neighborhood in the suburbs to see how we do. See how it works out."

"Yeah, worked out great," I say.

She looks at me. Laughs.

"What was that you said about something warm to drink?"

Five minutes later we're at a strip mall. Most of the stores are closed, but there is a pizza place that's still open. We go in, order a slice each and coffee. There are only a few customers, so we've no trouble getting a table.

"So Tennessee," I say.

"Yup," she says, biting into her pizza with obvious relish.

"What happened to your accent?"

"I moved to New Jersey when I was ten, my dad worked for a power company."

"What? So really you're a Jersey girl?" I say, surprised.

"Well, I don't know about that, I was born in Tennessee," she says a bit defensively.

"I get it, you're one of those people ashamed of Jersey, so you say you're from Tennessee?"

"I'm not ashamed, I just feel more like a southern girl, at heart," she says with that infectious grin.

"Yeah?" I say, gently mocking her.

"No, look, I lived in the south for eleven years, barely six or seven in Jersey before I went to college in Boston," she says.

"You met Charles at Harvard?"

"Yes, how did you know that?" she says.

"I just guessed. You mentioned that he went there too, when Robert talked about ROTC."

"You're quick," she says.

"No, not at all," I say.

"I met him there. He was teaching a class on economics, it was very boring. I was a science major, you know, but I thought I'd try something different."

"He was a professor?"

"No, don't be silly. He was a graduate student. You never get a professor, ever. You'll see, you'll get taught by PhDs at Red Rocks."

"Oh, yeah, I think someone said something about that. Term doesn't start for a few weeks yet. Uh, so you loved his class and you married him?"

"Do you want to hear the whole boring story?" she says, completely distracted by her pizza, which is dripping melted cheese everywhere. She dabs her mouth with a lead violinist's fingers. Again, that feeling about her. Those vulnerable eyes. And those toned arms, like the skin of an F16.

"I do want to hear the whole story, you seem like a terrific couple," I say.

"Thank you. Well, ok, Charles got his PhD, left Harvard, we hadn't gone out then at all, in fact, I don't think he liked me. He gave me a C, which screwed my GPA. He went on to Yale Law School. Then he moved back to Colorado. Went to work at the law firm. He's from here, you know. Anyway, he and Robert set up CAW and worked very hard to get it off the ground, everyone thinks their dad does everything, but they hardly see him. It was all their own work."

"So I believe," I say.

"It was. Anyway, it was the most bizarre coincidence, I left college and I didn't know what I was going to do with my life and I did a few things in marketing and in PR but nothing really exciting and my mom went, uh, had been in the hospital, she had an accident, and it was a very bad time and I was skiing at Vail and who should I run into but Charles, who remembers me from that class. And I tell him he ruined my GPA and he laughs and he tells me what he's doing, he's just set up this organization and it's really struggling and he says I should come work for him, and I do and it's then that we fall in love and get married. Just like that. And CAW becomes this big success and everything works out."

She finishes her speech as she finishes her slice. Telling it all has completely transformed her mood. She's said it like it's some Horatio Alger story of rags to riches rather than what it is, bored kids of a millionaire, fucking around with other people's money so they can slime their way into Congress. And once again I wonder how much she knows. Everything? Does she support Charles, even if it means murder?

"But someone told me you don't work at CAW anymore. And yet here you are out on the coal face?" I say.

"Yes, after we got married Charles decided it wasn't a good idea for two married people to be in the same working environment, so I quit and we hired a brilliant girl, from your part of the world, actually; but now with the move to Denver we need all the help we can get, so I've had to chip in."

"You've got an Irish girl working for you? I never saw her around the office," I say, sounding excited and surprised.

"Actually, we've had a bit of bad luck with that really. We had two terrible things happen in the last few weeks. No one's mentioned it to you?"

"No."

"No. I suppose that's for the best. It was just terrible, right when we were moving from Boulder to Denver. Awful."

"Ok, you have to tell me what happened, you can't leave it like that," I say.

"We had two people killed. They were both murdered in their own apartments, people broke in and killed them, as brazen as that, one of them was in broad daylight. Mexicans. I think they must all be part of a gang or something."

"So what, did they steal their stuff?"

"I think that was the reason, burglary, it was awful, if

anyone robbed me, I'd just tell them to take every-thing, you know, there's no point in dying over a purse or something," she said, and shivered.

"Yeah."

"It's this town, you never know which are the good neighborhoods and which are the bad. They all look the same, don't they? Vulgar, tedious place in many ways. I never really go out anywhere and I exercise at the gym."

"I see a good bit of the city, it seems ok," I say.

"I don't care for it. Any break we have, we go to Vail. I'll bet you know more about Denver than I do and I've lived here three years," she says, sucks down some more of her coffee and plays with the melted cheese on her plate. It's kind of sexy. But then everything she does is kind of sexy.

"What time is it?" she asks.

"A quarter to ten, we don't have to go over there for a while yet."

"Do you want to split another slice?" she asks.

"Ok," I say.

She gets up and goes over to get one. The first slice was hard enough going down, but I want her to be happy. She comes back and plonks the half a slice on my plate.

"It's very good pizza for the sticks," she says.

"What was the Irish girl's name, it's a small world, I might know her?" I ask.

"Victoria something, she wasn't really Irish-Irish, she was Indian, you know, from India, it was a difficult name to pronounce, I met her once, I think, she was nice, she was born in Ireland, but her parents were from India."

"Well, I can't say that I knew any girls like that, our school was pretty white. I don't think we had any immigrants, not even from Scotland or anywhere," I say.

"You would have liked her, she was nice."

"I know this is a grisly topic, but who was the other person that died?"

"Oh, Hans was a vice president in charge of mass mailing. He was a bit of a drinker, no one's quite sure what happened. He fell off his balcony. They saw him arguing with two Mexican men or something. The police shot at them, still looking for them. The whole business is just awful. You're hardly touching your pizza," she says.

"To tell you the truth, I'm not that hungry."

"You said you would split a slice."

"I only said that because I knew you really wanted one," I say, giving her a big grin.

She laughs and wrinkles up her nose in mock rage.

"Well, I am tricked and angry," she says.

"Apologies," I say. "Look, why don't you have it?"

She thinks about it for a second or two.

"You're not eating it?"

"Nope."

She grabs the pizza and bites into it.

"No sense food going to waste," she says.

I really enjoy watching her eat. She finishes the slice with obvious delight and wipes her hands.

"What do they eat in Ireland? Corned beef and cabbage?" she asks.

"Actually, no, I'd never heard of that till I came here. But the diet is just awful, anyway. Fried everything. Fried sausage, bacon, eggs, potato bread for breakfast, chips for lunch, fish and chips for dinner. Lot of butter, lot of cream. Blood pudding, ice cream. Beer. Belfast is like *Logan's Run*, no one's alive over thirty, they all have heart attacks."

She laughs a little.

"Maybe the Catholic guilt kills them," she says.

"Well, not us, my parents were hippies, they were Jewish, but we didn't get any religion at all."

"Is O'Neill a Jewish name?"

"Grandfather a convert," I say.

"Really," she says, looking intrigued. "Didn't you get teased in school?"

"Not really, no one paid me any attention at school, I did well in my subjects, flew under the radar, everyone thought I was just a bit of a weirdo goof-off."

"Well, we like weirdo goof-offs in America," she says charmingly.

"I hope so," I say.

"We do," she says, reaches across the table and pats my cheek.

She's being ironic, but the gesture is so intimate, it takes me aback for a second or two. Her fingers are sticky.

"I got cheese on you," she says, grabs a napkin, wipes it off.

"Thanks."

"Oh my God, Alexander, a long, horrible, freezing night, huh? Every goddamn door was worse than the one before," she says, giggling. A lovely sound, the opposite of her brother-in-law's guffaw. Hers is like a string quartet improvising on a theme by Mozart.

"I know," I say.

"I don't normally do the doors, I usually sit in the van with Charles to keep him company. Please tell me people aren't that eccentric."

"I had a guy with a gun open the door the other night," I say.

"No?" she says, appalled.

"Yes," I insist.

"What did you do?"

"I played it cool, he thought he was James Bond. Bit bloody frightening."

"My God, did you tell Charles?"

"No, it was my very first night, I didn't want to sound highly strung, you know?"

"If it had happened to me, I think I would have resigned on the spot," she says, laughing. I sit in my chair and she plays with the cheese, stringing it from the plate to her mouth, completely unself-consciously.

"Ten o'clock, we better get back to the others and their tales of woe," Amber says.

I go outside as she dashes to the bathroom. I watch her through the window. On the way out, she flashes her smile at the pizza man and he grins at her and comes around the counter to open the door. In the moment when he's obscured by a pillar she deftly puts her hand in the tip jar, takes out half the notes, and puts them in her pocket.

"Thank you," she says breezily, as she leaves.

❖   ❖   ❖

We had walked nearly the whole way back to the rendezvous point when Amber noticed black spirals of smoke coming from the stoner kids' house.

"That's not pot, is it?" Amber asked.

"No, it's not, their fucking house is on fire," I said, and began to run.

We got to the house in seconds, but now the fire had taken hold. Sheets of flame coming from underneath the front door, a side window buckling from the heat— all the neighbors bloody oblivious.

"Amber, go to the closest house, call nine-nine-nine," I said.

"What's nine-nine-nine?" Amber asked.

"Jesus, whatever it is in this country, the fire brigade, call the bloody fire brigade."

"Nine-one-one," Amber said in a daze.

"Yes, just fucking go."

I had to physically shove her in the direction of the house next door.

It looked bad. The wind and the open windows had really stoked the fire and as I got to the front step I was hit by a wall of heat. I staggered back, put my jacket over my arm and head. I pulled my shirtsleeve down over my fingers and pulled the screen door. The front door was unlocked, the handle searingly hot. I pushed it open.

A horrible sight.

The kitchen was on fire at the back of the house and the walls and carpet were burning. Jets of orange flame shooting up the stairs.

The living room was in to the right. Stairs to the left. Impossible to breathe. I ran down the hall, got about two feet, dropped to a crawl, fumbled for the handle, and shoved my way into the living room. My lungs aching, sparks falling on my back and hair.

Both kids lying on the living room floor, unconscious. The room wasn't on fire yet, but thick black smoke poured in from a door to the kitchen. I stayed down on my knees, breathing. Behind me a huge tube of fire came hurtling down the hall, and I slammed the door. Something crashed down in the back room.

A couple of breaths of that smoke could knock me for six. But I had no choice. I got to my feet, picked up the TV set from off an upturned wooden crate, threw it through the front window. I kicked away the rest of the glass, got to the floor again, breathed. Stood. I picked up the first kid in a fireman's lift, hoisted him on my shoulder, ran with him to the broken window, tossed him out.

The second kid groaned.

"It's going to be ok, you little shit," I said, and picked him up too.

My legs buckled, but I managed to get him across the room. I tossed him out and leaped after him into the garden. The street full of neighbors now. They dragged the boys out of the garden, helped me to my feet and down the path. A couple of them clapped and patted me on the back.

I dry-heaved and spat, someone gave me a water bottle.

I saw Amber. She ran over and threw her arms around me.

"Oh my God, oh my God," she kept saying, over and over.

Two fire tenders arrived and in a couple of minutes they had the blaze under control and out. An easy one for the fire department, considering the number of wildfires they were increasingly having to deal with in this second summer of drought.

A cop showed up and paramedics took the kids to the hospital. They both had suffered smoke inhalation but would be fine. A paramedic asked me if I wanted to go to the hospital but I said no. He gave me a hit of O_2. I coughed and heaved and he gave me Gatorade instead. Amber helped me up.

"How did you do that, how did you know how to do that?" Amber asked, incredulous.

I knew, but I didn't tell her. My cop training had taken over. I'd been a cop for six years, not six months. It wasn't me, it was automatic pilot.

"I don't know," I said, "it just seemed like the right thing to do."

"Are you ok? Are you hurt? Maybe you should go to the hospital? What do you think?"

"I'm fine," I said.

While I recovered, we sat there on the curb with all the other onlookers. Amber held my hand and give me sips from a water bottle. A couple of minutes later a police officer came over to interview me. Tall, skinny, alert, he looked a little like trouble. I got to my feet. He asked me if I was ok. I said I was. He asked what exactly had happened. I began to tell him as simply as possible. He wrote everything down and in the middle of a sentence he suddenly stopped me.

"I know you," he said.

"You do?"

"Yeah, I know you from somewhere, I can't quite place it."

"Well, I don't think I know you," I said, guessing that the cop recognized me from the bloody artist's-impression wanted posters down at his station house.

"Yeah, it'll come to me in a minute. What's your name?"

"Um, it's Seamus Holmes," I said.

Amber looked at me, startled, but said nothing.

"Where do you live?"

"Uh, two-oh-eight Broadway, apartment twenty-six," I said.

"Ok, Seamus, what kind of accent is that?"

"Irish."

"Irish, huh?"

"Yeah."

"Not Australian, right?"

"No."

"Hold on a minute," he said, and walked off.

He went to his car and said something into his police radio. I was getting quite scared now. He walked back slowly. His face expressionless, giving nothing away.

"Just something I had to take care of there," he said.

"Ok," I said.

"And what do you do for a living?" the cop asked.

"Uh, I'm a schoolteacher, I coach, uh, soccer," I said, the first thing that came into my head. Also a stupid thing. If he asked what school I was at, I was sure to blunder.

"What school you at?" he asked.

"Kennedy," I said.

"Is that near Washington High?" he asked.

"Reasonably near," I said.

"Yeah, I know it, ok, and you just saw the fire and went barging in?"

"Yes," I said.

He nodded, was about to ask something else, and then his face lit up.

"Sheeat, I remember now, you play in the Cherry Creek Soccer League, right? I knew I recognized your face from something."

"I play soccer," I agreed.

The cop grinned. "I knew I knew you from somewhere."

"Yeah," I said.

"I better cancel that radio call," he said to himself.

"What?"

He looked at me. His face much more relaxed.

"Oh, nothing, it was to do with something else. I knew I knew you. Shit. And, hey, man, before the fire department gives you a lecture, which they will, I just want to say you did good getting those kids out of there."

"Thanks."

A TV crew from Channel 7 showed up searching for people to interview. They were getting in the way of the fire crew, and the cop looked distracted.

"Officer, is it ok if we leave, it's getting late?" I asked.

"Hold on," he said, not looking at me, "I gotta just take care of this and then I can let you go."

The Channel 7 crew marched right onto the lawn, started to do a live feed. The cop straightened his tie. This was his chance to get on TV. He marched over and chatted to them for a couple of minutes.

And then, to my absolute amazement, who should get out of a red Toyota Camry on the other side of the street but Detective David Redhorse. All five feet of him. Jesus Christ. Now I understood. Redhorse was looking for us. He had stuck up a wanted poster at the cop shop or put the word out asking the police to hold for questioning any young men with Australian-sounding accents. So after Klimmer's murder, Redhorse had gone to the train station to stake it out. He had seen the pair of us run onto the train and decided to follow. We seemed a little suspicious. But then we'd talked to him and his suspicions had been allayed a little. He thought we were ok. I was even injured, but it wasn't a gunshot wound and the facts they knew at that stage were that the suspects were Hispanic and (because the cop had fired and seen me fall) that one of them had been hit by a bullet.

Still, something had been nagging at Redhorse, he'd checked out our story and hadn't liked it and then come looking for us at the Holburn Hotel. Of course we weren't there. It had clearly worried him. Two Australian boys who perhaps looked a little like the two Spanish boys that had killed Klimmer. John had cut his hair, but there was nothing he could do about his height. Maybe it didn't mean anything, but it was something that he wanted to follow up.

And Redhorse himself scared me. A digger. A good peeler. His Denver Nuggets cap was on slantwise, his jeans and T-shirt were dirty, like he'd come from dinner or yard work, but appearances were deceiving, I could see that.

Redhorse lit himself a cigarette, took in the scene, and started making his way across to the cop.

"Let's go," I said to Amber.

I walked her fast along the street. We hurried down a long alley.

When we turned the street corner, Amber grabbed me. She led me under a big overhang at the entrance to an elementary school. She threw me up against the wall.

"You lied to him," she said.

"I did."

"You're an illegal immigrant. All that stuff on your

résumé is fake, isn't it? Everything except for the address on your paycheck."

"Not everything was a—"

She kissed me. She thrust her body against me and kissed me hard. Leaning up on her tiptoes, biting my lips. She took my hands and placed them on her breasts and we moved together backward into the shadow of the overhang. Her hands searched under my shirt and she touched my back and chest with her fingernails. She grabbed my ass with her right hand and pulled me closer. With her left she began unbuttoning my jeans.

"Right here," she said. "Right now."

"Madness," I said as I grabbed for the zipper on her black jeans. She stopped me and pulled down her jeans and then her panties. She held me and shoved me inside her. She was dripping wet. I leaned back against the wall and she leaned on me and climbed on me and I fucked her the way only a junkie can. Need and desire and displacement and hunger and concentration and pain.

"You're killing me," she said.

"I—"

"Don't stop," she said.

And when I came, she came, and I groaned and she yelled and bit her finger and laughed.

"I'm breathless," she said.

The whole thing couldn't have taken five minutes. She kissed me and zipped herself up. I buttoned my jeans and looked at her and caught my breath. Amber had a little crazy in her: this, the stolen money in the pizzeria. A Venus in a sweatshirt. Everything you could ever think and more. And yet a sadness about her too, a sense of loss, a hunger that needed filled.

"We better get back," she said.

She took my hand and we walked in silence along the streets, past the bungalows and mock Tudors and ranch-style houses, past mailboxes and strip malls and dog walkers and lovers and illicit men watering their lawn under cover of night.

She let go of my hand when we made it to the van. All the others inside, waiting impatiently. Robert wound down his window.

"Come on, you two, it's been a trying evening for everyone, l-let's get home," he yelled.

I sat near the window. I stank of smoke. Everyone was polite, ignored it, didn't mention it. Amber said nothing.

They dropped me on Colfax.

I watched them turn the van.

Amber in the front passenger seat.

You should run, Alex, I told myself. Run, now. Now that you've seen Redhorse. You should go.

Time had passed since Klimmer's death and the cop resources were stretched thin. We could have gotten out of town easily. A million different ways. And yet I knew it was too late. The hooks were in.

Amber.

Stupid to remain.

I knew I wouldn't tell John about Redhorse and I wouldn't tell him about her.

The van drove off. Through the window I could see her brushing that golden hair.

I stood there. Coughed.

The whores. The homeless. The wide street. The black sky. The taillights diminishing. Standing there staring after the van, even when it had long since gone.

9: THE SUTRA OF DESIRE

Haze covers Lookout Mountain. A calm sky. Aegean blue. Jets bending diagonals. The stillness becoming deeper and more taut. A silent vacancy. An absence from airport to aqueduct. It's early yet. A stray dog. A tailless cat. A girl in a black stole.

The foothills close as a spider on the ceiling.

Hawk's-eye view.

A street made more straight by the perfect right angles formed at intersections. Light sucked sideways from the vast eastern sun.

Worry has you by the hair.

Enemies from compass point to azimuth.

But not on this morning of ivory cloud, azure heaven, and the friendly boiling local star.

And only a moment ago this was the mythic plain, a migration path for bison and the Comanche nation.

Imagine an archer the instant before release. Before the Spanish, before the horses. Poised and under discipline of sudden death. That same feeling. The template for success or disaster. Blood, either way.

Mosquitoes above the windowsill.

The dead sunflowers.

The *thock* of arrows in the stampeding herd.

The braves running on to catch more game. The butchers remaining with their long knives of antler and bone.

"Noo nu puetsuku u punine," they call to one another before they part.

That was then. The city's pulse a drumbeat of cars and feet. A million people breathing in unison as the alarm sounds seven.

It's not worse, merely different.

The right angles, symmetry. The smell of cannabis, garbage, eucalyptus. Urine.

My father would say that the Comanche missed out on the great secret of the universe. The linking of the five most important numbers in mathematics by the formula $e^{i\pi} + 1 = 0$.

My father.

What does he know?

Nothing.

Voices in the living room.

The pair of them.

Laughing, talking.

And then the silence betrays a more intimate encounter still.

A knock. A third voice.

Two men and a girl.

Happy.

She's cooking.

They want me to come out but they think I'm sleeping. They're letting me lie in. Still, the smell of food is bringing me back to life.

Even a junkie has to eat sometimes.

But if I don't go out, the world out there can't hurt me.

If I don't go out.

I go out. . . .

I don't know what Ethiopians eat for breakfast, but it seemed unlikely that it was this. Areea had made us French toast with fried eggs, links sausages, and bacon. Faux maple syrup and coffee, too. Pat and I didn't have the greatest appetites at the best of times, but John wolfed his portion and there was no denying that everything had a delicious flavor.

All very amiable. Areea in the middle of a story about her life in Ethiopia and why, of all places, they'd come to Denver. Apparently, it had the second-biggest Ethiopian community in America, though it was hard to concentrate since she was wearing a miniskirt that showed off her long, dark, beautiful legs, which complemented her flashing eyes and beautiful smile.

Still, everything clicked along until she and John started kissing again.

"Not at the breakfast table," I protested.

"Alexander is right," Areea said, removing John's big hands from her bum.

John gave her a kiss on the cheek, and turned around to look at us.

"Well, boys, are ye not eating, how's the grub?" he asked, smacking his lips.

"Everything is just wonderful," Pat said.

"It is," I agreed. "You're a great cook, Areea."

"Oh, it's nothing," Areea said, "American food is easy to make."

She went to the kitchen to get more coffee.

"Isn't she great?" John moaned happily with a goofy expression on his face.

"Jesus, you're not in love with her, are you?" I whispered under my breath.

"I might be," John said with a grin.

"You bloody eejit. You realize, of course, the relationship has no future," I said.

"What is it with you, Alex? You're such a grumpy boots every morning," John replied.

Pat lit himself a cigarette and stared up at the ceiling. I clenched my fist under the table. I felt I had been very patient with John. Not one time had I brought up the fact that he had pushed a man over a balcony and bloody topped him.

"I'll support her, I'll look after her, I'll get a job," John said thoughtfully.

"Yeah, you're doing a fine job now," I muttered. "Me working my ass off all day long and you smoking pot and making love, living the life of bloody Reilly."

"Why is someone else's happiness such a burden to you? It's the fucking ketch, robs you of feeling for your fellow man, don't you think, Pat?"

"I'm keeping out of this, boys," Pat said, and continued staring at a point above his head.

I took a sip of the coffee. John was a wanker, but maybe he was on to something there. I shrugged. I didn't want this to develop into an argument. The situation was as much my fault as his.

"Sorry, John. Look, my head hurts, my sinuses are aching, my feet are killing me from all the walking. Problems, you know?"

"The sinus problem is from the pollution," Pat said. "They should be dealing with that and the fucking drought, not going after minorities in this state."

Areea came over with another pot of coffee.

"Wonderful," Pat said, and gave her a grin.

"You have sore feet?" Areea asked me, and we all reddened with embarrassment, hoping that she hadn't heard the rest of the conversation.

"Yeah, I do, I never walk this much normally."

Areea took a long look at my feet and offered to give me a foot massage. I looked at John, I didn't want to get into macho head games with him, but John nodded to show he didn't care. I retired to the couch and Areea proceeded to torture the soles of my feet with her incredibly strong fingers. Ten minutes later she was done and my feet felt much better.

"Wow, that's really amazing, you're totally multitalented," I said.

"That's not all she's good at," John said. He and Areea dissolved into giggles.

"Honestly don't know what she sees in you, she can't even get a green card off you," I said to him.

Areea asked Pat if he wanted a massage too. Pat refused out of politeness because his feet were in a bad way, but Saint Areea insisted, ignored his calluses and an open sore and gave him a gentler massage than me, but still effective nonetheless.

My watch said twelve and, sadly, it was time to leave this scene of domestic tranquillity. Pat begged me to have at least one martini before I went, but I couldn't. I'd had a weird high this morning, inverted and almost a bad trip, and I wanted to stay off the booze. It turned out that the heroin supply in this town was very patchy and you never really knew what you were getting. Manuelito, my dealer, always complained about it. Around here the crack cocaine was of the finest quality but the smack could be dodgy. Smackheads were all in New York: singers, starving artists, Goth girls, anorexic fashion models.

I was reluctant to go, though. I was tired and this was the best part of the day, hanging out in the morning with John, Pat, and Areea, chatting, messing about, sharing the fire escape with Pat, looking down on the world.

Of course, last night I hadn't been able to sleep. Two nights of that now. Ever since Amber.

Amber. Hypocritical me telling John off.

For it was all about her.

It's an old trope, the peeler who falls for one of his suspects or a witness or a victim. It's a cliché. They even tell you about it in the police academy, apparently it's very common in domestic abuse cases.

I should have had more sense, anyway. After seeing Redhorse, I should have scarpered. Smart thing to do. But Amber was the magnet. She had caught me.

Something about her that could not be denied. Smart, beautiful, sexy. Maybe if I'd been older I would have been immune. I should have run. But I didn't want to. And there was that feeling I'd had that she was somehow Victoria Patawasti's polar opposite. A looking-glass version of her, a Victoria in the parallel world. WASP, blonde, prim as a counterpoint to Victoria. Both incredibly clever, but Amber lacked Victoria's wit and Amber did not have Victoria's sense of humor, how could she? Victoria, who had been the only Paki in the whole school, darker even than her brothers, she needed a defense mechanism right from the start. She'd verbally taken apart anyone who'd screwed with her. Sarcastic, ironic, cool, in fact. I shouldn't have let her go. And this was before ketch and Mum's illness— no excuses. I suppose I was too immature, too caught up in my own universe.

Too clever by half, the teachers used to say about me, and they said the same about her. But she went on to be head girl. I wasn't subtle, that was my trouble, how could I be, growing up in that crazy house with those pseudo-hippie parents and aloof siblings—subtle would have gone unnoticed. And also, she was out of my league, destined to go to Oxford University, graduate with a first, and eventually be head-hunted by a nonprofit who would offer her a green card, free rent, a good salary, responsibilities, rapid advancement, and a chance to live in the USA. Aye. Fucked up then, fucking up now.

I sighed, went out.

Colfax Avenue. Heat, light, pollution, three Mexican guys being questioned by a motorcycle cop. A protester outside Planned Parenthood wearing a fetus billboard. Bikers in the park dealing pot.

The CAW building.

The Haitian concierge sitting at his desk and reading a green pamphlet, which was the latest security briefing from the Denver Police Department. He looked at me, smiled.

"*Ça va?*" he asked.

"Ok," I said, hoping there wasn't a description of me in there.

I pushed the button for the fifth floor. The elevator dinged. I got on. The day began.

◦　◦　◦

That night, for the second time that week, I was paired with Amber Mulholland. We were soliciting in a town called Evergreen right up in the foothills. Big houses, lawns, American flags, kids on bicycles. It was odd that Amber and I would be together, for a couple of reasons. First, I had been working at CAW sufficientl long now that I didn't need training or a partner anymore. Second, Amber told me when she did go out she did it only to keep Charles company. And yet here we were again. I wasn't complaining. I hadn't seen her for a couple of days, not since the night she'd caught me in a lie and I'd seen her steal and we'd rescued the kids and had hard, crazy sex up against a wall. I wanted to see her, I needed to see her.

She was wearing a white crew neck over khaki slacks. A little cooler here in the foothills. Needless to say, she looked stunning. We walked away from the van, and when the others were behind us, she turned to me. Her face flushed, rosy, biting her lip.

"Alex, listen to me, I lost my head the other night. I love Charles, I don't know what happened, but it can't ever happen again. I blame myself, the fire, the excitement, I don't know, I was overcome, if you value my friendship you won't mention it, please."

I didn't know what I was expecting her to say. But not this. Not the brush-off.

"Ok," I said.

"Friends?" she asked, and offered me her hand.

"Friends," I said, concealing my amazement at her behavior. It seemed so wrong, so immature, so silly. And yet maybe that's what adults did. We walked in silence for a half minute and took out our maps.

"I think we'll do better tonight. Tonight we have the Glengarry leads," Amber said with a little smile. . . .

She proved correct. A short night, but good work. Two hours, ten members each. A hundred and fifty bucks for me.

It was only on the way back to the van that we managed a real conversation. I tried to be lighthearted.

"You know what this neighborhood reminds me of?" I asked her.

"What?"

"It's the sort of place a lot of Spielberg movies begin in, you know, picket fences and kids playing and stuff and then something ominous happens, aliens come, or a poltergeist, or government agents, something like that."

"I don't really go to the movies," she said.

"No?"

"No."

"Oh, that's right. You said you like the theater," I said.

She nodded and the conversation died. With annoyance, she brushed the hair away from her face. How dare one strand of hair be out of place again. She knocked her hair clip to the ground. I picked it up, gave it to her. Our fingers touched. She smiled at me. I swallowed.

"Thank you," she said.

"Look, about the other night, I'm glad you didn't say anything to the police," I said.

"It's ok, I understand. You're from Ireland, you want to work, and you don't have all the papers, nothing to be ashamed of," she said, sympathetically.

"Not every American takes that attitude," I said.

"Well, I do, I come from pretty straitened circumstances myself," she said.

"Your parents weren't well off? Thought you went to Harvard?"

"I worked hard," she said firmly.

"Tell me about your background, if you don't mind," I said, and again she returned my smile.

"It's very complicated," she said carefully. She blinked a couple of times, angled her head away from me.

"I'd like to know," I said.

"Well, my parents were divorced, you know," she said.

"That can be very hard on a kid, did you have brothers or sisters?"

"No."

"What did your parents do for a living?" I asked.

"Dad was a mechanic, he went to college part-time, and he became a union rep and did well. Mom worked in a place called Dairy Queen, which you probably haven't heard of, I haven't seen any in Denver."

"So you were solid working class?" I asked with a smile, since some people can take offense at that kind of question.

"I suppose so, I don't have a, uh . . ."

"What?"

"Nothing."

"What?" I insisted.

"I don't know why I'm telling you this, but I don't have a relationship with my dad, we haven't spoken in years."

"How did that happen?"

"Well, he divorced my mom and he's a real operator, he had good lawyers and she got screwed over and got nothing. That's the first thing. And then when I was going to college, he'd promised he would pay but he stopped paying. He wouldn't give me anything until I went to see him, to beg in person, but I didn't want to do that because of what he did to Mom."

"I'm sorry. He sounds like a bastard," I said.

"Yeah. He was, still is, probably. I don't want to talk about it. What did your parents do?"

"My parents were both teachers, math and English. Dad's retired, Mum's dead," I said.

"Oh, I'm sorry, uh, what did your mom die of? I mean, if you don't mind . . ."

"She had cervical cancer, it was misdiagnosed for a while and when it was diagnosed it was probably too late, they tried some alternative treatments, but those things don't work," I said simply.

"I'm very sorry to hear that," she said. "How old were you when she died?"

"I was eighteen, it was my second year of university, it was really hard, my siblings were in England and my dad was doing all this political shit, Mum was practically on her own, it was awful, really. She was tough, though, she said we should all get on with our lives."

"I'm so sorry," Amber said, and stopped for a minute to give me a look of real sympathy. She touched my hand again. I squeezed hers.

"My poor mother might as well be dead," she said, her face sad with the memory.

"What's the matter?"

"She's only sixty-eight, but she has early-onset Alzheimer's, hardly recognizes me, it's awful. Charles had her flown out here to Denver, to a wonderful place. Oh, my goodness. Actually, I don't want to talk about that, either, it's terrible."

I nodded sympathetically. But sharing that had brought me closer to her.

"To be honest, I don't really like it here in Denver that much," she offered after a while. "It's a poor excuse for a city."

"If you don't like it, why do you stay?" I asked.

"Oh, Charles has to be here, for political reasons, you wouldn't really understand. All politics is local in this country. We have to be here."

"And does Charles have political ambitions?"

"I suppose so, don't we all?"

"Not me. You don't really hear about many national figures coming out of Colorado, though."

"No, no, you don't, the last was Gary Hart and we all know what happened to him."

"The girl on the boat, that scandal thing," I said.

"Monkey Business," she said.

I swore inwardly, for we were already back at the van. Everyone else there, Charles beaming, wearing Dockers, deck shoes and a button-down Oxford shirt. His hair gelled. He looked younger, like the millionaire commodore's wanker son at a yacht club function. And of course he *was* a millionaire's son and he *was* a wanker. I had to bite down a real hatred for the man. He bounded over, kissed Amber, shook my hand.

"Well, folks, hope you're ready to party," he said.

"What is it, Charles?" Amber asked excitedly.

"We just signed our ten thousandth member," he said, and gave her another big kiss.

"That's wonderful," Amber said, her face lighting up with pleasure.

"It is, ten thousand members and the timing

couldn't be better. Momentum is what we need right now. And we have it. Ten thousand members, if we could use the mailing list and hit them up for a hundred bucks a pop, we could have a million dollars in our PAC before anyone else even begins to raise money. . . ."

Charles suddenly realized he was being indiscreet. He looked at me and forced a grin. He turned to Amber, kissed her again.

"Darling, Robert and I have been thinking, we're going to have a big party, honey, tell me it's ok, but the offices are so boring, I was really thinking we could go to our house, it's big and nice, comfortable, everyone would love it, but if you don't think so, we could go to the offices, tell me what you think?"

"If that's what you want, Charles," Amber said a little reluctantly.

"Terrific, I'll tell Robbie and Abe," Charles said, and ran back to the others.

"So we're going to your place?" I asked Amber.

"It's not as clean as I would have liked, the maid only comes every other day, I hope we're not embarrassed," Amber said.

o o o

Amber was not embarrassed. The house was spectacular. An Edwardian pile on Eighth and Pennsylvania, the heart of Capitol Hill, a block from the governor's mansion. Easily six thousand square feet, with a big open-plan living room decorated in what I took to be southwestern style: Indian artifacts, prints, throw rugs, pastel furniture. A Georgia O'Keeffe painting of an adobe house. Pottery that looked to be pre-Columbian. It must have cost a bloody fortune, which meant the brothers couldn't really have been as poor as Klimmer claimed, although wealth is a relative thing. Perhaps they weren't that well off in comparison to their fabulously wealthy father. But even so, all of us humble campaigners were awed.

Twenty of us in here easily, but we hardly filled the space. Charles ordered a crate of champagne and food deliveries from several restaurants. We all mucked in, setting a table with caviar, French cheese, Mexican dips, hot plates, paté, and the like. After a couple of minutes I found Charles, gulping from a flute of champagne.

"Wonderful house," I said, "just the place for a future congressman."

"What?" he asked, grinning merrily.

"You're moving into politics, I hear," I said.

"Alex, walls have ears, I see. Don't breathe a word of that. Please. But yes, it's an exciting time, a very exciting time. You know, Robert thinks they're going to ask me to give a speech at the GOP leadership seminar in Aspen on the sixteenth. I don't know how I'll manage it. Can you imagine, six months ago no one had heard of CAW. We couldn't buy publicity and now, well, I hate to bring it into the realm of the personal, but things are looking up for me. I should have listened to Amber a long time ago."

Charles was getting a little excited. I got him another champagne.

"So Amber wanted you to go into politics?" I asked, handing him the glass.

"She's very clever, Amber, did I tell you how we met? Completely by accident, although I'd sort of known her before. Teacher-student relationships, frowned upon, you know. Anyway, yes, what a time. The first thing was to move CAW from Boulder to Denver. It seems like years rather than weeks ago. Couple of setbacks. We had those two terrible tragic incidents. Good God."

His tongue was really loosening, but before he could tell me any more Amber appeared, took Charles by the arm, and tried to lead him over to the window.

"Sorry, Alex," she said, "there's something we have to take care of."

"No, don't go," I said, "I never get to talk to the big boss anymore, this is my big chance to weave my way into his consciousness."

"Yeah, what's so important, darling?" Charles said.

"Well, I think we—someone knocked over a glass of champagne, you know what that will do to the carpet," Amber said.

"Oh my God, Amber, leave it, this is a party, Rosita will do it tomorrow. Not tonight, we're celebrating," Charles said.

"Do come on, Charles," Amber insisted.

They both disappeared and, try as I might, I couldn't get into conversation with either of them the rest of the night. The best I could do was Robert, who was not drinking and indeed looked quite somber. He was talking to Abe about politics. I joined the conversation.

"Mind if I butt in? I find the American political system fascinating," I said.

Robert looked me up and down as if deciding whether I was worth speaking to.

"And, Alexander, are you from the North of Ireland or the S-South?" Robert asked.

"The North," I said.

"And that's part of the UK," Abe said.

"Yup."

"So you vote for the London p-parliament," Robert said.

"Yes," I said.

"Interesting. Alex, we were just talking about the elections, here, n-next year," Robert said.

"They vote for the president and the House and the Senate," I said.

"No, not the Senate, Alex, only a third of the S-Senate," Robert said.

"But it will be the big year," Abe said, "a presidential election year. The GOP candidates are already battling it out. Dole will win, of course."

"I know, how could you miss it, it's in all the papers," I said.

"You'd be surprised how many people don't read the p-papers. Or they read exclusively about O. J. Simpson. Only about fifty percent of people eligible to vote actually vote in this country, I think in Ireland it's around seventy to eighty percent."

"I don't know," I said.

"Dole will lose," Abe said, "and Charles will help pull the party back to the center, we'll all do well out of this."

Robert looked at Abe as if he were saying too much.

"Oh, I've told Alex about August sixth, we can trust him," Abe said.

"Good heavens, how many other people have you t-told?"

"Just Alex."

Robert turned to me.

"Alex, p-please don't say anything to anyone. Abe should never have told you. We d-don't know for certain that Wegener is going to announce his r-retirement, it wouldn't do to j-jump the gun."

"He's retiring, Charles'll have the drop on everyone, the state chair wants him, the GOP needs him. Nobody should forget that this is the party of Lincoln and Teddy Roosevelt, not just Reagan and Bush," Abe said.

"I'd rather you didn't t-talk about this," Robert said.

Abe looked a little put out.

"Ok," he said glumly.

"You too, Alex," Robert insisted.

"Won't breathe a syllable," I said.

"Robert, can I have a word?" someone asked.

Robert excused himself and headed across the room. Abe was embarrassed and made an excuse to leave me too.

As illuminating as the conversations with Charles and Robert had been, the real shock story of the night, the real revelation, the real scoop, was to come as the party was winding down and I was on a trip to the bathroom. Never has a bog run been so profitable in my life.

Some people, it is said, keep their Academy Award in the toilet, others provide reading material in a little magazine rack next to the throne, still others attempt to affect a comedic air by plastering the toilet walls with cartoons or purchasing kitschy or otherwise risible bathroom equipment. It is more of a British thing than an American thing. Brits take equal parts delight and shame at the contemplation of bodily functions. But some Americans feel the urge to introduce levity into their bathroom arrangements. Perhaps those who have gone to prestigious Anglophile universities.

The Mulhollands had thought it a good idea to place, on their bathroom wall, framed photographs of themselves in younger days. Preferably those from the awkward teenage years. There was Charles, face covered with acne, standing beside a snowman, whose face he had also unself-consciously covered with pebble acne. There was Amber dressed in a barrister's wig and gown, playing a male part in the operetta *Trial by Jury*. There was a grinning Charles dressed in shorts and a striped jersey standing next to a dozen other boys, in front of a massed bundle of equipment, with the legend "Governor Bright Academy Lacrosse Team, 1973."

Under the photograph in tiny print, each boy's full name was spelled out. Charles William Mulholland, George Rupert Dunleavy, Steven Philip Smith, Alan James Houghton . . .

It took me a second to recall where I'd heard the name Alan Houghton before and then it did come back. Oh yes, I remember. The missing blackmailer.

Hubris, putting a photograph like this on public display?

Not necessarily. Probably no one ever took time to read the names. But even so, I wouldn't have done it. Perhaps Charles wasn't as clever as I thought.

I washed my hands and face, grinned, decided it was time to go.

Robert saw me to the front door and with forced, deliberate calm, I said:

"Wonderful party, mate."

◦   ◦   ◦

The next morning, I skipped the Areea-John lovefest breakfast and Pat's martinis and after a nice hit of Afghani black tar heroin I walked to the Denver Public Library and did a search on Alan Houghton. Nothing. Next I tried the Governor Bright Academy lacrosse team. A lot of stories, but the big one, the one that interested me, happened back in 1973 when Charles would have been sixteen.

The Denver Post gave me the gist, but the *Post* itself had only two short articles and after a couple more questions, it didn't take long before I was looking at the more extensive coverage in microfilmed copies of the *Denver Dispatch,* a now defunct newspaper that had covered the foothill communities to the west of the city.

The *Post* index had told me that an incident involving members of the lacrosse team had happened in May 1973.

Governor Bright Academy dated back to 1890, an all-boys boarding school in the southwest of Denver that, although not in the same league as Andover or Exeter, was far and away the best school in the state and indeed attracted pupils from all over the country. Bright took the boys at age eleven and kept them until they were seventeen. Academics were important, but Bright also encouraged each pupil to take part in a team sport. American football, soccer, baseball, ice hockey, basketball, lacrosse, and even cricket and rugby were offered. Those pupils who couldn't make a team took up fencing or cross-country running or some other similar endeavor. Winter Fridays were devoted to skiing. Although Bright was a boarding school, its regime seemed to be popular with its pupils and almost half went on to Harvard, Yale, or Princeton. Academic excellence was important, but sporting achievement was rewarded with scholarships and other perks.

The lacrosse team was one of the most prestigious in the school. Lacrosse is a game unknown in Ireland, so I did some side research to find out what it was. *Le jeu de la crosse.* A French-named Indian game, popular among private schools. Played by the elite, mainly in the Atlantic states and Colorado.

The incident had happened on May 1, 1973, but had gone unreported by the Post and Denver Dispatch until two days later.

Maggie Prestwick was the daughter of the stable manager. Bright had its own riding school, with a half dozen show horses and another half dozen ponies for trail hiking. Tommy Prestwick, a single father, had a grown-up daughter at college and Maggie, who lived with him in the house over the converted stable block. Tommy had a lot of responsibilities and Maggie, he told reporters, was an independent girl who he thought could look after herself. He hadn't noticed she was missing until the morning of May 2. He called the principal, who called the police. Bright, I suspected, had good relations with the Denver police department and they could be expected to be discreet.

Of course, the outcome of the police search was not good. My heart sank as I read the microfilm.

Along with a grainy picture of a derelict building, the May 3 issue of the *Denver Dispatch* had, as its front page lead, this:

> Margaret Prestwick, the 15-year-old daughter of Tommy Prestwick, the stable manager at Governor Bright Academy, was found dead yesterday evening at the site of Rookery House, a former hotel, a mile from the Bright campus. Police are not releasing details of the incident and a spokesman for the Denver Police Department, Officer Anthony Sut-

cliffe, said that it was "too early to determine the cause of death or whether Margaret Prestwick had been sexually assaulted." However, a spokesman for the Denver Coroner's Office said late last night that Margaret Prestwick had been the victim of foul play. . . .

In the next few days, the *Denver Dispatch* discovered further details of the incident. Margaret Prestwick had not been raped, but she had been sexually assaulted and then strangled. There were no scenes of struggle outside the property and the speculation was that Margaret had known her assailant and had arranged a liaison with him at Rookery House, a hotel that had suffered extensive fire damage years before and had lain empty since. In the weeks that followed, the *Dispatch's* sense of frustration grew as little progress seemed to be made with the crime. The police interviewed many people, but no one was charged and there were no arrests. It must have been an important story within the community, for even two months later, the *Dispatch's* crime reporter, Danny Lapaglia, was still writing about the unsolved murder.

This Fourth of July, the campus of Governor Bright Academy is quiet. School has been out for two weeks and the new term does not begin until after the long summer vacation. When school does begin, the new students at Bright will doubtless have heard of the ghastly events of the first week of May, when the daughter of the school's former stable manager was brutally strangled a mere mile from where this reporter sits. As the weeks have gone by and the Denver police have seemingly run into a wall, it is no wonder that Tommy Prestwick, the murder victim's distraught father, has resigned, leaving Bright Academy to be close to his only surviving daughter in New Orleans. . . .

The story disappeared until November of that year, when Danny Lapaglia came out with a scoop. By this time, though, his article was only the lead on page five.

This reporter has learned that the Denver Police Department interviewed all the members of the Governor Bright lacrosse team in connection with the murder of Margaret Prestwick in May of this year. . . .

The article went on to explain that a tiny piece of a lacrosse team tie had been found in Maggie's teeth. Great significance had been attached to this. Every boy at Bright wore the same school uniform, black blazer, black trousers, white shirt. However, any boy who was a member of a team was permitted to wear his team tie rather than the school tie. If, indeed, the murderer was a member of the lacrosse team, that could leave only thirteen suspects. In Bright there were three soccer teams and two basketball teams, but only one lacrosse team, with ten players and three reserves. Only thirteen pupils in the whole school were permitted to wear the lacrosse team tie. All thirteen had been thoroughly interviewed but none had admitted to any knowledge of the murder. The police had not ruled out the possibility that a pupil who was not on the lacrosse team had used a team tie as the murder weapon.

But the police didn't have the information that I had. That twenty years later Alan Houghton from that lacrosse team had been blackmailing Charles Mulholland from the same team. Maybe the blackmail was about something else, but maybe it was not. It certainly was worth looking into further.

I didn't know how I felt. Ecstatic that I might have a lead, but it was a lead that would mean Charles, Amber's husband, had killed more than once. Was Amber in any danger? In any case, I had to find out more.

I tried to speak to Danny Lapaglia, but his widow explained that he had died of cancer in 1983. Probably be a waste of time after twenty-two years but, anyway, I called in sick at CAW and took a trip out to the school.

It didn't board anymore and half the pupils now were girls. Quite far out, too, the taxi ride cost twenty dollars. A beautiful campus: ivy-clad buildings, a swimming pool, a sculpture park. Only a short drive along Hampden Avenue to the foothills of the Rocky Mountains.

I told the headmaster's assistant I was thinking of sending my adopted son there and he showed me around, but he'd been there for only two years and couldn't be pumped for information. He let me walk the grounds. They didn't own horses anymore and the stable block was now a garage for school buses. I walked in the hundred-degree heat across a dried stream and a brown field to where the old Rookery House hotel had been. Signs everywhere pointing out the danger of wildfires.

The old hotel was gone and a housing development had obliterated any hope of finding clues or insights into Maggie's murder.

It was only during the walk back across the dusty field under the unforgiving Colorado sun that I saw why the boys had met Maggie at the Rookery House. The Bright campus was on a hill that commanded the surrounding area. Two boys in Bright uniforms could be spotted from miles away coming over these fields. Except for this one field that led to the Rookery. For this field lay behind a small mesa that sloped down and away from the Bright campus. On the downslope side the little dry stream to the Rookery and the Rookery itself were completely cut off from Bright. Once you got over the brow of the mesa, you disappeared from view. Nice spot for a rendezvous.

Was it possible she had agreed to meet both of them? It seemed unlikely.

In the photograph, Charles was handsome, tall, poised, Alan stubby, askew, asymmetrical, and unattractive. If I had to take a stab at it, I'd say that Alan had tagged along unannounced. What had happened next was anyone's guess. Impossible to say then, impossible to say now. . . .

I went to the school office and asked if I could

browse through the alumni magazines to see how Bright pupils did in life. They were happy to let me have the last twenty years or so of the annual. It was even indexed. Alan Houghton appeared three times. In 1984 he was living on the rue Saint-Vincent, trying to be—guess what?—a painter. In 1989 he was in his hometown of New York "working in the theater." In 1992 he had moved to Denver, where he had bought a studio to "continue his experiments in the arts." A grainy photograph from the 1980s showed a haggard young man, with a fixed grin and something that might be a brown toupee on his head.

He had moved to Denver, perhaps to be near his good friend Charles. Perhaps to start hitting him up for money. Who knew? But that might be it.

The bell went for the end of school.

"What time is that?" I asked one of the secretaries.

"Three-fifteen," she said.

Three-fifteen. If I hurried, I could still get into the office.

I would. I wanted to see Amber, too. I wanted to untangle those thoughts of her that were crowding my mind.

I called for a taxi and made it there by just after four.

Abe was about to give me a lecture about lateness, but Amber intercepted me. Black jodhpurs, black cashmere sweater, boots. Hair tied back. Maybe not the most comfortable of sartorial choices, but it looked bloody great. She looked like a high-class dominatrix. As cute as a box of knives.

"Alexander, I'd like to speak with you," she said.

"Ok," I said, and I found myself wondering why my perception of her personality was so influenced by her taste in clothes.

She walked me over to the sofa that had just been set up in the reception area of the CAW offices.

"I'd like to ask you a favor," she said.

"Oh, yeah?" I said, as those lovely turquoise eyes blinked in fast succession.

"Charles is being asked to speak at a Republican Leadership Conference in Aspen," she said.

"I know," I replied.

"Charles doesn't want me to go, thinks I'll put him off," she said, smiling.

"I can understand that," I said.

"Anyway, it's the same night a touring company of *Dancing at Lughnasa* is coming to Denver and I hardly ever get to go to the theater. Robert can't go. It's a big hit and it's about Ireland. I thought, I mean, I wondered if you wouldn't mind escorting me. I don't want to go alone. I have two tickets. And I thought, because it was about Ireland, you'd be interested."

"Of course," I said, stunned.

"Thanks," she said, and left the room without another word.

I shuddered. Hot and cold. She had me jumping through hoops. Intentionally or not.

To compound it, she didn't come into the office at all for the next few days. In fact, I didn't see her again until I met her outside the theater in a rented tuxedo. I was there twenty minutes early. She was late. A limo dropped her off.

She looked incredible in a slightly risqué, low-cut black dress and heels. She had had her hair done, too, pulled back and pleated and curled over on itself. Perfumed, bedecked with pearls over an impressive cleavage, she could have been going to the bloody Oscars or just a dinner party next door. My dinner jacket was old and too long in the sleeves and judging from the other patrons I was woefully overdressed.

"Thank you so much for coming," she said.

"Not at all," I replied.

"I'm glad to get out, I'd be worried about Charles all evening," she said.

"Sure."

"You're not nervous, are you?"

"I'm not nervous. Why would I be nervous?"

"Don't you get nervous for the performers? Hoping they'll hit their lines and their marks?"

I shook my head. We went into the show.

The audience said "Ssshhh" as the lights went down.

The actors. The play. Amber's bare arm next to mine. I hardly paid the story any attention at all. The only thing I noticed were the worst Irish accents I'd heard outside of an Irish Spring commercial. It went on for a long time.

The audience liked it, though, and there were four curtain calls. Amber clapped with the best of them.

We filed outside.

Amber wanted to walk home. She was very happy and it was a gorgeous night.

We walked south along Sixteenth and despite the play, despite the lovely evening, despite the champagne cocktails at intermission, Amber was talking about Charles.

"You can imagine how excited he was, he won't be on television or anything like that, but it's a real honor to be asked to speak, bigwigs are going to be there, Robert Dornan, Alexander Haig, he's on the bill right after Newt Gingrich."

"Great."

"Charles, naturally, is diametrically the opposite. He represents the moderate wing, you know. He called me this afternoon, very excited. Of course, he's been to Aspen a million times, but he's not a natural public speaker."

"Maybe you *should* have gone with him," I said.

"He thinks it will be worse if I'm in the audience, better in front of a bunch of strangers, he says."

"I don't see Charles as the nervous type," I said.

"Oh, you see, that's where you're wrong, Alexander, he's extremely shy, he's very much like Robert in that respect. He's quite introverted. In many ways, it's all a front, his whole persona. He does it to get the best out of people. Really, he's very sensitive, shy. 'Course, you must keep that to yourself."

"Of course I will," I said indignantly.

We talked a little about the play and the neighborhood. On Pennsylvania Street, she pointed out the fancy nursing home where her mother stayed. A big, white, modern, soulless building.

"Charles pays for everything," she whispered reverentially.

"That's nice," I said.

"He flew her in from Knoxville. It's one of the finest homes in the state, she gets the best of care, it's so sad," she said, her voice breaking a little.

"It is," I agreed. "Alzheimer's is the cruelest way to go."

"I can barely bring myself to visit, once a week is about all I can manage," she said, overcome by sadness.

That topic had killed the conversation, and we walked in silence the rest of the way to her front door.

I wished her a good night.

"Oh, come up for a quick drink," she said, slurring her words slightly and frowning a little at herself. Tipsy from the walk and the aftereffects of champagne, I assumed. She tapped in her security code, the cast-iron gate swung open; I followed her inside.

"What a night," she said.

"Aye."

"I wish Charles could have been there, it's always the way, isn't it, everything always happens at the same time," she said.

"Yeah, life is like that," I agreed.

"Do you want a drink?" she asked.

I didn't, but I said, "Anything."

"Charles has a collection of single malts, I don't

know a thing about whisky, would you like one?" she asked.

"I suppose in Tennessee you were all drinking bourbon?" I asked.

"What?"

"You know, because you're next to Kentucky, Jack Daniel's, that kind of thing," I said.

"Yeah, well, we weren't big drinkers in my family. My father, well, he was a recovering alcoholic, you know, we didn't really allow it in the house. . . . Anyway, it doesn't bother me, do you want a whisky?"

"Ok."

If she wasn't accustomed to alcohol, that explained how she could be tipsy. But why mention this out of the blue? Christ, maybe she was in a confessional mood. What else did she want to talk about? Maybe more about shy, introverted Charles? I would have to go softly-softly.

"Do you want anything in it? Ice or water?" she asked.

"No, nothing, thank you."

She brought me a glass, smiled innocently, happily.

I chastened myself. No, she hardly seemed to be breaking under the strain of angst about a double murder. Maybe I was overanalyzing everything. You're not supposed to do that, you're supposed to get the information first, then collate it, and then think about it. Not leap to conclusions on inadequate facts. I relaxed, sniffed the whisky glass. Peaty. I took a sip: peaty with a seaweed tinge and a sugary harshness. From Islay or Jura.

"How is it?" she asked.

I noticed that she hadn't poured one for herself.

"It's good, it's from the Inner Hebrides, you can tell because of the peaty aftertaste."

She removed her pearls and put them on a sideboard. She kicked her shoes off and sat on the leather reclining chair next to the sofa. She really was extraordinary looking. Beautiful in a way that Irish girls aren't. Healthy, sunny, fresh. She was the whole of America. Her big wide smile, her golden hair, her long legs. Even more attractive now that the thoughts of her poor mother had exposed her a little to me.

Her fingers tapped on the leather arm of the chair.

I got up, poured her a glass of whisky to see if she would drink it.

She sniffed it and took a big sip.

"Oh, Alex, that was a lovely play, Ireland sounds very romantic. Charles went there when he traveled around the world."

"Yeah, he told me, he went to Dublin," I said.

"Oh, yes, of course, he went everywhere. I've never even left America, if you don't count Puerto Rico," she said wistfully.

"And you don't count Puerto Rico, because it's still part of America," I said with a grin.

"Yes, I suppose it is, isn't it. What is it? It's not a state, is it?"

"It's a colony," I said.

"No, I don't think so," she said dismissively.

"It is," I insisted.

"No, I don't think we have any colonies," she said dreamily, her mind clearly on something else.

"You do, and Puerto Rico's one of them, you got it from Spain, I think," I said.

She bit her finger and looked at me.

"You know, Alex, when we first went out campaigning in Englewood, that night of the fire, the first time we'd talked really, apart from the interview, I was very impressed with that thing you said."

"To the policeman?"

"No, when we talked to that dreadful woman. You said that thing about African Americans."

"I honestly don't remember what you're talking about," I said.

"You said that African Americans had invented jazz and blues and rock and done lots of things," she said.

"Oh, I stole that from somewhere, I'm sure, it's hardly an original thought," I said.

"Yes, but clearly you have the sentiment, don't you? You believe that. I mean, well, you know what I mean," she said.

"I don't think so," I said, laughing, and looked at her legs crossing themselves, her hand fixing her dress.

"No, of course not, I'm not saying it very well. In fact, I don't know what I'm saying. I just mean that you, you have real empathy. Does that make sense?"

I examined her. What was she doing? What did she mean by that? Was she complimenting me by an unspoken comparison to someone else? Was she really talking about me, or talking about herself? Maybe in a roundabout way she was trying to tell me something about Charles. Charles is not like this. He is not like you and me. Charles is cold, single-minded. Charles is a—

"Is it because you grew up in Northern Ireland, was it very hard living there with all the bombings and everything?" Amber asked softly, dripping the words out with precision, brushing the hair from her face. That accent of hers always throwing me. Not New Jersey, not the South, not Boston. A gentle echo of Charles's patrician tones. Slightly affected. She took another drink of his whisky.

"Not that hard, you just got on with things, you got used to being searched going into stores, that kind of thing, people are very adaptable," I said.

"Did you see any of that bad stuff?"

"Not really," I lied.

"You didn't see anything?" she asked, her lips closing into a pout.

"Once when I was a kid they blew up our local toy shop and we got discounted train sets and Lego. They were all fire-damaged, but it was mostly the packaging. Really, it was actually a good thing."

"Oh, my goodness, they blew up your toy shop? Why would they blow up a toy shop?"

"I don't know," I said, studying the reaction on her face, which was sympathetic. Upset for me.

"I bet you saw a lot more than you're saying," she said, smiling.

"No, not much."

"I bet you're just being brave and stoic like in the play," she said, scratching at the skin under her gold watch. Taking it off.

"Honestly, it wasn't that bad," I said.

"No. I know all about it. That's why you're here illegally. That's why you lied to the police, because you don't have a green card. I don't mind. I wouldn't tell anyone. I know how difficult it must be. I read the papers. Ireland. It's awful over there."

"Well, it can be hard," I agreed.

"It's what the play was all about. And what a story, huh? Incredible," she said.

"Yes, I forgot that it was set in Donegal. Donegal is very beautiful. Stark, there's still some Gaeltachts out there, villages where they still speak Gaelic," I said.

"Do you speak any Gaelic?"

"No. Well, a little."

"Go on."

"An labhraíonn éinne anseo Gaelige?"

"What does that mean?"

"Is there anyone here who really speaks Gaelic?"

"Did you learn that in the Gaeltacht?"

"No, I went to a Protestant school. The Protestant schools teach Latin, the Catholic schools teach Gaelic, I just picked some of the language up from a book. I'm pretty good at languages. The one thing I am good at."

"Tell me more about yourself," she said.

"You know everything, you saw my résumé."

"We both know that was closer to fiction than truth, right?" she said, again with a smile.

"Yeah, I suppose."

"You know, despite his many travels, Charles is hopeless at languages, most Americans are, you know. I have Spanish, though," she said.

"That's cool, it's always good to know a language."

"I think I'd like to learn Irish, it sounds beautiful."

"It can be pretty guttural. It's not beautiful like Italian."

"Ireland's nice, though? Donegal, you say, is lovely."

"It's really nice, you've got the Atlantic Ocean, big, empty beaches, the Blue Stack Mountains, Saint Patrick's Purgatory on Station Island."

"What's that?"

"It's a pilgrimage site, you can wipe away your sins if you go there on a pilgrimage, you walk around the island barefoot and when you're done you're free of sin. Seamus Heaney wrote a very famous poem about it."

"Did you go there?"

"What makes you think I have any sins?" I asked.

She laughed at this. A big sincere laugh. And it wasn't that funny. She took a sip of the whisky and then another and then she grabbed my glass.

I touched her hand.

She looked at me.

And, oh God, I wanted to kiss her, I wanted to hold her, I wanted to be with her. I wanted her to tell me everything. I knew it would be all right. I wanted her and I wanted to have sex with Charles's beautiful wife while he was out of town. To punish him.

"Maybe I should go," I thought and said.

"Oh, don't go, I was just about to try a different whisky, another glass won't do me any harm, and I can't drink alone," she said.

She poured us both some Laphroaig. The conversation failed. She crossed her legs. Her skirt hiked up a little.

"So, no, I never went to Saint Patrick's Purgatory, it's only for Catholics, really," I said.

She looked at me, inspected me. She seemed to make a decision, poured herself some more whisky, added ice, knocked it back. But then said nothing, sat back down on the sofa. And asked dreamily:

"Is Belfast close to Donegal?"

"Geographically close, you know, less than a hundred miles, but the roads are quite bad, so it takes about three hours to get there."

"And you never went to Carrickfergus, even though it's only about five miles from Belfast, I checked that on the map."

I studied her again. Nothing betrayed on her face. No subtlety, no fear, no repression of hidden emotion. Normal.

"No, like I said, I've never been to Carrickfergus," I answered as carefully as if I were a bomb disposal expert, cutting the blue wire, not the red one.

I waited for her to bring up Victoria Patawasti. Was she about to crack? Was she suddenly going to tell me everything because I was a compatriot of the dead girl? Was all this Irish stuff getting to her, filling her with guilt about what she knew? Her lips did not quiver, her eye was steady. No, she wasn't going to blurt out anything like that, instead she surprised me by saying something quite different:

"I suppose you know you're very handsome, too skinny, maybe, but very handsome. Tall, dark, and handsome, in fact."

"How do I reply to that?" I asked, embarrassed despite myself.

"You say thanks for the compliment and then you compliment me. It's basic civility," she said.

"Ok. But I don't want you to think that I'm saying this because you asked me to give you a compliment, I'm saying this because it's perfectly true. You are the most beautiful woman I've ever met in my life. I'm not good at saying things, but you don't just look beautiful, you have that rare thing that gets said too much, and I'm sort of regretting saying it right now, but the thing called inner beauty, too. You have it. It's a purity of spirit, I can just tell that you are both lovely and good. Since I saw you first, I've felt bewitched, it's like that stanza from Yeats, 'It had become a glimmering girl with apple blossom in her hair, who called me by my name and ran and faded through the brightening air. Though I am old with wandering through hollow lands and hilly lands, I will find out where she has gone and kiss her lips and take her hands. . . . And pluck till time and times are done the silver apples of the moon, the golden apples of the sun.'"

"That's incredible," she gasped, genuinely touched.

I knew half a dozen Yeats poems, all memorized to

impress a different girl in a different world. But it had done the trick and I knew I had to deflate the moment, so I finished off the whisky, gave her my best winning smile, and said:

"Yeah, Amber, maybe I'm cynical, but it's true that when you've got an Irish accent and you're trying to impress a woman and as long as she's not Irish or a hard-bitten professor of literature then Yeats will generally do the trick. 'He Wishes for the Cloths of Heaven' is by far the most popular choice, but I like 'The Song of Wandering Aengus,' it's got that great last line, the chicks love it."

She looked at me for a second, fury on her face, and then I saw that it was mock fury and then she started to laugh and laugh. Laugh so much tears were running down her face. Relief? A huge pent-up flood of emotions suddenly let loose? I was going to ask if she was ok, but before I could, she was standing up and she was reaching out her hand to mine, and I gave her my hand and she pulled me to my feet and kissed me. Hard, passionate, angry kisses. Her mouth was hungry with desire. She was drowning, she was suffocating, she was dying, she was living again through me.

I carried her to the bedroom and laid her on the bed. I pulled her dress down on one shoulder and kissed her arm and the top of her breast. There was a scar on the shoulder, a tiny imperfection in all that beauty. It made her more desirable, not less.

She wriggled out of the dress and undid her bra and ripped off my jacket and shirt. And still having my wits about me, I dimmed the lights, to hide the track marks. She looked up from the bed.

"I need you, Alexander, I need you, now, tonight," she moaned.

I didn't say anything. I took off my trousers and her panties. Her body pale, slender, carved in white marble, her hair like the faery gold; her red mouth open, so hungry, there was never anyone so hungry.

I kissed her neck and between her breasts and she pulled me close, her nails in my back holding on to me as if we were in danger of being torn apart. Sucked away into a vortex by terrible forces, the malignancy of Charles, by the blackness pursuing me. We were alone in this land of light. Secure. As long as we stayed together it would be good. Outside there were horrors, waiting like traps. But not here, not here. Here we were safe, safe, in this bed, in this one night.

"We're shipwrecked," she said, and I, agreeing, added nothing.

The bed and the silk sheets and her smooth skin and those eyes, blue like that ocean in Donegal. And her hands in my hair and on my back. And her voice in those soft harmonized American vocals.

"Oh, Alexander, you don't know, you have no idea."

"I want to know," I said.

"No, no," she said.

"Tell me," I said.

"No."

"Tell me," I insisted.

"Kiss me," she demanded.

My hands stroked her long beautiful legs and her belly and her arms. And I held her close and I kissed her and she tasted of champagne and whisky and ice.

And I kissed her and she didn't speak and I came inside her and her body ached, hurting with pleasure and loss and she sobbed and we lay there in the dark, panting, breathing, holding each other.

And then she climbed on top of me and we made love again, and the midnight hour came and went.

"Hold me," she said.

And I took her in my arms and I kissed her, and she smelled of booze and that perfume and her own sweat and the smell of me. She fell asleep. A drunk sleep. Exhausted.

This girl, this woman, here with me in the long, dark, lovely night. Beautiful. And I looked at her. This girl, whose husband was a hundred and fifty miles away in Aspen. This girl, whose husband maybe killed Maggie Prestwick or aided Maggie's killer on a May morning twenty-two years ago. This man who almost certainly did kill his blackmailer and then committed another brutal slaying on the girl who found out about his slush fund. And it was neat now, tidy. Of course, we had helped, John and myself, killing the only person who could prove anything. We had wiped the traces. And now he could do anything. He could even run for Congress. And win. There would always be rumors, there would always be stories, but nothing that could be proven, nothing that would stick, and with his good works established, and his politics sensible, he would rise. And she would rise with him. From this foundation of blood and lies. Both of them bound by the black rite of this marriage. It would take place, it would happen. Unless I said something, unless I did something, unless I broke her away and let her know the truth about her husband, the truth about Victoria Patawasti. About Victoria, about Amber's shadow, her mirror, her sister, the ghost that brought us together. Yes, and Maggie, too.

How much did Amber know? How much did she want to know? Is that why I'd slept with her? To find out the truth.

And she lay there snoring, and I knew what I was going to do.

A crime.

It could kill her.

It could fucking kill her.

I eased myself out of the bed. I went to the kitchen and got an ice cube.

I found my jacket. I took out the needle, the spoon, I got some water, my alcohol swab. I boiled the heroin, drew it up through the cotton wool. It would be her foot, she'd never notice and I'm the master, I always find a vein, every time.

But ketch and alcohol do not mix. Just ask any of a dozen dead rock stars. It can stop the heart. Can I take her across the line? What if she's done nothing? Can I do that to her? Can I take her across and still have the right to save her, protect her?

I found a vein, put the ice cube on it, to numb it.

She didn't wake. I took off the ice cube, swabbed the spot with alcohol, injected the heroin above her heel.

She moaned for a second in her sleep.

I let her absorb it, I watched her chest move up and down.

Her breath became shallow, she began to sweat. Was her heart going to fib? I sat there, frightened for ten minutes, but then she came out of it. She was in the center of the high. There were things I had to know and this might be the way.

I woke her.

"Amber," I whispered. "Amber."

She looked at me, smiled.

"Amber, I want to ask you something."

"Ask me anything," she said drowsily, happily.

"I want to ask you about Charles."

"Ask me anything," she moaned.

Heroin isn't a truth serum and the memory doesn't blank afterward, so you have to be reasonably subtle, not shock them enough so they'll remember.

"If Charles wanted to get into someone's computer, could he do it?"

"Computer?" she asked, her eyelids heavy, her lips in a pout, quivering, under the opium paralysis.

"Yes, Amber, a computer. Could he get into someone else's computer?" I asked quietly.

"Carrickfergus," she said.

"What?"

"Carrickfergus," she said.

"What does that mean?"

She groaned, started drifting off. I didn't have much more time.

"Ok, forget that, what about Charles?"

"Charles."

"Yes, look, if Charles was going to kill someone, how would he do it?" I asked gently.

"He wouldn't do it, he wouldn't kill anyone."

"But if he had to, if he had to kill someone."

"He wouldn't," she said.

"Are you sure?"

"Yes."

Her eyes fluttered, closed. Damn. I looked at her. That was enough, I couldn't risk anything more, she'd remember, I'd kiss and tell her she was beautiful and say something about, oh, I don't know, Africa, lions. In the morning it would all be jumbled up. She wouldn't recall. It hadn't worked or maybe it had and she knew nothing, she was as innocent as the—

"Throw it," she said lazily from her sleep, her eyes still closed.

"Throw what?"

"Throw the gun, get rid of it," she insisted.

"Where would you get rid of the gun?"

"Have to get rid of it, Italian gun, throw it away, anywhere, Cherry Creek. Get rid of it."

"Why there?"

"I don't know, the nearest river, get rid of it, get rid of it. . . ."

She began to snore again.

She knew, then, she knew Charles had killed Victoria. She had told him to throw away the gun.

I could imagine the scene. He's just killed Victoria, he comes back. "Oh, Amber, something awful has happened, it was an accident"—and he's still got the goddamn gun.

Congressman Wegener's birthday announcement is coming up, they have too much to lose. Maybe he didn't mean to kill her. Maybe he went to confront Victoria and things got out of hand. Amber keeps a cool head. She orders him back out into the snow to get rid of the gun. He throws it in the water and it's washed away, like what else? Her conscience. Her humanity.

I stared at her sleeping form, at—what was it Yeats said?—"that terrible beauty," and I thought, Am I better than you? Me, who took a chance on killing you, to get that?

Had a wee while left.

I looked her over. I examined her, as if she were a corpse. That scar on her shoulder had been a tattoo she had had removed. It was about the size of a silver dollar. I could tell from its shape that it had been a harp. Working-class girl, with a harp tattoo. Shanty Irish girl, bit of a klepto, marries old-money Charles? Then she reinvents herself as patrician fabulous? She didn't give much away. Just that accent and the way she ate pizza. I admired that. Liked that even as I hated her for what Charles did to Victoria. Hated her and wanted her, too. My muscles ached. My body writhed. I wanted a hit.

I still had time.

I forced myself to have a scout around. The predictability of the decor. What did it show? What a good job the cleaning woman did? Charles's shallowness, Amber's impression that this was how the other half lived. No cultural cringes, no giveaways. I went to the garage and checked their car. An E-type Jag. Had Charles killed Alan Houghton on Lookout Mountain? That's where they'd found Houghton's car. Charles could have arranged a meeting up there, killed him, put the body in the trunk and dumped it somewhere, a lake, a canyon, the foundation of a construction project. I popped the trunk, checked it, but it had been long since cleaned. A spare tire, a tire iron, and a Leatherman multitool.

Back to the house. That photograph of Charles playing lacrosse. But screw the murder, I wanted more about her. I searched the drawers, I smelled her underwear, I went through her things. Lingerie, fishnet stockings, tasteful stuff from a high-class boutique. But then at the back, a leather panty with an attachment for strapping on a dildo. I rummaged around. Nothing else. Kinky little minx. I went up to the bed and touched her breasts, kissed her. I watched her. I could have killed her with that dose. Thank God, she was alive, breathing easily.

Got up, searched some more. Looking for back story, photographs, but there was precious little. The past was wiped. Something to be ashamed of, maybe. Finally, in Charles's study I found a box of college stuff. I rummaged through and found a few pictures of an Amber Doonan in a Harvard production of *Twelfth Night*. Further down another yearbook. No Amber Doonan, but a photograph of Amber Abendsen, a talented actress in the drama society. She had changed her name. Why? Could she have married someone before Charles?

A talented actress, the caption said.

What else about you, Amber? What else could I know about you? I found her purse and rummaged through it. Driving license, credit cards. A notebook with all the pages blank. More to know but too late now.

Too late now. I was shivering. I put the box away. I went back to her. Breathing. Lovely. I needed a hit. I couldn't bear to look at her without a hit.

I threw the used needle in the garbage. I cleaned the vessel in the bathroom sink. I cleaned the spoon, let it air-dry. Waited, patient. I took the ketch, I boiled it, I found a vein. Alcohol and heroin do not mix, I thought as I injected myself. I stowed my kit back in my jacket, I lay down with her on the bed.

I climbed on top of her, I touched her belly, breasts. She could barely respond, but I had to have her.

I eased my way inside. . . .

Early morning. Sunlight the color of her hair, filtering through the wooden slat blinds. She's awake, looking at me. She smiles when she sees me wake.

"Hey," she says.

"Hi. You look great," I reply.

"Really? I don't feel well at all," she says.

"What's the matter?"

"I'm just a bit under the weather, groggy."

"I'm sorry to hear that," I say, and look at her.

She seems a little yellow. I kiss her and touch her legs and incidentally check out her left heel. If you miss the vein you can leave a big blister, but I didn't miss the vein and it seems fine down there.

"I don't feel a hundred percent but I know what will help. Let's make love," she says.

"Ok."

I kiss her and climb on top and we make love, but I'm still under the influence of the smack and I let her be on top and her back arches and her big breasts heave and drip sweat, and we come together and we're happy.

I laugh and she laughs.

"Well, that's position twenty-one in the Kama Sutra knocked off," I say in an Indian accent.

"What did you say?" she asks, suddenly sitting up.

"I said that that's position twenty-one of the Kama Sutra knocked off."

She wraps the blanket around herself and rubs her eyes. Her leg moves in such a way that it is no longer touching mine. She shivers. She looks at me in the half-light with those cat blue eyes. She turns away. I've screwed up somehow. She yawns.

"You better go, Charles might be back soon."

I stretch lazily and nod.

"Gosh, yes, it's seven o'clock, you better go, we have a maid service that comes," Amber says.

"I'll see you this afternoon?" I ask.

"Yes. Come here, Alex, kiss me," she says.

I lean over, kiss her. Thinking: She's beautiful, she's frightened, but she's basically good, and somehow, somehow, it's all going to be ok, it's all going to work out for the best, for her and for me and for everyone.

Of course it is.

10: THE REMOVER OF OBSTACLES

Denver already up. Dollars being made in oil, high tech, commerce, land spec, tourism, and the like. I noted the cars, counted the SUVs, the Jesus fish and the odd "God Hates Gays" or "Abortion = Murder" bumper sticker. At Einstein Brothers I bought a mixed bag of bagels. Carried them to the building, walked up the five flights.

"Alex, what about you?" John asked.

"Not too bad, mate," I told him.

Areea smiled at me. She was always here now. Before her job, after her job.

"Good morning," she said.

"Hi," I said.

John took the bag of bagels, split it open, and toasted three of them.

"Where's Pat?" I asked.

"He's putting his face on."

Pat always spent at least an hour getting his appearance into some kind of shape for the day ahead. There were sores to be covered, a beard to be shaved extremely carefully, there was rubbing alcohol and pancake to be applied to his skin.

"I'll just take a half, John," I said as I went into the bedroom to boil my heroin and shoot up.

"Ok, pal," he said. He didn't ask where I'd been all night, or what was going on. This was one of John's good qualities.

I found a clear track of vein, injected myself, lay down on the bed.

"Did you fall asleep?" Areea asked a couple of hours later.

"Yeah," I said.

John gave me a look and shook his head. "You're running late," he said, "and your bagel's freezing."

"Where's Pat now?" I asked him.

"He's not feeling well," John said.

"No?"

"Yeah."

"I'll go visit him."

I walked down the hall to Pat's. I was a bit late, but I had to ask him something.

He was wrapped in a blanket in the living room, sipping raw gin from a pint glass. His face drawn, tired.

"Get you anything, mate?" I asked.

He shook his head.

"Listen, I've got a question. It can wait if you're not up to it," I said.

"Fire away. I'm better than I look."

"Where does Cherry Creek go?"

"The river or the shopping mall?" he asked, stroking his stubble, his dead cheeks.

"The river. How could a shopping mall go anywhere?"

"It meets the South Platte at Confluence Park."

"And then what?" I asked.

"Platte, Missouri, Mississippi, Gulf of Mexico."

"Shit, ok, I see."

"Why you wanna know?"

"Oh, nothing, just curious."

"You wanna know anything else, sip of gin or a martini?"

"Nah, I have to go, actually."

"Don't think of fishing there or anything, just a couple of feet deep, best of times."

"Ok, Pat, I have to head. Are you sure I can't get *you* anything?"

"No."

"Gotta go to work," I said apologetically.

"Sure," he said. "Oh, nearly forgot, last night I got a call about you."

"What?"

"Yeah, some Native American dude from the Denver Police Department called up, wanted to know if I had anyone stay over with me on the night of June twenty-second. Maybe two Mexican, Australian, or Irish guys."

"Shit, and what did you say?"

"I said nope, said I used to take paying guests but it wasn't worth the hassle anymore."

"And what did he do?"

"He thanked me, said it was just a routine inquiry, and hung up."

"His name was Redhorse, right?"

"Yeah, something like that," Pat said.

"Did the right thing, Pat, he's looking for us since—"

Pat put up his hand to stop me. His eyes cold, certain.

"I don't want to know," he said. "The best thing is if I know nothing."

"Ok. Probably best if you don't tell John, either," I said.

Pat's eyes widened, but then he nodded and I said goodbye. I'd forgotten all about Redhorse. Or, if not forgotten, I had put him out of my mind. If I had any sense at all, I'd see that now was the time to quit, to get out of town. But I was so close. So close. And the hook was deeper than ever. *She* was deeper. . . .

Incredibly, at the CAW offices Charles was there, looking a bit bleary-eyed but showered, his hair gelled back, wearing a fresh linen suit, white shirt, and tie.

"Alexander," he said with a big grin, "you like cigars?"

"You had a baby?" I asked.

"Sort of," he said, laughing. "I gave my first public speech last night."

"How did it go?" I asked.

"Very well. Here," he said and give me a silver tube.

Charles explained that he'd given the speech to a packed hall in Aspen, made lots of contacts, and then driven back this morning. He had even met Newt Gingrich and Senator Dole. He said that giving a speech wasn't that much different from lecturing, or presenting a brief, or doing a rap at a door, except that you had to read off a Teleprompter, which took some getting used to.

"Wow, that's cool, did you write the speech?" I asked.

"Robert and I wrote it. Robert wanted to come and, of course, Amber wanted to come, but, I don't know, I thought it might be easier if I was there on my own. Amber tells me you escorted her to that play she's been going on about."

I nodded. He smiled. There he was. Together, tall, confident, just the sort of person who gets elected to Congress, whose past indiscretions are swept under a rug, never to see the light of day, the sort of fucker who pops up on a vice presidential ticket five years from now. I don't know what kind of a person Maggie Prestwick was, but I'll bet she was worth ten of Charles. Victoria Patawasti, I know, was worth a hundred.

"Come on, we're having a meeting, everyone's invited, including the campaigners," he said.

"How democratic," I muttered.

The meeting was just a pep rally for Charles. He talked about his speech and the conference, how he'd met half a dozen senators, congressmen, and governors. He told us that we should all be ready to see some big changes in CAW in the coming months. CAW was going to be adopted by influential people within the GOP as a counterweight to Greenpeace and the Sierra Club, who were firmly in the Democratic camp. It would mean more money, more work, more potential for growth. He didn't mention August 6, but he was itching to, I could see that.

My eyes flitted down the table to Amber. Dressed in burgundy slacks and a tight silk cream sweater, her hair piled under a beret, it was a look I hadn't seen her pull off before. She resembled Faye Dunaway in one of those films from the seventies. She mustn't have had time to fix her hair before Charles had unexpectedly shown up. That would have been fun if he'd appeared even sooner, interesting seeing her talk her way out of that one. Would Charles's violent streak extend also to the killing of his wife and her lover in their marital bed? No, a bit too clichéd for him. It would not serve his future self.

The meeting broke up, and although Amber looked nervy, I needed to speak to her. I pushed through the crowd.

"Nice hat," I said, just as Abe bumped into her, making her spill her tea.

"What?" she said, glaring at Abe.

"Sorry," Abe said, chastened.

"Forget it," Amber said, recovering her poise and giving me a nod.

"What did you say, Alex?" she asked.

"I like your chapeau," I said.

"Thank you, Alexander."

"You look like Faye Dunaway," I said.

"Faye Dunaway?"

"Yeah."

"Doesn't she always play the villainess?"

"No, I don't think so. She was the victim in *Chinatown*."

"Well, that's not good either," she said with a tight smile.

"Hey, it was cool about Charles, wasn't it, apparently he was a big hit," I said.

"He was, I really should have been there, it was selfish of me to go to the play," she said almost to herself.

"But you would have put him off," I said.

"Yes, that's what he said," she muttered.

"Next time, maybe he'll want all of us there, as his confidence grows," I said.

"Perhaps," she said, and looked at me for the first time. Abe, Robert, and Charles began laughing at something. I took the opportunity to lead Amber to the windows at the far side of the room. I kept my eye on the trio behind us. Maybe we were looking at the gray clouds, debating the possibility of rain. Denver needed rain badly.

"How soon did he get there after I left?" I whispered.

"About an hour, it was close," she said.

"Jesus," I said. "But everything was ok?"

"No, I don't feel well at all. After you left, I threw up. Revolting," Amber said.

"Maybe the whisky," I said, but of course I knew it was the heroin. That was a dumb move on my part, I was lucky I didn't give her a bloody heart attack.

"Alexander, I don't know what to think about last night," she said softly.

"I know, I know," I said stupidly.

"It's confusing. I, I think, perhaps, we shouldn't try to see each other again for a while," she said.

I looked at her. She was so beautiful and at a loss. I was surprised. I thought she was going to say either "Alexander, I need to talk to you" or "Alexander, this was a terrible mistake" or "Alexander, I can't see you again." But not confusion. That was unexpected.

"Do you want to see me again?" I asked.

"I don't know," she said.

"I had a wonderful time," I said, perplexed.

"Me, too," she said, and smiled so sweetly that it made my dick skip a beat. Was I falling in love with her?

"And you hid everything? And he has no idea?" I asked.

"No idea, he was talking all about his speech, all about himself," she said.

"Good," I said.

She touched my hand. This, I saw, would be one of those moments I would always remember. Robert, Abe, Charles, fifteen feet from me. Charles's wife touching the back of my hand. Five people in this room. Charles laughing. Amber looking at me with sadness in her eyes. What was betrayed on my face? What emotions was I revealing? Could she read me like I was supposedly reading her?

Aye, the moment.

The room. Denver out the window. The Rocky Mountains. The rest of the great North American continent curving away to the horizon.

Amber.

Amber's husband. Victoria Patawasti's killer. With those hands. With that fingertip he squeezed the trigger. With that laughing face. Standing there, grim, in Victoria's apartment. Standing there. Perhaps admiring his handiwork or perhaps recoiling at the horror of it. Stepping back, remembering to drop the driving license, walking out, closing the door, taking the elevator, holding on to the gun. Amber, the devoted wife saving the day. Drop it in the nearest river. Cherry Creek. Drop it. Get rid of it.

Amber. Her lips parted slightly. Breathing out. Her finger on the back of my hand. If time could freeze then we all survive and the bad things don't happen and it doesn't get worse. But time can't freeze. . . .

Amber lifted her finger from the back of my hand, leaned back. Charles was looking at us.

"What are you two conspiring about over there?" he asked, grinning.

"Maybe it's going to rain. Make a change. Be nice, be like real Irish weather," I said, meteorology always a good fallback.

"When we were in Dublin it didn't rain at all, did it, Robert?"

"It did not," Robert agreed. "We c-could do with a good downpour here, forty days and forty nights, if we're lucky. They haven't let me water m-my lawn since March of last year."

Amber turned away from the window and walked back to the others.

"I'm very proud of you, darling," she said to Charles.

"Maybe we'll all get to go to the next conference, or even the convention in San Diego," Abe said, getting between Charles and her.

"It's possible," she said, examining the tabletop like it was the Risk map of the world and she was in trouble in Central Asia. She couldn't look at him. I walked over and joined the merry group.

Charles finished his conversation with Abe, put his arms around his wife, and lifted her up in the air.

"I was really something, honey," he said.

"I'm sure you were," she said, laughing.

"No, really, they were terribly impressed, not just with the speech but the handouts, the whole package. I do believe we are on a roll," Charles said.

"That's wonderful, darling," Amber said, and kissed him on the lips. He kissed her back and I decided to fade into the background. I had never seen Amber kiss Charles in the office before. Not in front of everyone. Perhaps she was just happy for him, perhaps it was because of me. I wanted to deck the bastard. The girl killer. And his accomplice.

"It's all thanks to you, darling," Charles was saying.

"No, darling, it's you, all your hard work," Amber said.

"I love you," Charles said.

"And I love you, darling," Amber said as I finally made it out the conference room door. I was seething. I wanted to get away from everyone. In the main office, Robert had found a cigar clipper and was offering it to anyone who wanted to use it. Abe and he were smoking provocatively under the No Smoking sign. I went to the bathroom, filled the sink, dunked my head, held it there longer than was strictly necessary.

A long, boring day stuffing envelopes.

That night we drove all the way down to Colorado Springs again. Robert, Abe, and Steve West taking the vans, both Charles and Amber staying home. Amber still not feeling well. Robert bossing us about. Like a lot of weak people, Robert was a bit of a bully.

When I'd got enough memberships, I went to look for Robert. I had a couple of things I wanted to ask him. He was glad to see me, he wasn't making much headway.

"I'm done, Robert, I did every house twice, got fifteen members, I thought I'd keep someone company, you're the first one I've found," I said.

"Fifteen members, good job, very good job. Charles w-will be pleased," Robert said.

I hung out and did some of his doors for him. In between we talked about the woeful state of his garden and how well CAW was doing. Finally, I got him off the environment and onto the topic of crime. Two or three questions in, I asked the lead.

"You know, I worry about some of the girls or someone like Amber out on her own, going door to door, you never know who could answer, once when I knocked someone came to the door with a loaded gun. Or there's vicious dogs. Shouldn't she have some protection?"

"Amber? Oh, don't worry about her, she can look after herself. She's a b-brown belt in one of those martial arts."

"Yeah, well, not if the guy has a gun. The guy who hassled me the other night. He thought he was James Bond, he was carrying a Walther PPK."

"Oh, well, I know Charles gave Amber a p-pistol when she moved to Colorado, the gun laws are very liberal here, not like Boston, both Charles and m-myself own rifles, although neither of us were any good. Papa tried to take us hunting once, dreadful, we both cried. They drummed us out of the ROTC, you know—"

"Yeah, so you said. So Amber carries a pistol?"

"I don't know if she carries it, she should, a .22-caliber revolver."

"She owns a .22?"

"Oh, yes. Charles had it handmade in Italy. Gold inlay. Work of art, really. His and her initials. Beretta, I think. Anyway, I d-don't know much about that; Charles and I both learned how to shoot rifles. Totally different thing. We're both NRA members, have to be if you're going to run with the big boys in the GOP. Keep that under your h-hat, by the way, August sixth, Alex. Just a few weeks away, hush hush."

I smiled, talked about the NRA and hunting, changed the subject back to the weather. . . .

So had Charles killed Victoria with Amber's .22? Had Amber told him to toss it in the nearest river—Cherry Creek? If so, by now it was nudged halfway down the goddamn Mississippi River for all I bloody knew.

I chatted with Robert about politics and CAW and other things, but he was done with his revelations.

We met the others, stopped for pizza, drove the long ride home.

Colfax Avenue. My building. On the third floor I was so exhausted I had to stop for a breather.

With heavy legs I made it up two more flights.

I opened the apartment door, went in. All I wanted to do now was sleep, but I could hear John and Areea, in my room, screwing. That shit, what did he think he was doing? I was going to go in and kick the bastard out, but I stopped myself. Why should I interfere, what business was it of mine? They couldn't do it in her place because of her folks, they could hardly do it in the pullout bed in the middle of the living room. John had every right to be in the bedroom. I sighed. But if I gave in tonight, I would be giving him the room with its cooling cross breezes for the whole rest of the summer. I eased myself onto the sofa and listened to them. They weren't talking, they weren't being dramatic, they were just having good, beautiful sex. Slow and wonderful lovemaking between two people who were very fond of each other. When was the last time I did that? Last night? I wasn't sure.

I sat there and wondered what to do. Was Areea going to stay there all night? It seemed unlikely, sooner or later she'd probably slip back down to her apartment.

I felt I had intruded and it made me uncomfortable. The apartment had only limited space and you could hear everything. I backed out of the living room and walked down the hall, closing the door quietly behind me.

I looked at my watch. It was twelve-fifteen. I walked all the way along the corridor and around the bend to Pat's place.

I knocked gently on the door in case he was asleep.

"Yeah," he said, almost immediately.

"Pat, you're up," I said.

"Alex, is that you? What's up?"

"John-Areea-fucking-my-place."

Pat opened the door. He was wearing his day clothes, but he had wrapped a huge duvet about him. It wasn't cold, I felt the chill more than most and it wasn't bad, so Pat must have been really feeling under the weather.

"Drink?" he asked.

"Sure," I said.

"What?"

"What are you having?"

"I'm drinking rum and coke, it's a nostalgia thing," he said.

He poured me a glass, and I sat on the sofa in front of the TV.

"What's on?" I asked him.

"You ever see the *Tonight* show?"

"Yeah, once or twice, I think," I said.

"Used to be good, now they got those Dancing Judge Itos on all the time," Pat said.

I had no idea what Pat was talking about, but he switched over to Letterman anyway

"What was that?" Pat asked during a commercial.

"A beer ad," I said.

"No, I heard something," Pat said.

I listened, but I couldn't hear anything. Letterman came back on. A few minutes later we both heard a girl's scream.

"What the hell was that?" I said, getting up.

"You better check it out, tell John to keep his woman under control, and if it's a bad scene come back," Pat said calmly.

* * *

A bad scene. I trudged down the corridor, got my key, but the apartment door was already open. Even in the ambient light coming through the windows I knew that it felt wrong. Something smelled bad. There was something the roaches liked.

I hit the light switch. Blood on the doormat and floor tiles and a smeared blood trail that led from the front door and down the hall. Someone had been stabbed or shot, had fallen, had lain there for a moment, had dragged himself backward down the hall.

"John," I said. I ran in.

The blood pooled in the living room in an ugly, confused mess that led to the bedroom.

"John," I called out.

I heard movement.

I skidded into and opened the bedroom door. It

smelled like a butcher's yard. I turned on the light. Blood everywhere, on the bed, on the floor, on the walls. John, leaning halfway out the window of the fire escape. He was naked, there was a hunting knife sticking out of his chest, sticking out of his heart. John had tried to pull it out, but it was a six-inch serrated blade.

Incredibly, he was still breathing.

Tiny, impossible, desperate breaths.

Blood on his tongue, forming bubbles. Blood in his eyes, hair, everywhere.

Suddenly I couldn't stand.

I sat on the floor, next to him, my jeans soaking up John's blood. I took his cold, naked, gore-coated hand.

"John," I said.

His head turned to look at me. He was trying to speak. He couldn't speak. He couldn't breathe. He was in pain, shock. His mouth moved, blood trickled out of it, his teeth coated, his lips dyed.

I don't know what I was thinking. I tried to pull out the knife. But the pain writhed through him. He thrashed, gasped. I took his hand again. I wanted to run away. I couldn't look at him.

I had seen crime scenes before. I had watched my mother die. But I had never seen anything like this. Not the murder of a friend, his body warmth still leaving him. I pulled him close. I held him.

"Pat," I screamed down the hall, "Pat."

John's eyes glazed. He started to convulse.

"John, I'm going to call for help, I'm going to go get help," I told him.

"Sssssstay," he managed, heroically, to say, and his dead man's hands held me tight.

I looked at the knife. No, no sense trying to remove it. Wouldn't help. The blood from his chest wound was a trickle now. I pulled him closer. I held him. Oh, God, John, I am so sorry. I got you into this. I got you into this. His body shook, shuddered, he reached for what? The window, the closet, something.

"What is it?"

He pointed.

"What is it?"

His arm reached out and fell, his head slumped forward onto the window ledge.

He was dead.

I looked at him. The knife, his white face. I closed his eyes.

A whimper.

And I turned to look at the closet.

Areea.

I opened the closet door. Crouching there. Naked. Covered in his blood. She was terrified. She screamed when she saw me. Stood, pushed past me, I tried to grab her.

"Wait, what happened? Tell me what happened!" I yelled at her.

Her breasts, her long arms and legs, all soaked red. It looked like she'd just given birth. She slid past, dry-heaved when she stepped over John, ran naked across the living room and down the hall. I went after her, slipped on John's blood, skidded, fell heavily on my side.

"Wait," I called after her, "what the fuck happened? Wait."

She didn't come back. I got up and ran down the hall and then halted. No point. No fucking point. I stopped there and looked at the footprints in the blood. Hers, mine. No one else's. The murderer had not followed John into the apartment. Not even a hint of an extra footprint in the fresh blood trail into the apartment.

And I saw how it was done.

The murderer had knocked at the door, John had got up, walked naked down the hall, opened the door, been stabbed once, immediately, in the dark of the landing. The killer, of course, didn't know that I lived with a roommate and assumed that the figure at the door was me. One massive puncture wound, right in the heart. John had had no chance. He'd fallen backward into the apartment. The killer had bolted down the stairs, run out of the building as fast as he could. Not a professional hit. A professional would have stepped into the apartment to confirm the identity, removed the knife, cut John's throat, and taken the murder weapon with him.

An amateur, who not only killed the wrong person but had run away so quickly he couldn't even be sure that that person was dead. Maybe someone who had only one hour's sleep in the last forty-eight. Maybe someone who was exhausted, had just driven back from Aspen and was told by his wife that I had to be gotten rid of.

So I *had* fucked it up with Amber.

I had said something. Given myself away.

But what, what had I said? Not the time. Think about it later.

"John," I moaned, and found that I was weeping.

I went back into that terrible room.

His head was resting on the window ledge. He looked so uncomfortable I lifted him and put him on the bed. I was utterly drenched with blood now. His eyes, horrifically, had opened again.

I closed them a second time. Sat there. Stunned. Frozen. Minutes went by, perhaps hours.

"Poor Areea," I said.

They had stabbed John at the door and he had crawled down the hall and Areea had screamed and we had heard her. She had held him and as he gasped for air, she had opened the window and then she'd heard me coming in.

She'd been frightened, thought it was the killer coming back. Hid.

It had all happened in a couple of minutes. Even if she hadn't been panicked, frozen by fear, and managed to call 911 immediately they couldn't have helped him. A puncture wound in the heart.

Where was she now? Downstairs, cowering in her apartment, showering, composing a story that she had been there all night.

What to do? I was dripping blood, making everything worse.

Pat.

I went to the bedroom, stared at John, sat down again. I kicked off my bloody shoes, grabbed a pair of sneakers and put them on. I carefully made my way across the bedroom and skirted the blood trail. I walked to Pat's and knocked on his door.

He opened it. He took a look at me, staggered back into the apartment, dropped the remote control.

"Jesus, Mary, and Joseph," he said. "What the fuck happened?"

"They murdered John," I said.

"Oh my God."

"They killed him," I said.

"Fuck. Who? Who murdered him? Are you ok?"

"I'm ok."

"Jesus Christ," Pat said.

"Areea was in there, she's downstairs, hiding, I don't think she saw anything," I said automatically.

"Alex, who killed him?" Pat asked.

"Charles," I said.

"Who's that?"

"The guy I'm after," I said.

"You better tell me everything," Pat said, "but first we'll go down and see if he's really dead. You civilians don't know shit."

Pat followed me along the corridor. John was really dead.

"You should never have moved him," Pat said. "The cops will book you for sure."

"I didn't do it, Pat," I said.

"I know. Charles did. Whoever the fuck that is. Ok,

ok, what are we going to do? Ok. First things first. Are we calling the cops? We're not calling the cops, is that right?"

"I don't know, Pat," I said.

"They'll book you, Sonny Jim, better tell me who Charles is, what you got on him."

I took a breath and told Pat everything. Everything. From the very beginning. Me, the peelers, the ketch, Commander Douglas, Victoria Patawasti, Klimmer, the lacrosse team, Maggie Prestwick, Charles and Amber Mulholland. I was good at giving a précis, it only took five minutes.

"You've no proof of any kind?" Pat asked.

I shook my head.

"It's my fault, Pat," I said.

"It's not your fault. It's ok," Pat said, trying to digest all the information I had thrown at him, trying to think. His face was alert now. He held himself upright.

"Jesus, Pat, it's a nightmare," I said.

"So you're an ex-cop, huh. I knew you were something. And John's dead and Areea's terrified, right, ok. Ok, what do we do?"

"I don't know," I said.

"Ok, ok, this is what we do. You get up and go to my apartment, go straight to the shower, don't touch anything, get in, take a shower, take your clothes off in the shower, leave them there. Shower and get the blood out and when you're really clean, do it all again. Use a towel to dry off and leave it in the bath with the bloody clothes. When you're done, pour yourself two fingers of gin. Ok? You did good not getting any blood down the corridor."

"What are you going to do?"

"I'm going downstairs to talk to Areea, she's bound to be messed up. Talk to her, talk to her family. Tell them it was a burglar but if we want to keep the cops out of it, we gotta take care of this ourselves. They don't want the cops as much as we don't want the cops. They'll get questioned, passed on to INS, deported. We gotta take care of this in-house. Tonight."

"What do you mean, Pat?" I asked.

"Don't worry about a thing, we'll take care of this, no one else involved," Pat reassured me, suddenly becoming stronger before my eyes, taking on something of the old DFD lead paramedic, someone with responsibility for other things than himself. But even so, I wasn't convinced.

"I just assumed we'd call the cops," I said.

"Alex, listen to me, they will arrest you, they'll say you were jealous of John and Areea, you're covered in his blood, you have motive, opportunity, I swear to you, there's a very good chance you'll go to prison."

"If I tell them about the Mulhollands. . . ."

"They won't believe you. . . . Christ, Alex, you should know that, the cops want simplicity, there's a simple explanation for everything. This isn't a big fucking conspiracy, this is a simple case of homicide. You can get those knives anywhere."

"I have an alibi, a witness."

"Who, me? Come on. You were his roommate, he

was fucking the girl you loved, you killed him with your own knife. At the very least, you're going to jail. I suppose you don't have fifty grand for bail?"

"No."

"Alex, listen to me. You're fucked."

I nodded, too tired to debate it, too tired to see if it was the right thing to do or not. I went to Pat's, stripped, soaped myself, showered. Sobbed up against the wall. Found one of Pat's robes, put it on, went down the hall. Walked back into the apartment. No one there. The smell of blood, vile, pervasive.

I trudged downstairs. Knocked on the Ethiopians' door.

It was open. I went in. Pandemonium. The whole family up. Pat talking to Mr. Uleyawa, the sons beside him, aghast, afraid, Simon translating what Pat was saying. Areea, wrapped in a blanket, curled on the sofa in the fetal position. Her hair soaked. She had showered or bathed. She'd been terrified but she wasn't stupid, she'd gotten that blood off her.

A bucket sat beside her, she had been throwing up. Her mother and grandmother stroking her hair as she shivered and wept.

She gasped when she saw me.

"Areea," I said.

"Get out of here, Alexander," Pat said, "I'm taking care of things."

I walked over to Areea. She backed into the cushions, afraid of me for a moment. The grandmother tried to stop me from touching her. I knelt by the sofa.

I could smell blood on her still. Or maybe that was my imagination.

I touched her hair.

"It must have been terrible," I said.

She sobbed. I let her cry for a minute. The conversation in the room ceased.

"Areea, I'm sorry about this, I'm very sorry."

"Alex, don't," Pat said, cautioning me about saying anything.

Areea put her arms out and I leaned in and hugged her. No, not blood. She smelled of shampoo and skin, she had been scrubbed raw. We held each other for a minute. Her wet hair dripped down my back. Pat began speaking to Simon again in low tones, Simon translating it for his dad in singsong Ethiopian.

"Areea, listen to me, listen to me, did you see anything?" I said. "Did you see who did this?"

Areea shook her head.

"Tell me, tell me what happened."

Her mother gave her something to drink from an opaque glass. She swallowed it. She looked at me and tried to smile a little.

"John and I were in your bed," she said.

"I know," I said. "What happened?"

"We were sleeping, we were falling asleep."

"And then?"

"There was a knock at the door. John thought it was you, he said: 'Silly bugger's dropped his keys.'"

I smiled at her.

"And then what, Areea?" I asked gently.

She grabbed my hand and held it tight. So tight that it hurt.

"John got up, he left the bedroom, he closed the bedroom door. He walked down the hall, he did not come back. I did not hear anything, at first. I wondered what was keeping him. I thought he was talking to you. I waited for five minutes. The fan was on in the bedroom, so I could not hear him and then I did."

She burst into tears.

Pat came over, touched me on the shoulder.

"Alexander, you're doing yourself no good here, I'm trying to get this organized, you're dripping wet, you should go back upstairs," he said, calm, sensible.

"In a minute, Pat, in a minute," I said.

Pat gave me a significant look. He didn't want me to say anything. He had made a story for Simon and he didn't want me to mess it all up.

"I'll go back in a minute, Pat," I said.

Pat walked back over to Simon and began talking to him again, urgently, explaining something, telling them what happened and what they were going to have to do.

"Areea, tell me," I said.

"John was at the bedroom door, he had crawled all the way from the hall, he was bleeding. He could not speak. He could not say anything. He was bleeding. The knife. Oh my good God. Oh my good God."

She cried again. I let her. She shook.

"I am sorry, Alexander, I was so frightened. I was too frightened to leave the bedroom. I helped John inside.

I held him. I was too frightened. I know I should have called the ambulance. John was dying. I was so frightened."

"It's ok, Areea, they couldn't have helped him, the doctors couldn't have helped him. He had lost so much blood, there was nothing any of us could have done."

"No, no, no, it was wrong, I should have got Patrick and used his phone, I was so frightened, I am so sorry, I am so sorry," Areea said.

"No, it's ok," I said.

Areea began digging her nails into my hand and then abruptly she let go and began digging her nails into her own face. She began screaming. Her mother tried to stop her, she was writhing on the sofa. Her mother and grandmother held her down. Pat practically lifted me to my feet.

"Alexander, can't you see you're making things worse here? Go upstairs, Jesus, look at you, there's still blood in your hair, I told you to have two showers. Go, now."

Areea was sobbing and I wanted to hold her and tell her it was ok. My fault, not hers. My fault. My stupidity that had got John killed. My carelessness. It was nothing to do with her. Pat frog-marched me to the front door of the apartment.

"Listen to me, Alexander, I am a sick man, but if I have to drag you up five fucking flights I will, now get the fuck out of here," he seethed at me, furious.

I went upstairs, took Pat's advice, had another shower. The hot water was gone. It was cold. I relished the pain of the freezing water. Pat was nowhere to be seen. I put on a pair of his jeans and a T-shirt. They were too big for Pat now and too big for me. I walked out into the hall to see what was happening.

Pat, two of Areea's brothers, and her dad, carrying John's body, wrapped in sheets out of the apartment.

"Alex, get out of here," Pat said.

"What are you doing, Pat?" I said, panicked, frightened, protective of poor John.

"Alex, leave this to us, fuck off," Pat said.

"No, Pat, what are you doing? The police," I said weakly.

"Hold on, boys," Pat said. He took me by the arm and led me back to his place.

"Listen, Alex," Pat whispered, "I told them John had been murdered by a burglar, ok? Crackhead, looking for dough, ok? I told them Areea would have to tell the police what she knew, that she would get arrested, that they all would get arrested, deported. That they have to help if they don't want to go back to fucking Ethiopia."

"What the hell are you doing, Pat? What are you doing with John?"

"We're going to take John to the big trash Dumpster from that building renovation on Fourteenth. Throw him in, cover him up with garbage bags, timbers. They empty that thing every Friday, take it right out there to the landfill in Aurora. With any luck, he'll never be found."

"Fucking hell, Pat, there must be some other way."

"No other way, Alex. We can't get the cops. You'll be

questioned, arrested, I promise you, I know the system. Areea will be questioned, arrested, they'll deport her and her family, you'll get done for homicide, I'll get fucking evicted. It's the only way."

"I don't know, Pat," I said.

"Did you drink that gin?"

"No."

"Go do it now, go do it."

I found the Bombay Sapphire bottle, poured myself a half a glass of gin. Pat left. I poured myself another glass, resisted the temptation to let ketch take over and sort this one out by itself.

When I stepped outside the apartment, the Ethiopians and Pat had John in the corridor and were maneuvering him down the stairs. He was wrapped like a mummy, in five or six sheets and blankets. No blood was soaking through, which wasn't surprising considering how much he'd bled in the apartment.

"John, oh God, I'm so sorry," I found myself saying.

"Alex, if you're going to help, you got to pull yourself together," Pat said.

I walked down the hall. Of the Ethiopians only Simon spoke good English. The father said something to me and Simon translated.

"A bad business," he said, as if discussing a fall in the stock market or a war in a far-off country.

"Yes."

"Just like with O. J. Simpson's wife," he said.

I glared at him. Clenched a fist. Pat put his hand on my shoulder.

The two big Ethiopian boys looked at me with expressionless faces. Maybe they thought I had killed him, or Areea had killed him in an argument. Anything . . .

"Alex, if you want to help, take the front, my place, and I'll direct traffic," Pat said.

I took Pat's place at the front of the body. John was well wrapped in blankets, but I could feel his legs.

We walked him down the five flights. There were four of us. Surprisingly easy. Too easy, it should have hurt more. We paused in the lobby.

"I'll check the street," Pat said. He went out onto Colfax.

"We have to hug the shadows and get quickly around the back of the building. We'll be exposed in the street for about thirty seconds," Pat said.

I had no idea of the time but one thing was for sure, there wouldn't be many random cop cars going by. Cops seldom came around here, almost never at night. Still, a taxi or bus driver might alert the authorities.

"It's all clear," Pat said.

We carried John outside and walked with him around the building to what Pat had called a Dumpster. We froze as a car drove past on Colfax, but it didn't stop. Simon muttered something to his brother. I hoped they weren't going to leg it, leave us with the body.

We heaved John into the skip and Pat told Simon to lift his brother in there so he could cover the body with debris. Matthew, the older boy, climbed up the side of the skip and lowered himself in, and spent a few minutes covering John with garbage bags, bits of wood and debris from the building. We stood there, looking foolish, feeling guilty. Matthew climbed out and gave us the thumbs-up.

We walked back to the apartment building.

"I have to see Areea," I said.

"In the morning," Pat said.

"I have to speak to her tonight," I insisted. "It must have been terrible, I want to speak to her. While it's fresh."

"In the morning," Pat said again.

Pat was a mess. Unemployed and unloved and abandoned by his friends and dying of AIDS, but at this moment his head was clearer and he was made of sterner stuff than me. I bowed to his common sense.

"Of course," I said.

All of us walked up the five flights. The Ethiopians went into my apartment.

"I've told Mr. Uleyawa that they're going to spend as long as it takes cleaning up the blood, not that you'll be staying there anymore, not that anyone will be staying there anymore. But just to be on the safe side," Pat said.

"Why won't I be staying there?" I asked.

"They know where you live, asshole. You'll be staying with me tonight, out first thing in the morning," Pat said. "I have a place in Fort Morgan, it's a one-room, it's full of my old shit, but you'll be safer there. Get you on the first bus."

"Gotta thank the Ethiopians," I said.

"No, don't say too much, they think we're doing it for Areea, we're covering up for her, for all of them, don't disavow them of that notion, we don't want them talking. Ok?"

We went to Pat's. He poured me a large whisky but I didn't drink it.

"She told him, Pat," I said. "She told him, Pat, she didn't have any qualms, I mistook her, I didn't see it, Jesus, she must have told him, too much of a coincidence. I don't know what I said. I said something, I fucked up, I killed him."

Pat put his fingers on my lips, showed me to his bed. I was too exhausted to protest. I boiled some ketch, injected it, crawled into his bed, and stared out the window at the sky over the park, stared all night until the black slowly evaporated and the stars went out and the ugly gray dawn stretched its tentacles across the sky. . . .

° ° °

The bus to Fort Morgan left at ten. It was nine-thirty, but I had to see Areea before I left. Pat was opposed.

"No time," he said, helping me on with my rucksack.

Downstairs. A knock. Her mother led her out. She'd been crying all night. She looked terrible. Where the blood had been, her hands and arms scrubbed raw.

"Areea, listen to me, I need you to understand that it wasn't your fault. There was nothing you could have done, you understand that, don't you?" I said.

Areea didn't say anything. She stared at me. She

opened her mouth but then closed it; her expression spoke volumes. She, for one, did not believe Pat's story about a burglar. In the night she had absolved herself of blame. She had placed it where it belonged. On my shoulders. Areea's cold intelligence had seen through everything, cut to the quick of things. She looked at me for a hard minute. Her eyes burned. I let her go. Backed away. Closed the door. So there I was, indicted. Given a responsibility I wasn't sure I would be able to fulfill.

In any case, I had to leave.

The bus station. A scout around for cops. None.

The bus.

Denver slipping behind me, with all the farce and horror and catastrophe; desiccated sunflowers on the plain, drying prairie, the South Platte River. I slept.

"Fort Morgan, Colorado," the driver said.

I got out.

The I-76, the river, a sugar factory, and unemployment were the salient features of Fort Morgan. Too far to commute to Denver, too close to the city for a thriving motel strip or highway spill-off trade. It had nothing much going for it. No mountains, no scenic beauty. Drugstores, diners, a couple of bars, depressed-looking, prematurely aged farmer types.

Pat's apartment was in an old redbrick building next to a large graveyard that ran beside the highway and the river beyond. One room. A dirty window, a working phone, a sink, a hotplate, a mattress on the floor, and everywhere a whole shitload of gear Pat had stolen from the Denver Fire Department. The guy had lifted everything: a uniform, a first-aid kit, two fire extinguishers, six pairs of fire-retardant gloves, a respirator, smoke bombs, burn cream, boots, and the pièce de résistance: a Kevlar vest that the firefighters wore when putting out fires in riot areas. Some handy stuff there for the motivated individual.

I stewed in the cramped Fort Morgan apartment for a week. One hundred degrees every day and a dry mistral from off the endless plain, dust from Mexico when the wind blew from the south and from Canada when it switched to the north.

I bought chili and dumped it in a pot. I didn't know what I was doing there. I was waiting. I was letting time slip by. I knew I wasn't going back to Ireland now. I mean, it could have been easy. I could have disappeared and never have had to deal with him or her again. I didn't know why they wanted me dead, I had no proof of anything, I wasn't going to the police with that thin tissue of suspicion and innuendo that would have gotten me laughed out of any precinct house. What was going on in his head? Did Charles think I knew more than I did? But if so, he must have known I wouldn't have fucked around, I would have gone straight to the peelers. I had nothing. Why bother to kill me? It made no sense. But then it's hard to know what goes on in the brain of a psychopath. Regardless, I could have vanished, I'm sure he thought that I was dead, he had stabbed me in the fucking heart. No report in the paper, but that didn't mean anything. Jesus,

I could be lying there still. Anyway, I was dead. And I could have stayed dead and they would never have thought of me again.

Pat had three books in his apartment: *The Man in the High Castle, Respiratory Injury: Smoke Inhalation and Burns,* and the *I Ching.* I read the former two and rolled the latter and the forty-second hexagram had nine in the last place. Misfortune: Do Not Act.

But it nagged at me.

What had I said to Amber that had finally blown the gaff? What had I done? And what about the lack of proof? If I knew anything, what game did they think I was playing? Did they think I wanted to blackmail them? Was that why I'd said nothing, I was biding my time, positioning myself to be the new Alan Houghton?

I used the phone. I had Pat now as a confidant. Pat took more interest in the case than John ever had. He was sharper, too. Pat had heard of the Mulhollands. He was fascinated by the whole business, especially the murder of Margaret Prestwick.

He reckoned that Charles had just panicked. Amber tells him I know about Victoria, I'm not who I say I am. He realizes I'm after them, panics. Whether I have enough evidence to go to the police is irrelevant. The congressman's resignation announcement coming up. The water cannot be muddied. I must be stopped. . . .

Gothic, but probably true.

Whatever the reason, Charles had read me completely wrong. That's not how I would have done things. I would have kept my mouth shut. I would have built my case slowly and steadily and then when I really had something, some actual, honest-to-God proof, I would have given it to the peels, gratis, let them handle it. He had read me wrong and Pat was probably right. Charles had freaked. Decided he had to finish it that night. Exhausted, nervous, resolved.

Colfax. That goddamn broken lobby door. Five flights. John with a knife in the heart. Charles, you fool, if only you could have taken a day's rest. Slept on it. You would have seen sense. No reason to kill me. John didn't have to die in my place. I had nothing. If I had, you'd have been in goddamn handcuffs. You and the wicked queen, too.

A week. A long week. I was running out of ketch. You couldn't get smack in this cow town. And at the end of it, I had thought enough. I was resolved.

I told Pat what I was going to do.

And once again, he was the voice of reason. And as I plotted and as I planned every day, he told me to forget it and to let it go.

But I couldn't, not now. It all had led to this. I had to see him in person, that was the only way. I had to. Why? What would I do when we met? Kill him? I didn't know. But I had to bring things to a head. I had to see the fucker. Had to. A compulsion. A madness.

Pat raged, fumed.

He told me to take the weekend to think it over before I did something so dumb. And Pat was a wise person and I would be a fool to ignore his advice and I did think it over, but I knew I was going to do it.

I told him.

Again Pat begged me to reconsider, but he knew it was too late and once he'd heard my plan, he resigned himself and decided that he should help, so at the very least I wouldn't get topped as easily as John.

"Sit tight," Pat said, "I'll be on the next bus up."

I met Pat off the bus. The ride had been rough on him, he was pale, sick. I cooked him Campbell's cream of mushroom soup. He ate some of it. Opened his overnight bag. Removed a bottle of gin and a .45 automatic Colt pistol.

"This is for you," he said, giving me the gun. "It was my dad's. Army issue. He was a lieutenant in World War Two. I've checked it, I shot it at the range. Works good. Anything closer than fifty feet. Blow their fucking head off."

"Thanks," I said. I felt better about it, I had a gun and a Kevlar jacket. I'd be safe. We went onto Pat's narrow fire escape, looked at the graveyard and the river, and talked.

"What makes you think he'll come alone?" Pat asked, pouring gin into a coffee mug.

"Oh, he has to. This whole thing has been about blackmail. He can't involve anyone else. He'll come alone, it wouldn't make sense for him to bring in other people now," I said with confidence.

"Take the gun, and wear that Kevlar vest, he'll try to kill you," Pat said.

"I know," I said.

A bright hot plains–Colorado afternoon. Blue sky. We walked together to the pay phone outside Walgreen's. Pat accompanying me at a snail's pace, but insisting on going in a last ditch effort to dissuade me. I dialed the number. I got through to the Mulhollands' answer phone. Read from my piece of paper:

"I want to meet. This is a one-time-only offer. You didn't kill me. I am not dead. You fucked up. You know who this is. I want to meet on my turf. Alone. Tomorrow night, midnight, the cemetery in Fort Morgan, Colorado, the shelter in the center of the graveyard. Alone."

I hung up the phone.

* * *

The next day. A thunderstorm came in about ten o'clock. Thunder and sheet lightning that shook the whole building. It began to hail, golf-ball size.

"Nasty," I said, looking out the window, just for something to say.

"Yup," Pat said. "On the radio they said it would be freezing rain and hail. Whoever heard of such a thing in July? It's El Niño, that's what it is. Won't do any good, though, we need six months of sweet Jesus rain, need it bad."

"I know," I said.

"But look at that. Can't see for shit out that window. I won't be able to check the cemetery. Dumb-ass plan. I knew it. I bloody told you. You'll be on your own," Pat said grimly.

"I'll be ok."

Pat muttered and made some coffee. We watched the clock. Midnight crept around.

"Well, I better go," I said.

"Can I just say one thing?" Pat asked.

"Aye."

"This won't solve anything," Pat said, his melancholy eyes teary, sad.

"Pat, I'm going to get this fucker, he killed my best friend, I have to do this, I have to bring things to a head."

"You don't have to do anything, Alex," Pat pleaded.

"I do," I said.

"Why not just go home," Pat said.

"No."

"What do you possibly think you can get from this?"

I thought for a moment. What did I want? I wanted to confront him, I wanted to yell at him, I wanted him to confess, I wanted him to go to the police, to turn himself in, I wanted to see his face, I wanted closure, I wanted him dead. I wanted a million things.

I put on a sweater, a coat, the Kevlar vest, and a wool hat to keep out the rain.

"Are you sure he'll be alone?" Pat asked.

"He has to come alone. This is all about blackmail. They can't involve anyone else. You'll see," I reassured him.

"Be careful," Pat said.

"I will."

I left the apartment, walked downstairs. I crossed

the street to the main graveyard entrance. Went in. My plan was to skirt the tree-lined stone cemetery wall on the river side. It rose to a dense woody embankment overlooking the graves and from there I could see everything, yet because of the trees I couldn't be seen. Charles wouldn't know that. He wouldn't know Fort Morgan. He'd show up, go to the shelter in the center of the graveyard, wait for me, but I'd already be there watching him.

I inched along the wall. The hail had become freezing rain. Pitch black. I couldn't see ten feet in front of me. I stopped in the trees fifty feet behind the shelter.

Midnight. A few minutes after.

A figure in a white coat. Too small to be Charles. Who? Amber? He sent you to do the dirty work? He sent you to clean up his mess?

I watched her. I waited. She came closer.

Amber. Is that really you? I kept behind the trees. Had to be her. I smiled. I moved nearer, still hidden by the undergrowth. I slithered down the embankment until I was only twenty feet away, cloaked by the trees and the night.

"Amber," I said.

She didn't hear. She leaned on a hooped pillar, provided for people to tie up their horses.

I said it louder: "Amber."

She spun around, looking at the graves, and then she peered into the thickets of dense wood, staring right at me, not seeing me. The hood on her coat up, but definitely Amber. No one else had that poise. That deep embodiment of sex. One of the main weapons in her arsenal. And as I stood there looking at her, thinking of that, gazing at her, it came to me and I knew what the mistake had been. What a naive boy I was. From Ireland. From the sticks.

"Amber."

"Alex?" she said. It *was* her.

"Amber, I know now what I did wrong," I said.

"Come out, come down here and talk to me like a civilized person," she said with self-assurance.

"It was that remark, that joke. Wasn't it?"

No reply.

"That Kama Sutra twenty-one joke. Goddamnit. You froze up after that. And you told Charles. And he came to kill me."

"Come out of there and talk to me face-to-face," she said. Cool, icy. I liked that.

"Kama Sutra twenty-one. Victoria said that to me once. Victoria Patawasti. She said that as a joke to make me laugh. To relax me. A joke against herself. You know, because she's Indian. But she said it to you, too, didn't she? You slept with her, didn't you? You fucked her to get her to tell you her password. Or if not to tell you, to give you information to work it out? I'm right, tell me I'm right, Amber."

"Come over here and I'll talk to you, I can barely hear you," she said, quiet and calm. Of course she wasn't going to confirm or deny anything in case I had a tape recorder. I knew that.

"'Carrickfergus,' you kept saying. Was that it? Does

that ring a bell? Was that her password? Maybe, maybe not. Who cares. It doesn't matter. You got it somehow. Seduced her, got her to trust you. You were Charles's whore. And it was more than just the password, he wanted to know if she could be bought."

"You must be drunk or something, Alexander, I don't know what you're talking about, I want to help you, I think you might be mentally unbalanced, you're talking nonsense, come down here, come out of there, I can help you," she said.

I barely contained my anger.

"No, you stand there and fucking listen to me," I said.

"But I don't know what you're talking about, I'm really sorry, Alexander, you're out of your mind," she said softly, patronizingly, like a social worker or a nuthouse nurse.

"You know exactly what I'm talking about. Alan Houghton, the first obstacle. Victoria Patawasti, the second. And you seduced her and she wasn't sure, but you're so goddamn beautiful. You fucked her. Probably with that strap-on dildo you used to have."

"That's disgusting, you must be drunk or on drugs or something. Please, Alex, believe me, I have no idea what you're saying," she said.

"Liar. You fucked her. Charles told you to do it. Maybe it was her first time with a woman, she was nervous, so she made that joke. That same fucking joke. Her on top, you below. 'That's position twenty-one of the Kama Sutra,' she said. And stupid me. You remembered it when I said it."

"Oh, my God. I don't know what you're talking about. You're quite delusional," she said, calm and lovely and irritating.

"When I did that Kama Sutra joke, you knew I'd slept with her too, that I knew Victoria Patawasti, that I'd slept with her and that I'd come to avenge her, to seek you out."

She didn't speak, she didn't budge, she stared at me, silent, unmoving. Infuriating.

"Tell me I'm wrong, you bitch, you bloody bitch," I screamed at her.

But she said nothing. Shook her head sadly. Smiled. It was the final straw.

I climbed out of the thicket. I walked down the embankment toward her. I took out the .45, chambered a round. She dropped something, a signal. Hit the deck, put her hands over her head, a glint of her white teeth grinning in the dark and rain.

The shooting started and I was hit immediately in the chest and shoulder.

I tumbled to the bottom of the embankment. Gasping. Blood over my hands. Bullets flew out of the dark, thumping into a tree a half meter to my left. Others flew by from a different angle, big and churning like machine-gun rounds. The rain poured down. It hurt to the touch. My hat gone. Amber gone. Dazed. I looked for a way out but the air was as thick as coal.

I stood again. Easy target. Petrified. I dived for cover. I got behind a gravestone. Caught my breath. A scream of objects came whistling by out of the trees.

An arc of fire. A shotgun. Jesus. So that's shooter number three: a guy above me blocking off the exit.

They had planned it out. Trumped me, checkmated me. They had anticipated that I would come early, that I would be in the trees above the shelter and along the wall. They had seen all this and had placed two assassins in the shelter next to Amber and one in the trees behind me so I could not escape. The men below had me from different angles and the man up at the wall could shoot down on me from a flanking and elevated position.

I had lost all the advantages that I had come here with: surprise, tactical superiority, the high ground.

Automatic weapons. M16s. Coils of tracer in the black sky. A hungry pack of bullets seeking me out. The cemetery far from streetlights, and Fort Morgan cloaked in low clouds. Thunder. Rain. No stars. No cars. No help.

They found me. An object smashed into me and I went down again. My eyes saw white. I bit through my tongue. I rolled to the side. I'd taken another hit. Above my left knee this time. I reached down and my hand came back with blood. Shotgun pellet. I couldn't tell if my patella was smashed. A lot of blood. I yelled and burst into tears. Scrambled away. Pathetic. I had failed. For Victoria, for me. For everyone. I, who was so goddamn smart. Jesus. My eyes closed. She was cleverer than me. I could see that now. I had been bested. Arrogance. Hubris. I blinked. Crawled behind a big tomb bedecked by angels. The men were moving too. Getting a better position. I had to move. I slithered toward the embankment, under monuments, gravestones and Celtic crosses. A sign told me that I was in section K, block 1, wherever that was.

My head was light. I couldn't breathe. A tunnel collapsed my vision into a single fatal exit and the downpour took on a dreadful cadence. Funereal and mocking.

I should have listened to Pat.

No, it went further than that. I had fucked this up from the start. From the very day I landed in America. And now I was going to die.

At least it would be my just desserts. The punishment for such incompetence should be death. I took another breath.

"Lost him," one man yelled.

"No, over there somewhere," another replied.

"I'll go around," said the first.

Trapped, but I would try for it. The least I could do. I got up, I staggered on. Impossible. Shambling. Ahead of me somewhere in the pitch black were steps that led to the back entrance to the cemetery, the closed gate, the wire fence. Twenty or thirty widespaced cuts into the side of the hill, filled with pounded stone, leveled. I could have run them in thirty seconds on a good day. Now, at night, in the middle of a storm, with a shoulder wound, a leg wound, and with at least three gunmen less than the length of a basketball court away and zeroing in on me, it would be a bloody epic. Three men, one armed with a shotgun and the others using bloody automatic rifles.

I made it up about three steps, slipped on the dirt, fell. Tumbled down the hill, slewing in the mud. My head hit the side of a cast-iron litter bin. Sickening pain, a big cut above my ear. The shotgun tore up the air to my left.

"There he is," someone yelled.

I slithered behind a stand of trees. I couldn't see them but somehow they could see me. Maybe they had night scopes. Or, more likely, maybe they just knew there was nowhere else I could be. I gasped for air, panicked, waited for the big hit.

The rain a knife blade. My scalp on fire. My knee screamed, my chest gurgled, the wind blew down. I threw up in my mouth. Junk sick.

I saw a storage shed for lawnmowers. I crawled behind it. Safe for a few seconds. I took a deep breath. Calmed myself. Options. I wasn't dead yet. I had the dark. I had a gun of my own. And the rain so thick it was nearly impossible to see. The boys would have to come close to administer the coup de grâce.

I did a quick triage. I'd been hit in the chest, but the vest had protected me.

The shoulder wound was a ricochet off the Kevlar. I felt around, it wasn't serious. I was bleeding, but no major blood vessel had been punctured and it hurt like hell—a good sign. The shotgun pellet in the leg wouldn't kill me. I put my finger through my soaked jeans to the skin. A lot of blood, but I could wiggle my toes. My tendons and nerves were ok. All that shooting and I'd really only been fucking grazed.

More shots, yells of organization: "Where'd he go? Where's that fucking light? Who had the light?"

Only male voices. Amber, of course, was well out of this. Back at the car. Gone. Already left town. I took out the .45. Blacked out for a second. Where was I? I was in the middle of a graveyard. Shooters above and to the side of me. Three points of a triangle and I was at the center. They were good. Pat had been right. I was an idiot, an amateur dealing with professionals. It made no sense, Amber, why would you hire three more potential blackmailers? Goddamnit, it made no sense. Forget it. Had to get out. If I could make it to the fence on the far left of the cemetery. About fifty yards. Could I walk it? I'd have to crawl. Ok. Ignore the pain. Let's go.

Caked with filth, I slithered my way over graves, cleaning the vomit out of my nostrils, sliding carefully along the ground.

Suddenly someone shouted triumphantly: "There he is."

They turned a dazzling portable spotlight on me. One of those with thousands of candlepower.

And I knew if I didn't move I was a dead man.

An M16 threw fire at me from the trees. I struggled to my feet and ran for the fence, ignoring the pain from the pellet above my knee. The rain made it difficult to see, to get purchase on the ground. I slipped and fell between the pillars of a massive tomb. Bullets smashed into the marble, sending chips everywhere. I ran for the fence, dodging between graves, taking cover between granite tombstones. Shots and fire overhead. A man in front of me. I was heading straight for him. His back to me, a big dark shape in the night and rain.

An automatic rifle churned up the mud ahead of me, smacking into granite, tracer bouncing everywhere, like fireworks.

"Frank, stop shooting, you're going to hit fucking Manny, Frank, cut it out," a voice yelled.

I ran toward the man.

"Jesus, Frank, didn't you fucking hear me? Stop shooting."

The M16 abruptly stopped.

"Manny, Manny, he's over there, he's right there."

The voice was yelling desperately, behind me and over to my left. The big light came full on me again.

"There he is, Manny, turn around." Another voice.

"Where?"

"Manny, he's right there, at that big cross behind you."

Manny, in front of me, turned at last when we were fifteen feet apart. White guy with a beard and a flat cap. Soaked through. Probably waiting here for hours. He began raising his shotgun. He hadn't kept it leveled because he hadn't wanted water to get into the barrels.

That's what killed him.

I straightened my weapon, pulled the trigger. Pat's big Colt banged. Flame from the heavy barrel. I'd cleaned it, but this weapon hadn't been fired in combat since the Battle of the Ardennes. I screamed,

charged him. Ran into the dark, shooting. Half a clip.
Like an insane man. Blinding flashes from the .45.
When my eyes cleared, no sign of Manny, he was
down.

Yellow fire all around me from the M16s. The
Fourth of July and Guy Fawkes night and a riot drill
and every other nightmare rolled into one.

I could see gravity in the parabola of the tracer. The
bullets smacking into the wire fence around the cemetery. Ringing off the concrete walls, bouncing a thousand feet into the air.

I ran like a shit-kicker now. I sprinted to the cemetery fence. I needed both hands, so I dropped the .45.
I climbed over the five-foot wire mesh, fell to the
ground, scrambled across the car park on the other
side.

More tracer, more bullets. M16s in the middle of
the town. But this was Fort Morgan after midnight,
during a thunderstorm. Empty.

I kept running. The car park was well lit up. They
found me easily in the lights and shot at me but the
shots were wild, they rang and screamed off the railings, and the shooters didn't focus them properly. They
were excited, not taking their time.

I saw a Volkswagen camper van parked on an over-
look near the river.

I yelled. "Help, is there anyone there? Help."

I ran to the van and banged on the window. Bullets
slammed into the side of the vehicle, puncturing tires
and windows. Glass and metal shards smacking into

me. A bullet careened off the Kevlar vest, knocking me
to my knees.

"Fucker," one of the men screamed behind me.

I got up and turned to see two men climbing over
the cemetery fence. They had shoulder-strapped their
rifles. Bearing down. Big men. White guys. Heavy, but
tough. Where had they come from? All the trouble
they took to silence a simple blackmailer in Denver,
and Charles somehow hires three professional killers
to shoot me?

I ran past the sugar factory, the Walgreen's, a video
store. The shops all closed. The street deserted.

"Come back, you fucker," they yelled, shooting pistols now.

A bullet clanged into a stop sign. I ran on, wounded,
slowing as they gained.

Only one thing for it now.

Only one way out. The river. I cut across the deserted I-76.

I sprinted to the end of a lane and vaulted over the
safety railing that led to the embankment over the
South Platte. I stole a final look back. They were still
shooting at me as they ran.

I took a breath, jumped.

A moment in the river-cooled air.

I landed in the water.

Sank like a fucking stone. . . .

Coldness.

Smothering, death-bringing cold. Annihilating, elec-
trocuting cold. The air crushed from my lungs.

My body writhes. Shots in my wake. I gasp for breath. I swallow greasy, frigid water and sink and am rocketed downstream. I fall through the poisons and heavy chemicals toward the choked sandy bottom, clutching, screaming, down-down-down.

I touch bottom, I'm dragged along rocks.

My blood freezing, my eyes open.

So this is how it ends.

In this river. With these gray claws and ash tide. The Platte with its hard line and dead current. This river. Like the gun, to the Mississippi, the Gulf of Mexico, the Atlantic. This river. To its black, tenebrous heart. And I go to you and I see you in the dark. I see your traces along the trail that you have beaten to the Great Perhaps. And are you there, Victoria, and are you there, Mum? It's cold, it hurts. And I smile. This river. This time.

But no.

Not yet.

That will come.

But not yet.

My fingers find the Velcro straps of the Kevlar vest. I pull them, the straps loosen, the Velcro rips, the vest falls off me and I tumble upward to the surface. I suck a desperate breath, float for a minute in the fast-moving water, before smacking into a rock on a sandbank. I lie there for half an hour.

Wade across the shallows to the bank.

Walk.

Shivering, oblivious to the rain, shoulder wound, leg

wound. Two miles back to Fort Morgan. Empty streets, neon signs, and not another human soul.

Adrenaline fighting against blood loss and exhaustion.

Three floors to Pat's apartment. The door.

"Help me," I manage and Pat turns, horrified, toward me.

And I fall at his feet and slip into that other realm where things made sense and the guilty suffered and equity lived and we all were saved.

11: THE LAST INCARNATION OF VISHNU

Ash on the fire escape. Images. A black cloud. My mother's hand. Her cold fingers. What will you do, son?

I'll join the cops, Ma.

No, no, don't do that, it'll upset your father, stay at university, it's for the best.

Ok, I will, Ma. I will. . . .

Them's brave boys that are out in that, John mutters.

Aye, I say.

We sit and drink and the smoke comes slowly overhead like a continent. Ash from the big wildfire near Greeley. John walks to the rail and is almost lost in the vertical cliff of choking smog that hangs in a blanket above the buildings. A stink of fire. Water-carrying planes flying overhead. I'm waiting with him on the narrow fire escape steps. I'm standing and hugging myself and he is hunched over and spitting down onto the dead potted plants of the floors below.

We both smell of smoke. He passes me the bottle and I take it in my left hand. The American whiskey tastes sour. I gulp down a big swig of it and the fake heat evaporates the cold out of my ears. I give him the bottle back and he swallows down the rest. For a minute I think he's going to throw it onto the ground and see if it smashes, but instead he sets it carefully on the iron slats of the fire escape.

We can maybe get ten cents back on that bottle, I say.

He turns to look at me and shakes his head, his shaggy hair still as his face moves. It's a weird effect, not unconnected to the booze. I laugh a little.

I'm drunk and cold, I tell him.

If you're cold, you can't be drunk, ya big wean, alcohol numbs the senses, he announces in a tone of pissed authority.

Bollocks, I think. But I don't want to argue with him. After all, he is dead.

Let's go in, he says, this overhang is barely giving us any shelter. This smoke can't be good for your lungs. Gimme a hand to get this thing open.

He gives me his cigarette and tugs on the window and tries to pull it up. It sticks on the first shove and he has to thump it. A heap of red ash falls on us from the wooden board covering the air conditioner on the next floor.

Hey, watch what you're doing, John, I say.

Relax.

He bends his body and pushes past me, climbing in through the window, over the grille of the security gate.

Aye, like you couldn't wait for me, I say sarcastically and look around at this sorry excuse for a town, the orange sky, the old buildings, shriveled and spectral. And all I can think about are the gray waves that separate us from our home. A moat between me and the braided dark.

Eagla, mathair, eagla, I whisper into the stinking air.

Are you saying something? he mutters from inside.

No.

Aye, well, get in and we'll get this window closed, so we will. Quit your gabbing and get moving, he says suspiciously.

I put a leg over the metal trough. It's sharp and comes up to my groin, so I can't lean on it. I end up falling in and landing in a clatter on the floor.

Keep your comments to yourself, I say before he can call me an eejit.

You care about my comments, he says, with a sly grin on his pale face. Anyway, it's late and it's time we were in bed, he says.

I am in bed, I say.

And he looks at me, surprised.

So you are, he says. What are you doing?

I'm recovering from drowning and from Pat taking a shotgun pellet out of my leg and the fact that I'm going off ketch forever.

You're not.

John, I have to. They're having a fund-raiser, a ball. We saw it on Channel 9. And I'm going. And this time I won't screw up. This time I'm going to kill him. I'm quitting ketch. Pat's helping me.

John looks at me skeptically.

You couldn't kill someone, he says, and don't say you

killed that guy in the cemetery, there was no report about it in the paper, they must have taken him with them.

I gave him half a clip, I protest.

How many hit him? John mocks.

The dying man, who has been in the corner the whole time, looks up at me. His flat cap is askew, shotgun by his side, he's still soaked, but with blood, not rain.

Enough hit me, he says.

John snaps his fingers in front of my face.

Ignore him, he says. Continue.

Pat's making me healthy, I say.

Sure, he's in no fit state himself, he says.

He's fine. End of conversation. All right?

Aye.

And now I have to see Ma, and I have to reveal the black secret at the heart of the Troubles.

That's ok, just don't say that thing again.

What thing?

I am the Last Incarnation of Vishnu, the Avenger, Storm Bringer, Lord of Death.

Ok. I won't, I say, and pause for effect and then announce: I am the Last Incarn—

He turns off the light. . . .

.   .   .

Ma is in the ground six weeks, and I'm on the Scotch Quarter being interviewed. They're accepting my application to join the police. It has annoyed my lefty, progressive father, and that's the beauty of the thing.

"Alex, we always want someone who has experience of the law and your A levels are outstanding, do you have anything you want to say?"

Do I have anything I want to say?

My eyes fluttering . . .

The bedroom spinning.

Pat gives me the bucket and I throw up.

"Neither poppy nor mandragora will ever medicine to thee that sweet sleep which thou hadst yesterday."

"What?"

"Not poppy, not mandragora (whatever that is) will give me that sweet sleep of yesterday. I see that now. Heroin takes, never gives. That and that alone can explain so many mistakes since coming to America."

"And you say heroin is to blame?"

"Yes."

"But earlier you said heroin saved your life?"

"It did."

"How?"

Like this:

I'd been a policeman for nearly six years. A full detective for three. I had gone straight into homicide. As Commander Douglas of the Samson Inquiry will tell you, this is practically unheard of. Being groomed, and I knew it. I was being used, but I wanted to be used, I wanted to make my way up. There were factions within the RUC that didn't like the way things were. Fine, use me to further your ends. My talents, my skill. My *techne*.

All the way to the black heart of the Troubles.

A secret. Ostensibly, the rival paramilitary forces of the Protestants and the Catholics, the UDA and the IRA, were deadly enemies; but in the late eighties and early nineties, while they were killing each other in bombings, shootings, massacres, something brought them together.

Heroin.

Ireland was an island and it was impossible to get drugs there, especially when the paramilitaries had a thing for killing drug dealers and proving that they were as legitimate of respect as the police. But in 1993 at a secret meeting in Jake's Bar in Belfast, it was decided to divide up Ulster between them. Heroin was just too big a moneymaker to ignore. Had to be secret. Had to be hush-hush. The IRA's backers in Boston and New York and San Francisco would have been upset if they had known the IRA was in the drug-dealing business. And the UDA's backers in Belfast and Glasgow would have had similar qualms.

After six years as a police officer I was appointed DC/DS, Detective Constable/Drug Squad.

Heroin, the gateway drug, was giving the paramilitaries millions and they were still bombing bars and factories and driving people into their arms for protection. That was why people like Victoria Patawasti had to leave Northern Ireland in the first place.

Yes, thinking, remembering it.

Lying here, in this bed, Pat bringing me soup.

"Are you ok, son?"

"I'm ok, Pat. Hey, it's snowing."

"No. It isn't, Alex. It's just ash from the wildfire, don't worry about it, just relax, they have it eighty percent contained."

"Look, Pat, the snow," I say, but he's gone and it's night. I put my head out the window and the snow stings me in the iris making tears that skitter down the lines of least resistance on my face, half-freezing before they slide off my chin.

I can stare right through the clouds, through the dark. The snow is coming not from the sky but from the blue-faced moon, where the Celts believed the dead go. You sent it, Ma. Drizzling from the ether and the high atmosphere and down the roof onto this bed. It moistens my lips.

Morning.

"Eat your soup," Pat says, and kisses me on the forehead.

"The case," I tell him.

I followed it for months, it wasn't that important, but it led to a suspect. Was it all a setup? My mentor was Chief Superintendent William McConnell. Big man, forties, old school. I trusted him.

"Alex, follow this where it leads, I'll back you up."

"I will, sir. I will."

Stakeouts, undercover, but more the paper trail. Made an arrest. Stuart Robinson, a CPA. Ha. Just like how they got Capone. Does no one ever learn the lessons of history? I cracked him, I broke him, I trapped him in his own lies. He gave me names and I found it out. It was waiting to be found out. I don't flatter myself. I saw it, a black secret. The IRA, the sworn enemies of the police, worked with a tiny corrupt unit within the police to control the flow of heroin into Ireland. The IRA and dirty cops. The bad guys and the good. Samson was on the right track. Buck McConnell, Commander Douglas were on the right track. It was all true. It went to the highest levels of the cops. Dangerous information. And what did I do, reading the accounts, that rainy night in Carrickfergus in my apartment overlooking the marina. What did I do?

I could take the evidence outside the RUC, to Special Branch in England, and forever live my life a fugitive, knowing that one day they'd get to me, they always do.

One bright morning in Perth, Australia, I go out to get my paper and a man with an Irish accent says hello, Alexander, and shoots me in the head.

Or I could bury the case, pretend it never happened.

Maybe I am a coward. I sat on it, in indecision, and that night . . .

Pat comes in with tea. Chitchat. I stroke my beard. I have a beard again. It's been days. Weeks?

"You were saying?" Pat asks, liking when I talk, he says it helps me.

"That night . . ."

Heavy fog had smothered the wind and for once the gossipy yachts, dinghies, and small craft were silent.

My apartment at the marina. The quiet woke me. Gulls and distant foghorns up in Belfast. I sat in the bed and weighed my options. I was sweating, afraid. Death and exile on the one hand, or do nothing and forever live in shame. I heard the sound of hobnail boots on the marina pontoons. I grabbed my service revolver, but I put it down again.

The interrogating room. Classic twist. The roles reversed.

"I'm saying nothing until I see a lawyer."

"You won't be seeing a lawyer, Alex, you're being held under the Prevention of Terrorism Act."

"I want to speak to Buck McConnell."

"Chief Superintendent McConnell has taken early retirement as of this morning."

And I knew if I blabbed they'd kill me. They suspected that I knew the names of the corrupt cops but if I confirmed it, I'd be dead. They held me for two days and I said nothing and they released me. It gave them and me time to think.

What do I do, go to Scotland Yard, Special Branch, to the newspapers? I'd be hunted, killed. Say nothing, wait for the shoe to drop, I'd be hunted, killed. Run? Where?

I walked home from the barracks, afraid of every passing car.

Yes . . .

Pat sponges me down and cleans me off. Gives me green tea that he says is loaded with antioxidants, I throw it up. Why was it so hard going off junk when I wasn't a junkie? Pat helps me to the toilet and I drizzle diarrhea and sob.

The bed.

The apartment overlooking the boats. Death one way. Death the other. Racking my squirreled-up brains.

And I hit upon a solution.

A third way.

Brilliant. The scourge would save me. The biter bit.

I found my undercover stash and like I'd watched, but never done, I injected myself with heroin and tracked up and down my arm until it looked like I was a junkie. Hit, rest, hit, rest, needle marks. And then I signed into the police station, broke into the evidence room, and got caught stealing half a click of heroin under my jacket. I was arrested on the spot. They found the track marks and it was such an obvious cliché, they bought it, the drug squad officer who uses. Maybe to establish credibility with dealers undercover, maybe because he was tempted, maybe he was weak. But it happened. Pathetic. Caught fucking red-handed. Where do these eejits come from?

And the higher-ups saw too. I was a junkie drug-squad officer. Caught stealing. How to handle it? Prosecute me?

No.

I would resign in disgrace, my file would be closed, we would hush it up.

Perfect. If I shut up and behaved myself, we'd leave it at that. And if I tried to whistleblow, I would have no credibility, no one would believe me, a junkie peeler caught stealing ketch from the police evidence room.

No need to kill me now. I wasn't blabbing, I wasn't going to anyone. I could never make my case. I had a record and no moral weight and I would live.

I had saved my life. And every day I kept using and I kept buying and I was safe.

Heroin had saved my life.

Or it had for six months till Commander Douglas from the Samson Inquiry came along and made me an offer I had to refuse. . . .

Pat nods. Rambling and arse backward, but Pat has got the gist of it.

"So why can't you go home now?" he asks.

"They think Commander Douglas will compel me to testify anyway, my evidence alone would not be credible, but it will add to the overwhelming weight of evidence Samson has compiled. They have to plug the hole in every dyke. Have to kill me, just in case. I'm not safe anywhere."

"That's why, Alexander, it's better that you stay here and do nothing and get well," Pat says.

"Pat, I have nothing there, I have nothing here. The reason I'm getting well, the reason I'm quitting junk, is so that I can fucking shoot Charles Mulholland, the killer of my two friends. Don't you see, man's crazy. Gotta be stopped. I've got to do it before the announcement on August sixth, before he gets to run for Congress. If I can do it, I can wipe the slate clean."

Pat wipes my brow and cleans me with a sponge. Spoons tea into my mouth and shakes his head.

"Alex, the announcement was yesterday. You've been here for ten days. It's too late. Congressman Wegener has already announced that this will be his last term. The mayor of Fort Collins isn't entering the race. It's a coronation. Charles Mulholland will be running for the GOP nomination unopposed. It's all over. It's too late. Let it go."

"What? Too late? Oh yeah, I forgot, I forgot, that's not the plan, new plan, kill him at the fund-raiser, kill him then."

"Madness," Pat mutters. "You didn't listen to me before, listen to me now."

I owed Pat a lot. He had operated on my leg to remove a shotgun pellet and then kept me alive despite the fact that I'd been suffering hypothermia, shock, blood loss, and then junk withdrawal. Pat was no surgeon, either, a paramedic, and paramedics aren't trained for that kind of thing. But he'd done enough. And in any case, I didn't hear him. I was taking advice from a higher authority. The verse of the Gita echoing in my skull: O Arjuna. Why give in to this shameful weakness? You who would be the terror of thine enemies.

The terror of thine enemies.

∘　∘　∘

It had taken several more days until I felt confident about walking the streets of Fort Morgan again. I had kicked heroin and my leg was healed and I could walk and run. We had looked out for dodgy characters, but there were none. The hired guns had seen me sink in the South Platte and, as Pat says, but for the two years of drought and the river's historic low level, I surely would have drowned.

But, anyway, I was in the clear. They thought I was dead for the second time. You can't ignore a chance like that. My next move was the story on Channel 9. Charles was having a fund-raiser, a summer "white attire only" ball at the Eastman Ballroom in Denver. It showed Charles's savvy. The historic Eastman Ballroom hadn't been used for several years, everybody said a big event like this might help keep away the developers. Regardless. That's where I would set the world to rights.

And I was certain about Charles and I knew it was him, but one thing troubled me still. What had happened in the cemetery made no sense. Charles would never have hired contract killers to ambush me. First of all, how could he have met them? Every third hit man in America is an undercover FBI special agent. Second, as I'd thought at the time, what was to stop them blackmailing Charles once he became famous?

Something wasn't right.

So, free of junk for the first time in nearly a year, I told Pat, "We have to go back to Denver."

He protested, raged, refused.

We packed our stuff. Rode the bus, arrived at Denver, took a taxi to Pat's old apartment building. The

Ethiopians were gone, the lobby smelled of urine and was filled with garbage. Someone had tried to break the new locks on the inner door but fortunately had not succeeded.

We settled into Pat's place. I couldn't go back to the apartment where John had been killed. . . .

And the world harsher. Denver, a big, hot, unpleasant city, and I got hungry now and I could read people when they were angry and I couldn't ignore filth and dirt. Ketch softened the edges of everything, soothed you, blurred things like an impressionist painting. With ketch, Streisand was always singing and Vaseline was always on her lens.

I researched the stories of Robert, Charles, and Amber Mulholland. Old-fashioned police work. Phone calls to Harvard, to Cutter and May law firm, to the Mulholland Trust. Legwork at the Denver Public Library.

Robert and Charles checked out. They left traces all over the papers. Well known. The kids of a multimillionaire. Father divorced, the trust funds, the private schools, the Ivy League education, both PhDs in economics/political science. There were no surprises.

The surprise reserved for Amber Mulholland.

Hardly any information at all under that name. Her wedding in *The Denver Post* and *The New York Times*, but very little else. I remembered that photograph in the yearbook in her apartment. During her first year at Harvard, she had changed her name from Amber Doonan to Amber Abendsen. Now, why had she done that? She had mentioned some kind of problem with her father. But it had puzzled me at the time. Which was her real name? There was an easy way to find out. . . .

I put on a shirt and tie and showed up with a dozen white roses at the nursing home Amber's mother was housed at on Pennsylvania Street.

A very young security guard with a buzz cut.

"Yeah, maybe you can help me, I've got roses for a Mrs. Doonan, but then that's crossed out and it says Mrs. Abendsen?" I said in my best approximation of an American accent.

The guy barely looked at me.

"Room 201," he said.

"What name is it?" I asked.

"You had it the first time," he said.

The home was upscale. Plush carpets, a mahogany handrail, nurses in crisp white uniforms. I knocked on 201. I went in. A frail, silver-haired old lady, sitting in a chair, looking out the window, stroking a sweater curled in her lap like a cat.

"I've got some flowers for you," I said.

She didn't turn around. Didn't look up.

"Flowers," I said again, but she didn't even appear to be aware of my presence in the room. How old did Amber say she was? Sixty-eight? She seemed just a little older, but clearly, the disease had hit her hard. There was no way I could ask her anything but there was no point in wasting an opportunity. I put the flowers down and scouted the room. A few pictures, prints.

Cautiously at first, I opened her chest of drawers. Amber's mother didn't move.

Old-lady clothes, adult diapers, nothing special, but in the top of a cupboard that she couldn't reach—personal effects. China figurines, Hummel characters, bits of crystal, a few postcards. Several from Amber. Nothing of interest until I found an envelope filled with papers. The mother lode. Literally. Her birth certificate, born Louise Abendsen, Knoxville, Tennessee, 1927, her high school graduation certificate, her marriage license to Sean Doonan on October 31, 1955, and divorce papers from him on January 1, 1974, when Amber would have been about eight or nine.

Louise stared out the window, not stirring as I looked at this, the most significant piece of information so far. For on the divorce papers it said "Custody to the father, Sean Doonan, on the grounds of Louise Doonan's present incarceration at the Huntsville State Correctional Facility." The divorce papers made a big play out of the fact that Mrs. Doonan had gone to prison three times in the previous ten years for shoplifting, petty theft, drunkenness, and other crimes that the papers said "were signs of an unbalanced temperament." The papers also made a point of explicitly denying "Mrs. Doonan's claims that Sean Doonan was in any way involved in organized crime."

"Flowers," Louise said, not moving from her spot at the window.

I said nothing.

"Flowers," she said again.

She was getting agitated. Time to go. I had plenty here to work with anyway. The information almost made me feel sorry for Amber. Screwed-up mother, dodgy father. I put the envelope back. I looked at Louise. I knew I couldn't leave the flowers, in case someone wondered where they'd come from, so I took them with me and dumped them in a trash can down the hall. I felt bad. The guard didn't look up as I walked out.

The rest of the pieces weren't difficult to fill in. The New Jersey and, indeed, the New York papers had heard of Sean Doonan. A notable, but unindicted, member of the Irish mob in Union City. He had been implicated on several counts of union fraud, numbers rackets, protection rackets. He had never been convicted of anything.

After their divorce, Amber had gone to live with him full-time. She had clearly run a little wild. Amber Doonan's name showed up in the *Union City Gazette* in connection with arrests for vandalism and car theft. I had interlibrary loan at the Denver Public Library get me a photocopy of the relevant issues of the *Gazette*. A grainy black-and-white photo that showed a defiant, pretty punk girl with a pierced nose and a shaved head.

Amber, however, had either done brilliantly on her SATs or her da had pulled strings, for she had been accepted to Harvard. As I'd already discovered, in her second year Amber began calling herself Amber Abendsen, her mother's maiden name. Young Ms.

Abendsen won a Boston Drama Festival Prize, and I even found a photograph in *The Boston Globe* that showed a girl with long blond hair in a Gucci blouse. Neither her father nor her mother attended Amber's Harvard graduation, something two of her college classmates commented on when I phoned them. It didn't surprise me now.

It seemed that Amber had reinvented herself in Boston. She had disowned her parents. Shanty Irish mobster dad, convict, drunken ma. She had made herself anew. She was moving in different social circles, ashamed of where she'd come from. She'd removed that harp tattoo. Cleaned up her elocution. But you could take the girl out of the bog, but not the bog out of the girl. The stealing of the tip money, the random fucks, she had a little throwback in her. Or was that a racist thing to say? A classist thing. Maybe.

Regardless, from *The Denver Post,* it appeared that neither of Amber's parents came to her wedding. Probably Charles understood why Amber wanted it this way. At the time of the wedding, her ma was back in jail and her father had been on TV as part of a prolonged trial that had just collapsed. His face had again been in the New York papers. Indeed, Amber's father, Sean Doonan, was a nephew of Seamus Patrick Duffy, who was now the reputed leader of the Irish mob in New York City.

The more clear blue water between her and him the better, if she wanted to move in the dizzy circles around Charles Mulholland.

And all this would have been irrelevant but for one thing.

Now I probably knew where the gunmen in the park had come from.

My phone call must have precipitated it. Scared them. Charles and Amber at their wits' end. Charles had messed up; even though he'd stuck a knife in my heart, I wasn't dead. And Amber knew that to protect her husband and her future there was only one thing to do. She had to contact dear old Dad. It was possible. Why not? It seemed she had been telling the truth when she told me she didn't have a relationship with her father. Eight years of estrangement would have had to come to an end. She needed his help. She needed someone in whom she could place absolute trust, who would not blackmail her and Charles, who could supply three professional assassins to meet her husband's tormentor in Fort Morgan, Colorado. Charles had taken care of everything, but this loose end had to be taken care of by someone else.

So maybe she had picked up the phone. Knew that he would trade it for future favors, but even so. Dad I need your help. . . .

So it was another fuckup on my part, I'd arranged the meeting in the graveyard a day in advance, plenty of time for Doonan to fly a hit team to Denver, to drive to Fort Morgan, to scout the territory, to lay the trap. What a fool I'd been. And perhaps Charles had bullied her, frightened her. If I was right, it must have taken some persuading to get her to talk to her da, especially after all she had gone through to be rid of the past. But she had agreed. The future, too important. A politician's wife. A rising star. Yes, Charles, I'll call Da, he'll take care of it, he'll kill Alex.

Thanks, Amber. I am not one to hold a grudge. But, my dear, prepare your screams. Your Jackie Kennedy face. In three days Charles is going to be lying beside you with a bullet in his skull.

◊ ◊ ◊

I needed a weapon, so I went to see my old dealer, the Mexican kid who worked behind the Salvation Army shelter on Colfax. Entire books have been written about the relationship between a user and his dealer. Burroughs, De Quincey. Lou Reed has written songs about it. Mine was uncomplicated. I liked Manuelito. I had quit now and no one was interested in ketch in Denver, so I didn't blame him when he gave me a bit of the old cold shoulder at first when I went to see him.

"Manuelito," I said with a big grin.

"Manuel to you," he said sourly. His baby face trying to force a frown.

"Listen, I quit smack, don't bring me down."

He shook his head.

"Man, you know, heroin isn't even worth the risks anymore."

"I know," I said, and we chatted about the dreadful state of affairs the world was in when kids wanted to do crack and then go out and rob some old lady, rather than taking honest-to-God Afghani horse, which was so pure these days you could smoke it, mellow out, chill, harm nobody but yourself. On the subject of the dangerous world we lived in, I told him I needed a piece and he told me about an unlikely place to buy one.

"There's a guy called Tricky, lives a couple of blocks away from the police headquarters on Federal Plaza, I'll take you over."

We went to see Tricky. A wiry, high-strung Guatemalan kid who had so much energy he made me nervous. Also a bit tense to be looking at shotguns, Armalites, pistols, and a machine gun and thinking about committing a political murder a hundred yards from the police HQ and a divisional office of the FBI. Tricky wanted me to take the machine gun off his hands, but in the end I settled for a long-nosed .38 revolver similar to a gun I'd had in the peelers. Stolen from a gun dealer's in Mexico, Tricky said. As good as untraceable. Pistol in hand, I thanked the two boys and went back home.

Pat wasn't doing so well these days. He told me not to worry, saying that some weeks you were good and some weeks you were bad. His doc told him to expect that. It would be a sine curve of health, up, down, up, until the final cataclysmic plunge.

He coughed most of the time now and as I got stronger and put on weight, he balanced me out, getting paler and losing weight. Most nights now I fed *him* soup and did my best to keep his apartment clean.

Pat and I were really getting on and I felt a bit guilty about leaving him. But leave him I must. Either for jail or the afterlife or maybe even for Ireland. In case of the latter, I had changed my airline ticket once again, deciding that if I survived the assassination, I'd fly to Dublin that night on my real passport.

And I might shoot Charles and get out, but more likely I'd be killed at the scene or arrested. Congressman Wegener would be there and a senator from one of the logging states and they were bound to have protection. Peelers and FBI and maybe a few private security guards.

"Hey, Pat, does Colorado have the death penalty?"

"No," Pat said, with a little cough. "But you won't get that far," he added with an ironic grin.

He was wrapped in his blankets. He had a cold. A cold can kill an AIDS patient. He'd given me the list of numbers to call if we had to run him up to Saint Joseph's.

"Do you want some tea?" I asked. Pat shook his head.

"Did you take your AZT?"

"Everybody I know on AZT is dead," he said.

"Pat, do us all a favor and take your prescription. I don't need you dying on me."

"I'll take it, don't freak. I'll be fine, I'm a survivor," he said, his eyes lighting up to convince me. . . .

Two days before the fund-raiser.

Pat was very sick in the morning and I didn't get out to inspect the Eastman Ballroom until the afternoon.

Six blocks north of Colfax on Comanche Street. A large, boxy building with grille-covered, high-arched windows. Plain all the way around, but at the front a lovely art deco facade: marble columns that held up a statue of two seminaked figures who were either ballerinas or angels or prisoners on a starvation diet. It was a beautiful structure, though, elegant in its simplicity.

The ballroom sat on its own block, opposite an empty ball-bearing factory and an old warehouse. The closest apartment building was four blocks south and derelict. I couldn't quite understand how the neighborhood had worked; the sidewalks were large, the streets wide. No traffic, no people, no apartment buildings. Perhaps this had been the equivalent of a factory town and when the factory had closed, it had killed the neighborhood completely. Definitely an area waiting for redevelopers to swoop in and convert everything into condominiums.

The CAW "white attire" ball was by ticket only, but I felt I couldn't take the risk of attempting to buy a ticket, even under a fake name, since I'd have to have it sent to my Colfax address. Someone would put two and two together.

I'd have to find another way in.

I stared at the Eastman Ballroom entrance. A dozen steps led up to a set of double doors under the columns. There'd be ticket takers up there, and if I tried to bluff my way past, I knew it would all go wrong from the start. If I tried to shoot my way in, that would give Charles plenty of time to get to cover. I walked all the way around the building again and leaned against the wall of the old ball-bearing plant.

A dry, sunny Denver day and the factory made big, bold shadows on the road and sidewalk. It wouldn't be a bad idea to actually go inside the ballroom, have a check and see what the layout was. But then, what if there was a guard or a cleaner or even someone from CAW making preparations? Why show my face to a security guard when I didn't have to?

I took a final look and walked away, in case people started taking an interest in me. I hadn't come up with anything. Maybe I'd try and bluff my way in regardless, I'd say I'd lost my ticket. We'd see. The one thing I now definitely decided that I wasn't going to do was to wait for him on the sidewalk while his limo or taxi pulled up. Since there were absolutely no pedestrians in this weird part of town, I'd be totally suspicious.

The getaway was another problem. Car could get roadblocked in the nasty Denver traffic, so I went to Kmart and bought a hundred-dollar mountain bike and a fifty-dollar lock and chain. If I could get out of the ballroom somehow, I'd bike quickly to Colfax, and once on Colfax, I'd be safe.

If I could get the fuck out.

◦   ◦   ◦

We didn't talk the whole day. Pat tried to make me eggs for dinner, but I took over the cooking. He couldn't eat, I couldn't eat. When night fell, I dressed in the white suit I had bought from the Arc Thrift Shop for five dollars. A third of the price of the dry cleaning bill. I grabbed the bike from the hall. Pat looked up from the *Rocky Mountain News* with a face full of tears and said:

"Have you got your passport?"

"I do."

"Your tickets?"

"Aye."

"Your gun?"

"Yes."

"And you want me to toss the rest of your stuff?"

"Yes."

He sat for a minute, swallowed. Now even his hair was graying. I went and sat beside him.

"Alex, there's nothing I can say to stop you?"

"No, Pat."

"Ok, then, give me a hug."

We hugged, Pat kissed me on the cheek.

"I'm worried about you, Pat," I said.

"Fuck that, mate, worry about yourself, I'm not dead yet," he said.

"If the police come for you, Pat?"

"I'll handle it, Alex, I'll be ok," he said, his face in a fixed grin that neither of us believed. I nodded, stood, and looked at him, I didn't want to be talked out of it. I didn't want Pat to convince me of anything, but I needed something. I needed some word.

"Pat, you don't have to tell me I'm doing the right thing, I know you don't think I am doing the right thing, but at least tell me you understand. You knew John, you saw what Mulholland did to him. And Victoria and maybe another girl. You know that. Tell me at least that you understand."

Pat looked at me, smiled weakly.

"I understand," he said softly, tears streaming down his cheeks.

I picked up my backpack and left the apartment for the last time. I never saw him again. . . .

I rode the bike along Colfax and up to Comanche Street. At the ball-bearing factory, I dismounted. It was darker now, and with no streetlights I would have been practically invisible, apart from the white shirt, white tie, white seventies suit, and white pimp hat. And I still hadn't figured out a way of getting into the CAW party.

I locked the bike. Hid my bag with my change of clothes and passport.

I walked to the Eastman Ballroom. A lot of activity at the front of the building. Town cars, limos, taxis. Rich white people getting out, the women wearing too much jewelry, the men paunchy, older.

I walked around the back, waited, tried to think. Maybe get in one of the fire exits. I skulked in the shadows of the derelict factory, my mouth dry.

An hour went by. I didn't even have smokes.

Getting tense. Sooner or later, I'd have to go around the front and try to bluff my way in. I didn't want to, I figured it wouldn't work, but soon I'd have no choice.

I counted a final fifteen minutes on the watch. I could hear a band playing inside.

I started making my way to the front of the building and just then I got a break. An emergency exit opened and a man in a dinner jacket came out for a smoke. He left the exit open, lit his cigarette, and then decided to take a leak up against the dimly lit ball-bearing factory wall. I crossed the street out of the shadow.

"Hi," he said.

I nodded.

I went in the open emergency exit, walked down a concrete corridor, pulled a door, was in the ballroom.

A large floor, a closed balcony, a band up on the stage, a chandelier, tables ringing the ballroom with waiters in dinner jackets bringing hors d'oeuvres and booze. About two hundred and fifty people. Half of them dancing whitey fashion to light jazz and Muzak versions of Rat Pack standards. The rest sitting at tables or standing to the sides, chatting, flirting. White dresses, white suits, a couple of people in more creative white lab coats, white boiler suits. Dull as dishwater. Exactly the sort of thing you'd expect at a fund-raiser for an organization like the Campaign for the American Wilderness: middle-aged, wealthy, satisfied, not a person of color who wasn't carrying a tray. Trophy wives and girlfriends. Grizzled men in their forties and fifties who had dodged the draft, made money in real estate, swung from left to right, and whose dream was to someday make the cover of *Cigar Aficionado*.

I zeroed in on a group of tables near the stage. Charles, sitting there in a white morning suit, Amber in a dazzling cream dress. Everyone in orbit about her. God, I'd forgotten how beautiful she was. I couldn't see Robert or the retiring Congressman Wegener, though there was a fat man in a white vest, flanked by goons, so that was a possibility. The congressman had been getting death threats for his antigay stance. The guys with him might be armed. It wouldn't matter, I'd be quick. Amber was talking to a man who looked so like her, aged thirty-five or forty years, that I knew instantly it was her father. He and a couple of hoods with him were wearing black jackets with a white buttonhole. It made them look like the wait staff. I smiled. I might have been right about my assessment. Maybe I'd brought them together. Having had to find men to kill me had been the great family rapprochement. Touching. The taller of the two goons looked like one of the shooters from Fort Morgan a few weeks ago.

A waiter came by with caviar on a piece of Melba toast.

"Sir?" he asked.

"Thanks," I said, and forced myself to relax. I unclenched my fists and pretended to be looking at a large 1930s WPA mural of people dancing in various eras of history. I saw that the best route to Charles would be to avoid the dance floor and make my way clockwise through the crowd along the ballroom's circumference.

Ok, no more dicking around, I told myself.

Now or never. I checked in my pocket for the gun and the smoke bombs from Pat's apartment. I pulled down my pimp hat and walked completely into the room. . . .

Time slows. The world blurs. Movement. People. The disco lights come on. Snatches of conversation:

"Oh, he did it, O. J. killed her first and then the waiter. . . . Winter Park is so over. . . ." "Not Heston, not Sinatra, the worst wig in television is Jack Horkheimer, he's this astrology dude. . . ." "Clinton will win for certain. . . ." "Norm McDonald plays a great Bob Dole. . . ."

Couples dancing. Perfume on the women. The band onstage. The lights. The people. But I can see only one. Charles, talking to a man who is doing something to a microphone stand. There are to be speeches later.

Well, I can safely say the audience isn't going to have to suffer through that.

I ease my way through the crowd.

No one pays me the slightest bit of attention.

Closer.

Closer.

I get bumped by a flapper.

"Sorry," she says, gives me a winning smile.

"Not at all."

Twenty feet from his table.

I feel for the gun again. Swallow. I feel sick.

Time slows further.

My legs begin to tremble. Can I do this? Can I kill another person? Didn't I kill that guy in the cemetery?

I had the hate. I had it. Victoria alone would have been sufficient. But John and possibly that girl Maggie too? So close.

Fifteen feet. No dancers between me and him. I can see his eyes, his confident sneer. A direct line, a clear shot. He's standing next to Amber. He scratches his ear, takes a drink of champagne. His last. My veins are throbbing, I can count my heartbeats. One, two, three, four . . .

I blink. Loosen my fingers. Sweat in beads rolling down my palms. My knee hurts. I have stopped breathing.

Ten feet.

I touch the .38. I cock it in my pocket. I force my legs to stop shaking. The metal of the gun is warm, the grip drenched with sweat. Did I load it? Of course I did. I pull it out.

Time stops.

I grin.

I'm really here. This is really happening. This is it. It's too late now. You can do what you like, Charles. Grab your rosary. Sing your songs. Your existence is hereby erased.

People are moving behind me, talking. The music plays. A drum solo. The room sways slightly.

My throat is dry. I try to swallow, but when you're not breathing, you can't swallow.

Charles leans forward to hear something, I begin to lift the gun.

Charles turns his head slightly.

I momentarily catch his eye.

My grin widens.

He looks away. There's a lot of things going on in this room.

Charles says something to a man with enormous whiskers. The man looks puzzled. Charles has begun an anecdote or joke, but he has lost the plot, he looks confused, he begins to stutter, like his brother. I bring the .38 to full extension, Charles's confused face in the middle of the sight.

Amber leans in. Charles relaxes. Amber, beautiful and clever and hard. She says something and the man laughs and Charles looks at his feet and perks up and finishes his joke. And suddenly I see the whole dynamic of their relationship. Everything depends upon her. She's not just the one behind the scenes. She's the one that gives him confidence. She's the one that lifts him up. It's her. The heroin concealed it from me.

And then the gun feels weak in my grip as suddenly I see it all.

It's Amber. Of course. It's her. Jesus.

Charles could never have killed anyone. Too effete, delicate, too sensitive, he wouldn't have had the bottle. And Amber under the ketch already told me as much. She told me everything already. I just didn't see it. That perfect skin, that razor smile, those quirks, that steely look.

It's her.

Charles probably never killed anyone in his life. Not John, not Victoria. Probably not Maggie, either. If it was one of those lacrosse boys, it was more likely Houghton. Charles just doesn't seem the type. Of course, the blackmail game would still be on. Charles meets Maggie, Houghton shows up. There's an incident. Houghton's word against his. But no, I don't think he did it. Charles is no killer.

Not even bloody John. I had assumed a man had done it, but why? Look at her. Strong, fast, fit, lithe, a fucking martial artist. Why not her? Tough enough and lucky enough to get one blow right in the heart.

Amber stroking her hair in midflirt with the powerful man next to Charles, who I recognize as a famous senator. And then I laugh. I really laugh. She had outplayed me from the very beginning. She had seduced me, to enable me to unveil myself. She had been hot and cold, all to get me off my guard, to find me out, make me slip. She was the detective, trying to figure out who I was and what I was doing here. Maneuvering me into a situation so that I would slip, reveal that, yes, I did know Victoria, I was on her trail. Ha. Me thinking I was mining her for information and all the time it was the other way around.

Amber, her mother a thief, her father a player. School of hard knocks. A real piece of work. Her body was the weapon she had used on Victoria and me, but her mind was the really impressive instrument.

How long have I been standing here? With my arm outstretched and the big coat sleeve partially but not wholly concealing a gun held in my hand.

One second? Two?

But in that moment, that brief increment of time, I see everything. From its very beginnings. After years of paying off Alan Houghton, Charles confesses or lets slip to his wife about the blackmail. Amber knows Charles is her ticket from the shanty-Irish muck. An old-money WASP with political ambitions. There is only one thing to do. She decides to kill Houghton. The easy way would be to tell her da. But she's burned that bridge. She will do this on her own. Her da is the past she's escaping from. She will make her own future. She plans it all. She plans the murder. She's learned well from her da's success, her ma's failures. Yes. Handle this on her own, keep Charles out of it, keep Dad out of it, she'll do it by herself. Just as she worked hard to get into Harvard, reinvented herself, probably forced the coincidence whereby she and Charles would meet at Vail. This was one more obstacle to be overcome.

Yes.

Then Victoria Patawasti finds out about the slush fund. Victoria leaves a trail in the accounts. Charles notices that someone has been looking at the secret account file. He panics, tells his wife. Of course it could only be Victoria and silly, poor, doomed Victoria writes up her suspicions in her computer. Only Charles, Robert, and, what was that Klimmer said, yes, Mrs. Mulholland, only those three ever went into Victoria's office. Amber has to know what Victoria knows. Seduces her, gets her to reveal her password and what she knows. And once the decision is made to kill Alan

Houghton, Victoria has to die too. Victoria can't be bought. Amber has to act quickly. Hector Martinez is working at the CAW offices. Maybe he drops his license, maybe she rifles through his wallet. It doesn't matter, she gets the license and knows she can use it to set up an innocent man. She kills Houghton and Victoria on the same night, sets up Hector as a burglar. Brilliant.

Does Charles know about it all? He must have told her that someone had been looking at the secret account. Is he in on the murders? Did Amber tell him? Did he have anything to do with Maggie Prestwick's death? Does it matter? I don't think I even care now.

And only after she botched my murder did Amber see she was at the limit of her power. She needed professional killers to kill me. The risk of hiring unknowns—who could blackmail her—was too great. Who to turn to? Daddy. Because she needed him. Because blood was thicker than water. A rapprochement. Oh, Amber. It had to be you.

I move the gun sight from him to her.

And I hold it. Hold it. My finger on the trigger. The sight between her shoulder blades. For a second. Amber's fair face. Her golden hair.

Beautiful.

Another long second.

A squeeze.

And then.

And then I release the tension on the trigger.

No, Amber, you will not make me do the wrong

thing again. I was weak before. I failed. In Ireland. But not here. Not this time. Some other way.

I begin lowering the gun. A man at her dad's table sees me, reaches inside his jacket, pulls something out.

I finally breathe.

A blast like a firecracker.

The man next to me is thrown backward into a woman holding a champagne glass. Blood gushes from his back. There is a ghastly silence and then people start to scream. The other man beside Amber's father draws his gun, begins to shoot. The men next to the senator and the congressman pull out their guns, shoot across the room at Amber's father's table. Panicky fast shots thumping into the walls. Shooting from all directions, all around.

People begin screaming, diving for cover. At least half a dozen men now are shooting at once, seemingly at random, in a panic, at me, everywhere. Bullets from semiautomatics and big-caliber revolvers, the sound horrendous in the enclosed space of the ballroom. People yelling, terrified, running, trampling one another, falling to the floor. A bullet hits a spotlight and a fire starts behind the band. The fire alarm goes off.

Charles and Amber have dived to the floor.

I drop a smoke bomb.

Confusion, more gunshots.

The sprinklers start spraying water and the water makes the lights fuse, flicker, go out.

Now the screaming really starts.

Yellow emergency lights come on above the fire exits. I run for one.

I sprint across the darkened room, unhindered, untouched. Something comes whizzing over my head and crashes into the wall. There's the sound of shooting and a yell to cease fire. Not an unarmed person left isn't screaming, isn't diving under the tables.

I push on a metal bar and the door flies open. I run down a corridor, open another fire door, and am suddenly out in the night. I hammer across the street to the ball-bearing factory. I wipe the gun clean and throw it through one of the broken factory windows. I tear off the white jacket and pants, change into jeans, an Eddie Vedder shirt, black jacket, sneakers. I unlock the bike, ride like crazy. I head east, I just keep going. I don't look back.

In two minutes, I don't hear the fire alarm, I don't hear anything, I'm on big empty streets going anywhere. A fire truck shoots past me heading for the Eastman Ballroom.

I ride through the unfamiliar landscape of northeast Denver until I come to a bus stop. I ditch the bike, I get the bus to the airport bus stop.

I take the airport bus to Denver International.

That big teepee structure. The windows. The sun behind the Rocky Mountains. The blue sky. The stars. I queue up at the British Airways desk. I get my boarding card for the direct flight from Denver to London.

I find the toilet and throw up. I wash my face. I

smack the hand dryer off the wall. What a disaster. What a terrible balls-up. I go to the gate.

I get on the plane. Sit in my seat. The plane idles for a long time, gets delayed, loses its place in the queue. The captain explains why. Something mechanical. We wait. My heart going like a rivet gun. I bite my nails. We finally get another takeoff slot. The plane taxis, turns, roars down the runway. Lifts into the night, leaving behind the city, the plains, and, eventually, Newfoundland and then North America itself.

John's body in the landfill in Aurora and Amber safe and alive. Unharmed, and as strong and as beautiful as ever.

12: THE HIDDEN RIVER

Through the window it's morning. Night slinking away over the lighthouse and the milk churns and the cliff path. The moon's breath, cold, in the gray light that in the east they call the wolf's tail.

Across the Irish Sea, the peak of Ailsa Craig and the hills of Galloway.

A line of yellow in the sky.

A smattering of vessels, fishing boats, tankers, and big container ships waiting for the pilot to guide them to the container docks of Belfast. Closer to the shore, a lobsterman, pulling nets, swearing so loud that you can actually hear him.

A man is coming up the road.

This isn't my house. I've come here, to hide as best I can. Dad was useless as usual, but Mr. Patawasti suggested their cottage up the Antrim coast if I wanted a place to rest.

There is only one way to the house.

Along the cliff, around the lighthouse. Coming over the boggy fields would be a nightmare.

An assassin has to come up the one narrow road.

That's the beauty of the thing.

And he's here. I can't tell if he's being furtive. There

isn't enough light. But I can see him. Glimpses of him between the thorns and the blackberry and the bramble bushes. Walking fast. Not running. That's how I'd come too. At dawn. In the half-light. I would never have spotted him but for the fact that all I do in my waking hours is look out at the sea, the cliffs, the path.

And now the decision.

There is a shotgun over the fireplace. I checked it as soon as I moved in. Twelve-gauge. Nice. Clean. For shooting foxes, badgers. A box of shells near the range. It would be easy to slip out the back, circle behind the cottage, and take him as soon as he gets to the front door. Easy.

And yet.

I sit here, the gun untouched, the shells untouched.

I'll let him come, I say, and smile. Aye, I'll welcome him.

For I have failed in everything.

The debacle in the Eastman Ballroom. I didn't even fire my weapon. More than a dozen people injured, two nearly died, and, of course, Charles and Amber completely unharmed. More famous now than ever while an inquiry sorts out what on earth happened. No one really knows, but they think a security guard panicked and started shooting at a man he thought had a gun.

Charles has been on 20/20 and even Larry King, displacing for a moment the round-the-clock O. J. Simpson coverage. CAW's profile has been raised a hundredfold. I couldn't have given them a better gift.

He's a shoo-in for Congress, a rising star. He's got a chance of running for governor or even being the balance on the GOP presidential ticket at some point in the future.

I have fucked up utterly, in all ways.

I fell in love with heroin, I fell out of love with truth. I was beguiled by a killer, smarter than me. I let down my old love, failed her, too, failed my friend.

So come, assassin.

I'll wait here.

Come. And he does.

Who would they get to kill me? Would they have told the IRA that I was a senior police officer, or an independent drug dealer, something like that? The IRA, the UDA, it doesn't matter. As long as they are efficient.

I look out the window. The Scottish coast, the ships, the birds, farther up the channel the barest outline of the Mull of Kintyre.

And the worst part is, the day I got back to Carrickfergus Mr. Patawasti had come around and thanked me. Congratulated me for a job well done. Dad had told him that I had helped Hector Martinez's lawyer get him off. Mr. Patawasti had said that although I hadn't found the person who killed their daughter, at least I'd helped set an innocent man free, got the police looking for the real killer.

I almost threw up.

I had to get out of there. Get up here. Where I would be safe. For a while. Until now. I suppose it was inevitable they would find me. Northern Ireland is a small place.

The assassin.

Closer. I can make out a few details now. He's wearing a parka raincoat and a flat cap.

Breathing hard.

His breath curling into the morning air.

His footsteps heavy.

His gray face.

He opens the gate and walks to the house.

He knocks on the door.

Which is slightly unusual.

I open it.

"You're a hard man to find, Lawson," he says.

I recognize him at once. It's Commander Douglas from the Samson Inquiry.

Not an assassin, then, but just as bad. As good as a gun. As good as a bullet in the brain. Just more complicated.

"So this is where you've been hiding for the last couple of months," he says.

It's more like a couple of weeks, but I don't quibble with him. He sits in the chair by the window. Lights himself a cigarette. It doesn't calm him down.

"Well, since you've no phone, I thought I'd drive up here myself and let you know. I wanted to see your fucking face. You're just like every other paddy in this fucking country. Be in the papers tomorrow, Lawson, you're off the fucking hook."

"What do you mean?"

"The first question you should ask is how I found you."

"How did you find me?"

"Broke into your house yesterday, found a letter your father was about to post, careless, very careless."

He blew smoke aggressively in my face.

"You want to get me a drink?"

"There's only water," I said.

"Forget it then. Typical. Anyway, so you're off the hook, Paddy, we won't arrest you, and your own lads won't kill you. You're free as a fucking daisy."

"What are you talking about?"

"Only the collapse of the entire Samson investigation into the Royal Ulster Constabulary. Only thousands of man-hours of work and millions of pounds down the drain. Only the destruction of a good man. Not to mention a couple of dozen senior Northern Irish coppers getting away with graft of the most outrageous kind. I tell you, it's no coincidence, I see the work of MI5 in all of this."

"Yes, but what, how?" I asked, getting frustrated.

"Samson's been arrested for fraud, criminal mischief, falsifying documents, and, get this, statutory rape. Apparently, Tony Samson's casebook wasn't as clean as we all thought. He just did things every other copper did, cutting a few corners here, losing papers there, you know, fitting up a few hoods who deserved it. He's been arrested and the whole inquiry has of course collapsed, all the preliminary findings are suspect now, it's all going to be scrapped. The PM has already said he wants this finished, we've been instructed to close our files and send them to the Home Office for permanent seizure, or at least until after the thirty-year rule releases them again to the public domain. Yes, Lawson, you might have to watch your back sometime around 2025, but until then . . ."

"I still don't understand," I said.

He looked at me, disgusted. Took off his cap. Spat on the floor.

"Thought you had that big IQ. They fitted him up. Samson has been arrested, for corruption. Ironic, eh? Oh, aye, and they even threw one at him for having sex with his sixteen-year-old baby-sitter. His career is over, the inquiry is over, you won't be forced to testify. The story will break on today's evening news. You fucked us. You sneaky Paddy bastards, I don't know how you did it, but you fucked us."

I sat for a while. The RUC, or MI5, or the Home Office, or someone else entirely had seen that Samson was going to blow the lid off corruption within a section of the police in Northern Ireland, had seen that it could jeopardize Northern Ireland as a political entity in and of itself, had therefore begun digging for dirt on Samson himself, had found enough to bury him. His whole inquiry was compromised, useless. He was just like me now, the poor bastard.

And it really was over. No one would compel me to testify. Nothing to testify about. I was what I'd always been. A drugged-out, worthless, wasted cop. I was safe.

"Tell me one thing," Commander Douglas said.

"What?"

"Off the record, Lawson, why did you resign?"

I believed him. I didn't mind telling him.

"It's very simple. Buck McConnell was my mentor in the peelers, he pulled me along. He used me. He put me in the drug squad, figured I'd shake things up. I did. I found out that several senior RUC officers were allowing the IRA and UDA to traffic heroin and e, protecting them, regulating the market, I could have blown the lid off a dozen big careers, but they found out about me. They weren't sure if I was loyal or if I was going to go to Special Branch. I wasn't sure if I was going to go to Special Branch. I didn't want to be killed, I didn't want to live in fear in some witness-protection program, so I took a third way out. I destroyed my credibility. I injected myself with heroin, enough times to convince them I was an addict. Then I stole heroin from the police evidence room, I got myself caught stealing, they said they wouldn't prosecute if I resigned. I resigned in disgrace."

Commander Douglas grimaced, stamped his cigarette out.

"Very clever, Lawson, you made yourself a pariah. Sneaky. You're all alike. I don't know why we stay in this bloody country. It's like the fucking Raj and you're the niggers."

I said nothing, Douglas rubbed his hands over his face. His eyes narrowed, closed. A comic effect in a man incapable of comedy. He sighed, nodded to himself.

"Well, you fucker, you don't get off that easy," he said.

He pulled out his gun and pointed it at me.

"You were lying," I said, surprised.

"No, I wasn't lying. It's all true, you're off the hook, with Samson, with the Brits, with your own side. Off the fucking hook with everyone. Everyone except me."

"But you can't do anything, the investigation's over."

He nodded in agreement. Sighted the revolver.

"You fucking bastards, ruin a good man like that, you just sitting up here waiting for your pals to do the dirty work. You fucking coward. You fucker. Biding your time. Well, Paddy, let me tell you about this gun. It's not a cop gun. It's off the books. If I shoot you, no one will ever know who did it."

I looked at him, looked at the gun, saw that he was serious. Did I want to die now? Now that I was free? Things were different. I wasn't sure. Douglas got up and walked over toward me. He put the gun against my temple. Was he really this fucking crazy?

The touch of the cold steel. This is not how I want to go. Every second of every day someone dies. Every minute someone's murdered, someone's murdering. But not now, not me. Not this place.

"I could kill you, Paddy," he said, furious. "I could fucking kill you easy. A squeeze of this here trigger. Nice gun. Browning. Yes. I'd enjoy it. I would."

His face was dispassionate, resolved. He meant to do it, he would do it. His eyes, ice. It was a decision he had made in advance.

He took a step back so the blood spray from my skull wouldn't get on his clothes.

I knew he'd do it. For I was everything he hated about this country. I was the distillation of all that rage. I was the symptom and the disease.

"What do you want?" I asked.

"What do I want? What do I want? I want what I've always wanted. A fucking bit of cooperation. One fucking Paddy who knows right from wrong. I want to know the name of the copper running the heroin, I want to know his name. Give me that. Fucking give me the name. I don't care if *they* fucking kill you. I don't care if the investigation *has* collapsed. I want that fucking name. I'm going to count to three."

For emphasis, he clicked the hammer back on the revolver. One slip of his finger and I was dead.

"One," he said.

The barrel and the sweat. This little room. The sea outside. His mouth fixed, resigned, one way or the other, it didn't matter. If I didn't give him the name, he'd top me.

"Two."

That face, that scarred hand, the paratrooper wings on his wrist. That gun. Would this be the last impression in my retina, the last memory in my brain?

I gagged. I was afraid.

No.

"Thr—" he began.

"John," I said.

"What?"

"John Campbell. Big guy, blond hair, only a constable, part-time RUC. He's the one you're after. Carrickfergus Police Station. You won't find him, though. He's already run. He's in America. But he's the one, he ran all the drugs, he was the kingpin. Low-key character. He's the one you want. Constable John Campbell, smart guy, wouldn't even take promotion. Stayed out of the limelight. He's the one all right, the one you want."

I swallowed, felt sick.

Douglas looked at me for a second. Revulsion crept over his face. He knew mentioning that name had cost me something. He believed me. What a coward I was. Douglas spat. And I hated myself. Doing down John like that to save my skin.

Another betrayal.

Douglas nodded, took his finger off the trigger.

"Piece of shit," Douglas said, put the gun in his pocket, picked up his hat, walked out of my life forever.

∘ ∘ ∘

The river begins on the roof of the world. All the great rivers of Asia are born there. The Hindus believed that their gods were born in the Himalaya and went there to die. The Tibetans felt that the air was so full of spirits that not even the clean vision of the Buddha could purge it.

The plane flying over the Hindu Kush. Over the opium fields of Afghanistan. I look out the window.

The Flower of Joy. I remember. Sip my orange juice.

A round-trip ticket from London to Delhi costs five hundred pounds. I didn't have that kind of money. But Dad did. Dad, amazingly, had gotten fifty-eight votes in the local council elections. He got his deposit back, for the first time ever. And he promised me he'd lend me the dough if he got the money back. I held him to his word. India? Why not. What else was there? The plane flying over the hazy brown Indian subcontinent.

Touching down. The Morris Ambassador taking me from the airport. The heat, the orange sky, the pollution so palpable it coats your tongue. Child beggars at the traffic stops, filthy and in rags.

"Jao," the taximan says, which means piss off.

The insane streets around Connaught Place. Connaught—the wildest of Ireland's four provinces, an appropriate name for central New Delhi.

The hotel. Pancakes from southern India. Delicious. All the food, in fact, incredible. And if you put a lot of spice on and don't drink the water, you don't get sick.

Two days in Delhi, amazing grub, sights. At the hotel on CNN International I happen to see Charles Mulholland in an interview. He ends it by saying that a friend is taking him and his wife for a yachting vacation in the Virgin Islands. A wealthy and influential friend, no doubt. Cigar smoke, cognacs: So tell me, Charles, what are your long-term political ambitions? . . .

The train station. Black and nightmarish in the morning mist. Beggars by the legion, the homeless, the lame, the halt.

The wrong train, directions, the right train. The second-class car. Breakfast. Toast, tea, marmalade. A hot napkin. *The Times of India*, the *Hindustan Times*. Hindu matriarchs, blue-turbaned Sikhs, Muslim businessmen, Jain priests, Buddhists, students, hippies. Like a scene from *Kim*.

A delay. The moving train. The squalor of the suburbs, more beggars, shantytowns, muddy fields, an elephant, vultures, and the brown flat earth of the Ganges Valley all the way to the horizon.

The Ganges is not the longest river in India, certainly not the most beautiful. The continent takes its name from the Indus, so why is the Ganges the holy river of India?

Because the gods say so.

The Ganges begins as a gurgle on a mountaintop. Glacial peaks, permanent snow, spring flowers, yellow, red, blue. It's a foot wide, this river. If you lay your body down across it, you can stop the flow, you can dam Mother Ganga.

From the mountaintop it moves on inexorably down onto the sienna plain, where everything becomes the color of mud. And down into the holy cities of Varanasi and Allahabad. The latter given that name by the Muslim conquerors who supposedly did not believe in that sort of thing.

Varanasi is the city of Lord Shiva. To die in Varanasi is a great thing. Shiva will look favorably upon you and your next incarnation will be a blessed one.

But holier still is the upstream city of Allahabad.

The most sacred site in India. Indeed, when the world is destroyed, only one place will remain and that is Allahabad—Prayag, to give it its Hindu name.

Allahabad is sacred because it is the confluence of three holy rivers. The Ganges, of course, but also the Yamuna and the Saraswati.

The Yamuna is the second holy river of India. Mahatma Gandhi's body was burned by this river. Three prime ministers also were cremated by its banks in sandalwood funeral pyres, their ashes drifting from the burning ghats into the sacred waters.

The Yamuna and the Ganges meet in Allahabad. An important place. The hometown of the Nehrus. The hometown of Victoria Patawasti's family.

The train stops. I get off. I walk around, looking at fort ruins, at Jawaharlal Nehru's house, at Victoria Patawasti's house.

I visit her paternal grandparents, who are both alive. They have fourteen grandchildren, two of whom have been incarnated already into another form. I spend the day with them and I stay that night in their big turn-of-the-century mansion, exquisitely designed to take cooling breezes off the river.

We talk and we drink nimbu pani soda and we eat sweetmeats.

And Dr. Patawasti tells me the story about the Hidden River.

The river Saraswati flows only in Heaven or, say some, underground. It is the river of Paradise, of the gods, the Ganges and the Yamuna are only its earthly mirrors. They are imperfect. The Saraswati is perfection itself. But Vishnu so loved the world that he allowed the Saraswati to bend down to Earth at one place, at only one spot on the whole globe. At the point where the Ganges and the Yamuna meet. And if you bathe here, your sins are wiped away. Indeed, so sacred is the water that not only your sins but those of seven generations backward are wiped clean too.

"My sins will be wiped away?" I ask.

"Do not even think of bathing in that river," Mrs. Dr. Patawasti says, "you will catch cholera and die. The peasants defecate and throw their waste in these supposed holy waters. Industrial plants, tanneries, all pump their poisons into the rivers. Dead cows and buffalo are in this water. Why are there no fish? These rivers are toxic."

"There are many fish," Dr. Patawasti says. "Mark Twain said that the cholera bacillus cannot survive in the Ganges."

"Say that to the thousands who catch cholera and typhoid every year," Mrs. Dr. Patawasti says, a furious look across her face.

"Still, my sins, and seven generations backward," I say.

"The scriptures are far from clear on this," Mrs. Dr. Patawasti says, "if you ask me it's a swindle to bring in tourists to the Kum Mela."

"That is an outrageous thing to suggest," Dr. Patawasti says.

Mrs. Dr. Patawasti looks at me seriously. Gray hair,

thin, but more than a hint of her former beauty in the dark skin and pale eyes. What Victoria would have looked like at age seventy-five.

"Young man," she says to me, "do not swim in the river, I beg you. And don't you encourage him," she says to her husband.

"I don't know, all my sins," I say again.

Mrs. Dr. Patawasti groans, Dr. Patawasti laughs. . . .

Early morning. The family still asleep. A bicycle rickshaw. My shorts, sandals, T-shirt, a wide-brimmed hat.

Houses, dirty streets, dust. Children staring vacantly at me, others grinning, playing with a football.

The Ganges, brown and solemn. The Yamuna, yellow and sluggish.

The bank of the Ganges is littered with refuse. Newspaper, cans, rags, bits of old boats.

I pay the rickshaw man, look for a boatman.

People are washing their clothes, doing Puja.

I step over a dead dog.

The boatmen spot me, come racing over, and I find one I like.

We negotiate twenty rupees to row me out to the junction of the two rivers. To the point where the Saraswati comes down from Heaven and cleanses sins and past mistakes and makes a man anew.

He rows me out in a leaky boat, with mended oars and rowlocks made of hemp.

The head of a water buffalo floats by.

The boatman is named Ali. Thin, dark, nervous, dressed in a ragged white caftan.

We talk about the rivers and the legend of the Hidden River and Ali gives ambiguous and noncommittal answers. I suppose he's seen many Westerners get rowed out here with the intention of bathing, take one look at the water, and then sensibly chicken out.

We stop at one of the many wooden pillars that are set into the river specifically for bathing pilgrims. We tie the boat. I strip. I lean over the side and dip my feet into the water. I lean on the edge of the boat. Ali leans on the other gunwale to prevent a capsize.

I let myself slip down the side of the rowboat and immerse myself up to my chest.

The water embraces me, and I let go the side of the boat.

I can feel the current from both rivers. The Ganges is warm, the Yamuna colder. It's shallow. My feet touch the bottom and I walk along it.

Ali laughs delightedly.

A hundred feet to the right I can see another large animal carcass floating past. I dunk my head under. I come up, breathe, the sun is bright, the water glitters. Ali thinks this is hilarious.

I dunk my head under again.

And this time I know it's the right place.

The Platte wasn't it.

This is the right river.

I am here at last.

The water washes over me.

I open my eyes, it is hard to see. But my vision is perfect and I do understand, I understand the purpose of it all. To bring me here, on this day, at this time, now.

I see, and I am resolved. I have failed. I did not bring redemption, I did not bring justice down from heaven. I did not have Victoria's killers put to rights. It has been a catalog of failure. As a son, as a policeman, as a man with a second chance, as a human being. I have let the guilty slip through my fingers, indeed enhanced their position. I have let my friends die. I have not done anything with this life.

Take from me my sins.

And I see her.

Ma. She dies. Her cold fingers. Her fingertips. They let her die. His words of comfort, meaningless. All of it, meaningless. How stupid not to know that lesson. You can't save her. No one can save her.

And I'm here.

At last.

This river of death. This continent of death. My feet stand on the mud. My sins have been ones of omission. I have let things happen. Sure, you could say that I saved Da, that he would have fallen apart if they had killed me, but it was cowardice. I was afraid. And I took the easy way out and let things happen. And to cap it all, I slandered John to save my neck again.

And now all I have to do is open my lungs. Open my lungs and let the river cleanse me.

And my body will writhe and my trachea will scream—water there instead of air—and my heart will beat but there will be no oxygen in the blood returning from my lungs. No place for the CO_2 to be expelled.

And my heart will beat; but it will eventually cease to work. My brain will soldier on for a minute, perhaps two, starved for oxygen, crying out for it, for air. And then it, too, will slow and the chemical reactions will cease and I will lose consciousness, perhaps seeing that white tunnel that people see when the neurons fire random images in the cortex.

I will float there and in another ten minutes the last of the electrical activity in my brain will stop forever. And I will be nothing. Appropriate, wasn't it, the Hindu mystics who invented the concept of zero?

I reach down and grab the mud between my fingers.

The river flows and my smile widens and my mouth opens. Thick filthy water pouring over my tongue and into my throat.

I gag and force open my jaw with my fingers. I expel the last of the air and I breathe in.

The pain is terrible. Like an electric shock. My lungs howl and my body bucks against this terrible intrusion. I war against the pleading of my lungs and brain. I fight against the urge to surface.

And again I swallow.

I am coming to you.

Mum and Victoria, John.

That holy trinity of loss.

I am coming to you.

Even though I know what awaits is not you, not sleep, but annihilation. In this brown filthy water. Dirt on my teeth. Fire in my nostrils.

But I'm coming anyway.

This place, this is the time.

The river pours in.

Yes.

To you.

John.

Victoria.

Ma.

My hair.

A hand.

The sun.

A hand pulls me up out of the water by the hair.

A voice:

"You must not be fooling around in this water. You are catching dreadful things. Do not be believing stories about the purity of this water. It is foul. I am Muslim. I am above such superstition. This town is called Allahabad. There is no God but Allah. There is no God but Allah. There are no spirits. There is no magic water. There is no Hidden River."

"No?" I sputter, coughing, puking, spitting the water from my mouth.

"No, come, I will pull you in."

Before I can reply, his big hands tug me into the boat, and I cough and vomit water and gasp for air.

He looks stern, shakes his head.

"You are seeing what I am explaining?" he says with disgust.

"Uh—"

"Very dangerous, very dangerous, you are not seeing the dead cow?"

"No."

I spit some more, cough. He wags his finger.

"So what do we do now?" I ask him after a while.

"You are sitting in the boat and drying off in the sunshine and I am rowing you to shore. No. We are not doing that. I am rowing you to hotel, where you are showering that filthy water off your body. *Insh'Allah*, you are unharmed. *Insh'Allah*."

"Ok," I say.

The ocher river. The yellow sky.

I lie back in the boat.

Ali looks at me and laughs at my foolishness.

He doesn't know it, but he's given me my life back. I lie there and I am at peace, lullabied by oars and the gentle harmonic motion of the boat, drifting on the golden waters of the Ganges, on the edge of sleep. Saved. Alive.

Ali is still talking:

"Those Hindus are crazy men. There is no vanishing river. The Saraswati was a real river long ago that dried up. They do not know their history. The Prophet, may his name be blessed, cured us of such pagan superstition. The Hindus see magic where there is no magic, they see—"

I sit up suddenly in the boat.

"What did you say?"

"I said that they are crazy men who—"

"No, no, about the Saraswati?" I ask.

"A real river. It dried up centuries ago."

"Dried up. A drought, of course. That was why I survived the Platte. A drought. The creek. Pat tried to tell me it's only two feet deep at the best of times. She wouldn't know that. She despised the place, thought a river was a river. Don't you see? Don't you see?"

Ali looks at me, uncomprehending.

"I am rowing you to shore," he says.

"Yes, yes, yes," I say excitedly.

◦　◦　◦

The Patawastis were still asleep. Their twelve-year-old servant boy making tea. He ignored me when I grabbed the phone and dialed the international operator. I talked to her for a while and finally she gave me a number in Colorado. I dialed it, got through to the switchboard.

"I'll put you through to his voice mail, ok?" the switchboard woman said.

"Ok," I said.

"This is the voice mail of Detective David Redhorse. At the tone, please leave me a message and a number and I'll get back to you."

I spoke fast:

"Redhorse, you don't know me, but I've got information. On June fifth, 1995, in Denver, on the night of that freak snowstorm, Victoria Patawasti was murdered. Her killer was Amber Mulholland, the wife of Charles Mulholland, who is running for Congress. Amber killed Victoria and walked the gun down to Cherry Creek and threw it in. Probably the closest part of the creek to Victoria's building. Amber thought it would get washed down to the South Platte River. But there's been a drought. She doesn't know the city, doesn't know Cherry Creek is only a couple of feet deep, and now it must be completely dry. It's a special gun, a Beretta, with her initials on it. Do you see? The gun is still there. It's got to be. El Niño's brought freak weather. Snow in June. A bone-dry spring and summer. Look in the creek, not too far from Victoria's building. Find the gun. The forensics will match. The gun dealer in Italy will tie it to Charles Mulholland. What else? Yes, motive. Amber killed Victoria because Victoria found out her husband was stealing millions from the charity to pay a blackmailer named Alan Houghton. He's disappeared, but there might still be something in CAW's computers. Anyway, the important thing is the gun, find the gun, find the gun, find the bloody gun."

I hung up the phone. Yes, goddamnit, yes.

I got myself a drink. I went onto the balcony overlooking the Ganges.

Dozens of men and women doing Puja, letting the holy water trickle through their fingers for the rising sun. And the Ganges itself a vast trunk road. Kids, priests, metalworkers, water buffalo herders, cycle rickshaw drivers, boatmen. I sipped my nimbu pani, sat down, watched it all.

And I don't know—maybe it was escaping death or maybe it was being in India—but just then I saw how it could be. How it should be.

The final act. . . .

Seven time zones west of Belfast, twelve time zones west of Allahabad, two policemen check their arrest warrant and extradition papers and board a plane from Denver to Atlanta to the U.S. Virgin Islands.

The plane lifts off from Denver International Airport, circles to gain altitude, and heads east. For the policeman in the window seat it's his first time ever in an airplane. David Redhorse is afraid to fly. But this is too important. Time is of the essence. The Mulhollands are taking a well-needed break on a luxury yacht. At the moment they're in U.S. territory, but tomorrow they're going on to the Bahamas. You couldn't solve every case. That Klimmer one had gone dead, but this, this was a juicy high-profile murder.

Redhorse looks out over Denver and Aurora and Boulder and the Rocky Mountains. He stares down at the South Platte River and at Confluence Park, where the South Platte merges with Cherry Creek. The gold nuggets in Cherry Creek, the whole reason for Denver's existence in the first place.

Cherry Creek. After getting the phone call, Redhorse took one of the police department metal detectors and searched the dried-up creek. He found the gun in about fifteen minutes. Forensics matched the pistol with the bullet they took out of Victoria Patawasti. And Beretta told him who owned a fancy gun like that. The wife of Victoria's employer: Amber Mulholland. The gun. The murder weapon.

"There's the creek," he says.

His partner, Detective Miller, doesn't reply. He's

reading the newspaper. The engines whine. There is a terrible grumbling noise.

"Undercarriage coming up," Miller says kindly.

The plane hits turbulence and falls sixty feet. Redhorse bites down a yell and looks around. No one else seems alarmed in the least.

The aircraft straightens out.

Redhorse unclenches his fists and when the "Fasten seat belt" sign turns off, he goes to the toilet, stands on the seat, disables the smoke detector, pulls out a pack of cigarettes, and smokes.

CODA: TWO YEARS LATER—OXFORD

Rows of bicycles. The leafy quad. An empty punt floating down the Cherwell. It's seven. The vast majority of the students are still asleep. But I have to be up. I have work to do. I'm on the hardest degree program in the university. The Bachelor of Civil Law. A three-year law degree taken in one year. Final prep on my paper before the tutorial. But first, breakfast and the news. I walk to the porter's lodge and pick up the papers for the common room. Five British broadsheets, five British tabloids, and two American papers: *The Wall Street Journal* and *USA Today*.

Coffee, scone, clotted cream.

And the story.

Only on page four of *USA Today*, this morning.

The repercussions of the plea bargain.

It's an open secret in Colorado that the DA has been as lenient toward the Mulhollands as propriety has allowed him to be. Indeed, observers of the Victoria Patawasti murder trial praised Amber Mulholland's team of attorneys for getting the DA to accept a guilty plea on a charge of second-degree murder with diminished responsibility for an alleged crime of passion. Amber, however, won't come up for parole for at least twenty years. Her husband, though, has escaped jail time for his guilty plea to charges of fraud and embezzlement.

Page four of *USA Today*. A few columns.

No one cares.

There are bigger fish to fry. Rumors about President Clinton and another sex scandal. A new IRA cease-fire in the works.

Even in Denver it's not that big a story. The Jon-Benet Ramsey murder case has seized the headlines. Worse things have happened. Worse will come in the southern suburbs at a school called Columbine. But for now the media is done with the Mulhollands, the Patawasti murder, and the bloodletting in the ball-room. The latter is already passing into legend. Indeed, the Eastman Ballroom itself has been torn down to make way for condominiums.

I close the paper, push it away. Yawn, stretch, get up, leave the common room, find my bicycle key. Unlock the bike. Cycle down Fyfield Road.

Yes, it's over. Done. Nothing to do with me.

Gone.

Only the continuity of violence remains.

Denver was born in blood: the native Cheyenne massacred at Sand Creek, the Comanche and Ute driven beyond the mountains in a vale of tears.

The Patawasti case is over and the ballroom incident

is closed, unsolved, unsolvable, soon to be unremembered.

No one should be surprised.

In the end, all of history's songs will be lost in the depths of time. And the great streams of memory will be as hidden as the rivers of forgetting.

Scribner proudly presents

THE DEAD YARD

Adrian McKinty

Coming soon in hardcover
from Scribner
Turn the page for a preview of *The Dead Yard* . . .

The cell was deep underground, a yellow bulb in the ceiling giving off a little light. Cold, damp. Impossible to tell if it was day or night. But I'd been in worse. Much bloody worse. They fed you three times a day, there was a bog that flushed, and the fauna situation was manageable.

I was sitting on the cot reading *How Stella Got Her Groove Back* for the third time when the cell door opened.

I stood.

A man and a woman. A tall man carrying a chair and a water bottle. He was wearing a linen jacket, white shirt, Harrow tie. It was difficult to see in the dark but he looked about thirty-five, forty at the outside, hard-faced, blond-gray hair. He held himself like a high-ranking army officer: straight spine, shoulders back, stomach in. He unfolded the chair and sat down. A revolver peeked out next to his armpit. Interesting. The woman also had a chair. She was late thirties, wearing a sundress and sandals with red hair tied behind her in a ponytail. She was heavy but attractive—Rubens plump, not lesbian-biker plump. She took out a notebook and sat back in the shadows. He was the man and she was the assistant. They fell immediately into their roles, which wasn't smart, but despite that I still didn't like the look of either of them.

"You're British," I said to the man.

"That's right, old boy," he said in a plummy public school voice. Not for him the attempt to tone down the upper-crust accent and give in to the increasingly common Estuary English pronunciation. It told me a lot about him—arrogant, proud, the Harrow tie not a joke but a reminder of a birthright. A wanker, more than likely.

"I suppose you're from the embassy," I said. "I'm completely innocent, you know. I wasn't involved in anything. I was on holiday. First bloody holiday in years."

"Beastly piece of luck, I'm sure. But the Spanish don't

care, you will be tried, you will be found guilty, you'll get five to ten years, I suppose. The new prime minister, Mr. Blair, has said that he supports fully the Spanish government's intention of making an example out of the soccer hooligans who once again have blighted the good name of England," he said breezily.

"I'm not English," I told him.

"It doesn't matter," the man replied quickly.

"It matters to me."

"Well, it won't make any difference. You will be convicted," he said.

"Listen, mate, if you came here to give me a lecture you can piss off," I said, lifting up my trouser leg and scratching under the straps that held the artificial foot to my calf. I'd lost the foot five years before in a lovely piece of jungle surgery in Mexico. It had saved my life and I was thoroughly unself-conscious about it now.

The man smiled, picked at a piece of fluff on his shirt, looked behind him at the secretary, cleared his throat.

"I imagine, Brian, that you do not want to spend the next ten years in some ghastly prison on the mainland," he said softly.

"No, I bloody don't," I said, trying to conceal my surprise with passion.

He pulled out a pack of cigarettes.

"Do you smoke?"

I shook my head. He lit himself a cigarette, offered one to the woman, who also declined. But he had me now. It was an interesting situation and I had to admit that I was intrigued. No guard had accompanied the two Brits. They did not appear flustered, angry. There was no pompous talk. Something was going on. Were they releasing me? Maybe Dan Connolly from the FBI had heard about my predicament and pulled a few strings.

"You've been living in America?" the man asked.

"What the hell is your name?"

"Jeremy Barnes," he said, blowing a Gaulois in my direction.

"Oh, and I'm Samantha Caudwell," Samantha said in an

even more upper-class accent than Jeremy's. The sort of snide Queen's English Olivia de Havilland used when she was badgering Errol Flynn in those films from the 1930s.

The smoke from the cigarette drifted over. Only pseuds and poseurs smoked Gauloises. Jeremy, however, seemed not to be either of these.

"You've lived in Paris," I said, surprising Jeremy with a good guess. Jeremy looked a little taken aback but quickly recovered his poise.

"Yes, yes indeed. They told us you were good," Jeremy said.

"Who's they?"

"The FBI. The US Marshals Service. We've read your file, Brian, or should I say, Michael. We know everything about you."

"Aye?" I said, trying to appear casual.

"Yes. Shall I tell you what we know?"

"Maybe you should tell me a wee bit about yourself first," I said.

"No, I don't think so, old chap. Would you like a drink?" Jeremy asked and threw a flask onto the cot.

"I'd like water."

Jeremy tossed me the water bottle.

"Good idea. Water first, then the brandy," Jeremy said.

"Ok."

I drank the half-liter bottle of water, unscrewed the hip flask, and took a sip of brandy. I threw the flask back.

"Your name is not Brian O'Nolan. Your real name is Michael Forsythe. You went to America in 1992 to work for Darkey White. You ended up killing Darkey White and wiping out his entire gang. You turned informer and the American government set you up with a new identity. I gather that recently you've been living in Chicago," Jeremy intoned placidly.

I said nothing.

"You speak fluent Spanish. That, and only that, can possibly account for your desire to take a vacation in the Canary Islands," Jeremy mocked.

"I'll ask again. Who the hell are you?" I demanded.

"Mr. Forsythe, I am the person who could get you out of this cell, today. Right now in fact. In the next five minutes you will have to make a decision. That decision will be either to come with me or stay here, get tried, get convicted, and then spend the next few years in the Columbaro Maximum Security Prison in Seville. Perhaps you'll choose the prison. Miguel de Cervantes began *Don Quixote* there. A fascinating place, apparently."

"Who do you work for?" I insisted.

Jeremy finished his cigarette. Slowly lit another.

"What do you see?" Samantha asked from behind Jeremy.

"What do I see?" I repeated.

"Yes. Tell us," Jeremy said.

I sighed. Leaned back. What game were they playing?

I looked the two of them over. They were relaxed, confident, obviously serious. This was a test.

"Ok, I'll play if you want to. I guessed Paris because of your fags. Easy," I said to Jeremy a little warily.

"What else?" he asked.

"You went to Harrow. Not on a scholarship, your father probably went to Harrow and his father before him. Your granddad probably used to tell you stories about how Winston Churchill was in the remedial class when he was there."

Jeremy laughed and choked on his cigarette. I continued.

"You're wearing a linen jacket. Expensive, but more than that, a kind of uniform. You knew you were going to have to go to Spain to see me, but you took the time to change from English clothes into something more sartorially suitable. Why? Why not shorts and T-shirt, or a polo shirt, or a cotton shirt and chinos? Hmmm. You feel you have to wear a jacket because you're on duty. You look like an army officer but you're in civvies. Maybe you were in the army or maybe the RAF, you don't seem like a navy man anyway. . . . So why are you here? You work for the government. You and your wee secretary have flown all the way to Spain. You don't have a tan, you're not even red, you came here right from the airport. To see me. Huh. Why? A job.

You need me for a job. You've come to make me a job offer."

Samantha whispered something to Jeremy. He nodded. I was impressing them with this bullshit.

"Who do I work for?" Jeremy asked.

"I don't know."

"Think about it."

"Why should I?" I asked petulantly.

"Why indeed?" Jeremy said, smiling.

"Ok, let me see. . . . Christ, I have it, it must be the Old Bill. You work for the cops."

"Not the police, why would the police want you?"

I sat forward on the edge of the bed. Yeah, he was too much of a patrician for the cops. He was a highflier, he worked for—

"British bloody Intelligence," I said.

Jeremy's jaw opened and closed. Samantha moved a little closer. Jeremy turned round to look at her.

And then I saw I was being dicked. I'd been wrong. Samantha was the superior officer. Jeremy was the underling. She was watching both of us, using him as a barrier to assess me, seeing if I was right for whatever it was they wanted me for.

Well, enough of that for a game of soldiers.

"Hey, Sammy, why don't you do us a favor, get your boy out of here and we can talk business," I said.

Jeremy looked startled. Samantha tried not to appear nonplussed.

"We do think we're clever, don't we?" she said, mispronouncing her Rs in that way they teach you at only the most elite of English boarding schools.

I said nothing.

"You may leave, Jeremy. Please wait for me outside," she ordered. Jeremy stood, winked at me, and knocked on the door. The guard opened it and let him out. Samantha moved to Jeremy's seat and picked up the file he had left on the chair.

British Intelligence. Well, well, well. I suppose they

wanted someone with insight into the workings of the rackets in Belfast. If the peace deal everyone was talking about came off, then they'd want to make sure all those bored paramilitaries in Ulster didn't move into organized crime and drugs. I could be very useful on that score. Or, maybe they wanted someone to spruce up their training programs for undercover ops. I could probably do a job like that. I was army trained and I'd interrogated the shit out of people before. Might be a nice little earner if I played my cards right. The FBI kept me safe but they didn't exactly keep me flush.

Samantha skimmed through the folder, pretending to notice things for the first time.

"I don't have all day, you know. I'm very anxious to find out if Stella can learn to love herself again," I said, holding up my novel.

Samantha smiled and continued to thumb my file.

"You've been quite the naughty boy, haven't you, Michael?" she said, her tone as condescending as if she were a Victorian missionary and I, a recidivist cannibal chieftain caught with a hut full of human heads.

"Depends what you mean by naughty."

"Killing several unarmed people in cold blood."

"You want to tell me my life story or you want to get on with it?" I said, irritated.

"Don't get cross. I'm here to help you," she said.

"You're here to bust me out of this joint," I sneered.

"That's right," she said, crossing her legs and accidentally hitching up her skirt a notch.

Really not a bad-looking *chiquita* if you liked that sort of thing and, if truth be told, I did like that sort of thing. You could tell that underneath the prim, proper, repressed, King and Country exterior . . . the rest of the sentence is cliché, but I'd bet money it wasn't far off the mark.

"Michael, first of all, I feel that it's very important that I'm honest with you. You're obviously too smart to fall for a line, so I'll tell you how it is. Although it looks like we have all the cards, in fact I have a poor bargaining position. If time were not a factor, you would need us much more than we would need you. But, alas, time is a factor," she said in that round-about diplomat way again.

"Honey, if time is a factor, you better be a bit less oblique," I said, leaning back on the cot and noting that from this angle I could see right up to her panties, which were white cotton and soaked with sweat.

"I do apologize. Of course you're right. Let me explain, Michael. Jeremy and I work for MI6, British Intelligence overseas, which, in case you don't know, is the equivalent of the CIA and a—"

"I know who you are," I interrupted.

"Good. Well, I am in charge of a section within MI6 called SUU—the Special Ulster Unit. MI5 deals with Irish terrorism in the United Kingdom, but SUU looks at Irish terrorism in Europe and the Americas. We report directly to the home secretary. We largely bypass the MI6 bureaucracy. We have had many successes. Well, several successes . . ."

"Ok. Where am I supposed to come in?" I asked.

"For the last six months or so, Her Majesty's government has been in not-so-secret negotiations with the IRA to resume their cease-fire agreement. The election of Mr. Blair has changed little except for speeding things up. The negotiations have been going well. The IRA's Army Council is becoming convinced that this is the right thing to do at the right time. The Clinton administration has been helpful. Things are moving quickly now and the IRA seems to be on the verge of announcing a complete cessation of hostilities and a resumption of the cease-fire."

"I read the papers," I said.

"Well, yes, it hasn't exactly been the best-kept secret in the world. And we're jolly well hoping that it's going to come off. The problem is that the IRA's Army Council is worried about causing a split in the IRA. IRA splinter groups are not uncommon. The council wants to eliminate the hard-line elements before they announce a cease-fire. We believe this announcement is going to come by the end of the month, perhaps even in the next few days. In Northern Ireland and in the Republic of Ireland, the British and Irish governments will turn a blind eye to a purge of IRA extremists. This is not the case in America. As you may be aware, the IRA has several well-organized cells in the United States. Most will abide by the Army Council's decision. Disband, disarm, sleep. But one, we know, will not. The IRA would like to wipe out the extremist SOC, Sons of Cuchulainn. The FBI and the American government will not permit such a purge to take place. They would rather go the legal route of evidence gathering and prosecution."

"Cuchulainn, love. It's pronounced KuckKulann, not Cushcoolain," I said with a smug grin. Samantha ignored me and soldiered on.

"It's a tiny group, almost a cell really, but, we believe, extraordinarily dangerous. And well off. Neither we nor the FBI have any agents at all with the Sons of Cuchulainn. None. We are desperately short of manpower. And for reasons I'll explain in a moment, time is of the essence. We have agents within the IRA, the INLA, the UVF. But we urgently need an agent, someone to go to America to join or spy on the Sons of Cuchulainn, to gather evidence and help in their prosecution, if of course they are doing anything illegal."

"I have an ominous feeling that I see where this is going. That someone, that poor bastard—let me guess who you have in mind."

"Michael, your folder only appeared on my desk the day before yesterday. It was handed to me by someone in the Foreign Office. But I have to say I was jolly impressed."

I wasn't really listening now. Whatever financial package they were going to offer wasn't worth the risk. An IRA cell. They had to be kidding. Samantha continued as I stared up her skirt and contemplated her oddly seductive voice.

"Yes, Michael, your handlers speak very highly of you and you were in the British army, which was good and although, um, unfortunately you were asked to leave Her Majesty's employ rather prematurely, you completed a reconnaissance course and received some special operations training."

"I failed that recon course, and the special ops course

ended with me in the brig for assaulting a civilian," I said blithely.

Samantha was not to be put off.

"That's neither here nor there. The fact is you were in the army, which is good, and you were also a low-level gangster in Belfast, which is even better. And you worked for the Irish mob in America, which is best of all. You could be an ideal person to infiltrate the Sons of Cuchulainn for us. Dan Connolly of the FBI says that you're one of the best that he's ever seen. Proficient, merciless, bold, surprisingly disciplined."

"You talked to Dan, huh? Nice of him to sell me down the river."

"No, no, Dan was very complimentary. . . . Michael, I have to tell you, I'm going out on something of a limb here. Dropping everything, flying to Spain, talking to you. But now that I've met you I honestly think you could be the one to do this job for us. To infiltrate this cell and gather information and help put them away before they ruin everything. If they manage to do a bombing campaign in America, the Protestant terrorists will have to respond, the IRA will have to reply to that, and oh my goodness the whole cease-fire and all our hard work will be jolly well up the spout."

"How jolly sad," I said, irritated enough to take the piss.

"And naturally if you did do this for us, we would convince the Spanish government to drop all charges against you," Samantha said with a satisfied wee grin. She sat back in her chair, crossed her legs, blocking the crotch shot.

I also smiled. Who the hell did they think they were dealing with? Did they think I was some eejit Paddy just off the bloody boat?

"Why don't the FBI infiltrate this group of yours? It's their country," I asked for starters before moving on to the main course.

"The FBI won't touch it with a ten-foot pole," Samantha said, her eyes narrowing.

"Why?"

"Our plan is to insert an agent as soon as possible. Before

the Sons of Cuchulainn begin their campaign, which we strongly believe will commence once the cease-fire announcement comes. In other words, we have to have an agent in their ranks in the next couple of weeks. The FBI feels that an attempt to hurriedly insert an agent in this manner and in this climate would be too rushed and too dangerous," Samantha said calmly.

"The FBI, in other words, thinks it might be a bit of a suicide mission," I said, my smile broadening.

"Er, yes," she muttered, embarrassed.

"And just to be clear, if the operation weren't dumb enough already, of all the people in the world, you want me—a man who has a contract on his head from the Irish mob in New York—to attempt to infiltrate an IRA splinter group," I said and laughed at her.

"Mr. Forsythe, I don't think—"

"Don't Mr. Forsythe me, Samantha; thanks for thinking of me, thanks for taking the trouble to fly out, but I think I've heard just about enough. Run along now. I'll do my time quietly in Seville. I've been in a lot worse places than that. Nice to have met ya," I said.

I leaned back on the cot and put my hands behind my head. I closed my eyes. Let them sweat for a bit. Let me think.

Samantha considered the situation.

"Perhaps I have oversold the problems. All we want you to do is gather evidence that would lead to a prosecution. The fact that you are from Belfast but have experience in America, the fact that you've been in the British army, the fact that you come highly recommended by the FBI. All this is to your advantage."

"I think, Samantha dear," I said with sarcasm "you're barking up the wrong tree, love. As I've patiently explained, I'm already wanted by the Irish community in America. Seamus Duffy has a million-dollar bounty on my head."

"I am perfectly aware of that, Michael. But you must understand that the Sons of Cuchulainn are a separate entity from the Boston Irish mob. The mob dislikes and distrusts anyone whose motives are political rather than fiduciary. They have very little time for fanatics. And the Boston mob itself is a rival to the New York organization and they maintain few links. There will be at least two layers of separation between you and your former associates. You'll be quite insulated from Seamus Duffy and his agents in New York. And in any case, from what Dan Connolly tells me, Duffy is more than occupied with his own internal problems rather than looking to settle old scores. You're yesterday's news, Michael. It's been five years. No one remembers you. That's not to say that you won't be taking any risks. No, we must be clear from the get-go. Oh, good God, no. This will be extraordinarily risky indeed. Even if they never found out that your real name is Michael Forsythe, they would kill you at the drop of a hat if they discovered that you were linked to Her Majesty's government in even the remotest way."

She paused, ran her hand through that peachy auburn hair. No rings on any finger. Not married, not engaged.

"Did you hear what I said, Michael?"

"I heard. You're doing your case no good. What you're basically saying is I'd have to be mad to take this job, because I could get killed in half a dozen ways," I said, leaning back on the cot again and resting my arms over my eyes.

"Well, I'm not one for odds, but yes, I'd say that even a competently trained professional agent with years of experience would have a rather higher than average chance of being compromised in a time-imperative operation such as this one," Samantha said.

I yawned in the face of her candor.

"And compromised means killed," I said.

"I'm terribly sorry but I have to be frank. I feel it's only fair that you appreciate the risks. Of course I do not think you will be killed or compromised in any way. It's very unlikely that McCaghan would bring you into the inner circle. We just need tidbits of information, anything that will help prevent a potential bombing campaign. And yes, ordinarily, I'd do something dramatic, I'd leave the cell, give you a day or two to think it over, maybe get the Spanish to rough you up, hector you a bit, but as I've said time is a factor here. An ideal opportunity for an insertion has presented itself. If my plan is going to work at all you absolutely have to be in Revere tomorrow."

"Revere Beach, Boston? You must be joking, honey. If I go near a Paddy neighborhood like that, I'll be killed."

She shook her head and gave me a brilliant smile.

"No, you won't. I wouldn't send you if I thought that. The Sons of Cuchulainn are beyond the pale in Irish American republican circles and after the IRA hit tomorrow, they're going to be even more beyond the pale. They'll be pariahs."

"IRA hit?"

"Michael, please don't worry about your former problems. We'll dye your hair black, give you dark green contact lenses, something like that; that's not my field exactly, but we'll gussy you up so that your own mother wouldn't recognize you."

"Sure."

"You'll only have to be in Boston for one day. Then we'll fly you to an FBI field office in a secure location. And then in a week or so your formal assignment will begin. The most difficult part of an operation is the entry. Believe me, I've done dozens. And what we have going tomorrow is a perfect entry for you. It's an opportunity not to be missed. Instead of months of preparation, we can get you buckets of credibility in a single night. Indeed, if we pull this off, I'd say the risks of being compromised are considerably reduced."

"What exactly do you want me to do in Revere?"

"You're going to save a girl's life," Samantha said with a cough.

"What?"

"The IRA is going to try to kill her father, and you're going to save her," she said, looking at the floor.

"That sounds bloody risky to start with."

"Not really. Look, Michael, we need you. We had one other person in mind but . . ." her voice trailed off.

"Let me guess. He's turned you down," I said.

"Well, yes. That's why this whole Spanish angle has been particularly fortuitous for us. You know, not everyone agrees with me, I'm taking a bit of a risk flying here to see you. There are some within the department who don't agree with the idea of recruiting outsiders. Especially a potential loose cannon such as yourself."

I was fed up with her now and I'd thought about it enough.

"While I really appreciate the faith you have in me, Samantha, thanks but no thanks. Now I think I've been pretty polite with you; if you would do me a favor and tell your pal in the Foreign Office that I still haven't seen a lawyer and could they please arrange for me to see one ASAP I'd be much obliged."

She looked disappointed.

"A lawyer?"

"Aye. I want to plead and get this shit over with."

Samantha frowned, undid her ponytail, and let the hair hang down her back. She started doing her hair up again, glancing at me with what could almost be described as pity.

"Michael, obviously I haven't made the entire situation transparent. You're caught between a rock and a hard place. The Spanish government will see to it that you go to jail. And what's more, when your time is up, the Spaniards will extradite you to Mexico, where I believe you are a fugitive from justice."

That was her trump card. The one she'd been saving.

I sat up on the bed. Horrified.

I'd been arrested in Mexico on a charge of drug smuggling but I'd escaped from the remand prison before I'd come to trial. I could be looking at twenty years there for the drugs, plus God knows how much for bloody jailbreaking.

Cold fear ran down my back. I'd been so cavalier with Samantha because I knew the Spanish angle was bullshit. Who gets ten years for being a football hooligan? Even if I got convicted they'd sentence me to three or four and I'd do two at the most. Probably less. *The Sun* and the *Daily Mirror* would quickly be filled with horror stories about all the poor Brits and their mistreatment in Spanish jails. Even the worst offenders would never serve close to ten years. And me, a side player with zero physical evidence to back up the police case, I'd be out in easy time and probably well on my way to winning damages at the European Court of Human Rights.

But Mexico, that was another matter completely.

I was in a world of shit if I went back there.

"The FBI won't let you send me to Mexico. We have a deal. I'm a protected witness," I said, trying to keep the tension out of my voice.

Samantha read from the file in front of her and shook her head.

"You have been given exemption from the crimes you committed in the United States. You certainly could not have been given exemption for criminal acts committed in a third country. Last night I called up my counterpart in the Mexican intelligence service. He would be more than happy to have you back in Mexican custody and the Spanish government would be delighted to extradite you. They have excellent relations with Mexico, as you can imagine."

I stared at her.

Any residual lust evaporated, replaced pound for pound with enmity. There was no way I was going back to Mexico. The place where Scotchy, Andy, and Fergal all had died in horrible circumstances. The thought of returning to that prison at all was like an ice dagger in the heart. You know what they do to gringos in Mexican prisons? Let your imagination do the work and then add a little on top because I'd already goddamn escaped.

But I didn't want to work for her. Suddenly I felt trapped. Panicked. My mind sprinting through scenarios. Not Boston but not bloody Mexico, either.

Aye. Maybe there was another way.

What was it that Goosey had said? We could live out in the wilds of Tenerife forever. Fish, eat fruit, maybe escape by boat.

I formulated a tiny, desperate, pathetic plan.

Move fast.

Last thing anyone would be expecting.

Up, run at her, kick her off the chair, grab it, smash it down on that ponytailed skull. Jeremy hears the commotion, comes rushing in, let him have it with the goddamn chair too. Grab his piece, cock it, point it at the guard, put the gun in my pocket, but keep it on him, and get the guard to march me right out of the prison, telling everyone that I was being transferred or released. Walk right out, casual as you please. Take his money, steal a car, go back up into the volcano country. Wait out the search.

In von Humboldt's book I read that the indigenous people kept going a guerrilla war against the Spanish for over a hundred years. Easy, up there on the mountain fastness. Hunt out a cave, lay low until the heat cooled down, come back into town, find some drunken German tourist, mug him, steal a passport, money, plane ticket, Tenerife to Frankfurt, Frankfurt to New York. Get back to safety in the good old USA.

Not a great plan.

Not even a good one.

But this bitch wasn't going to threaten me.

"Since you put it that way, I suppose I have no choice," I said, readying myself.

"Oh, I am pleased. I'm sorry about the coercive aspect of all this, it's just beastly that Her Majesty's gov. has to be in the blackmail business, but there it is. Indeed, it couldn't have worked out better. Jeremy was right, what made you come to Tenerife in the first place, don't you know it's notorious for riots and disturbances? Vulgar, awful place," she said with an amused expression.

"I was reading Alexander von Humboldt and Charles Darwin and they paint it in a different light," I replied and offered her a conciliatory hand and a big broad smile of acceptance.

"Well, bad for you, but good for us, old boy, Sword of Damocles, Scylla and Charybdis, call it what you will," she said and gave me her hand too.

I grabbed it and pulled her violently off the chair, she screamed, dropping her pen, folder, and water bottle. I threw her to the ground, kicked her to one side, and grabbed the chair. I lifted it over my head and positioned it to bring it down on her spine.

A terrible pain in my right foot—which was not the one I'd left behind in a jungle village in the Yucatán. A searing explosion of nerve endings and when I looked down I saw a penknife sticking out of my Converse sneaker.

Jesus.

Before I could react, she'd kicked me behind the right knee and I fell to the cell floor, banging my head on the edge of the metal bed.

I groaned. Jeremy opened the door and looked in.

"Good heavens, what on earth is happening? Need any help, Samantha?" he asked.

Samantha picked up the dropped file, righted the chair, and sat down. She moved herself away from me so I couldn't pull the penknife out and threaten her with it.

"I'm fine, darling, but young Michael is going to need medical assistance," she said softly.

Jeremy called for the guard, produced his gun, and pointed it

at me.

I pulled myself back up onto the cot.

I breathed deep, swore inwardly, pulled out the knife, and sent it clattering to the floor.

"What I'll need," I began between clenched teeth "is a letter from the Spanish government stating that all charges have been dropped. So you won't be able to hold that over me indefinitely."

Samantha smiled.

"I'll get our lawyers working on it immediately," she said.

"And I'll want a document from the Spanish, British, and United States attorneys general that I will not in the future be extradited to Mexico under any circumstances," I said.

"I will get working on that, too," Samantha said. "Is there anything else?"

"Aye, a guy called Goosey who was picked up with me, him out as well," I gasped.

"I'll also see to that."

"I have your word?"

"You have my word," she assured me.

"Fine, in that case. I'll do it."

"Good," Samantha said and snapped my folder shut.

Within an hour, I was stitched, sutured, shaved, and sitting on a taxiing RAF Hercules transport plane that would be taking me to Lisbon. From Lisbon, the direct flight to Boston Logan.

Samantha sat beside me, organizing her briefing notes.

The big Hercules taxied down the runway. A military aircraft, tiny slit windows and you sat facing backwards.

Samantha passed me earplugs. I put them in. Looked out.

The harsh volcanic mountain, the outline of banana plantations, the aerodrome. The propellers turned, the transport accelerated, lift developed over its wings, and we took off into the setting sun.

The blue water. The other Canary Islands. Africa.

We flew west over Tenerife, and through the safety glass and smoke I could see what the hooligans had wrought on Playa de las Americas and what the concrete-loving developers at the Spanish Ministry of Tourism had done to the rest of the island. Humboldt for one would have been displeased. Samantha saw my grimace, patted my knee. Her big pouty red lips formed into a sympathetic smile.

"Don't worry, darling. It's going to be all right," she soothed and, of course, as is typical when someone in authority tells you that, nothing could have been further from the goddamn truth.

Not sure what to read next?

**Visit Pocket Books online at
www.SimonSays.com**

Reading suggestions for
you and your reading group

New release news
Author appearances
Online chats with your favorite writers
Special offers
And much, much more!

All the clues point to Pocket Books for a good read...

Hoax
Robert K. Tanenbaum
All the bling in the world can't help New York City DA
Butch Karp solve the murder of a rising rap star...

Maximum Security
Rose Connors
Should an attorney ever defend her lover's ex?

Blood Hollow
William Kent Krueger
A beautiful high school student has been murdered,
and it will take a miracle to find her killer.

Blood Knot
S.W. Hubbard
Tough love escalates to murder at a school for
troubled teens.

The Man Burns Tonight
Donn Cortez
Wild pandemonium is traditional at Nevada's
famous Burning Man festival. But this year there's
murder on the Playa...

12911